The Adventures of the
Posse of Little Horses

Oxbow Lake the 2nd

ShipWreck Publications

If you don't laugh at our books,
you're probably dead . . .
or should be!

ShipWreckPublications.com

A Copyright Notice Like No Other

This book is a work of fiction created in the fevered mind of the author or authors. Thus the characters, incidents, and dialogue are not real in that sense of the word. Any resemblance to actual persons, events, real or imagined, or living and/or dead is entirely coincidental in the interpretation of that word most favorable to the author or authors.

To prove my or our point, the author or authors did NOT use the incident in which certain individuals were accused of having some kind of relations with a burro, which actually didn't occur in real life anyway. The opinions, ideas, notions, emotions and feelings expressed in this novel may or may not necessarily be those of the author or authors, the publisher, those who participated in preparing this novel for publication, those who read the novel, and/or those who do not.

One Toke Over The Line
Words and Music by Michael Brewer and Thomas E. Shipley
Copyright © 1970 by Universal Music - Careers
Copyright Renewed
International Copyright Secured All Rights Reserved
Reprinted by Permission of Hal Leanord Corporation
ISBN: 9780983976608
Library of Congress Control Number: 2012904764

This edition is published by ShipWreckPublications Corporation.
Cover design and illustration by Karen Mathis
ShipWreckPublications Corporation
9745 Fox Chapel Road
Tampa, FL 33647
Visit our website at www.ShipWreckPublications.com

PRINTED IN THE UNITED STATES OF AMERICA

Dedication

I dedicate The Adventures of the Posse of Little Horses to my cat Rocket "Lefty" Garcia, who accompanied me to my writing desk all those mornings at 4:30 AM and did not return to his early morning hunting until he was satisfied that I was hard at work.

Spanks And Thanks

First and foremost, we do NOT thank the many, many publishing agents of that debilitated, incestuous profession who rejected our wonderfully humorous, satiric and entertaining novel without having read any of it as they were too busy to do so because they were searching for the next great teen witch-fantasy vampire zombie murder-mystery spy novel involving a female CSI investigator who will become the next president of the United States after her heart-warming sex change operation so that she can become the first transgendered gay cross-dresser to become President of the United States... a novel to be written by a gay single parent Ivy-league father who is on welfare (a creative and novel touch) because of Vice President Dick Chaney. We actually look forward to this novel when it is published as we'd like to know which bathroom the author of this great tome will have his transgendered gay cross-dressing president use.

We would, however, like to thank my cat Rocket "Lefty" Garcia who inspired and encouraged us, in spite of not reading well, and who, even given his lack of reading skill, recognized a great novel in the making... unlike the above debilitated and incestuous profession. Poor Rocket has since gone to the great litter box in the sky having succumbed to that most dreaded of feline fatal fates, Cats' Bobheimer's Disease.

We would like to thank that great publishing mogul Robert A Ward III for publishing this novel through his ShipWreck Publications Corporation. He is a man of great vision and taste.

We owe a great deal (or at least a little deal) to Alan Beebe and Tom and Sue Wolfe for reading the manuscript for the novel and not saying they didn't like it. Whatever the deal, our thanks are unlikely to result in monetary remuneration for the three of them. We also thank published authors Steve Hamilton and David Silverman who, after reading the manuscript, did not encourage us to commit suicide as the most likely way to create the sympathy necessary for us to have even an outside chance of getting the novel published.

Then there's Lisa Lazzaro, who was kind enough to send us a quote that we use to advertise the novel. (See the 'Praise For' section of the book.) Finally, thanks go to Karen Mathis, the Creative Director at ShipWreckPublications, who designed and created the wonderful cover for the novel

Oops, we almost forgot to thank Gordon Gensler, whom we tricked into editing the manuscript and who, even after realizing we'd tricked him, did an excellent job making a silk purse out of what we sent him.

At this point, we feel obligated to request that Colin Lazzaro-Smith and John Robinson return the manuscripts that we sent them and which they did not read and to warn them that we know people who will encourage them to do so in ways they may find unpleasant should they not heed this warning! We provided them with self-addressed and stamped envelopes. In a rather weak justification for their lack of action which we do not... I repeat, do not... accept, they claim that the United States Post Office might refuse to accept the packages as said packages may contain pornographic drug-related literature, which we kind of deny.

Unsolicited Praise for Oxbow Lake's

THE ADVENTURES OF THE POSSE OF

LITTLE HORSES

"I re-ckon Oxbow Lake is a pen name. Is that damned idiot Ward A Bobb the 3rd ashamed of his work?"
- *Sam Clemens (channeled through Bob Dylan)*

"If I were alive, I'd have written it myself, only differently and better!"
- *Mark Twain (You Dead Tube)*

"The Adventures of the Posse of Little Horses does not make me regret committing suicide."
- *John Kennedy Toole (Giggle Beyond Internet Site)*

"The bastard plagiarized my Ride a Cockhorse after I died so I know that at least part of it is good."
- *Raymond Kennedy (scratched on a bar near Columbia)*

"Worst punctuated novel I've ever read. The man's obsessed with ellipses... he's out of his freakin'... elliptical mind!"
- *Lisa Lazzero (freelance professional punctuator)*

"It has some damn short sentences which is damn good. Too bad they don't make any damn cents."
- *Ernest Hemingway (channeled through Groucho Marx)*

"He's my intellectual mini-me. Mr. Oxbow Lake the 2nd knows how to really torture a thought."
- *Marquis De Sade (channeled through VP Joe Biden)*

"To get this novel published, Oxbow will need at least two sets of knee pads."
- *Senator John "Bluto" Blutarsky (Animal House séance)*

"I find Oxbow Lake's novel to be vulgar and despicable, and I have only read the first page."
- *Charles Dickens (channeled through Hugh Hefner)*

"Against the assault of laughter nothing can stand."

-- *Mark Twain*

Thursday, June 26

Renting a bower of love for fun and games…

Charles Fontaine, the best man to be, stood somewhat unsteadily before the check-in counter of the Adirondack Motel. Looking like a young Marlboro Man of years gone-by in an Ivy League Mexican odd sort of way, he peered from beneath a rather large sombrero at an old man with a large beer belly standing behind the counter. He steadied himself by placing his left hand on the counter and said rather thickly, "One of girls over at Hermitage retreat sent me. Said I could rent room here for a little bachelor party for my posse. One our guys getting married this weekend."

The old man scratched his beer belly with both hands, winked and said, "That sombrero a souvenir from a little senorita siesta over at the Hermitage?"

Somewhat puzzled by the unexpected question, Charles stepped back from the counter, folded his arms defiantly and replied, "No, I've had hat long time."

The fat man laughed and asked, "Reserve a room for tomorrow?"

Charles shook his head up and down vigorously indicating yes and as he did so, the large brim of his sombrero dipped backward and then forward, the forward dip causing him to lose his tenuous balance and slowly fall toward the counter. He reached for the counter with both hands to break his fall and again steady himself. Having regained his somewhat tentative equilibrium, he pushed back from the counter and again stood unsupported.

The fat man behind the counter asked, "How about a suite of rooms? We have a real nice suite with full accommodations... full service kitchenette, large living room, beautiful bedroom. It even has a hot tub. Great place to party. Actually it's our honeymoon suite, but it's available this weekend."

"How much?"

"Its five hundred bucks a night, but you gotta take it for the entire weekend... Friday, Saturday and Sunday. It's a package deal. So it's fifteen hundred, but I can give it to you for a thousand plus tax... in advance. Anything you break, you pay for."

Charles put both hands on the counter and his face disappeared beneath his sombrero's brim as he dipped his head in thought. Then the sombrero rose revealing his smiling face and he asked, "Honeymoon suite?"

"Yup, the honeymoon suite. It's called the Shangri-La."

Charles' face again disappeared beneath the brim of his sombrero as he lowered his head and scratched the back of his neck with his left hand. After several moments of apparently deep thought, up popped his sombrero revealing his face yet again and he said, "What the hell. It'll solve two problems. I can give lucky couple Saturday and Sunday as wedding gift. I'll take it." He said to himself, "The Stuntman can begin life of marital bliss with lovely Leslie Wright at the appro... appro... approprat-ly named Shangri-La. Good a place as any for him to wet his dipstick in the virgin queen." And he handed the fat man his credit card.

The fat man processed the credit card and handed Charles a credit slip as well as a bill to sign. He asked, "And who's the lucky couple? I gotta have their names for the register."

"Jamie Stein... Steinkraus and Leslie Wright... Mr. and Mrs. Jamie Steinkraus." And he slowly spelled out the last name as the fat man typed the names into the motel's computer system.

Having completed the transaction, Charles turned to leave. However, there before him and blocking his exit stood an obviously very nervous, short and slender young man with a swarthy complexion who was dressed in a dark business suit, white shirt and red tie. He wore a pair of wire rim glasses behind which his eyes were constantly shifting back and forth. Stuck beneath his nose was a large and obviously false black mustache, which he kept pressing with the fingers of his left hand to keep in place. He appeared to Charles to be suffering from some form of untreated attention deficit hyperactivity. Charles thought to himself, "Damn, dude looks like Mexican Groucho Marx in business suit."

The young man smiled nervously, pushing at his false mustache, and said, "No bachelor party is complete without the traditional entertainment such an event calls for." And he handed Charles a large brown envelope. The fat man behind the counter laughed and left the room.

Charles took the envelope, pulled the top open, reached in and pulled out an eight-by-twelve color photo of a beautiful, dark-haired and quite well-endowed young woman dressed in a very short traditional Mexican dress, the kind with the slit up the middle that revealed her luscious upper thighs. She was looking directly into the camera and smiling.

Charles blurted out, "What beau-ful eyes."

The young man said, "It is not only her eyes that are beautiful... no?"

Charles replied, "No... mean yes... yes... all of her is beau-ful."

"She looks very young but she is an experienced entertainer. She has performed at many bachelor parties. For two hundred dollars, she will perform her dance of the running of the bulls at your party. Only two hundred dollars... an excellent deal... and if you wish her to perform something extra, you can negotiate such extras at the party."

Charles slipped the photo back into the envelope after several attempts and handed it back to the young man. He reached into his back pocket, took a step back to steady himself and pulled out his wallet. He removed two one-hundred dollar bills, which he thrust into the free hand of the surprised Mexican version of Grouch Marx, who, unlike the original, was at a loss for words, apparently having expected to do some haggling over the price.

As he pushed his wallet into his back pocket, Charles said, "Friday round six… here… Shangri-La" and staggered out to his rental car. The young man stood holding the two one-hundred dollar bills looking very un-Groucho like as he nervously pushed at his false mustache with the sleeve of his left arm.

They're not losing a daughter but gaining a posse…

The rotund father of the bride, Professor Jeremiah Wright, leaned his rather large and jowly head forward and peered through his great bushy eyebrows into the full-length mirror before him. Unable to see his image, he leaned his head yet closer to the mirror. When he took this action, the weight of his large forward leaning head being added to the weight of his large forward-leaning belly, one of the Newtonian laws of physics took effect and he tumbled toward the mirror. As he tumbled, he muttered a rather cryptic "ut oh." However, he was able to prevent an inadvertent and more than likely unsuccessful tumble into Wonderland with his right hand, which left yet another large handprint on the wall next to the mirror.

It then dawned on him that his problem of perception was not one of distance but of focus, for he was not wearing his glasses, which thankfully happened to be in his left hand at the time and not his right. When he remembered to wear his glasses, he wore the kind called pince-nez, which is a fancy way of saying "pinch nose." You've seen these glasses in old historical pictures. They're the kind that one pushes down on the bridge of one's nose and attaches to a piece of one's wearing apparel with a safety string to prevent them from falling to the floor when they lose their grip on one's nose. The professor righted his ship, pushed the pince-nez down on the bridge of his nose and tugged at the blue velvet safety string to be sure that it was securely attached to his vest. He then peered back into the mirror from a more upright position.

He muttered to himself, "Unruly, unruly, unruly," as his eyes focused on his large, grey handlebar mustache. His fingers reached into one of his many vest pockets and pulled out a monogrammed ivory mustache comb which he pinched between the thumb and middle finger of his left hand. He carefully leaned his head forward and delicately ran the mustache comb down his whiskers, working his way across the mustache. Satisfied that he had conquered his unruly whiskers, he smiled and returned the mustache comb to its vest pocket.

Looking admiringly at his image, his jowls jiggled as he shook his head yes. With some effort, he pulled his plaid vest down over his considerable girth, smiled again and said to his image, "Good day, Mr. Theodore Roosevelt." His colleagues at Columbia University never tired of telling him that he bore an amazing resemblance to an older (and unmentioned but thought, very rotund) literary TR, and the professor never tired of hearing it. His students, taking a somewhat different view, thought he looked more like an absent-minded Captain Kangaroo of super-sized proportions, who like the good captain wore funny glasses.

His wife Rose, who not so coincidentally happened to be the mother of the bride, entered the bedroom and asked the question "Aren't you ready yet?" As with most of her questions, the tone of her voice was more appropriate for a command with a very specific and expected response in mind than a question. She stood across the room from him with her hands on her hips. She was a short, slender, athletic woman who hyphenated her name and insisted on being addressed as Mrs. Rose Fazzano-Wright. Those who did not know her might consider her quite good-looking in spite of her years and her rather severe demeanor. Those who knew her referred to her as The Barracuda, but only when talking about her. She continued, "Get it in gear," adding "Did you have to wear that brown corduroy suit again? I knew I should have laid out your traveling clothes for you."

Professor Jeremiah Wright looked into the mirror, crushing his jowls with his chin as a hurt expression slowly formed on his face. "Dear, I think that my present attire makes me look quite professorial. Quite appropriate for an adjunct professor of English literature at a prestigious Ivy League university."

Rose replied, "Well Mr. Adjunct Professor of English Literature at a prestigious Ivy League University... get your Ivy League adjunct professorial butt down to the garage. At the pace you're moving, our daughter will be married and have given birth to several grandchildren before we get out of Manhattan"... the last part of her statement being yelled over her shoulder as she spun and exited the bedroom.

The good professor took one last long look into the mirror and lumbered from their apartment to the elevator with a gait reminiscent of an old brown bear. Upon his arrival at the elevator, this lumbering old brown bear found it out-of-order. He then lumbered to the stairs and lumbered down five flights of them to the basement garage of their co-op. By the time he reached the landing to the garage entrance, he was sweating profusely. He stood for a moment to catch his breath and then pushed the entrance door open. There standing before him was Rose with her hands again on her hips, cool as a cucumber. She said, "What took you so long?" He started to reply, "The elevator is broke..." but before he could finish, she interrupted him, "It's broken for everybody. Not just you." Before he could fruitlessly respond, even the thought of a response became fruitless, because by the time he inhaled in preparation for speaking, Rose was already across the garage standing behind their ten-year-old Volvo and alongside a huge pile of suitcases of various sizes, a large garment bag and sundry other bags and baskets. She yelled to him, "I packed everything we'll need. I hauled all this stuff down here while you were admiring yourself in the mirror. It's your job to load up the car"... with great emphasis placed on the word your.

The good professor thought very calmly and quietly to himself, "How could we possibly need all that stuff for a three day stay?" Why, you wonder, did he control the intensity of his thoughts when Rose was present? Quite simply in an attempt to keep those thoughts to himself and from Rose. Over the twenty-seven years of their marriage, he had become convinced that she could read his mind if his thoughts were too pronounced or as he termed it, too loud, for he was a great fan of Stephen King, one of his two concessions to modern popular fiction, and under the subtle influence of Mr. King had come to believe that much like young Danny Torrance in The Shining, Rose too could "shine". He believed that if his thoughts were like whispers instead of shouts, she would be unable to tele-pathically hear them. Most of the time his thoughts must have been on the rather loud side, telepathically speaking, because Rose seemed to always know what he was thinking.

Rose responded apparently to his thought, "Don't complain about the luggage. We have to be prepared for all contingencies. Our daughter only gets married once... at least I hope she'll only get married once, even if it's to that turkey Jamie Steinkraus. I don't want things to get screwed up." He thought to himself, "Golly, she shined again and I thought very quietly to myself." Rose interrupted his very quiet thoughts yet again, "Stop standing there trying to fig-ure out life. Get over here and load the darn car."

Following Rose's first order, he hung the large garment bag from the hanger over the rear door in the back seat, for it held all of Rose's dresses, including several choices for the wedding ceremony. He loaded the luggage and the various other bags and baskets into the Volvo under Rose's very careful supervision, having to remove items and rearrange them many times as Rose tried to maximize the efficiency of the loading without much consideration for the stress on the loader, the only constant being the large garment bag which remained in its original position. Luggage went into the trunk, out of the trunk, into the backseat and back to the trunk. Baskets and bags were stuffed and shifted about and, no matter how Jeremiah arranged things at Rose's very precise directions, a large piece of luggage always remained orphaned on the garage floor behind a fully loaded Volvo.

In frustration Rose yelled, "Damn it, you'll have to tie a suitcase to the roof." She emphatically pointed to the orphaned suitcase on the floor and said, "I want this one inside the car. It has the rest of the clothing and the other necessities I'll need to dress for the wedding." And so, after the trials and tribulations of even more supervision, Jeremiah unpacked the Volvo yet again and repacked it so that the large suitcase with the rest of Rose's wedding necessities was loaded inside the Volvo and, as it turned out, the suitcase with Jeremiah's clothes was tied to the Volvo's roof with ropes that went through the two partially open rear windows around and over and around the suitcase yet again, with one end of the rope ending up tied to the front bumper and the other tied to the rear bumper in an arrangement that would have pleased the mythical, yet all too real, Rube Goldberg. Jeremiah pictured Tom Joad, whose image bore an amazing resemblance to a Henry Fonda, smiling down on them as Jeremiah squeezed into the driver's seat and the Volvo slowly groaned towards his side of the car as he sat.

Rose was already sitting in the front passenger's seat ready to command the next phase of their odyssey. She opened a folder and said "MapQuest says The Hermitage of the Adirondacks is 260.4 miles from here. We'll be taking the Thruway north. Turn left on Broadway, go up to 230th and take the I-87 ramp north to Albany. It's on the left."

Being well-conditioned to following Rose's directions, Jeremiah did as instructed and soon they were tooling north on the New York State Thruway in their very late model Volvo at a breathtaking 55 miles per hour with the wind loudly whistling through the two partially opened rear windows, a consequence of the necessity of tying Jeremiah's one piece of luggage to the roof.

Jeremiah yelled, "Where is this establishment?"

Rose watched the cars and trucks whizzing by them and yelled back, "It's outside Blue Mountain Lake. We'll take the Northway at Albany to exit 23. According to MapQuest, it's a 4 hour and 42 minute drive. That's without stopping and going at least 65 mile per hour. We'll be lucky if we get there in 6." There was only one area of the good professor's nonacademic life where Rose had totally failed in her effort to "bring Jeremiah up to snuff" as she put it and that was the speed at which he drove. No matter what she said or did, she could not get him to drive over 55 miles an hour and he frequently drove much slower regardless of the posted speed limit. Her failure here only served to highlight her success in virtually every other part of the non-academic areas of the good professor's life. She looked at the speedometer and sighed.

Jeremiah's curiosity about his daughter Leslie's wedding was raised for the first time. He had been preoccupied with the biography he was writing of the English novelist and poet D. H. Lawrence, and as was his habit, operating pretty much on autopilot concerning the events of the rest of his life, including, as it turned out, the arrangements for his daughter's wedding. It was an easy state of mind for him to inhabit given his own predisposition, especially when combined with that of Rose. He asked, "What kind of establishment is this Hermitage of the Adirondacks anyway?"

Rose yelled, "What'd you say?" Jeremiah dutifully repeated his question more loudly. Rose annoyed by both the question, the need to repeat it and the whistling of the wind that made repetition necessary, snapped back, "Weren't you paying attention for... say... the last year or so? After all, it is your daughter's wedding."

Jeremiah drove in silence for several miles in order to let Rose calm down before replying, and then said apologetically, "Well, I got the general gist, but I'm not sure I ever knew any of the details."

Rose liked informing him of the details of their lives in a manner and time of her choosing, for in so doing, she was exercising yet another form of control over him. There was the distinct possibility that she had never told him any of the details, but Jeremiah wouldn't have remembered them even if she had. He was oblivious to his wife's use of this technique and thus untroubled by it. He was steadfastly preoccupied with his work and this steadfast preoccupation was the secret to his sanity, what there was of it, and his happiness. Rose's instinct to inform Jeremiah only as she saw fit overcame her anger, so she decided to tell him about the Hermitage and selected details about the arrangements for their daughter's wedding.

"The Hermitage of the Adirondacks is a kind of religious retreat. The brochure says it was founded by a group of Russian Orthodox brothers who came over here in the 19th century to provide aid and spiritual comfort to the Russian loggers who immigrated to the Adirondacks."

Rose paused and carefully scrutinized the expression on Jeremiah's face to be sure that he was being attentive, and satisfied that he was, she continued, "The loggers were recruited by the logging companies and they logged much of the Adirondacks before it became forever wild."

Jeremiah drove and listened and thought and then asked, "I thought that forever-wild law virtually eliminated any development in the Adirondacks?"

Listening to him this time, Rose actually replied to his question, probably because the question advanced her plan for directing the conversation. "The law states that there can be no new building and development, but whatever is already there is OK. Since the brothers, in their religious fervor, had built a substantial settlement on the far side of Blue Mountain Lake long before the law was passed, their settlement was grandfathered in."

"And they can still operate even though the Russian loggers are long gone?"

"Apparently. The brochure doesn't address this, but my guess is they have maintained their religious charter and therefore the state can't fully control their operation. They rent out cabins and rooms in their lodges for what they call family retreats and other facilities for religious events like weddings. I think the brothers severed their connection to the Russian Orthodox Church years ago. Personally, sounds like a scam to me, but that's between the brothers of the Hermitage and the thieves in Albany."

As if Rose had scripted Jeremiah's side of the conversation, he asked on cue, "Do they have a church on premises?"

"No, but there's an open-air chapel and a covered pavilion for the reception. There used to be a church but it burned down years ago. The wedding's a package deal that includes a nearby lodge with a full kitchen and large dining room, a great room and rooms for the bridal party."

"My, my. Sounds quite expensive. Did we have to contribute?"

"You know, Jeremiah, you're as oblivious as a sleeping Rip Van Winkle, only you're oblivious whether your eyes are wide open or shut. No, we didn't contribute a dime, as I believe I've mentioned a time or two. Our future idiot son-in-law paid for the whole thing."

"My heavens! How could he afford it? He's still quite young."

"He's young all right, but he's also rich. Leslie said he dropped out of Columbia after their freshman year. Apparently he found college life too boring. I thought Leslie had seen the last of him. Turns out his deceased father had set up a rather large college fund which Mr. Wonderful used to invest in real estate back in Chicago where he's from. Using this college money, the know-it-all Mr. Jamie Steinkraus started buying commercial property. Leslie says he leveraged his holdings to buy a chunk of land in Manhattan which he then sold for a large fortune. He owns property all over the country. Maybe the world for all I know."

"He sounds quite enterprising. To meet him, one would never know."

"Well to know his friends is to know him. I met them once last year and once was enough. He hangs around with a bunch of drunken dropout freaks he calls the posse. For God's sake, Jeremiah, they 'possied up' as he tells it in jail… the Tijuana jail. I have no idea what Leslie sees in the man. I just hope she holds up through this ordeal. Maybe you could exercise a positive influence over your prospective son-in-law and his so-called posse, at least through the weekend. Try to keep his drinking and the influence of his ne'er-do-well friends to a minimum, and that includes my idiot nephew Louis."

Having said her peace and made all the points she thought necessary to get Jeremiah "up to snuff" for the upcoming wedding ceremony of their daughter and all the associated festivities, Rose ended the conversation and silence prevailed, only broken occasionally by Rose with a hoarse word or two concerning the directions for the drive.

The good professor, with his wife riding a frustrated and somewhat deafening shot gun, drove on at the breakneck speed of 55 miles per hour. Seven hours and 14 minutes later, after four stops necessitated by nature's call, they pulled up to the administration building for The Hermitage of the Adirondacks. With her head down, an impatient and angry Rose exited the car, ran up the stairs to the building and entered in hopes of quickly registering. After a good forty-five minutes she returned, red-faced and even more angry. "Can you beat that! The place is mobbed and who's behind the desk? A bunch of Mexicans who can barely speak English. The Russian Orthodox brotherhood's become senorita central. We're staying at a cabin called the TR. Mr. Money Bags had reserved the cabin for the groom's party but decided to stay in the lodge up by the pavilion." She looked down at the brochure and map she had been given by one of the administrative senoritas and said, "Drive up this road and take the first left onto a dirt road. It'll be about a half mile up the road on the right."

Jeremiah was overwhelmed and exclaimed, "The TR! How fortuitous! I have the feeling this is going to be a very eventful and exciting weekend!" He took the first left as instructed, drove up a dirt road and parked in front of a cabin. A large sign nailed to the cabin's porch proclaimed The TR. He sat admiring the log cabin and asked, "Pray tell, why is this fine log cabin called the TR?"

Rose, still annoyed by the difficulties she had encountered registering at, as she put it, "senorita central," snapped, "Take a guess, Mr. Adjunct Professor of English Literature?"

Jeremiah smiled, oblivious to Rose's agitated state of mind, excitedly proclaimed, "Teddy Roosevelt came often to the Adirondacks. Perhaps he stayed in this cabin during one of his fishing or ornithological expeditions? It looks to be wonderfully restored."

Rose replied, "Now that was a conclusion only a genius adjunct professor of English literature at a prestigious ivy league university could reach. Get out and unpack the car."

They both got out of the car, Rose quite deftly and Jeremiah somewhat less so and faced each other over the hood of the Volvo. They both looked up at the roof of the car. The ropes securing the suitcase on the roof were all in place, the only thing missing was Jeremiah's suitcase.

Order, order everywhere and not a drop to drink...

Jeremiah had laboriously unpacked the car. He had hung the garment bag in the closet of the master bedroom and had placed the bags, baskets and suitcases about the large three-bedroom cabin in various strategic locations as Rose had instructed… that is, all the suitcases with the exception of his, which had mysteriously disappeared from the roof of their Volvo on the drive to The Hermitage of the Adirondacks. He was exhausted and sought refuge in a rocking chair in the master bedroom where Rose was unpacking her clothes.

She stood in front of a chest of drawers refolding her array of various undergarments, blouses and socks that she had neatly packed in her suitcase. She stacked and stored the articles of clothing according to kind, color and size, as was her habit. An experienced sales lady in an upscale midtown fashion boutique could not have done it better. As Rose robotically refolded, stacked and stored her clothing, she said over her shoulder to Jeremiah, "They have a shop here that sells souvenirs and other incidentals. I think they sell some articles of clothing, sweat shirts and the like. After I get done here, I'll drive back to the administration building. I think that's where the shop is, and buy you some underwear if they have any for sale and whatever else I can find. Because of your size, I doubt we'll be able to get you another formal suit for the wedding on such short notice."

Jeremiah sat in the big rocking chair slowly rocking himself back and forth, his more than ample jowls rhythmically jiggling away as he rocked. He was close to joining the previously mentioned Rip Van Winkle but managed a periodic and strategic "yes dear" here and there as his eyes closed and he drifted off. Rose continued talking and launched into a litany of criticisms of his inability to secure his suitcase on the roof of their Volvo, none of which Jeremiah heard. Suddenly he was jolted back to consciousness by Rose's voice as she yelled, "Darn! There's no cell phone service in this godforsaken place." He thought it odd that God would forsake a place established by brothers of the Russian Orthodox Church and dedicated to providing a place for family retreats and other religious ceremonies. Of course there was that business of the brothers separating themselves from the Russian Orthodox Church and then using a technicality in New York state law to develop what many considered a resort which apparently made a lot of money. A second thought quickly overshadowed the first: perhaps God, being omniscient, would know this and much more unknown to mere mortals such as himself and even Rose, so the question of whether or not God had in fact forsaken The Hermitage of the Adirondacks remained open at this time in Jeremiah's estimation, regardless of Rose's contention.

Rose continued, "I hate to use the phone in the cabin. I'll bet the good brothers charge an arm and a leg for a call."

Jeremiah's mind continued: Maybe there's something to Rose's contention that God has forsaken the Hermitage? If true, this does not bode well for our daughter's wedding and all the matrimonially related ceremonies that accompany it.

Rose now directed her attention to Jeremiah as she placed an envelope on the chest of drawers, "There's your schedule for the weekend. Tonight's the rehearsal. There's a buffet dinner after. The rehearsal is scheduled to begin at 7:00 at the outdoor chapel. Imagine, an outdoor chapel. I still think they should be married in a church, a Catholic church. Well, that's water over the dam. After that the rehearsal dinner is at the lodge up by the pavilion where the rest of the wedding party is staying. When I get back we can walk to the chapel. It's just up the hill."

Jeremiah managed another somnolent "yes dear" as Rose continued, "Mr. Wonderful's best man, Charles something-or-other, has organized a bachelor party for tomorrow night and you're invited. The invitation's in the envelope. He left it for you at the admin center. I'm not sure you should go, but if you do, see if you can be a calming influence on Steinkraus and his freaky friends and that includes that idiot kid nephew of mine. How Louis got involved..." her voice fading as she looked about the cabin to be sure that everything was in its proper place. Having assured herself that all was in order, she continued, "It'd be nice if that so-called posse remained upright for the wedding and reception on Saturday." In the blink of an eye she was at the door and as she disappeared she yelled, "And keep that stupid corduroy suit clean. You'll need it for the wedding." And with that she was gone.

A rehearsal dinner or the Last Supper...

The dining room was crowded with people scurrying about to fill their glasses with beer and their plates with food. Some attacked the beer keg first while others went for the buffet table which nicely divided the crowd into two almost equal lines.

Rose and Jeremiah remained seated waiting for the crowd at the buffet table to thin out a bit. Rose kept her head on a swivel looking for her daughter Leslie to make an appearance. She pointed to the stairway to the second floor, nudged Jeremiah in the ribs and shouted, "There she is!" as she waved with her other hand. "Over here, Les! Over here!"

Leslie made her way to their table, being stopped many times along the way to receive greetings and best wishes from friends and family. She sat down at their table and sighed, "I feel exhausted." She was dressed in red shorts and a white tee shirt. Thankfully for her and particularly for her prospective husband, she had for the most part inherited her mother's looks and build and her father's disposition and intellect.

Rose smiled and said what she said to Leslie every time they met, "You should eat something. It'll help settle your stomach. Make you feel better." Jeremiah kept an eagle eye on the buffet line.

Leslie frowned and replied, "Mother, don't get started. Not today. I had a bite to eat in my room. Jamie brought me a plate after the rehearsal."

Rose looked around the dining room and asked, "Where is Mr. Wonderful anyway?"

Leslie pointed toward the beer keg in the front of the hall. Rose turned to see and there was Mr. Wonderful standing on a chair over the beer keg holding the keg's spout in his left hand. With his red scraggly beard and longish red hair, he looked much like a somewhat diminutive modern day Celtic chieftain. He kept the spout open and beer gushed into the glasses of revelers who stuck their cups beneath the pouring beer as they walked by. He blessed each reveler as they passed beneath him. Every now and then he'd raise the spout above his upturned head and pour beer into his awaiting mouth. Remarkably little beer reached the floor.

Rose looked at the beer pouring spectacle and said, "That's disgusting. He doesn't even use a glass, and those so-called friends of his. Just disgusting. Is that the sign of the cross he's making. He's supposed to be Jewish, I thought." She turned back to face Leslie and said, "The rehearsal went well, considering that not one of the three ushers showed up." Rose then added, referring to her nephew, "Wasn't Louis and his freaky friends supposed to be ushers? What happened to them?"

Leslie, knowing her mother's feelings about Jamie's friends in general and her cousin Louis in particular, replied softly, "Jonnie Hogg and Garcia Rosenbloom… they got arrested on the Northway for well…" She hesitated and Rose jumped in, "Arrested for what?" Leslie continued, "For urinating." After a pause, she added, "Well actually only Jonnie got arrested for urinating."

Rose's eyebrows shot up and back and she said in disbelief, "Urinating? Men stop to take a leak on the roadside all the time. What's the big deal? Surely even an idiot like Jonnie what's-his-name could manage that."

Leslie scrunched up her cheeks and said softly, "Well, it seems they weren't stopped."

Rose, unable to comprehend the situation, asked "Weren't stopped?"

After a long pause, Leslie said, "Yes. Jonnie was urinating out the window of the car while Garcia was driving. Seems they were going a little fast and passed a state trooper and Jonnie inadvertently urinated on the state trooper's windshield."

Rose finally got the picture. "Inadvertently! So while one of these characters was peeing out the window on a state trooper's windshield, the other was driving the car and speeding. How fast?"

Leslie looked down, obviously embarrassed, "I think that Jamie said he was clocked around 120 miles per hour. They didn't want to miss the rehearsal."

Rose shook her head in some combination of disgust and disbelief. "This is like a Dumb and Dumber reality show. Where are Mr. Dumb and Mr. Dumber now?"

"They're being held in Albany."

"Where's my worthless nephew?"

"He drove down to Albany to bail them out of jail. That's why he missed the rehearsal."

Rose said, "Jeremiah, have you ever heard of such a thing?" When she didn't get the dutiful response she expected, she turned and found the chair next to her empty. Jeremiah was in the buffet line.

Leslie reached across the table and put her hand over her mother's hand. She looked down at the table. Rose instinctively put her free hand over Leslie's and said, "What's wrong, Les?"

"I don't know." She paused and then said, "Well, I do know."

Again she paused and finally said in a barely audible voice, "Jamie and I have never been… well… intimate." She looked down at their intertwined hands and continued, "I've never been intimate with…" and after a long pause whispered, " anyone."

Rose gently patted her hand and said reassuringly, "You've been a good girl like you're supposed to be. Don't worry, dear, it's not that important. Your father and I haven't been intimate for years. These things have a way of working themselves out."

Leslie pulled back her hand and said, "I don't know how to work something like this out. I've done a lot of research and reading but it doesn't seem to click with me. Jamie's been very patient."

Rose didn't reply and turned to see where Jeremiah was.

Leslie tapped her mother's hand to get her attention and said, "You know, Janey and Angel are throwing a bachelorette party for me tomorrow night. You're invited. It's here, upstairs."

Rose replied without turning to face her daughter, "Les, I'm not into those kinds of things. Besides, I'm a little too old to be drinking too much and giggling late into the night with a bunch of girls."

The crowd had been eating, drinking and smoking at a furious pace. Jeremiah, no slouch he, was winning the putative eating contest, having already finished his third heaping plate. Rose, as usual, having only picked at a salad, was second to last with Leslie, also as usual, finishing dead last. There were many ties for the lead in the other two putative contests… drinking and smoking.

The great unwashed had divided pretty much into two distinct and equal groups: a rough and tumble, very boisterous suds-consuming crew and a somewhat quieter, mellower group, more like a closely knit community, that seemed to grow happier and more chatty as the pungent and aromatic herbal odor in the dining room grew more pronounced.

Jamie still stood on a chair above the beer keg pouring beer from the keg's spout into the glasses of the revelers who passed below him. He raised his head toward the ceiling, poured beer into his mouth and turned the keg's tap off. From his commanding view of both halves of his audience, he raised his hands and yelled, "Announcement! Announcement, folks! Important announcement!" At first half his audience groaned, believing that the keg was dead. Jamie, knowing his audience, at least this half of it, yelled, "Not to worry, folks. There's plenty of suds. Another announcement!" He wiped his sweaty forehead with his shirt sleeve, pushing his longish red hair away from his eyes, and then licked the beer suds off his red mustache and wiped his beard with the same shirt sleeve in preparation for speaking. The crowd quieted. Jamie waved to Leslie with the hand holding the keg's spout and yelled, "Les, come up here."

Leslie stood and slowly worked her way through the crowd until she stood before the keg of beer. Jamie looked down at her and yelled, "Les, I have a surprise for you. It's my wedding gift to you. I've kept the secret for a year, but I can't keep my mouth shut any longer." Here he paused for a moment to be sure all were paying attention. Most were and he continued, "You know how you hate the long cold winters in crowded Manhattan?" He jumped from the chair and stood next to her, "Well I bought a small parcel of land with a mountain-type chalet east of San Diego. Now we'll be able to escape the long cold winters of Manhattan whenever we want." He kissed her, raised his face toward the ceiling and took a long slug of beer from the keg's spout. The crowd went wild, not needing much of a nudge to do so, for they were happy for Jamie and Leslie and ecstatic now that the keg pouring could resume. Leslie struggled to smile faintly but neither Jamie nor the crowd in their collective happiness and ecstasy noticed her struggle.

A theatrical fertility rite gone real…

As was custom, the time of the bachelorette and bachelor celebrations had come. The bride and the groom were to have one last fling as separate social and legal entities before their lives were conjoined by society's matrimonial glue, and a very strong glue it would be. After tomorrow, should the bride and groom, either individually or in ironical unison, decide to unglue as it were, lawyers, the courts and large sums of money would be involved, and there was the distinct possibility that intimate biographical and even biological details of their lives would be made public in the process. The social and legal stakes were high, which may account for the emotional intensity enveloping the bride and groom and why their respective camps approached this night's celebration with a frenzy approaching madness.

The prospective bride, Leslie Fazzano-Wright, called Bookers by her close friends, awaited the bachelorette celebration with her typical nervousness. Even under much less stressful circumstances, she had great difficulty controlling her emotions. In May, she had collapsed the night before she was to accept her PhD in anthropology from Columbia University. Without the lotus-like help of the fruit of years of meticulous research by the pharmaceutical industry, she would have had to accept her degree through the US postal service.

Mother Rose thought her daughter too thin, and with great perspicacity, attributed this thinness to a lack of eating. To solve this problem, she thought the best plan of action was to exhort Leslie to eat more as often as possible, and this she did. Her encouragement frequently took the form of the following statement, "You're 15 pounds from being a knock-out,"… the unstated portion of this thought being "… and you're not one now."

However, in spite of what her mother said and what Leslie came to believe, young males viewed her as a slender and quite attractive female member of the species. Contrary to their intent, these motherly exhortations made this nervous Nelly in extremis even more so, and the more she worried about her appetite or lack thereof, the less she felt like eating.

Tonight Leslie's emotions ran high and predictably she skipped dinner. Just as predictably, she had taken a double dose of the lotus-like help of the aforementioned fruit of years of meticulous research by the pharmaceutical industry in an effort to avoid a collapse during her bachelorette celebration. And a fine celebration had been planned. The maid of honor, Janey Toussaint, or JT as close friends addressed her, and one of the brides maids, Angel Bangor, referred to as Buns for quite obvious reasons by everyone, had organized one last fling for academic Leslie. As Janey put it, "Let's show Miss Goody Two-Shoes what she's been missin'!" And with this as the organizing principle of the celebration, Janey and Angel had invited the other four members of their old high school clique known as the Seven Damsels in Distress (the other three being the aforementioned Leslie, Janey and Angel), set up a wet bar, acquired several means to relaxation, and hired live entertainment, which Janey described as "enlightening."

The seven damsels in distress gathered at seven o'clock, their traditional meeting time, to begin the festivities. As Janey put it with a broad smile, "Let's give the damsels some time to relax, have a glass of wine, smoke a little pot and chew on some munchies before they're enlightened." As Angel put it, "Oh boy, let's have a big drinkie poo and toke some weed!"

After Leslie and the other four damsels in distress had arrived and exchanged their various gossipy hellos and had a glass of wine or three, Janey called the celebration to order. "Circle up my damsels in distress! Circle up!" The damsels sat cross-legged on the floor forming a circle. Janey pulled two joints from her purse and said, "Damsels, lookie what ol' JT has. Pure California Gold!" Angel shrieked "Oh boy!" as Janey lit one joint, took a toke and passed it to Angel who sat on her left. Janey then looked passionately at the second joint and said, "And scored right here from one of the cleaning ladies. Who'd a thunk?" She then lit the second joint, took a long toke and passed it to her right. The joints passed each other at Leslie who took a short, shallow toke of each and passed them on. Bowls of munchies followed the joints about the circle and the damsels occasionally got up to refill their wine glasses.

The damsels talked constantly and from time to time apparently listened, for somehow vital communications seemed to mysteriously occur. Leslie remained quiet, barely sipping her wine and only taking several more short tokes as the joints passed by. By nine o'clock, the damsels were quite relaxed and Leslie, even though she had indulged lightly, was relaxed a bit beyond quite.

A loud knock at the door signaled the end of the relaxation phase of the festivities and the beginning of the enlightenment phase. Janey jumped to her feet, walked over to Leslie, pulled her up to a standing position and guided the somewhat unsteady soon-to-be-bride to the door.

Janey swung open the door and said, "This'll be right up your alley, Bookers!" There stood a tall and chiseled male exotic dancer dressed in a red loin cloth, a feathered headdress, two feathered and belled ankle bracelets and nothing else. His skin glistened in the dim light of the party room. In his right hand he brandished a short plastic stabbing spear to complete his costume.

Leslie looked up at him with stunned amazement and said the

first thing that came into her mind, "Golly, he's black." To which Janey replied, "Honey bun, you of all people should know that not everyone's white." Leslie tried to clear away the cotton that absorbed her thoughts before she could realize them. Slowly her mind seemed to focus. Standing before her was not some exotic male dancer but rather a great Zulu warrior who embodied the folkways of that people. Her mind wandered back to her doctoral research and the Zulu fertility rites she'd witnessed and which she'd written about in her thesis.

On Janey's cue, Angel, who had retreated to the far side of the room, turned on the stereo and yelled, "Go Jamal!" A faint heavy base thudded slowly as the sound of distant tribal drums filled the room. Leslie heard the other four damsels screech with joy, anticipation and hope. "Do you think it's true what they say?" giggled one of the damsels. "Dunno" replied another, "Hopefully tonight we'll be enn-lightened!" Leslie was in something akin to an hypnotic state as Janey guided her to the center of the room and gently pushed her into a kneeling position as she motioned for the remaining damsels in distress to push back and form a semicircle facing Leslie, who now knelt before them.

Leslie's great Zulu warrior jumped forward into the room with both feet, his ankle bracelets jingling as his bare feet hit the floor. He swirled forward until he stood over Leslie. His dark eyes peered down at her. The chatter in the room quieted and the beating of the tribal drums quickened and became much louder. Leslie looked up into those piercing dark eyes and then down at the floor. Sweat formed on her forehead. Her stomach muscles tightened and she was struck with a strange emotion. Her breathing quickened and she felt something akin to fear, a primordial fear, well up inside her, yet a fear leavened with a strange anticipation and desire. Angel again yelled, "Go Jamal!" which all heard except for the mesmerized Leslie.

This great Zulu warrior, taking Angel's cue, swirled around Leslie, his belled ankle bracelets beating time to the rhythm of the drums as his feet struck the floor. He stopped before Leslie who looked up at him with fear and anticipation in her eyes. Her great Zulu warrior towered over her. The tribal drums grew louder and louder. Leslie felt weak and feared she would faint.

As her great Zulu warrior beat time to the rhythm of the drums with his heels, bells jingling away, he thrust the short stabbing spear forward towards Leslie three times. Leslie felt a sharp pain in her groin and instinctively placed her hands between her legs. Her mind raced. She thought, "What is happening to me?" Then it struck her. She was being deflowered in a ceremony which she had witnessed and about which she had read and written. Her great Zulu warrior raised the stabbing spear above his head and shouted. With his other hand, palm up, he motioned for Leslie to rise, which she did slowly and somewhat unsteadily. From his spread stance, his hips slowly undulated forward and back as Leslie arose. Leslie felt her hips slowly undulate forward and back in response. Her now sweaty tee shirt clung to her breasts and she could feel the cloth rubbing against her nipples as she moved.

Her great Zulu warrior then swirled about the room. The other damsels shrieked with joy. Janey whispered to Angel, "Now comes the expensive part." And Angel, interpreting expensive to mean the very best, swigged her drink and yelled, "Oh boy!"

After circling the room, the great Zulu warrior stopped in front of Leslie and motioned for her to kneel, which she slowly did. He swirled so that he faced away from her and slowly danced about the semicircle, facing the other damsels. He reached across his waist and pulled the clasp to the belt holding up his loin cloth. The belt swung free and dangled from his raised hand. With a wide stance, he bent at the knees and began rising on his toes and then hitting his heels on the floor in rhythm to the tribal drums as he danced about the semi-circle of anxious damsels. Slowly the loin cloth fell to his feet. There he stood, his groin covered with custom white bikini briefs known as a cock sock in the trade.

Leslie could hear the almost painful yet quite joyful "Ooohs!" and "Aaahs!" emanating from the damsels whom he now faced. As

Leslie's great Zulu warrior swirled and faced her, she saw the reason for their distress… and joy. The so-called cock sock worn by her great Zulu warrior had a sheath-like extension which strained under the pressure of its contents. He then swirled about the room again and spun to a stop again facing away from Leslie. He reached for the custom briefs and ripped them away. For a moment there was stunned silence as Leslie swayed in her kneeling position to the rhythmic motion of the muscular black buttocks before her as her great Zulu warrior swayed forward and back. Then one of the damsels yelled, "My God, it's true! Oh, Jamal!"

Leslie's great Zulu warrior then swirled around again facing Leslie. As he hopped towards her, his huge black phallus bounced in rhythm to the beat of the drums. He stopped, towering over her. She looked up into his dark piercing eyes and raised the palms of her hands, gently cradling his huge black scrotum with her hands. She lowered her head and then looked up at the great phallus running her fingers along its length to its root where a leather ring clasped about the base of the uncircumcised beast. Heat ran through her body and centered in her groin. She rhythmically tightened and relaxed her stomach and thigh muscles and the muscles of her groin and buttocks in response to the undulations of the great Zulu warrior standing over her. She felt a desire that she had never felt before and could not describe with words. The muscles of her groin and buttocks now involuntarily contracted rhythmically and intensely. She gently pulled the foreskin back revealing a wonderfully shaped head. She looked into this great black phallic Cyclops, raised her head, looked into the eyes of her great Zulu warrior towering above her and swooned, crumbling unconscious at his feet.

A gathering of the Posse of Little Horses…

Professor Jeremiah Wright looked down at the formal, printed invitation through his pince-nez and read aloud to himself, "There will be a gathering of the Posse of Little Horses to honor our own Stuntman, who after tomorrow will be a one-trick pony."

There was today's date (June 27) followed by the time (7:00 PM) and the place (Adirondack Motel, Shangri-La Suite). To the left of the text was a drawing of two horses. One horse was rearing up on its hind legs above the other horse and looked as if it were about to attack, while the horse about to be attacked seemed ironically to welcome its impending peril.

Jeremiah stared at the drawing with his bushy eyebrows scrunched against his pince-nez as if he were trying to untie another of life's great Gordian knots. He thought to himself: "Stuntman. Hmmmm… Stuntman?" He pushed down at his pince-nez to be sure they remained in place on his nose and wondered: "Why in heaven's name is there a drawing of one horse attacking another on an invitation to a bachelor party? I wonder what the symbolism is? Such a metaphor makes no sense."

After several minutes of contemplation and still unable to make any headway in the metaphoric untying process, he looked down at the invitation, his eyes carefully avoiding the puzzling reference to a Stuntman and the strange drawing of two horses. He took out his pocket watch and stared at its face through his pince-nez. Sure enough, it was seven o'clock. He looked down at the invitation again, his eyes carefully avoiding the puzzling reference and strange drawing a second time, and checked the place. He looked up at the large neon sign by the road and it blinked a pale blue Adirondack Motel in a fine script. Then he looked back at the formally printed invitation, his eyes yet again carefully avoiding the reference and drawing, to check the room. Sure enough, he was standing in front of the door to the Shangri-La Suite. He knocked timidly.

After several tense moments, the door swung open and there stood a tall, well-built young man whose features were partially hidden beneath the brim of a large Mexican sombrero. The man lifted his head in laughter and then Jeremiah recognized him. It was Mr. Charles Fontaine, best-man-to-be, with a big grin plastered across his face. He shouted, "The father of the bride arrives! Glad you could make it, Perfesser! You're the first member of the posse to mosey in! Welcome to the Shangri-La Suite of the Adirondack Motel. Could there be a better place for a bachelor party than a place called the Shangri-La?" Charles waved the professor forward and yelled, "Come on in!"

Jeremiah stood before the doorway peering into what appeared to be a large living room. The Shangri-La was obviously a luxury suite of rooms. Charles yelled encouragement, "Don't be shy, Prof, step into the scene of tonight's crime."

Jeremiah cautiously stepped into a large living room and looked about in wonderment. He had never seen a motel suite such as this. To his left was a counter with two bar stools and behind the counter, a kitchenette with what appeared to be all the modern appliances one could desire. At the living room's center stood a large circular coffee table before a huge leather couch. A mosaic of an airborne cupid with arrow drawn decorated the surface of the coffee table. The large leather couch was an off-pink, a color apparently intended to complement the mosaic. Across the living room, were wide double doors. The doors were closed and over them was a relief of red hearts and yellow and purple flowers surrounded by an intertwining green vine with small pointed bright green leaves, and above the relief were the words "All for Love" in bold red script.

Charles raised his hands above his head and said, "Well, what do you think of the place?"

Jeremiah replied, "What kind of suite is this?"

Charles began to laugh uncontrollably. When he regained control of himself, he said, "You look like the White Rabbit about to fall down the hole into Wonderland. Prof, this ain't Wonderland and there ain't no Alice here. It's the god damn honeymoon suite!"

Jeremiah looked dumbfounded and managed a weak, "Honeymoon suite?"

"Yeah, I rented the place for three days. Tonight for the bachelor party, tomorrow night, after the wedding, Leslie and Jamie are going to stay here for a couple of days before they fly to wherever they're going for the rest of their honeymoon. Know where they're going?"

Jeremiah stared at the relief and muttered to himself, "The Shangri-La. How appropriate." Then he answered Charles' question, "I'm afraid I don't know. I think Rose said that Jamie's kept it a big secret. Apparently even Leslie doesn't know. At least that's what I think Rose said."

Charles put his hands on his hips admiring the relief of hearts and flowers over the double doors and said, "Well Jamie's been pretty tight-lipped about their honeymoon destination with the posse too. We don't know where they're going to end up, but I know where their adventure's beginning... You won't believe the bedroom... And the bathroom? It's got a humongous hot tub. The three days cost me a small fortune. It's my gift to the newlyweds."

Jeremiah handed Charles a wrapped gift, obviously a book. "I brought this gift for Jamie. It's a copy of D. H. Lawrence's Lady Chatterley's Lover."

Charles took the wrapped gift and tossed it onto the large pink leather couch and yelled over his shoulder, "Great," as he walked to the counter that separated the kitchenette from the living room. "Would you give me a hand setting up before the other horse's asses arrive? Little Horses are always late, myself excluded. I don't think the bastards can tell time... which is pretty stupid given they all have digital watches. But they'll all show up. If not for the Stuntman... for this!" And with those words he turned and held up a bottle of tequila. "I got eight bottles of this stuff for 25 bucks."

Jeremiah looked puzzled, "Who's Stuntman? I saw a reference to him on the invitation."

"Prof, I thought you knew. Jamie's Stuntman. It's his nom de caballito."

Jeremiah peered down at the invitation which he still held in his hand, "Oh, the Stuntman on the invitation is Jamie. Now the invitation is starting to make sense. By the way, that invitation is nicely designed and printed."

Charles was admiring the eight bottles of tequila, "Made a bunch of them to commemorate the great celebration. Ain't computers grand."

"What's the significance of the drawing of the two horses?"

"The two horses? Prof, look at that magnificent beast rearing up on its hind legs. Notice anything?"

"Nothing other than one horse seems angry and is about to attack the other horse."

"Prof, that ain't anger. That's desire. And that ain't just any horse. That's a stallion. And he's hung like... well... a horse. And that other horse... that's a mare."

"Oh my" was all Jeremiah could say as the metaphoric meaning of the drawing dawned on him.

Charles, still holding the bottle of tequila before Jeremiah, said, "Brand X, X and X. Never saw this brand before and I've seen a bunch. Found them in that liquor store next to the laundromat in town. There they were. Eight beautiful bottles covered with dust. Bought all eight for 25 bucks... twenty-five bucks. The guy in the liquor store just wanted to get rid of them. Great deal!"

Jeremiah walked over to the bar where Charles was placing one of the bottles of Brand triple-X tequila on a tray with two shot glasses, a salt shaker and a plate of lime slices. Without looking up, Charles said, "Back in a minute," as he walked over to the far side of the living room and knocked on the double doors to the bedroom. A man appeared and took the tray. The man had a very real, large black mustache and looked like a modern-day Mexican bandito. He wore a black tenement tee shirt and his biceps bulged as he held the tray. He and Charles spoke in hushed tones. Then Charles reached into his back pocket, pulled out his wallet and counted out a number of bills, placing each bill on the tray as he counted. The muscular modern day Mexican bandito look-a-like smiled broadly, shook his head yes and disappeared behind the double doors.

Charles literally danced back to the bar and clapped his hands. When he reached the bar, he rhythmically swung his fists in a chugging motion yelling, "Cha, cha, cha!" as he did so. He then said "And that, my Perfesser, is the entertainment, or at least the manager for the entertainment, and for a few more pesos, the entertainment has agreed to a little something special."

Jeremiah, still puzzled by the situation in which he found himself, said, "You hired entertainment?"

"Yup! A stripper. A bachelor party ain't a bachelor party without one. Grab three bottles of Mr. Brand X, X and X and put them on the coffee table." As Charles spoke, he grabbed two bottles by their necks in his left hand and one in his right and walked over to the large round coffee table, which dominated the center of the room, where he carefully placed the bottles around the airborne cupid. Jeremiah followed suit and placed another three bottles on the coffee table. Charles then evenly spaced the six bottles around the edge of the coffee table. He went back to the kitchenette and returned with a large tray containing six salt shakers and a large plate of lime slices, which he placed at the coffee table's center. He stood for a moment admiring his work and mumbled "That should do it for now."

Jeremiah and Charles plopped down on the large pink leather sofa to await the rest of the posse. Academic curiosity gnawed at Jeremiah and he asked, "Why brand X, X and X tequila? Why not one of the better tequilas like Curvos? I suppose a good tequila is more expensive, but I've read that a cheap one has a very harsh taste and causes terrible hangovers."

Charles smiled, "I think you mean Cuervos. Harsh is the point, Prof, and Cuervos ain't harsh. For a tequila to be right for a gathering of the Posse of Little Horses, it has to be harsh, as you put it. It has to slam you. It just so happens that cheap tequilas slam the hardest. This Brand triple-X is cheap and kicks like a mule. I've tested it. I was lucky to find this stuff. It's getting harder and harder to find really cheap tequila. Seems like the tequila industry has gone upscale. For us, it's not the price that counts. It's the kick."

Jeremiah scratched his chin in thought and said, "I don't understand. Slam? Kick?"

"That's right, Prof. Kick drives tequila's spirit to a man's very core where his soul resides, and enables the tequila to do its job. I call it the kick of truth."

Jeremiah sat for a moment staring at the coffee table before them and the six bottles of tequila evenly spaced around its perimeter. He was facing another of life's Gordian knots. This gathering of the so-called Posse of Little Horses raised questions he had not anticipated. Words thundered across his consciousness: stuntman, caballitos, tequila, the bite of truth? He decided to begin with the first word that had crossed his mind: "Is this in any way related as to why my future son-in-law is called Stuntman?"

"You betcha. He's the man, or rather he's the Stuntman! That's his nom de caballito."

"Why is he so called?"

"Prof, because he invented the Stunt, in many ways the raison d'être of our posse. Many others have claimed the title, but for the Posse of Little Horses... he's the one."

"So Jamie has earned this... what did you call it?"

"Nom de caballito"

"So Jamie earned this nom de caballito of Stuntman by inventing the Stunt, which as it turns out is the raison d'être for your Posse of Little Horses?

"Co-rect-a-mundo, my Perfesser!"

"And what may I ask, is this stunt?"

"You know about the ritual for drinking tequila, right?"

"Where one licks a slice of lemon, drinks a shot of tequila and then licks some salt?"

"Well you kinda got all the parts but you ended up with an ugly camel instead of a handsome caballito. First you lick the back of your hand just below the middle finger. It's got to be just below the middle finger, the one used for the single finger salute. Then you pour some salt on the wet spot. You lick the salt and quickly slam the shot of tequila, as we say. Then you bite into a slice of lime... not a slice of lemon but a slice of lime. It's got to be lime. The salt clears the palate by neutralizing the natural acidity of the mouth and the flavor of the lime enhances the after taste of the tequila so that you get full benefit of the tequila's kick."

"But that's not the stunt, right?"

"Riiiight! Jamie invented the ritual we call the Stunt. He's the man or rather he's the Stuntman! He invented our path to truth. First you lick the back of your left hand just below the middle finger. Then you pour a little salt on the wet spot. You snort the salt off the back of your hand, quickly slam the shot of tequila which you are holding in your right hand, slam that little horse on the table and squash the juice of a slice of lime into your left eye. That... my dear Perfesser... is the Stunt!"

"Slam the little horse? I thought you were the little horse? You slam yourself on the table?"

"No! Although that would be a nice touch. I'll have to remember that."

Charles walked over to the bar and returned with two long, thick shot glasses which he held up to Jeremiah. "These are called little horses in the world of tequila. In Spanish they're called caballitos. It's where we got the name of our posse."

Charles handed Jeremiah one of the caballitos which Jeremiah carefully perused, turning it slowly in his fingers. Charles cautioned Jeremiah, "Careful now, that's my personal caballito, my vessel of truth. Harm it not."

Jeremiah pushed his pince-nez down on his nose and looked at the caballito. "It says 'Charlie-O' on your caballito. Why Charlie-O?"

"That's my nom de caballito. All the members of the posse have one."

"What's it mean?"

"Prof, it's a long story." He took his caballito from Jeremiah and handed him the other one he'd brought from the bar. "This, Perfesser, is your own personal caballito. Keep it as a reminder of tonight's celebration."

Jeremiah held the caballito up and turned it so that it was

horizontal and read aloud the word "Perfesser", which was neatly printed in black along the side of the caballito.

Charles smiled. "My dear Perfesser, tonight you are an honorary Little Horse!" And with that, Charles gave Jeremiah a hardy slap on the back knocking his pince-nez from his nose and swinging by the blue velvet cord attached to the vest which covered his more than ample belly. "Perfesser, you already have a nom de caballito."

A knock at the door interrupted their little tête-à-tête and Charles jumped to his feet and yelled, "The rest of the posse has arrived!"

Slip Sliding in the bower of a Chicano love goddess...

Charles ran to the door and threw it open. There stood a short, squat young man, whose blonde head was crowned with the world's worst mullet, and a tall, thin, dark-complexioned young man with a large black mustache and a gigantic gold Star of David necklace prominently displayed about his bare, dark neck.

As they entered the room, Charles yelled, "Pig Fat! Joobie! Two sights that make my eyes sore... and I mean that. Sober, you guys look like shit on a stick."

The short squat young man mumbled, "Go fuck yourself," and pushed past Charles. The tall, thin, dark-complexioned man with the thick black mustache followed but with a slow mosey of a walk.

Charles made the introductions. "Little Horses, this is the Perfesser, Dr. Jeremiah Wright, Leslie's father. Perfesser, this redneck Okie is Jonnie 'Pig Fat' Hogg and this Mexican half breed is Garcia Rosenbloom. We call him 'Joobie', short for Jew-beaner. His old man was a Mexican Jew. Believe that... and a wetback to boot. Swam the Rio Grande to the U, S of A doin' a Mexican version of the Yiddish crawl."

Jeremiah stood and said a meek, "Hello, gentlemen. I am glad to make your acquaintance."

The two recently arrived Little Horses gave Jeremiah a nod and walked over to the coffee table. They took small leather pouches from their shirt pockets, opened the pouches and pulled out their own caballitos. Charles pointed to a bottle of tequila on the coffee table. "That one's yours, Pig Fat," and pointing to the bottle to the left said, "Joobie, yours is right there, to Pig Fat's left. No, no, Joobie, Pig Fat's other left." Joobie obediently moved to Pig Fat's other left.

The two Little Horses carefully set their caballitos before their designated bottles of Brand XXX tequila. Charles asked, "Hey Pig Fat, where's the Guinea and our guest of honor?"

Jonnie Hogg was carefully centering his caballito before his bottle of tequila and without looking up said, "They're outside. Took forever to... ," and before he could finish the sentence, the door swung open with a bang.

Someone shouted "Poncho Villa, we have arrived!" and two young men charged into the living room. Jeremiah recognized both young men, one being Louis Fazzano, Rose's nephew, and the other, Jamie Steinkraus, his prospective son-in-law.

Charles said, "Perfesser, you know these two as Louis Fazzano and Jamie Steinkraus, but for tonight's celebration, they're to be addressed as the Guinea and Stuntman."

Jeremiah mumbled a bewildered, "So it shall be," and sat back down on the large pink leather couch.

The Guinea, aka Louis Fazzano, who could easily have been cast as one of John Travolta's Brooklyn buddies in Saturday Night Fever, looked about the room, whistled loudly and said, "Damn. This place looks like a French whore house with a microwave. What's that say over the door? All for Love? Damn!"

Jonnie Hogg yelled to the newly arrived Little Horses, "Get yer asses over here so we can begin."

Charles asked Jonnie derisively, "What's barbequing your ass, Pig Fat?"

Without looking up, Jonnie replied, "A fuckin' afternoon in the Albany county jail. That's what's barbequin' my fuckin' ass."

Louis joined the discussion, and not reluctantly. "Shit, I had to drive down to Albany and bail you two assholes out. I'm the one should be pissed. And you two owe me five hundred bucks… each. Why the hell were you pissing out the window? That speeding ticket makes sense, but pissing out the window and littering?"

Jonnie wiped his nose with his sleeve and said, "I had to take a fuckin' leak."

Louis yelled back, "Well why didn't you piss into one of those beer bottles?"

"Couldn't."

"Couldn't?"

"That's right: couldn't as in could fuckin' not! We only had one bottle of Fitzgerald's left and it still had beer in it."

"You guys never buy just one quart. What'd you do with all the other bottles?"

"Chucked 'em out the window. That's how come we got ticketed for litterin' too."

Charles rejoined the discussion. "You were drinkin' Fitzgerald's? Shit, if you pissed in the bottle it'd have improved the taste."

Jonnie, as unrepentant as ever, retorted, "Well if you were goin' to take the next slug, I would have!"

Garcia Rosenbloom stood silently before his bottle of tequila smiling inscrutably during the exchange.

Charles pointed at the bottle of tequila sitting on the coffee table before Jeremiah and next to his and said, "Up, Perfesser, up!" as he motioned palms up toward the ceiling. He then pointed towards the coffee table and said, "Put your caballito there. The ceremony is about to commence!" Jeremiah stood and dutifully obeyed. Louis "the Guinea" Fazzano and Jamie "Stuntman" Steinkraus removed their caballitos from pouches as Jonnie "Pig Fat" Hogg and Garcia "Joobie" Rosenbloom had done and carefully placed them before their designated bottles of tequila. Charles checked the table to be sure all was in order and then placed his caballito before his bottle of tequila.

The posse of five Little Horses opened their bottles of Brand

XXX tequila and filled their caballitos, returning each caballito to its designated place on the coffee table. Charles said in rather reverential tones, "Our caballitos have become vessels of truth." Jeremiah followed their lead.

Each of the Little Horses licked the back of his left hand below the middle finger, grabbed a salt shaker from the coffee table and poured salt on the wet spot, returning the salt shakers to the center of the coffee table. Jeremiah followed their lead. The five Little Horses then thrust their right hands above the coffee table, clutched their hands into fists, all fists meeting above the center of the coffee table. Jeremiah timidly followed suit. As the fists met, the five Little Horses shouted in unison, "We don't need no stinkin' badges!" snorted the salt off their left hands, grabbed their vessels of truth with their right hands, slamming the tequila down, then slamming the now empty caballitos onto the coffee table, all in unison. Without hesitation they quickly and in unison grabbed slices of lime from the plate at the center of the coffee table with their left hands, quickly raised the slices of lime above their left eyes and squashed the juice from the slices of lime. They then threw the spent lime slices onto the coffee table and shouted "Fuck you!" shooting their right fists into the air with their middle fingers pointing to the ceiling in the familiar single-finger salute.

Jeremiah stood holding his vessel of truth and watched in stunned disbelief. He had witnessed a strange ceremony, more like a carefully rehearsed insanely irreverent Greek chorus. Jamie yelled to Jeremiah, "Prof, slam your vessel of truth!"

A dazed Jeremiah dutifully sipped from his caballito until the tequila was gone. At first he felt nothing and then a terrible burning sensation gripped him and he started to cough. Jamie slapped him on the back and said, "Prof, that's the slowest naked slam I've ever witnessed!" as laughter filled the room. Jeremiah smiled sheepishly and sat back on the large pink leather couch.

The salt poured, the tequila slammed and the lime slices squashed as the Posse of Little Horses and their one honorary member sat around the coffee table and drank tequila following the more conventional ritual. Jeremiah followed the lead of the Little Horses, albeit somewhat more slowly but fast enough to start to feel very warm. He liked the feeling… a lot.

Jeremiah, his academic inquisitiveness now even more stimulated and less inhibited, asked, "Why do you call the… caballitos… vessels of truth?"

Charles replied, "Because the caballito is filled with tequila and the tequila, once slammed, whispers to your soul, Know who you are. Be who you are. Thus the caballito becomes the vessel of truth. It bares your soul. It strips away the clutter. It teaches you your inner truth. It enables you to be who you truly are."

Jonnie smiled and interrupted Charles' philosophical discourse on the consumption of tequila, "Yeah, it enables you to be drunk!"

Ignoring Jonnie's interruption, Jeremiah mulled over what Charles had said and then asked, "What's the idea of packing a punch have to do with all this? From what I felt, the punch is painful. What's the purpose of pain in all this?"

Garcia Rosenbloom slammed another caballito of truth and said, "Othingnelito learscito wayasito hetito luttercito boutasito eryito oulsito ikelsito ainpito, istermito erfesserpito." (Nothing clears away the clutter about yer soul like pain, Mister Perfesser.)

Jeremiah looked at Garcia and back to Charles with an expression of great puzzlement. Charles asked Jonnie Hogg, "Hey Pig Fat, how many has Joobie slammed?"

Jonnie raised four fingers and wiggled his thumb.

Charles turned to Jeremiah and said, "Joobie's speaking a Mexican dialect of Pig Latin that he invented. He always speaks it after five slams. Say again, Joobie" and Garcia Rosenbloom repeated what he had said.

Charles translated for Jeremiah, "He says something like, loosely translated, pain clears the clutter from the soul," adding "I can understand beaner Pig Latin but I don't speak it very well."

Jeremiah replied, "That's amazing. Does he speak Spanish?"

Charles smiled, "No, but we think he speaks a little English."

Garcia Rosenbloom slammed his caballito on the coffee table after another draught of truth and said, "Herewisita ancingdita enoritasita, istermito harlieocita?" ("Where's the dancing senorita, Mister Charlie-O?")

Charles stood and raised his hands and waved for silence. "Joobie wants the entertainment to begin and I agree." With that, he picked up his bottle of Brand XXX tequila in one hand and his caballito in the other, walked over to the double doors to the bridal suite's bedroom, and gently knocked on the doors with his bottle of Brand XXX. The large muscular man in the black tenement tee shirt opened the door. Jeremiah recognized him as the entertainment manager he'd seen earlier, but there was a difference. The entertainment manager swayed a bit as he stood at the door and grabbed the door jamb for balance as he and Charles spoke in hushed words. The entertainment manager stepped back into the room. Charles turned, motioned for the others to follow and disappeared into the bridal chamber. With Brand XXX bottle and caballito in hand, the rest of the posse followed.

Just barely into the chamber the posse halted its already halting progress and gawked, for there before them was a large, heart-shaped bed on which lay a lovely and quite busty senorita in what appeared to be a traditional low-cut Mexican costume, the dress itself a somewhat shortened version for the senorita's legs were bare. The posse looked up and smiling down at them was a clear reflection of the busty senorita. Jamie looked up at the ceiling mirror and muttered, "Damn, Charlie-O, where'd you find this place?" Charles laughed and said nothing. The entertainment manager wobbled over to a side table where a large boom box sat and turned it on. Trumpets signaling the beginning of a bull fight blared forth.

The busty and lovely senorita waved for the posse to come forward. "Come, come, my gringo friends and be seated." Seven chairs were arranged in a semicircle about the large heart-shaped bed. The bandito entertainment manager plopped himself down in the chair farthest from the door. The lovely and busty senorita waved them forward again: "Come, come, my little gringo friends. I will not bite you... unless of course you want me to." Charles motioned for Jamie to seat himself in the center chair, the place of honor. Everyone else wandered to a vacant chair and sat.

The senorita rose to a sitting position facing Jamie, pulled up her knees and spread her legs slowly as she leaned back on her elbows. Her shortened dress slid up towards her belly. She looked at Jamie and said, "Do you not like what you see of your Juanita?" What Jamie first saw were the beads of sweat running down her forehead. His eyes slowly moved down her body, his gaze resting between her legs. The lovely Juanita said again, "Do you not like what you see, my little gringo friend?" Jamie slowly shook his head yes as he admired the bright red thong which formed an alluring camel toe that could not fully contain her lovely and very full bush of black pubic hair.

Juanita then swirled off the bed. As the music and cheering blared, the busty and lovely Juanita bent at the waist and as she did so, her breasts slid free of her dress. She placed her hands on either side of her head, sticking out the index finger of each hand as she pawed the floor with her feet as would an angry bull. She pawed the floor several more times in place, her large and firm breasts bouncing with each pawing. She then charged around the chair in which Garcia Rosenbloom sat on the far end of the row of chairs, rubbing the back of Garcia's neck with her breasts as she passed. Sweat poured down Garcia's forehead as he slammed yet another caballito of tequila and muttered, "Dito ikelito otito uckinsito noito hosetito esselsvita foita ruthtita." ("I'd like to suck on those vessels of truth.")

The beautiful mad bull then charged in front of Jonnie Hogg, paused, pushed her head into his lap and poked her index fingers into his thighs as she pawed the floor before swirling about and dancing behind Jamie. As she passed him, she gently nibbled on the back of his neck and he too slammed another vessel of truth after she passed.

Juanita kept swirling, now her back toward Charles. She bent over and pushed her bright red thong down to her ankles with her two forefingers, wiggling her hips as she did so. Charles threw back the sombrero shading his eyes to get a better view. The bright red thong fell to her ankles fully baring her plump and jiggling buttock cheeks a foot away from Charles' face. Looking over her left shoulder, she smiled and blew him a kiss.

She then stepped out of her bright red thong, grabbed it with the toes of her left foot, twirled and with a high kicking motion, kicked the thong through the air and onto Louis Fazzano's lap. Louis grabbed the thong and pushed it against his nose yelling "Toro! Toro! Toro!" as he did so. Then he too slammed another vessel of truth and said, "Nothing smells better than napalm in the morning."

Juanita, now naked except for her short dress, which was bunched about her waist, twirled before Jeremiah, clapping her hands above her head as she did so. Jeremiah held his full caballito in his right hand over his lap. Juanita looked into his eyes as she clapped her hands above her head and moved her hips in a slow grinding motion. Jeremiah's extended hand began to shake. The dress bunched about Juanita's waist slowly slipped down her body. As it fell to the floor about her ankles, she yelled "Olé!" Jeremiah, in an almost trance-like state, moved his caballito to his lips, spilling tequila down his now jiggling belly and onto his partially hidden fly as he did so. He slammed what was now a vessel of half truth in one fast yet unsteady motion. Juanita gently patted his lap and said, "Poor Señor Gringo, you have spilled tequila on your pants." Bending slightly at the knees, she spread her legs and said, "Perhaps seeing Juanita will help Señor Gringo forget his discomfort." A dumbfounded Jeremiah shook his head yes slowly as the naked Juanita spun to the great heart-shaped bed and sat down facing the Little Horses with her legs straddling the point of the great heart-shaped bridal bed.

Juanita leaned back on her elbows, spread her legs and said, "Do the little gringos not like Juanita's body?"

Charles yelled, "We sure do! How about some of those tequila body slams we paid for?"

Juanita scrunched back onto the bed and lay down. She smiled and said, "As my little gringo friends wish."

Charles turned to Jamie and said, "The guest of honor first."

Jamie poured himself another vessel of truth and staggered over to the bed, kneeling over the prone Juanita. The other Little Horses followed in their somewhat unsteady gait, surrounded the great heart-shaped bed and chanted, "Bod-ee slam! Bod-ee slam! Bod-ee slam!" Jeremiah remained seated and stared blankly at the scene as it unfolded before him.

Jamie held his caballito above Juanita and slowly poured its contents onto Juanita's belly button. Then he quickly knelt over her, supporting himself with his arms and licked the tequila from Juanita's belly button, quickly licking in circles around her belly button as the tequila spread across her belly. Juanita laughed as Jamie licked away and yelled, "Oh, Señor Gringo, that tickles."

Juanita kept laughing away as each of the Little Horses performed a tequila body slam on Juanita's welcoming belly to the chants of "Bod-ee slam, Bod-ee slam!"

Charles turned and noticed that Jeremiah was still seated in his chair and had not taken part. He yelled to Jeremiah, "Prof, you gotta body slam. If you don't, it'll bring bad luck to the groom. It's a long-held tradition."

Jeremiah, even in his present condition, remained concerned with what he considered important details and slurred, "How long this tradition held?"

Charles looked down at his wrist watch and said, "Twenty-seven minutes. But as an educated man such as yourself knows, twenty-seven minutes can be an eternity. Time is relative, but bad luck is forever!"

Jeremiah carefully if somewhat unsteadily poured tequila into his caballito, spilling as he poured. He put the bottle of tequila down by his chair and kicked it over as his staggered toward the bed. He turned and looked somewhat befuddled as tequila spilled on the rug around his chair. He had lost his concentration momentarily but regained his purpose as the chants of "Bod-ee slam! Bod-ee slam!" rang forth.

He approached the bower of love from the front, unsteadily lifted his left knee and then gently set it down on the left edge of the great heart-shaped bed's point. Juanita, to make things easier for the unsteady Jeremiah, scrunched down the bed towards him until her legs were on either side of him. As he leaned forward to pour the tequila onto Juanita's belly button, his other knee caught on the edge of the bed and he fell forward pouring his tequila onto Juanita's thick bush of black pubic hair as he fell. He landed face first between her legs and could taste the tequila. Juanita screamed, laughed and instinctively brought her legs together over Jeremiah's shoulders and around the back of his neck, trapping his head, face first, between her legs. He instinctively licked away at the tequila.

Juanita leaned back on her elbows and looked down between her two firm, large breasts at Jeremiah as he licked away. She looked up at the ceiling mirror, threw back her arms and moaned, "Oh, Señor Gringo, you know how to say gra… gra… gra… ci… a… a… aaaas!"

The Little Horses, apparently believing that Jeremiah's pubic body slam was intentional, cheered wildly, "Per-fess-er! Per-fess-er! Per-fess-er!" As Jeremiah munched away, his jaw tired as the weight of his upper body pressed down upon his face. He pushed up, slipped off the bed and fell onto his back, hitting the floor with a thud. He looked up. Garcia stood over him and yelled, "Erfesserpito, ouyito avehito ventinito a-ito ewenito odybito lamsito, hetito unatito ur- ritobito! Hetito unatito urritobito!" ("Perfesser, you have invented a new body slam, the tuna burrito! The tuna burrito!")

Jeremiah stared at the ceiling and saw a dark, luscious young love goddess smiling down at him. He heard the words "tuna burrito" shouted repeatedly. He slowly closed his eyes and fell into some- thing resembling a deep sleep.

Saturday, June 28
A rose is not always rosey…

Jeremiah slowly opened his eyes with great effort, the parting of his eyelids an act of pure courage. As he did so, light blasted his brain with pain. He saw above him what he thought looked like a familiar ceiling, but he wasn't sure as it circled above him. He desperately wanted to know where his body now lay. He wasn't even sure he was still alive, thus making it distinctly possible in his mind that he was not. Perhaps he was condemned to one of Dante's seven circles of hell. Or was it nine? The details of the Inferno escaped him, buried in the waves of pain that scrambled his thoughts. Through the pain he slowly turned his head to see if any of Satan's helpers were about. Then as his eyes slowly scanned the room, he froze in fear, for he was sure he was in hell, a living hell. There, primping before the mirror over the big dresser along the far wall stood… Missus… Rose… Fazzano…Wright… known to family, friends and even casual acquaintances by another name: The Barracuda. He thought to himself, "God, I wish I were dead."

He heard words. "Two strange young men dragged you in last night. A short, stubby reprobate and a tall Mexican wearing one of those gaudy Star of David necklaces. The stubby one looked like a poorly groomed redneck, if that's possible. The other one appeared to be a cross between Poncho Villa and Ichabod Crane. Was he Jewish?" Jeremiah groaned and after a short pause the words continued. "They dragged you in by your arm pits and dumped you into bed. I think the Mexican explained to me what happened, but he spoke a foreign language. I didn't understand a word. Sounded like a weird dialect of Spanish. Took me half an hour to get that stupid corduroy suit off that drunken body of yours. I cleaned it as best I could and pressed it this morning since it's all you have to wear today. It's hanging in the closet."

Jeremiah heard footsteps move away from him and then return. He heard a fizzing sound, then more words. "Drink this and get your adjunct professor's butt out of bed. I'm going to Leslie's room. I'm meeting her and the bridesmaids there to dress. She reserved a room at the resort's Blue Mountain Lodge down the road. You know, so that Jamie wouldn't see her before the wedding and she could have some privacy before the ceremony."

Jeremiah pushed up on his elbows and then very slowly and with great effort moved into a seated position. A hand, holding something, entered into his field of vision. He groaned and held out his left hand. He felt something cool thrust into his outstretched palm. It slowly registered that he was now holding a glass. The words continued. "You'll have to drive me to that lodge building. Drink. It'll make you feel better. You've got half an hour to get up to snuff."

He drank slowly from the glass. He felt the fizzing liquid cross his tongue as he swallowed and much to his surprise, his tongue found the sensation quite pleasant. Words resumed. "This place is gigantic. I had no idea." As the liquid slid down his throat, his stomach reacted quite differently. It found the fizzing liquid quite revolting. He spun off the bed and landed on his hands and knees. He crawled forward instinctively and found himself over a large porcelain toilet bowl as his stomach consummated its revolt on its own initiative and heaved the contents of his stomach into the large porcelain toilet bowl which he found before him. The revolt continued for some time. His stomach muscles ached from the contractions. The revolt finally ceased and he leaned his arms forward, put his head down and closed his eyes. Then he heard more words... those most dreadful of sounds… "You'll have to drive me to that lodge and help me find her room. I forgot to get the number. Can't be that hard to find."

He thought to himself, "Maybe I am in Hell." More words rained down upon him. "Brush your damn teeth. I can smell you from here." He leaned back against the bathroom wall and groaned. A shadowy figure filled the doorway. The apparition came forward and spoke still more words, "Drink this before you brush your teeth." He felt something warm thrust into his hands. He brought the warm vessel to his lips and sipped. The flavor of sweet, very sweet, black coffee slid down his throat. Then the apparition pulled open his right hand and thrust several small white pebbles into his now outstretched palm. More words. "Take these, you horse's ass." The apparition disappeared. He put the small white pebbles into his mouth and washed them down as he slowly drained the cup of sweet black coffee.

Jeremiah was hurting but the world was slowly coming into focus. He stripped off his underwear and stepped into the shower, turning the water on full blast. The cold water jolted his body and then he adjusted the water so that it was lukewarm. He felt the water pelting the top of his head, rushing over his face, rolling down his rotund body and slowly washing away his pain. He turned off the water and stepped out of the shower stall. Grabbing a large bath towel, he carefully dried himself and with some difficulty tied the towel around his midsection for the large bath towel barely reached about his huge waist. He robotically brushed his teeth avoiding the reflection in the mirror before him.

After these Herculean efforts, he turned and slowly lumbered out of the bathroom towards the bed. The thought of lying back down dominated what few thought processes were occurring in his brain. As he approached the bed, he noticed a pair of sweats spread out before him and a pair of sandals on the floor below. Any hope of lying down died a quick, painful death.

He stood before the bed looking at the sweats. Then more words rained down upon him. "I bought the sweatpants and shirt at the shop here. I could only get extra large, so you'll have to squeeze into them. I also got a pair of flip-flops. I think they'll fit."

As he reached for the sweat pants, the towel about his mid-section fell to the floor and there he stood naked as a gigantic jay bird. The Barracuda stood by the door next to a huge suitcase with a garment bag draped over it, watching him. Then more words shot forth, "You'd do well to get yourself a smaller belly or a longer thingy. Hustle it up. We're late."

Still too numb to feel insult to his masculinity or any other aspect of his being for that matter, he pulled the sweat pants over his naked body. He grunted and struggled as he did so since even extra-large sweatpants were a couple of sizes too small for him. It was only with great difficulty that he could stretch them over the rather corpulent lower half of his body. He began to sweat from the physical effort. He then pulled the sweatshirt over his head and grunted yet again as he forced it over the upper half of his rather corpulent body. Sweat poured off his forehead. Having succeeded in covering his body after much struggle, he now had to cover his feet. As he stood over the sandals by the bedside, he could not see them for his great belly blocked his vision. He slid his feet about the floor feeling for the sandals and after many attempts got his bare feet into them and slowly shambled over to the mirror.

He stood before the mirror above the dresser trying to gather his thoughts, wondering what the next step in his dressing routine should be. He noticed that he could not see well and after some thought realized that he was not wearing his pince-nez. He heard more words. "They're on the dresser. Hustle it up or I'll be late." He felt about the blurry dresser top until his fingers came upon a pair of pince-nez. He picked them up and pushed them down upon the bridge of his nose, ending this particular stage of his ordeal by pinning his pince-nez's blue velvet safety cord to his sweatshirt.

He peered into the mirror to confirm that he was still alive and noticed that the sweatshirt covering his upper half and the sweat-pants covering his lower half did not meet in the middle. A large, hairy band of white flesh, decorated with a huge belly button, separated the two halves of his attire. And the parts of his body that the sweats succeeded in covering did so as if they were a very tight body stocking. His sweats revealed every wrinkle, every indentation, every lump of his more than ample body. The sweats became a relief map for his physical being, and it was not an appealing map.

The running commentary continued. "You should have stayed in the room last night and rested like I did. You're too old for bachelor parties as you've more than amply proven. Quit admiring yourself in the mirror and grab the suitcase and garment bag." He did as instructed, followed his wife out the door and with great difficulty trundled the suitcase and garment bag to their Volvo.

Jeremiah stuffed the large suitcase and garment bag into the back seat of their late model but somewhat wrinkled automobile and then stuffed himself into the driver's seat. He awaited more orders. The Barracuda, already in the passenger's seat, did not disappoint him. "Take a left out of the parking lot and drive down the hill about a half mile. The Blue Mountain Lodge is the first building on the left." He did as ordered, exiting their parking lot, driving down the dirt road and pulling into the parking lot in front of the aforementioned Blue Mountain Lodge. The parking lot was huge and the only parking space he could find was a considerable distance from the lodge's main entrance.

He tumbled from the front seat of the Volvo and, with what seemed like a Herculean labor, slowly pulled the garment bag and suitcase from the back seat. With yet a second Herculean labor, he slung the garment bag over his shoulder and dragged the suitcase across the parking lot. He tried to keep up with Rose but the burden of the suitcase and garment bag with the added weight of his hangover slowed him considerably. Sweat beaded on his forehead. The wet patches under his armpits, and in other creases of his body better not mentioned, spread. He could feel the sweatpants vigorously rubbing against those rather tender better not mentioned body parts as he struggled forward. When he finally caught up with Rose, she was standing in the lodge's foyer before a large desk.

She looked at him and demanded, "Where's the clerk?"

Somewhat taken aback and not expecting to have to field this question or any question for that matter, he mumbled a reply after looking about the foyer. "Ah… looks like there isn't one." Much to his dismay the dialogue continued.

"Why not?"

"I don't know, dearest. What room is she in?"

"I already told you I don't know her room number. Now what do we do, Mr. Genius? I can't call her on my cell. There's no service in this godforsaken place."

Jeremiah could tell that Rose was in full panic. She was hotter than a frying pan with anger and frustration and quickly moving into her red zone, for her a very short and oft-traveled trip. He looked about and noticed a phone on the desk. He pointed to the phone and said, "Call the main desk in the admin building. They'll know."

On the faceplate of the phone was a list for all the lodge's services and their extensions. Rose found the number for the main desk and hurriedly punched the number into the phone's keypad as the phone jumped about the desk with the punch of each number. Jeremiah only heard one side of the conversation but even in his present condition it wasn't all that difficult to figure out the other side.

"Hello? I'm with the wedding party. I'm the bride's mother."

"Yes, the bride's mother. I'm supposed to meet my daughter at her room to dress for the wedding ceremony. She has a room reserved in the Blue Mountain Lodge, but I don't know her room number."

"I'm staying in the TR cabin."

"My name? Rose Fazzano-Wright."

"My future son-in-law, Jamie Steinkraus, reserved the cabin."

"That's right. Steinkraus… s-t-e-i-n-k-r-a-u-s."

"My daughter's name? Leslie Fazzano-Wright. Last name sound familiar?"

"You have no listing for a Leslie Fazzano-Wright?"

"No, he's not a bridesmaid. He's the groom. Not that it should matter to you."

"Could you please give me the room number?"

"So what if the names don't match? Just give me the damn room number."

"You can't? Why the hell not?"

"OK, then call the stupid room and tell her I'm here in the foyer."

After a long pause, the one-sided conversation continued, much to Jeremiah's dread.

"What do you mean there's no answer? This isn't a nudist wedding. She's got to put clothes on someplace and that someplace is a room in this stupid lodge. Damn it, call her again!"

After another long pause, Rose slammed down the phone.

By now, Jeremiah was sitting in a large leather chair facing the desk and a very angry Rose. He asked timidly, "No luck?"

Rose swirled on her heels facing Jeremiah and screamed, "What the hell do you think? And don't give me any of your B-S. You better not go ballistic on me, you horse's ass."

Driven by great fear and trepidation and the belief that a solution was preferable to a painful and losing confrontation, Jeremiah replied, "Did you get a hint as to her room number?"

Rose thought for a moment and then said, "I think the clerk mumbled 1245 as she dialed. That might be a room number."

"Right! Extension numbers are usually based on room numbers. My guess, that's first building, second floor, room 45."

Without replying, Rose spun on her heels and double-timed up a nearby staircase, two steps at a time, disappearing down the corridor at the head of the stairs. Jeremiah grabbed the suitcase and garment bag and hauled them up the steps. By the time he reached the top of the steps, he began to be envious of the mythic Sisyphus, for Sisyphus wasn't married to Rose. After that poor devil got done pushing the rock up the hill, all he had to do was walk back down the hill and push the stupid rock back up again. Without the benefit of Rose's direction, commentary and encouragement. Jeremiah did recognize one benefit from all this extra Sisyphean physical labor. He was sweating the alcohol out of his system. He dragged the suitcase and garment bag down the maze of hallways, right, left, right, following the room numbers until he reached a long hallway that dead-ended, and there at the far end of the hallway stood his own personal minotaur trying, as far as he could tell, to devour a door.

As Jeremiah approached, the banging got louder as did the shouting, "Leslie! Leslie! Open the damn door!" Once alongside the screaming and banging Rose, he noticed a Do Not Disturb sign hanging from the doorknob and offered, "Looks like the sign should read Cannot Be Disturbed."

Rose swirled about, yelled, "Shut up, you idiot," and took off back down the hallway heading for the foyer. Jeremiah slung the garment bag over his shoulder and dragged the suitcase behind him, arduously retracing his steps to the foyer. Once there, he stood silently, knowing that emotional Armageddon was a poorly chosen word away and that virtually any word he uttered would qualify as poorly chosen.

Rose stood silently for several minutes developing a new search strategy and then blurted out, "I'd recognize her voice anywhere. Wherever she is, she's bound to be talking. She never shuts up. All we have to do is walk down each hallway quietly and listen."

Before Jeremiah could speak, had he the courage to do so, Rose was already posted in front of the first door on the first floor hallway off the foyer, listening. She put her ear to the door holding up her hand to Jeremiah as he approached. She shook her head no and moved on to the second door. Jeremiah, reprising the role of an unfortunate Sisyphus, followed as quietly as possible as Rose put her ear to the next door. They proceeded up the hallway, Rose putting her ear to each door with Jeremiah following with the garment bag slung over his shoulder dragging the heavy suitcase behind.

As they proceeded up the hallway, Jeremiah noticed a map of the Blue Mountain Lodge on the wall, one of those building layout maps showing all the emergency exits with a big you-are-here arrow designating your present location vis-à-vis the rest of the building and the closest exit, which just happened to be alongside the map. He stopped, put down the suitcase, laid the garment bag over it and perused the map. He observed that the closest exit was to the right of the map, making the map in his mind somewhat unnecessary in relation to the need to find the closest exit. However, he was impressed with the total number of exits and rooms available and thought the map quite well-designed and helpful should someone desire to find another exit or a particular room.

Rose, having listened with no luck at all the doors on the hallway, returned to where Jeremiah stood. He offered a meek, "I don't want to be critical, but if someone opens a door and finds you with your ear glued to it, they could be offended. They might think you're an audio voyeur of some sort and complain to the resort's management, or even worse, take immediate vigilante action."

Rose gritted her teeth with the snarl worthy of a pit bull and said, "I dare the S-O-Bs..." but before she could finish, the building map on the wall behind Jeremiah caught her attention. Jeremiah pointed to the map and said, "We have an even bigger problem. I didn't realize it, but the Blue Mountain Lodge is actually three interconnected buildings, each one two stories high. There are hundreds of rooms."

She sighed, and said "You're right. It'd take way too long to listen at each door in all three buildings", much to Jeremiah's relief. He felt sure that their present insane search strategy was about to end, but he was wrong, very wrong. Rose continued, leaning heavily on her training as a programmer, "We'll have to reduce the number of target rooms with a second search algorithm." She thought for a moment and then smiled. "What do we know? We know the make and model of her car! We can walk through the parking lot in front of each building and chances are she'll be in the building where she's parked her car. Then we'll only have one third of the rooms for our primary search algorithm." She shouted, "Follow me," as she bolted through the exit next to the now superfluous map and out into the parking lot for the second lodge building.

Jeremiah stood for a moment girding his loins for the task at hand. He sighed the sigh not of a Sisyphean character but rather of an abused beast of burden. He had been downgraded from a figure of Greek mythology to a Disney character. He threw the garment bag over his shoulder, sighed again, grabbed the suitcase and pushed the exit door open with his elbow, edging his way into the second parking lot. By then, Rose had surveyed that parking lot and returned. As she passed him she yelled, "Her car's not here" and double-timed to the parking lot for the third lodge building. Jeremiah, now drenched with sweat, followed as best he could. By the time he reached the parking lot for the third lodge building, Rose had already completed her algorithmic search of same, passing him for a second time and yelling, "Her car's not here either" as she did so. She zoomed off to the parking for the first lodge building where they had parked.

Realizing that following Rose was a fool's errand even for a lowly beast of burden, he headed directly for the foyer where they had originally entered, huffing and puffing as he trundled along. By the time he reached the foyer's entrance, Rose was standing with hands on hips waiting impatiently for his arrival. As he pulled the suitcase up the entrance steps, she said to him, "Her car's not here either."

Once inside the foyer, Jeremiah let the suitcase drop to the floor, threw the garment bag over top of it, and plopped down into the large leather chair he had occupied before their great algorithmic adventure had begun. Rose stood at the desk and looked over at her beast of burden and yelled, "Now what, Mr. Genius?" as she fumbled through her purse. She pulled out a folded sheet of paper, unfolded it and started reading.

Jeremiah asked, "What's that?"

"A list of all the rooms and cabins rented by the members of wedding party."

Jeremiah thought for a moment and then said, "Rooms and cabin numbers are also extension numbers. Start dialing until you get one of the bridesmaids."

Rose looked down at Jeremiah and said, "You finally have a

decent idea" as she began punching numbers into the phone. She dialed a number and got no answer. Dialed a second and got no answer. After four or five more numbers, she shouted, "Hello? It's Rose. Where's Leslie?"

"At the administration building? Why?"

"Sign what?"

"The marriage license?"

"I'm in the Blue Mountain Lodge. The foyer."

"Her room here is in Building 1? Room 2-4-5?"

After a long pause as she listened intently, she hung up the phone.

"Her room's 2-4-5 in this building. It's the darn room we went to first. That was Janey. She said that Leslie had to go over to the administration building to sign the marriage license. She's picking Janey and Angel up and they're coming right over."

Jeremiah thought to himself, "Weddings reflect life. You always end up where you started after much thrashing about, one's life being the thrashing about."

Not long after Rose hung up the phone, Leslie and her bridesmaids Janey and Angel bustled into the foyer. Janey and Angel were chirping away but Leslie uncharacteristically said little.

Rose looked at Leslie and said, "Get all that signing business taken care of?" To which Leslie shook her head yes and walked towards the stairs. The two chirping bridesmaids, bubbling with small talk, followed. Jeremiah slowly stood, threw the garment bag over his shoulder, grabbed the suitcase and resumed his duties as family beast of burden. He followed Rose up the stairs as she followed the female portion of the wedding party, retracing their initial steps to room 245.

When the group had all arrived in front of room 245, Janey unlocked the door. The women stormed into the room. Jeremiah meekly followed, putting the suitcase down and laying the leaden garment bag on the bed. He rubbed his shoulder and wondered if Rose's dress not only looked nice but would also protect her from radiation should the need arise.

He retreated to the car and drove back to their cabin. As he entered the cabin, he noticed a large brown envelope on the floor. Someone had obviously slipped it under the door while he and Rose were out. Curious as to its contents, he opened the envelope and dumped the contents on the bed. A folded piece of paper and a bunch of color photos fell out. He picked up one of the photos and there he was, somewhat fuzzy but recognizable, his mustached face buried between the stripper Juanita's legs. He sagged onto the bed, bent over and held his forehead. His pince-nez fell towards the floor and then were yanked back from gravity's pull by the blue velvet cord he'd pinned to his sweat shirt.

He watched as his pince-nez swung back and forth below, his own personal pendulum of doom. They swung back and forth, their arc slowly decreasing until they hung motionless below his chin. As someone famous once said, "Nothing concentrates the mind quite like the prospect of hanging!" and Jeremiah's mind became quite focused, for he knew that his beautiful Rose had long, sharp thorns and that those long, sharp thorns could inflict terrible pain.

Then he looked down at the photos again and the accompanying folded piece of paper. He quickly grabbed his pince-nez, pushing them down on the bridge of his nose as he spread the photos on the bed. He again looked at the photo he had already seen. Much to his disappointment, he was still there munching away at the young and lovely Juanita's great bush of black pubic hair. In the background, he noticed the very fuzzy images of two young men yelling encouragement. One appeared to be Charles Fontaine, who yelled his encouragement from beneath the shadow of a sombrero, and the other a wild-eyed Jamie Steinkraus, who just plain yelled. The next photo pictured him still munching away at the young and lovely Juanita's thick, black bush, this time from a different angle, with the even fuzzier images of the other three members of the posse apparently cheering him on as well. He slowly checked the remaining photos. One appeared to be a fine picture of a thumb. Another, a wonderful picture of the floor. And the last, one of several pairs of well-shod feet.

He nervously unfolded the paper that accompanied the photos and spread it out on the bed. He then read the following note aloud to himself,

"5 grande or innernet will contak u for detail"

He mumbled indignantly, "Why would someone slip bad, incriminating photos and an illiterate note under my cabin door? Thank God, Rose was not here. This is doubly humiliating." Buoyed by his resulting doubled indignation, he showered a second time and dressed for the wedding ceremony in yesterday's clothing.

Jeremiah's plight: discovered and uncovered...

Jeremiah slowly walked up the dirt road from the TR to the entrance of the outdoor chapel. He pulled out his pocket watch and checked the time. It was eleven o'clock. He smiled to himself as he stuffed his pocket watch back into its proper vest pocket, for he was at the designated location at the designated time as so carefully and painfully instructed by his dear wife Rose. He had to await his daughter Leslie, her bridesmaids and his aforementioned dear wife and upon their arrival, perform his only official duty of the wedding ceremony, walk his daughter down the aisle to the altar. He had also been instructed to make the walk a slow one and not to trip while doing so. Ordinarily he would not worry about violating the instruction concerning tripping, but today he did, for the aisle was of unevenly crushed stone and he was still feeling the effects of last night's bachelor party. The walk down the aisle with daughter Leslie on his arm would require a level of concentration not usually necessary.

Still, the setting was breathtaking, for the outdoor chapel faced the beautiful Adirondacks. The sun blazed in all its glory with nary a cloud overhead. Jeremiah continued smiling and thought to himself, "Scenery such as this must have inspired TR." Then he pressed his hand to the breast pocket of his jacket and felt the incriminating color photos and the note that he had brought with him to show the

Posse of Little Horses. A frown spread across his face as he walked up to the posse who stood on the other side of the entrance to the outdoor chapel awaiting their official duties to begin.

The Little Horses were dressed in matching formal grey suits and from a sartorial point of view, appeared to be fully prepared to discharge their various official ceremonial matrimonial duties. From the neck up their preparedness did not match that from the neck down. Charles Fontaine, the presumptive best man, did not appear to be at his best, for he was leaning against a post on one side of the entrance, his eyes bloodshot and his stance somewhat unsteady. Jonnie Hogg and Garcia Rosenbloom stood upright without the support of posts and seemed steadier on their feet, although a keen observer of the human condition could detect that these two, in their present condition, were on the lower edge of that human condition. Jamie Steinkraus, the presumptive groom, was wearing the sombrero which Charles had sported most of last evening and large sunglasses, thus covering up any facial indications of unpreparedness which the aforementioned keen observer of the human condition would use to make a determination as to the groom's condition, vis-à-vis human-ity, although such an observer could entertain certain presumptions. Louis Fazzano did not appear at all.

Jeremiah looked at the posse and said, "I need all the Little Horses to help me. Where's Louis?"

Charles mumbled something close to English, but still requiring translation, which Jamie provided, "Went back to get the rings." He pointed at Charles with his thumb and said, "Numbnuts over here left them back in his room… he thinks." Charles smiled and slowly and sagely shook his head yes as if confirming an act of extreme competence on his part. Jamie continued, "What kind of help you need?"

Jeremiah pulled the photos and folded note from his jacket pocket as the posse, Louis light, gathered around him, "These photos and this note were in an envelope some ne'er-do-well slipped under my door this morning." Jonnie Hogg, after carefully perusing the first photo, observed, "Damn, Prof! That's a great shot of you inventing the tuna burrito. Who recorded the fuckin' historic event?"

Jeremiah pursed his lips, slowly shook his head no and mumbled, "I do not know."

Jonnie Hogg continued, "That Juanita chick has the greatest bush south of the border I've ever seen. You're buried chin deep into that tuna burrito. Can barely tell it's you except for those pinch-nose glasses of yours."

Garcia, now sober enough to return to speaking English but not so sober as to slip into his natural reticence, chimed in, "With each munch, I thought you'd lose those crazy specs of yours for sure. Man, how did you keep those babies stuck to your nose with all that munchin' you were doin'? "

As he looked down at the photo he was showing, Jeremiah absentmindedly replied to Garcia's question, "It's the spring on the nose piece. Keeps the pince-nezs very secure."

Jeremiah handed the first photo to Jamie. After carefully inspecting the photo, Jamie observed, "The damn photo's pretty blurry. That's definitely you and I guess that's Charles with the sombrero and looks like me in the background next to Charlie-O here. It's kinda hard to tell." Jeremiah then showed the posse the second photo, this one picturing Jeremiah from another angle buried nose deep between the lovely Juanita's legs with what was probably Jonnie Hogg, Garcia Rosenbloom and Louis Fazzano cheering him on in the background. Jamie whistled from beneath the sombrero and Charles mumbled, "Great fucking shot. Who took pi-tures? One of posse?"

Without answering, Jeremiah showed the third photo, this one picturing a thumb and the fourth, a picture of the floor and the final one picturing several pair of well-shod feet. Charles pointed to the last photo and said, "Those my boots!" He then scratched his head and answered his own previous question concerning the identity of the photographer, "Well that pretty much liminates us as photog... photog... fer. We're all in pi-tures."

Jonnie Hogg took the second photo from Jeremiah and after carefully looking at the details of the photo, said, "Hey, I think that's you, Joobie. And I think that other blurry bastard's the Guinea with his fuckin' eyes poppin' out his greasy head." Garcia smiled inscrutably.

Jeremiah then unfolded the note and by way of explanation said, "I also received the following note in the envelope with the photos. Correcting the note's text for poor spelling, lack of punctuation and poor sentence structure as well as several other egregious errors, the note reads, Five grande...with an e...or the internet will contact you for details."

As you the highly perspicacious reader know, the unedited note actually said: 5 grande or innernet will contak u for detail.

Charles looked down at the note and said, "Wass wrong with note?"

Jeremiah, holding the note in his right hand, moved his left index finger across the text, identifying each problem as he analyzed the note.

"The author of this note should have spelled out the word five and capitalized it I might add. He or she misspelled the words internet and contact, used an inappropriate contraction, u, neglected to make the word detail plural and did not place any punctuation at the end of the sentence. Probably should have used an exclamation point. And an article or two might have been nice. I could be critical of the use of the word grande and its spelling as well, but I let that pass since the note is obviously informal and thus the use of the colloquial grande, even when spelled with the e, can be viewed as appropriate in this instance. This note could have been written by any number of students in my freshman composition class or even by someone who doesn't speak and write English as their primary language."

Charles looked a bit puzzled by Jeremiah's textual analysis, which he actually seemed to follow, and asked, "What kinda article? Like in a newspaper explainin' things?"

Jeremiah, with studious seriousness, replied, "No, Charles. In this case the word article means the words a, an or the. The article the should probably have been placed before the now misspelled word internet."

Jonnie Hogg rubbed his chin thoughtfully and asked, "Who sent the fuckin' note?"

Jeremiah replied a quick, "Do not know. Luckily Rose wasn't there when I found the envelope."

Garcia Rosenbloom pointed to the word grande in the note and observed, "Isn't that the way you spell grand in Spanish?"

Jonnie Hogg added, "Who would spell like they were Spanish?" Then pausing for a moment, he continued, "Hold it... hold it... Mexicans speak Spanish. Didn't that entertainment manager dude look like he was Mexican? Why would he send you a fuckin' note?"

Jeremiah, leaping to the defense of the country's largest minority and half of Garcia Rosenbloom's ethnic and cultural heritage, solemnly countered, "Let us not jump to stereotypical conclusions. It could have been that young lady Juanita. She appeared to be Mexican as well."

The posse slowly shook its collective head yes, giving the impression to the casual observer that they agreed not to jump to stereotypical conclusions when analyzing the present situation. The more jaundiced observer would probably have thought they did it for the sake of appearance. However, given the intellectual and social proclivities of the posse, it is more likely that the group merely wanted to move the discussion forward, as evidenced by Charles' observation, "Who took photos probly wrote note. Couldn't a been that beaner bitch Juanita. She's in stupid pi-tures lovin' Perfesser's tuna burrito." The posse, this time joined by Jeremiah, again shook its collective head yes. Charles continued, "Musta been that bandito hombre, the enter... tainmnt manger dude, took pi-tures and sent note. Why he send it? Prof, read note again."

Jeremiah again read his edited version of the note, "Five grande or the internet will contact you for details."

The posse agreed that the five grande meant five thousand dollars although with the spelling of grand, they believed it could have meant pesos. It concluded that the five thousand dollars or pesos was a payment of some kind, but for what? Not to be contacted by the internet and for what details? It wondered: Why would someone pay five thousand of anything not to be contacted by the internet for unspecified details? The posse sank into confusion.

Then Charles pulled a shot bottle of tequila from his jacket pocket, twisted the cap off, threw the cap into the pews and drained its contents, dropping the empty shot bottle to the ground. Then he slurred, "Souns like two senses to me. What happns if you put some punshashon afer internet?"

Jeremiah yelled, "Eureka! That's it. The rather inept photographer and illiterate author of this poorly written note, assuming they are the same person, should have put the exclamation point after the word internet. It's not the internet that's going to contact me, but the illiterate author of the poorly written note. For arguments sake, that Mexican entertainment manager. But why?"

Jamie, who had remained silent throughout the entire discussion, held up the picture of Jeremiah slurping away as he performed his newly and inadvertently invented tuna-burrito tequila slam, said, "This is why!"

Charles took a second shot bottle of tequila from his jacket pocket, twisted the cap off, threw the cap into the pews and drained it, then using the empty bottle as a pointer, pointed it at the picture for emphasis and said to Jeremiah, "Some one's gonna put that piture of you on the innernet if you donn pay that Mexican ass-hole dude five grand. You're bein' blackmailed, thas what."

Jeremiah thought that Charles' use of the word asshole was unfortunate but pretty much agreed with his analysis as did the Louislight Posse of Little Horses. Jeremiah was being blackmailed and had to pay a five thousand, probably dollars, to someone to keep the picture of him inventing the tuna-burrito tequila slam off the internet and that he'd be contacted with the details on how to make the payment.

Charles reached into his pocket a third time and pulled out a ring case and said in disgust, "Shit, it's the stupid rings" obviously disappointed that he was out of shot-bottles of tequila. Just then Louis Fazzano screeched his fully restored 1958 red Edsel convertible to a halt in front of the entrance to the outdoor chapel and yelled, "Can't find those fuckin' rings anyplace!"

Nonplussed, Charles held up the ring box and yelled, "Mr. Guinea, not to worry. Have rings here" at which Louis began screaming every swear word he knew in both English and Italian, and he had a large bilingual vocabulary to call upon, as he peeled out, his fine automotive chariot disappearing around the bend and raising a cloud of dust as it did so. Charles opened the box and showed Jamie the rings, "See, here's rings." He added somewhat disjointedly as he closed the ring box and returned it to his jacket pocket, "Wonner how that Mexican ass-hole took those tuna burrito pi-tures?" returning the attention of the posse back to the problem at hand.

The guests started to arrive and form small clusters of humanity. Jonnie Hogg and Garcia Rosenbloom began performing their ceremonial duties as wedding ushers. As each group arrived, Jamie, while still holding the first picture, the close-up of Jeremiah buried in Juanita's bush as he inadvertently invented the tuna-burrito tequila body slam, yelled "Left!" or "Other left!" pointing with the picture to his left or right as he did so to indicate to the ushers where the group of arriving guests should be seated, pews to the left for friends and family of the bride and pews to the other left for friends and family of the groom.

When all of the guests had been seated, the posse, now at full strength with the arrival of Louis Fazzano, took up the question raised by Charles concerning the pictures. Louis, who had not seen them, whistled as Jamie showed the first picture to him and said "Prof, you could be in deep doo-doo! If my Aunt Rose sees that picture, your ass is grass. Where'd that picture come from?"

Jeremiah replied, "That, Louis, is the question at hand."

However, before the posse could delve further into this mystery, the female contingent of the wedding party arrived in a large black SUV decorated on the driver's exterior door panel with a huge sign that faced those congregated on the left and on the other left awaiting the impending wedding celebration. The sign read: Jamal's Exotic Dancing and Escort Service. Out popped the ubiquitous Jamal, now dressed in a chauffeur's uniform, apparently none-the-less for wear after the events of the last evening's bachelorette party.

Giggles from several of the female attendees seated in the bride's section of the congregation greeted him as he exited the vehicle. Jamal, now the chauffeur, opened the rear door to the SUV and helped each member of the female contingent of the wedding party out of the vehicle and onto the ground. The bride was the last to exit. She looked down at Jamal and froze. Jamal reached up and offered his left hand to help her step down. She grabbed his hand with the strength and tenacity of a long-distance trucker squeezing the steering wheel for dear life while speeding down an ice-covered hill. When her feet had safely planted themselves on the ground, Jamal tried to retrieve his hand but she refused to let it go. With some difficulty he used his right hand to tear his left from her grasp. The audience broke out in oohs and ahhs at the appearance of the bride and by her beauty that the battle of the hands went pretty much unnoticed.

As the female members of the aforementioned wedding party gathered about the SUV, Jamie handed Jeremiah the picture he held and said, "Prof, we'll have to continue this discussion later." Jeremiah stuffed the note and photos in his breast pocket, self-consciously smiling at the approaching and much dreaded Rose as he did so.

A nondenominational and unexpectedly religious wedding ceremony...

All the members of the wedding party were present and accounted for, save one rather important exception, the rabbi, without whom the ceremony, billed as nondenominational, would be most difficult to complete, nondenominationally or otherwise. I suppose that someone else could have stepped in since a ceremony billed as nondenominational was pretty much open to free-form improvisation, but the chances of that happening were quite slim as the person most capable of such a feat and most likely to attempt it was Charles Fontaine.

However, Charles was:

1. Already the best man (although he could under different circumstances have attempted to perform dual roles),
2. Barely able to stand (hardly a handicap given his experience handling such circumstances), and more importantly,
3. Still preoccupied with the question he had asked earlier concerning the origin of the tuna-burrito pictures (his inquisitiveness driven to obsession by a combination of curiosity and inebriation and thus the final straw).

So all awaited the nondenominational rabbi in the shadow of a large wooden cross which dominated the scene even though it was covered with white streamers to more or less camouflage its presence.

The Posse of Little Horses and Jeremiah stood in a cluster to the left of the entrance to the outdoor chapel and the female contingent of the wedding party stood in a cluster to the right. The guests, all having been seated in the correct sections for the most part, now stood facing the entrance in expectation of a wedding ceremony of some sort, expectations, inadvertantly, shared by the wedding party. A great buzz of chatter arose from the assembled multitude.

Leslie, beautiful in her white gown, looked a bit green about the gills in stark contrast to her appearance from the neck down. Rose, her effervescent self, looked quite nice in a take-charge sort of way. As she adjusted a strap of Leslie's wedding gown, she asked, "What's with the sour puss? This is your wedding not your wake. Did you eat a good breakfast? You know what happens to you if you don't eat a good breakfast." Leslie did not react to her mother's question and so Rose asked again being even more demanding and specific, "What did you eat for breakfast?"

Leslie shook her head in such a noncommittal way in answer to her mother's first question, that Rose could not determine whether her daughter was shaking her head yes, she had or no, she had not had breakfast. So Rose bore in to get the truth or at least an answer she deemed appropriate for the question she asked, "Well, Leslie, what did you have for breakfast?"

The brides maids Janey Toussaint and Angel Bangor looked every bit as beautiful as Leslie in their peach-colored gowns. However, they were as chipper as could be, anticipating a fun-filled day and night, for unlike Leslie, they had trained a number of years for the rigors of such events. After a long pause that made it obvious that Leslie was not going to reply, Janey jumped in. "Before we met to dress this morning, we gave her a cup of hot, black coffee with about ten teaspoons of sugar, five aspirins and a piece of toast, which she kept down. We were up late at the bachelorette party and drank some wine."

Rose studied Leslie's expression carefully and asked, "What else did you do?"

Angel, who had little distance between her brain, at least what there was of it, and her tongue, of which there was quite a lot, said, "You were a party pooper and missed the show. We hired one of those exotic dancers and he was verrry exotic and verrry entertaining. Wasn't he, missy." She pointed to Jamal, who remained standing alongside his SUV and said, "In fact, that's him over there. He's also a chauffeur."

Leslie looked down at the ground, spoke for the first time and said robotically, "I don't want to talk about it."

Rose, having had her question concerning Leslie's breakfast answered and ignoring the comment about the exotic dancer turned chauffeur, moved on to her next concern. "Where the hell's that Jew priest, anyway. No wonder the yids defrocked the mook. Go figure. A nondenominational Jewish ceremony conducted by an absent, defrocked rabbi. I don't like this entire business. They should be getting married in a church. A Catholic church." She cupped her hands, put them to her mouth to form a sort of megaphone and yelled over the canned music across the entrance way to Jamie, "Where's that Jew priest friend of yours? You know, that defrocked Rabbi! Is he gonna show up? Where in heaven's name is he?"

Leslie said a second time, just as robotically, and to no one in particular, "I don't want to talk about it."

Across the way, the groom and his party also awaited the arrival of the rabbi. Jamie cupped his hands and yelled back, "Not to worry. Malachi will be here." He looked down at his watch, whistled and said more or less to himself, "Where the hell is that fuckin' asshole?"

Jeremiah asked, "Why did Rose refer to the rabbi as defrocked?"

Jamie adjusted the sombrero on his head and replied, "I don't think 'defrocked' is the correct term. Your Rose is exaggerating, as I believe she usually does in her inimitable fashion. Malachi O'Sullivan was a rabbi in an Hasidic community in Chicago. He either left or they kicked him out. Exactly what happened is unclear, but speculation has it that his last name may have done him in. Brought up unanswered questions about his Jewish heritage. After all, there aren't many Hasidic Jews named O'Sullivan. I guess in Catholic terms he could be considered defrocked, but in Jewish terms, he's still technically a rabbi as I understand it."

Charles, still leaning against a pole for support, mumbled, "Less get thisss show on the road. I need a drink!" And sure enough, a figure appeared in the distance walking slowly down the road towards them.

As the figure got even closer, it became obvious to the wedding party that the figure slowly walking towards them was dressed in a cowboy hat. As he got closer, they could see that the figure wore jeans tucked into cowboy boots. As he got closer still, they could see that he wore a fancy cowboy shirt with a cactus and rattlesnake embroidered in bright colors across the front.

Jamie smiled and yelled to Malachi, "Sully, you're not rehearsing for the lead in High Noon! You're here to conduct a wedding ceremony, remember!" The defrocked rabbi fast drew an imaginary six-shooter and shot at Jamie. He blew imaginary smoke from the imaginary barrel of his imaginary six-shooter, placed it in his imaginary holster and then continued his High Noon walk past the wedding party and up the aisle to a sort of altar, best described as nondenominational, on which sat a bottle of wine and a large glass. He carefully lifted the cowboy hat off his head revealing a black yarmulke and gently placed the cowboy hat on the altar next to the bottle of wine. He waved for the ceremonial aisle-walking to begin.

Jamie, nudging Jeremiah and as he walked past, said, "Don't forget the bride, Prof," and hustled quickly and very unceremoniously up the aisle to take his place to the left of Malachi facing the audience, followed just as unceremoniously by the best man Charles Fontaine, who navigated the crushed stone aisle with great skill and aplomb given his physical condition.

Rose walked to the entrance to the outdoor chapel where her nephew Louis Fazzano met her. She put out her arm which Louis took. As he did so, Rose turned to Jeremiah and said rather loudly, "Walk slow and don't trip. Got it?"

Jeremiah sheepishly shook his head yes as Louis was more or less escorted down the aisle by Rose to the first row on the bride's side where Rose seated herself with great ceremony.

Jonnie Hogg and Garcia Rosenbloom performed their duties as ushers flawlessly so that brides maids Janey Toussaint and Angel Bangor arrived with little incident at the nondenominational altar. Now the wedding party, in almost all its glory, stood facing the gathered multitude with Malachi standing behind the nondenominational altar, the groom and his party standing to the rabbi's left and the brides maids standing to his other left. All that was needed to complete the wedding party was the bride. As a hidden stereo blasted a recording of Here Comes the Bride, Jeremiah walked over to the far side of the entrance to the outdoor chapel and offered his arm to his daughter for the walk down the aisle. She stood there robotically forlorn. Jeremiah smiled and placed her arm in the crook of his right arm and said, "Les, it's time. Are you ready?" Leslie shook her head almost absentmindedly yes, and father and daughter wobbled down the aisle arm-in-arm toward the nondenominational altar.

Several steps down the aisle, they were greeted by great blasts of light as the assembled multitude snapped pictures to record the historic event. Jeremiah, blinded by the light, instinctively put his free arm up across his face to shield his eyes, an act that made him look more like a celebrity being frog-walked into a criminal booking than a father walking his daughter down the aisle to her wedding. Leslie just stared ahead, more or less pulled along by her father's progress down the aisle, apparently unaffected by the flashing cameras. Rose yelled over the rather loud wedding march, "Jeremiah, put your arm down, you dufus. You're ruining the pictures. Smile and keep your damn eyes open."

Jeremiah, even though now thoroughly blinded by the light, did as commanded and yanked his arm down. However, in so doing he lost his balance and stumbled on the crushed stone beneath his unsteady feet, pulling Leslie down and forward to the left so that she spun around and ended up sitting in the lap of a spectator whom she had knocked into a seated position in the pew just ahead of where Jeremiah had stumbled. Fortunately, Jeremiah fell into the arms of the rotund Louis "Big Louie" Fazzano, Rose's brother, the namesake for her nephew Louis and the only male guest present who was bigger than Jeremiah. Big Louie grabbed Jeremiah before he could tumble to the ground and yelled, "Slow down, big fella." He set Jeremiah on his feet as the audience simultaneously held its collective breath and continued snapping pictures at a furious rate. Big Louie then leaned over and grabbed Leslie by the waist and set her alongside Jeremiah as the flashbulbs continued to pop. Having regained his feet, Jeremiah grabbed Leslie's arm and continued their hazardous trip down the aisle.

Arriving at the nondenominational altar without further incident, Jeremiah gave his daughter a peck on the cheek and guided her to her place on Malachi's other left next to the brides maids. Jeremiah then shambled over to the front pew and rather unceremoniously plopped himself next to Rose, the pew sagging beneath his weight. Rose gave him a look that in biblical-like times would probably have turned him into a pillar of petrified donkey dung. She hissed, "You horse's ass. I told you not to trip!" and turned her attention to the ceremony which was about to begin.

Jamie removed his sombrero revealing a black yarmulke. He handed the sombrero to Charles Fontaine who in turn handed it to Louis Fazzano who in turn handed it to Jonnie Hogg who in turn handed it to Garcia Rosenbloom who in turn put the sombrero on his head, ending what appeared to be a sort of abbreviated all-male Mexican hat dance.

Malachi O'Sullivan poured himself a glass of wine which he downed in one gulp. In so doing, some in the audience were led to believe that, given his last name, he had proven that his apparent Irish heritage was much stronger than his apparent Jewish heritage, thus justifying his imputed defrocking. Malachi then reached into his back pocket and pulled out a very thick pack of 3x5 cards which he shuffled like a deck of cards on the makeshift altar before him, randomizing their order. He raised his arms and announced to the gathered multitude, "This is God's text!" and began to read from the cards. After reading from a card, he placed it in the back of the pack of 3x5 cards and then read the next card, which God had apparently randomly selected. He praised the beautiful mountains before them, he praised the sky, he praised the multitude before him, he praised the bride and the groom and the best man and the other groomsmen and the brides maids, but not necessarily in that order.

Having praised just about everything praiseable in God's name, he began the formal part of the wedding ceremony. He refilled the wine glass and took a healthy swig. Then he asked the million dollar question to Jamie who answered loudly in the affirmative. He asked Leslie, who remained silent. He asked her again and she still remained silent, at which point Rose yelled, "Leslie, say yes!" Leslie remained silent but robotically shook her head yes as a sigh of great relief went up from the gathered multitude before and about her.

Jamie turned to Charles Fontaine and motioned for the rings.

Charles reached into his jacket pocket and pulled out an empty tequila shot bottle, which he tossed to the ground. He reached back into his pocket and pulled out the ring case which he opened and presented to Jamie. Jamie took Leslie's ring and gently placed it on the ring finger of her left hand. Charles then presented the ring case to Leslie who just stood there looking down at it. Jamie guided her hand over the ring so that she appeared to hold it while in fact it was he who held it. He then slid the ring onto the ring finger of his left hand and let go of Leslie's hand, which fell dangling at her side. Malachi took another swig of wine and offered the glass to Jamie who took a swig. Malachi turned and offered the glass to Leslie who remained motionless. He put the glass to her lips and gently tilted the glass so that a drop of wine touched her closed lips. He then finished off the wine himself. While still holding the glass, he raised his hands, Moses-like, to the sky and pronounced the couple man and wife. Loud huzzahs went up from the gathered multitude as a strong mountain breeze sprang up. The breeze blew the white streamers that camouflaged the great wooden cross towering behind them skyward forming a sort of white halo above the huge cross.

The receiving line slowly formed on the pathway up the hill toward the pavilion where the reception was to be held, but before the line could be completed, Charles yelled from the top of the hill, "They tapped the beer!" at which point a significant number of those who were to make up the receiving line, joined by a number of those who were to be received, raced up the hill, pretty much ending the receiving line before it ever got formed.

The best man speaks from the belly...

The various and varied hundred-and-fifty-odd guests made it up the hill from the outdoor chapel to the pavilion. They had downed a beer or three, worked their way through the buffet line with no significant injuries and now sat more or less at their designated tables under the outdoor pavilion before plates full of make-your-own burritos, lasagna and other ethnic delicacies. The sun shone and a slight breeze gently wafted through the pavilion keeping the attendees cool and refreshed as they chowed down.

The bride, the former Leslie Fazzano-Wright, sat next to the groom, the former Jamie Steinkraus, apparently her now betrothed, as the couple awaited their first formal introduction as Mr. and Mrs. Fazzano-Wright-Steinkraus. Neither ate and, although Leslie still had a rather pale and distant look, the couple appeared relatively content, for the wedding ceremony had gone off about as smoothly as could be expected given the participants.

The best man, seated to their right, chomped with great gusto on a huge burrito he had created. He smiled and chugged beer as he chomped. Between chomps he gave Jamie a knowing wink and said with great conviction, "A cigar is juss a smoke, but a brito is a brito!"

When all had had their fill, Charles stood and vigorously banged a spoon against his water glass to get the attention of the seated guests to begin the introductions and formal speeches. In fact he banged so vigorously that the glass began to topple. Thanks to the reflexes of the maid of honor, Janey Toussaint, the glass did not spill its contents onto the bridal table.

The best man stood somewhat unsteadily. He reflexively wiped his swollen and reddened left eye with his left hand as he stood and as he did so he began to lean a bit unsteadily to his right. To prevent the lean from turning into a gravity-assisted tumble, he grabbed the back of Janey Toussaint's chair with his right hand to steady himself. He looked about the pavilion and said, "I'm Chars … Chars Fon… Fon…taine, Jamie's fren and proud to be his bes man. Raise yer cab-litos of Mexcan sunshine and les drink to Mr. and Mrs. Jamie Fazz… Fazz…" He seemed stuck and the quick-reflexed Janey Toussaint, who apparently was also as quick-witted, whispered, "Charles, it's Fazzano," and the best man, taking the hint, repeated "Fazzano" and continued "Fazzano-Wrights" again pausing then finally gaining a bit of intellectual equilibrium, resumed is toast and shouted, "Steinkraut." Again the quick-witted Janey Toussaint whispered quite loudly "Steinkraus" and the best man robotically

repeated "Steinkraus." All but one of the guests raised the celebratory caballitos of tequila that had been provided to toast the bride
and groom.

From a neighboring table, Rose looked down at her caballito
of tequila as she watched the best man drone on. She said quite
contemptuously to Jeremiah, "I'm not drinking that swill, toast or
no toast." Jeremiah whispered in reply, "Dear, it's Cuervos, the very
best." To which Rose replied, "So it's the very best swill. It's still swill
and I'm not drinking it. And that idiot of a best man is making a fool
of himself and a travesty of my daughter's wedding toast."

As the best man raised his caballito and tilted his head back
to toast the apparent new social entity formed by the recent wedding ceremony, his face turned ashen. The knuckles of his supporting
hand turned white as he tightened his grip on the back of the quick-
reflexed, quick-witted maid of honor's chair. He was apparently still
feeling the effects of last night's bachelor party and the hair of the
dog that he had so copiously prescribed to himself before, during
and after the wedding ceremony, in what appeared to be a valiant
effort to overcome the effects of the previous night's festivities.

A look of fear and trepidation spread across the groom's face as
he realized that the heretofore semismoothness of the wedding pro-
ceedings was about to be threatened as the best man's eyes shut and
his body stiffened. With a primordial moan, the best man became a
veritable human Vesuvius, projectile vomiting onto the bridal party's
table. The groom of the apparently newly formed Fazzano-Wright-
Steinkraus social unit grabbed the other half of the imputed and
newly formed unit about the waist and dove to the left to success-
fully avoid the Vesuvian splatter. The two groomsmen seated at the
table, Jonnie Hogg and Garcia Rosenbloom, reflexively jumped back
and also avoided the splatter.

The two bridesmaids, Janey Toussaint and Angel Bangor, were
not as lucky since they were directly in the line of fire. Much of
the contents of Charlie-O's upper digestive tract now decorated the
ample bosoms of the two beautiful and previously unbesmerched

bridesmaids and ran down the front of their gowns drenching them. The quick-witted and quick-reflexed Janey Toussaint stood and screamed, "Oh shit!" In an effort to distance herself from the contents of Charles' upper digestive tract, she reached behind her back in one of those moves that only a woman can make and unzipped her gown. She wiggled free of the contaminated gown which now lay about her ankles. And there she stood in bikini panties and a see-through bra, which the audience saw through, much to the delight of approximately half of the audience and the shock of the remaining half.

Her not-as-quick-witted companion, Angel Bangor, followed suit and similarly unsuited as well. Her gown slowly slid down over her wide hips and more than ample buttocks, settling about her very high-heeled shoes. There she stood in a slim thong and a support bra that left much of what it supported exposed. Her thong had ridden up her hips, sinking the thong's crotch into her labia revealing as fine a patch of pubic hair as God had ever created north of the Mexican border and making it obvious to the audience that she was not a natural blonde.

The prostrate groom looked up at the oldies but goodies disk jockey they'd hired after some very hard bargaining over his fee and yelled, "Play some music quick, you asshole." The cheaply-hired oldies but goodies disk jockey, not one to refrain from indulging in a grudge, set the speakers blasting with a somewhat appropriate oldy but goody: "Tequila" by the Champs.

By now Jonnie Hogg and Garcia Rosenbloom had gathered what little sense they had available at this time, given the present circumstances and the lingering effects of the previous night's festivities, and scrambled to their feet. One of them, and to this day it is not clear which one, yelled "Camel toe!" Approximately half the audience broke into loud applause while muffled exclamations and nervous laughter could be heard from the other half.

The less quick-witted of the bridesmaids looked down at her camel-toed pubes, up at the audience, and smiled broadly. Then the two bridesmaids, with a nonchalance that only John Barleycorn, a low IQ, an incredible self-confidence, or some combination of these previous conditions could provide, stepped out of their gowns, grabbed them by the hem so as to avoid contact with the contents of Charles' upper digestive tract, and high-heel strutted across the dance floor dragging their gowns behind them. The applause of approximately half of the assembled guests grew even louder, applause which was punctuated with the rhythmic chant of "Cam-al toe! Cam-al toe!" The quick-witted Janey Toussaint waved to the crowd and yelled, "Back in five!" as they exited the pavilion, their buttocks swaying to the voice of the immortal fat man, for the disgruntled and clever disk jockey had put on "Ain't that a Shame" by Fats Domino as the two bridesmaids strutted out of the pavilion.

Jonnie Hogg and Garcia Rosenbloom, after watching the two bridesmaids strut across the dance floor in all their semicommando glory, regained their focus and noticed that the best man, Charles Fontaine, lay unconscious at the feet of the now standing Mr. and Mrs. Fazzano-Wright-Steinkraus. Jonnie yelled to Garcia derisively, "Joobie, let's get ol' Cha… Cha… Charlie-O the hell out of here before he upchucks again." And with that the two groomsmen grabbed Charles' arms and legs and muscled him across the pavilion dance floor to the new chant of "Char-lee-O! Char-lee-O! Char-lee-O!" as the guests turned their attention to the best man's ignominious, yet strangely glorious, exit. Jonnie, groaning under the burden, grunted to his partner, "Let's dump the bastard in his room. I don't want to miss the rest of the festivities. I'm starved. I could eat a horse," and they trundled the unconscious best man across the parking area following the bridesmaids into the nearby lodge.

The bride's father, Jeremiah Wright, realized that someone had to step in, for surely the show had to go on. He walked over to the bridal table where the bride and groom stood and said, "I think that we should continue. I'd like to say a few words." And with that he raised his hands gesturing for silence. The guests were about chanted out anyway and welcomed the chance to catch their collective breaths and rewet their whistles. Jeremiah continued, "I have looked forward to this day for a long time, perhaps too long a time, and thought that, as the father of the bride, I should pass on some words of wisdom to the bride and groom befitting their new status as man and wife."

He paused, pushed down on his pince-nez to better secure them on his nose and reached into one of his jacket pockets. He pulled out the tuna burrito pictures and blackmail note, realized his mistake, and quickly stuffed them back into the pocket from which they came, saying, "Oops, wrong pocket." With great ceremony, he again slowly reached into his jacket and this time pulled out a dog-eared moleskin booklet, the kind that Ernest Hemingway supposedly used to take notes. As he shuffled through the pages of the dog-eared booklet he continued, "As you know, I am a bit of a literary fellow and read a great deal… I thought to myself, what author would have the best advice for a new bride and groom? D. H. Lawrence popped into mind immediately for few writers have understood the intimate emotional and physical relationship between a man and his wife as did Lawrence."

The audience looked puzzled and someone shouted, "Is that the Lawrence who ran around Arabia killing people?"

As he fumbled through the pages of the moleskin booklet, he looked up, smiled, and said, "No, no, that was T. H. Lawrence, better known as 'Lawrence of Arabia'. He wrote too, but not about the relationship of men and women."

Another voice yelled, "Wasn't that Lawrence of Arabia guy queer? In the movie some Turk bastard porks him, I think."

The guests had continued to drink without the aid of toasts and were becoming a bit more boisterous. Another yelled, "What the hell kind of advice can a queer give to two normal people who just got married?"

The father of the bride looked out at the audience and replied, "T as in Thomas Lawrence is not the Lawrence of whom I am speaking." Unbeknownst to him he was entering a dialogue with a collective group of 150 inebriated guests.

"Then who the hell are you speaking of?"

"I'm speaking of the D as in David Lawrence."

"D as in David is a pretty dumb first name. I thought you said his name was D. H. Lawrence. Who in the hell is this D as in David Lawrence anyway?"

"He's a writer, a famous one!"

"Never heard of him. What'd this D as in David guy do?"

"Maybe you heard of Lady Chatterley's Lover."

"I saw that movie. He did the movie?"

"No, he wrote the novel upon which that movie was based."

Someone standing by the beer keg interrupted Jeremiah, "Hold it. I saw that movie and this cripple guy tells his wife to screw some other guy so that she can have a kid. Then she takes off with this other guy who screwed her. What kind of advice is that to give Leslie and Jamie? You tellin' yer daughter to screw some other guy on her wedding night?"

The crowd was turning ugly, particularly the groom's relatives and friends, who now believed that the bride was about to be advised by her father to make the groom, their relative and friend, a cuckold or, as was so eloquently put by an outraged member of the audience, "to screw another guy".

Panic crossed Jeremiah's face. He realized that immediate clarification was in order. "No, no! I'm not advising that. Here, I have a quote from someone who wrote about D as in David Lawrence's life." He looked down at his dog-eared booklet nervously and read, "Lawrence, as an acknowledged expert on the human heart, was asked to give advice to a friend's son who at twenty was about to marry his fifteen year-old girl friend." He looked up at his audience pensively as they listened very carefully to his every word.

Someone yelled, "Fifteen… sounds like cradle robbing to me. In this state that's statutory rape." The audience was again on the brink of ugly.

Jeremiah raised his hands to calm them. "No, no. This was a long time ago and people got married a lot younger then." The crowd, assured that neither Lawrence nor Jeremiah was promoting statutory rape, calmed and Jeremiah continued, "You know the kind of advice a young groom would want, advice about married life and not sex. And here's the quote: 'He… Lawrence… told John'… that's the groom… that he must keep the center of himself always alone and that if his bride crossed him in anything, he should…" at this point Jeremiah stopped and looked up as sweat formed on his brow. Something wasn't right.

The crowd now interested in hearing this pearl of wisdom about how to be happy and married at the same time, as much for themselves as for Leslie and Jamie, listened intently. Jeremiah's silence continued as did the sweat now pouring off his brow.

An anxious member of the audience yelled, "Should what?"

Jeremiah looked down at his notes and then at the audience and said, "I don't think this is the quote I had in mind."

The audience again approached the brink of ugly and someone shouted, "God damn it, should what?"

Jeremiah mumbled, "beat her."

Someone in the back of the pavilion shouted, "What'd he say?"

And someone sitting closer to Jeremiah yelled, "I think he said, 'beat her'!"

There was a long silence as the crowd digested Jeremiah's words of wisdom, and then the group of men standing around the beer keg in the back of the pavilion started cheering. Shouts from distinctly male voices echoed from the rafters: "Atta boy Jamie… you got the word… you're the boss, big boy…" and so forth.

The bride burst into tears and ran for the lodge followed closely by the half of the audience that did not cheer Jeremiah's words of wisdom, thus ending what had initially been a semi-nice wedding.

A just and fitting matrimonial memorial…

Jeremiah walked from his cabin up the gravel road to the outdoor chapel. He stood for a moment staring into the gloaming at the barely visible mountains behind the large timber cross which dominated his view. He thought of the events earlier in the day and shuddered. He worried about his daughter Leslie and wanted to make amends.

His thoughts were rudely interrupted by a large black SUV that sped around the graveled bend above him. As it approached, it screeched to a halt. The front passenger's window slid down and out popped a mop of long blonde hair. Jeremiah squinted and recognized the mop of blonde hair as that of the camel-toed bridesmaid Angel Bangor who had so conclusively proven earlier in the day that she was not a natural blonde.

She shouted, "A penny for your thoughts."

Jeremiah did not reply. The thought crossed his mind that selling Angel Bangor even one of his thoughts for a penny would be taking advantage of the poor girl. She'd be overpaying for all the use she'd get from that thought, and selling her two pennie's worth would be an act of cruelty, for he was positive that two pennies worth would lead to massive confusion and possible paralysis on her part. He shouted over the SUV's racing engine, "Party breaking up already?"

"Hell no! Things are hoppin' up at the lodge. Tell Janey I'll be back tomorrow afternoon." She slapped the outside of her door which featured one of those magnetic signs. It read "Jamal's Exotic Dancing and Escort Service," which Jeremiah made a mental note of. She disappeared into the black SUV, the window closed, the tires squealed and the black SUV sped down the gravel road, raising a cloud of dust as it went.

Jeremiah stood for a moment watching the cloud of dust and then turned and continued his trek up the graveled road toward the bend, passing on his right the now empty and littered pavilion which was dimly lit by several stray light bulbs. As he turned the corner he could see the lights blazing from the lodge. He squinted and thought he saw a man upside down, his legs perpendicular to the ground being supported by two men on either side of what appeared to be a beer keg. He could hear a loud chant arise, "One... two... three," as he continued toward the lodge.

As he got closer, he recognized the young man up-side-down and perpendicular to the ground over the beer keg. It was the inimitable Charles Fontaine, who apparently had sufficiently recovered from his afternoon collapse to rejoin the festivities. On either side of him, supporting his legs, were the two groomsmen who had performed a similar yet distinctly different service for the best man earlier in the day. The chant continued, "21... 22... 23."

To Jeremiah's surprise, not only was Charles Fontaine upside down, he was sucking on the beer keg's spout. Before him on the great stone stairway to the lodge, sat a large group of guests from the wedding party loudly counting. Jeremiah noted with some optimism that the group was mixed with both supporters and critics of his unintentional matrimonial jeremiad, that is, the chanting crowd of revelers included both men and women.

As he passed the beer keg, Louis "The Guinea" Fazzano yelled, "Keg stand!" An upside down Charles Fontaine looked up at Jeremiah and shouted, "and the god damn record for the god damn Fazzano-Wright-Steinkraus wedding!" The mixed crowd on the steps cheered wildly, chanting "Char-lee-O! Char-lee-O! Char-lee-O!"

Charles' two pillars of support tossed him upright and somewhat surprisingly he landed quite deftly on his feet. He pumped his fist celebrating his record performance, raised his arms over his head and danced in a circle giving a somewhat unsteady imitation of Rocky Balboa's solo jig in the City of Brotherly Love. Charles then stumbled to the base of the steps where sat his adoring audience and stopped. There before him on the stone wall running up the crowded great stone staircase sat a half-empty bottle of tequila ominously labeled Brand XXX, a shot glass, a salt shaker and a paper plate strewn with unevenly cut slices of lime. He poured himself a healthy shot of the Brand XXX tequila, put the shot glass to his lips, tossed his head back and slammed the tequila down. He turned to Jeremiah and said, "Wanna slam a shot of Mexican sunshine, Perfesser? We got salt and lime if you want."

Jeremiah replied a polite, "No thank you. Have you seen Leslie?"

"Not really."

"Know where she is?"

"Think so."

"Where would you think you could see her were you to be where she is?"

At this question, Charles looked very puzzled and asked, "If I were where?"

"If you were with her, where would you be?"

"In a shit-load of trouble, that's where I'd be!" A scowl appeared on Charles' face as he contemplated what Jeremiah had said. "Jamie said somethin' about what you said about guys screwin' that Lady Chatterley after I left the reception. You accusin' me of somethin'?"

Jeremiah quickly realized that without immediate clarification, his questions could again lead to some difficulty. "No, no, Charles. I just want to know where she is."

"Oh. She's in her room on the second floor, and I ain't with her, Joobie ain't with her, Pig Fat ain't with her, and The Guinea ain't with her. Hell, even Jamie ain't with her. Her mother's with her, that who's with her, and she's bawlin' her eyes out."

A look of puzzlement overcame Jeremiah. "Why is Rose crying?"

Now Charles looked puzzled. "Rose? Who said Rose was cryin'?"

Jeremiah replied, "You just did."

Charles again started to anger, "No I didn't. I said Leslie was bawlin' her eyes out. I never used the word cryin'!"

Jeremiah thought unspoken concession best under the circumstances and asked, "Is Leslie crying because of what happened this afternoon?"

"I'm not sure. The afternoon's kind of a blank. Whatever it was, it really pissed her off." Charles shouted to Jonnie Hogg, "Hey Pig Fat, why's Leslie bawlin' her eyes out?"

"I heard some asshole insulted her after Joobie and me carried a tequila-soaked sack of shit from the reception."

Charles sat down on the lowest step and looked up a Jeremiah as he poured himself another shot of tequila, "Ever try a tequila boiler maker?"

"I don't believe that I have. About Leslie."

"Oh yeah, she's in her room bawlin' her eyes out."

"Where's Jamie?"

"Sittin' outside her door drinkin'."

"Why doesn't he go in and comfort her?"

"Can't."

"Why not?"

"Same reason I couldn't be where she is to see her."

"The reason of which is…"

"She locked the damn door, that's why, and her mother won't let anybody in."

Jeremiah thought for a moment and replied with an absent-minded, somewhat puzzled "Oh" and proceeded up the steps to the lodge's great room. As he worked his way around the revelers scattered about on the steps, he felt a tug on his pant leg.

"Hey Perfesser, seen Angel?"

Jeremiah looked down and there seated at his feet was Janey Toussaint, the quick-witted, quick-reflexed maid of honor, looking as lovely as ever, although unlike this afternoon, pretty much clothed.

He said, "Angel?"

"Yeah, the other bridesmaid. My camel-toed companion."

"Oh, her. I just saw her. She asked me to tell you she'd see you tomorrow afternoon. She was in that black SUV, the one owned by someone named Jamal, the exotic dancer, the guy who chauffeured the bridal party to the wedding ceremony."

"What a bitch! I knew she'd run off with that black sausage. Biggest sausage I ever saw and I've seen a few."

"Sausage? I thought Jamal was a dancer and chauffeur?"

"Yeah, he's a dancing, chauffeuring meat market."

The puzzled Jeremiah continued his trek up the steps and into the lodge's great room. A much more sedate crowd sat and kneeled on the floor beneath the huge stone fireplace. From what Jeremiah could determine, these revelers were pretty much Leslie's friends, many of whom Jeremiah had seen on Columbia's campus. A bearded man, who looked and dressed like a ghost from the first Woodstock festival, sat before a low coffee table upon which sat a large flat stone propped up with a smaller stone. He was painting flowers around the edge of the large flat stone.

Janey Toussaint, who had followed Jeremiah up the stairs and into the great room, nudged him and whispered, "They're painting the stone that memorializes the wedding. There's this tradition here where the bride and groom return to celebrate their wedding on one of their anniversaries and the memorial stone is here to remind them of their wedding day."

Jeremiah pointed at the mantle upon which sat another colorfully painted stone, "Is that what that is?"

Janey looked up at the memorial stone, "Yeah. That's from last week. It's for Dick and John, Betrothed, June 21, whoever the hell Dick and John are."

Jeremiah sagely nodded his head. He looked about the room and sniffed the air. Somewhat absent-mindedly he asked Janey, "What's that smell, some kind of herbal incense burning?"

Janey looked surprised at the question and replied, "Perfesser, you oughta know that scent. It's the scent of happiness. We're not all tequila freaks. Some of us are civilized and smoke to get high."

The light went on in Jeremiah's mind. He sniffed again and said, "Oh."

The two turned their attention to the memorial stone on the coffee table. The bearded painter was completing the last flower of the floral design edging the stone. After putting the final touches on the flower, he took a long toke from a joint that someone had passed him. He stared at the stone for a moment, tilted his head to the side, scrunched up his face in puzzlement and said, "I don't think I can fit Mr. & Mrs. Jamie Fazzano-Wright-Steinkraus on one line… at least in letters large enough to be read." He looked down at a sheet of paper on the coffee table and moved his finger across the page as his lips moved. "There's thirty-three letters, three blanks, two hyphens and one ampersand. That's thirty-eight spaces if we leave out the periods after the Mr and Mrs. That's way too much!"

A group discussion ensued as the great unwashed delved into this most vexing problem. From a member of the great unwashed came, "Can't you split the name up at one of the hyphens?"

The bearded painter responded, "Not a good idea. Bad symbolism."

"Bad symbolism?"

"Yeah, they're united as one now, so the name on the memorial's got to be on one line." He pointed up to the memorial stone on the mantle, "Like Dick and John up there. They're on one line."

There was hushed agreement on this point, a point which both defined the problem and negated the most obvious solution. Progress on the memorial came to a grinding halt. All that could be heard was the sucking of many long tokes as the group girded its collective loins in preparation to attack the aforementioned most vexing of problems.

Jeremiah looked up at the Dick and John memorial stone, then down at the blank memorial stone with its beautiful floral border and then back up at the Dick and John memorial stone. A sentient smile spread across his face and he shouted, "Eureka!"

All eyes turned to him as he pointed to the Dick and John in-scription on the memorial prominently displayed on the mantle. "Use Leslie and Jamie. Just leave off the Fazzano-Wright-Steinkraus part. If the approach is good enough for Dick and John, it's good enough for Leslie and Jamie!"

The bearded painter fondled said beard in thought and said, "Hold it, hold it. I have nothing against Dick and John getting mar-ried. I'm a full supporter of single-sex marriage, as are we all. But Leslie and Jamie aren't gays or even lesbians. If we just say Leslie and Jamie on the memorial and someone saw the two memorials next to each other, they'd think that Leslie and Jamie were a gay or lesbian couple, and they'd mistake their marriage for a single-sex one. If they found out that Leslie and Jamie weren't gays or even lesbians, they could think that we were denigrating single-sex marriages. It'd be inadvertent, but the offended wouldn't know that and even if they did, they could still be offended."

A worried murmur ran through the crowd as this new consideration sank in. No one wanted to inadvertently denigrate single-sex marriage. Jeremiah thought some more as was his want, for it was important that his daughter have a proper memorial celebrating this special day in her life, and once he bit into a thorny problem, there was no letting go until he had torn off a chunk, no matter how painful the bite. He shouted, "Double eureka!"

Again all eyes turned to him. He continued, "What we need is semi-specicivity. Our guiding principle must be semi-specicivity."

At first Jeremiah's suggestion was greeted with stunned silence. The great toking unwashed was puzzled and finally one of its members expressed this puzzlement by yelling, "What the hell's semi-specicivity?"

Jeremiah raised his hands to mollify the crowd and patiently said by way of explanation, "Semi-specicivity is being specific enough to describe the situation but not being so specific that we imply negativity to an almost analogous situation."

Another puzzled murmur ran through the crowd as the great toking unwashed tried unsuccessfully, to understand this new guiding principle. The bearded painter broke the silence. "Point of clarification. Could you be more specific?"

Jeremiah, having torn off that chunk of this thorny problem, was carnivorously up to the challenge. "We want a memorial inscription for Leslie and Jamie to indicate that their marriage was between a man and a woman and thus a legal one, but we don't want to do so in such a way that we imply denigration of Dick and John's marriage. Has my clarification been specific enough?"

A murmur of approval ran through the great unwashed and the collective process of developing a solution to this most vexing of problems, using Jeremiah's principle of semi-specicivity, was underway. Someone yelled, "Just say Leslie and Jamie on one line followed by "A real wedding" with the date on another."

"Won't do. Implies that Dick and John's wedding wasn't real."

"How about replacing the word real with the word legal?"

"Can't do that. Implies that Dick and John's marriage is illegal. I think we all agree that as of now their marriage is more like extra-legal. Implying illegal also implies negativity."

"How about his: Leslie parens a woman end parens and Jamie parens a man end parens, new line 'Wed June 29,' new line 'supporters of single-sex marriage'."

The great unwashed cheered the anonymous proposal as brush dipped into paint and completion of the memorial for Leslie and Jamie's wedding was underway. A loud thud brought silence as all turned toward the door to see a prostrate and unconscious Charles "Charlie-O" Fontaine lying face down and unconscious in the doorway, his recovery from the afternoon's festivities having been somewhat short-lived.

The pozolli[1] thickens...

After experiencing the initial joy that any adjunct college professor of literature would feel for having guided a large body of students through the rigors of solving a complex moral, ethical, social and communications problem both collectively, individually and all simultaneously, Jeremiah absentmindedly felt his jacket pocket and the somewhat larger lump protruding therein. As he felt the outline of the lump with the fingers of his left hand, he was jolted back to the reality of his now even more precarious situation, for in addition to the tuna burrito photos and the illiterate first note, he now possessed a second note which he also considered quite illiterate. He found his way up the stairs of the lodge to the second floor and the door to Leslie's room. Gathered about the door to her room was the posse, including an unconscious Charles Fontaine, who was seated on the floor, head hanging forward, legs splayed across the hallway and back slumped against the wall on the far side of the door.

[1.] *Pozolli is a traditional Mexican soup or stew made from hominy, with pork (or other meat), chili peppers, other seasonings and garnish.*

As Jeremiah approached the posse, he heard Jamie say, "She won't talk to me. She won't talk to anyone. In fact she won't talk at all. Rose is with her now. Says the last thing Leslie said was "Life can be so unexpectedly exciting and disappointing at the same time" and that was hours ago. She won't say what in life has excited her or disappointed her. She's been crying ever since."

After a long pause, Louis Fazzano asked Jamie, "What are you going to do?" as Jeremiah joined the group.

Jamie looked blankly into space and replied a dejected, "Dunno. Rose says she gets these crying fits sometimes and that I should leave her alone for a while. Made it pretty clear I should vamoose the premises." Looking up he noticed that Jeremiah had joined the posse and greeted him with "Prof! I'm in a pickle here. It's my wedding night and I'm spending it in this hallway with these assholes," and pointing to the door with his thumb, continued, his voice tinged with something between frustration and anger, "instead of in that bedroom with your daughter… my wife."

Jeremiah unconsciously put his left hand to his jacket pocket and said, "When she gets like this, it's best to just wait it out. She'll fall asleep and when she wakes up, she'll be back to normal. Rose is right. For now, it's best to just leave her alone." He paused and then patting his jacket pocket he said, "I've received a second communication regarding those rather incriminating photos and this one is even more illiterate than the first, if that were possible."

As Jeremiah reached into his pocket to retrieve the documents and photos in question, Jamie put his hand to Jeremiah's chest and said, "Not here, Prof. I got to remove myself from the premises pronto." Tapping the ring finger of his left hand against the door, he continued, "Besides, Rose is on the other side of this door. Things could get very dicey for all of us, particularly you, if that door opens at the wrong time."

Jonnie Hogg broke in, "Let's go to the Adirondack Motel. You won't be needin' the Shangri-La anytime soon. We can sort out this blackmailing bullshit there without any assholes interruptin' us."

Louis Fazzano agreed. "Great idea. Listen, meet me at Lucille. I'm going to talk with my uncle, Big Louie. He has connections and knows how to deal with this kind of stuff."

The posse nodded its collective head in agreement, all except Jeremiah, who asked, "Who's Lucille?"

Louis smiled and said, "Prof, Lucille's my four-wheeled chariot," and then disappeared down the stairs and into the kitchen behind the great room where he was sure he'd find Big Louie. Jeremiah and Jamie followed Louis down the steps. Jonnie Hogg and Garcia Rosenbloom grabbed Charles Fontaine by the armpits, lifted him and dragged him along. As Jeremiah walked down the steps, he could hear behind him the thump, thump, thump of Charles' boots banging against each step as he was dragged down the staircase.

Much to Jeremiah's surprise, no one in the crowded great room noticed them as they waded through the throng of revelers. Not even the spectacle of Charles being dragged across the room attracted any attention, for the great unwashed were fully engrossed in a series of toasts and tokes to Leslie's and Jamie's memorial matrimonial stone, which now sat on the mantle of the huge stone fireplace next to that of Dick and John, the previous memorialized matrimonial celebrants. Jeremiah turned, raised his head and sniffed. The pungent herbal smell he had detected earlier was even more pronounced.

He was about to turn to leave when he saw Rose standing at the top of the steps waving frantically for him to come back up the stairs, which he did. She grabbed him by the arm and pulled him down the hallway. She whispered, "Leslie's having some kind of breakdown. Remember I followed her when she ran out of the reception after that ridiculous speech of yours. What in heaven's name was going through that thick skull of yours anyway?"

Jeremiah lowered his head and shuffled his feet in embarrassment and said in a barely audible whisper, "I feel so bad about what happened. I should have better annotated my references. Is she OK?"

Rose responded in a much louder whisper, "I don't think so. By the time I got up to her room, she had already locked herself in. I knocked and knocked and got no answer. I went back to the reception and got my brother Big Louie to come back with me and pick the lock. You're not going to believe what she was doing?"

A puzzled frown formed on Jeremiah's face as he drew his thick eyebrows together and asked, "I thought that she was crying uncontrollably?"

Rose pulled him closer and whispered quietly this time, "She was spread out on the bed, naked as a jay bird, with her hands between her legs... and well... she was... you know... playing with herself... like some twelve year old who just discovered you know what."

Jeremiah's face reddened for his mind had never allowed the concept of sexuality and the development of his daughter to reside in the same thought or even in the most distant of thoughts. Rose continued, "And when I entered the room, she just kept doing it and making those sounds. She didn't even stop when I yelled at her. She just kept doing it and mumbled the strangest stuff... something... I think... about Zulus and dancing. Made no sense. Thank God, my brother didn't come into the room. I'm so embarrassed."

An even more embarrassed Jeremiah, asked, "What is she doing now?"

Rose said, "After she... had her..." At this point, Rose paused and swallowed before continuing and then mumbled, "her completion, she just laid there smiling. I didn't know what to do so I gave her a double dose of her medication and she's been sleeping ever since. I'm staying with her tonight. What are you doing?"

Jeremiah looked sheepishly at Rose and said, "We're removing Jamie from the premises as you suggested. We're taking him to the Adirondack Motel to take his mind off all this... difficulty... with Leslie."

Normally Rose would have detected that Jeremiah was attempting to conceal something behind his sheepishness, but she was too preoccupied with Leslie's troubles to notice. She said, "Come back here tomorrow," and before Jeremiah could respond, she had spun about and disappeared behind the door to Leslie's room which slammed shut.

Jeremiah retraced his steps down the staircase to the great room where the celebration of Leslie's and Jamie's marriage continued unabated. He proceeded down the great exterior stone staircase which had served as the gallery for the keg stand contest earlier in the evening and to the small parking lot to the left. There Jamie and the rest of the posse had gathered before the red Edsel convertible that Jeremiah had seen Louis Fazzano driving earlier in the day.

Jeremiah walked up to the Edsel admiring it and said to Jamie, "This automobile is beautifully restored. I didn't get a good look at her when Louis drove up before the ceremony today, too many distractions, but upon a closer inspection she's a stunning automobile."

Jamie ran his hand along the front fender admiringly and replied, "This is Lucille. She's a 1958 two-door Edsel Citation with a white rag top to boot. Very rare. Has an E-475 V8 engine. She's The Guinea's pride and joy. Even doing most of the work himself, he's spent a small fortune restoring her. The red paint job alone cost him a pretty penny. She's in better shape now than the day she came off the showroom floor. This baby's a classic."

Jonnie Hogg and Garcia Rosenbloom had dragged Charles across the parking lot and now held him upright beside the Edsel, but at a distance they considered safe for the Edsel should Charles inadvertently initiate anything digestively untoward. Louis exited the lodge from a ground-floor side entrance and joined them with the news that his uncle would meet them at the Adirondack Motel. He looked over at Charles, who was still being held upright by Jonnie Hogg and Garcia Rosenbloom and said, "After this afternoon's performance at the reception that piece of pickled bullshit ain't gettin' in my car."

Jonnie Hogg looked at Louis and said angrily, "Well we can't dump him in the parking lot and Joobie and me ain't gonna drag this dead weight back up all those steps to his god damn room. Draggin' him down was tough enough."

Louis scratched his balls, as was his habit when facing a thorny problem that needed his immediate attention, and said, "Look, we can put him in the trunk." With that he walked to the rear of his pride and joy, opened the trunk and spread a tarp which he had stored there over the trunk's floor. Jonnie Hogg and Garcia Rosenbloom dragged the unconscious Charles Fontaine to the rear of the Edsel and dumped him rather unceremoniously into the trunk. As Louis slammed the trunk closed, he said, "That miserable sack of shit won't notice where the hell he's riding anyway. Besides it's a short ride to the motel. Hop in boys, it's off to the races." And with that Jeremiah pushed the backrest of the front seat on the passenger side of the Edsel forward and made several valiant attempts the get into the back seat. However, the two-door Edsel did not have the clearance necessary to make that very easy or perhaps even possible, given Jeremiah's girth. From the other side of the Edsel, Louis yelled, "Hold it Prof! You'll break the damn front seat. Let the other three assholes get in the back. You get in the front seat." Jamie, Jonnie Hogg and Garcia Rosenbloom deftly squeezed into the back seat, Jeremiah wedged his way into the front, doors slammed and off they took.

Louis couldn't contain himself as he commanded his pride and joy, "Lucille's a great ride. She's heavy fast, as they say, because of her weight, but once she gets toolin', she's fast as greased lightning." The posse, with Jeremiah in tow and Charles Fontaine safely contained, sped down the gravel road onto the main road and literally in five minutes found themselves parked before the Shangri- La suite of the Adirondack Motel. Right after them, a black Cadillac Escalade pulled up alongside and out popped a surprisingly agile Louis "Big Louie" Fazzano.

The posse, the rotund Jeremiah, and the huge but athletic Big Louie, gathered at the door to the honeymoon suite. Jamie frantically searched his pockets for the key to the suite and came up empty. He mumbled, "Fuck, Charles must have the damn key." He motioned to Louis to toss the car keys to Jonnie Hogg, which Louis did, and said, "Pig Fat, you and Joobie retrieve that bastard from the trunk and drag his ass over here," which they also promptly did but with some difficulty. Before a thorough search of Charles' pockets could be completed, the task being complicated by Charles' uncon-sciousness, the door to the suite swung open. Big Louie had picked the lock. He walked into the suite, turned and said, "Entre vous, boys," which "the boys" did.

Big Louie, with hands on hips, looked around the living room and said, "This dump is a mess. Smells like a Tijuana bar." Jonnie Hogg and Garcia Rosenbloom dragged Charles into the bridal chamber and dumped him on the great heart-shaped bed. The es-teemed Charles Fontaine looked more like a somnolent burnt offer-ing to Bacchus than a precious gift to Venus as he lay splayed on the great red heart-shaped altar of love snoring away.

Jamie scurried about the kitchenette and made coffee. The group poured itself cups of the strong, black java and retreated to the brid-al chamber. Big Louie looked about, sniffed and said, "This room smells like a Tijuana whorehouse." Jeremiah pulled the tuna burrito photos and the two notes from his jacket pocket and handed the photos to Big Louie who whistled as he eyed the first photo featur-ing Jeremiah. After a good long look-see, he said, "Christ, that's one fuckin' sugar bush." He turned to Jeremiah and said, "That you eating that hairy pussy?"

Jeremiah slowly shook his head yes and said "Actually I was try-ing to drink tequila."

Big Louie doubled over in laughter and managed "Drinkin' te-quila? I'm not sure that's what Rose'd call it. That's some shot glass you're slurpin' from. If ol' Rosey sees this photo, yer ass is grass. How the hell did you keep your specs on, anyway?"

Jeremiah took off his pince-nez and gently bent the glasses at the nose piece. "It's the spring," he explained and then pushed them back onto his nose.

Big Louie whistled again and said, "Some fuckin' bush. From the waist down that's one good-lookin' piece of dark meat. She Mexican?"

Jamie broke in, "Yeah, we think so. Called herself Juanita."

Big Louie again looked at the photo of Jeremiah as he moved to the right of the bed, and said more or less to himself, "This photo was taken from here." He looked up and said, "Who took the photos?"

Jamie answered, "We're not sure. We were what you might call preoccupied at the time. There was this guy who said he was the entertainment manager. A big, mean-lookin' hombre. He was here the whole time. Sat over there. Must have been him."

Big Louie closed his left eye and peered with his squinting right eye toward the bed, framing a picture with the thumb and forefinger of his right hand and said, "Yup. This photo was shot from here. It's grainy. My guess, a cell phone camera."

He looked at the remaining photos and determined that they had been taken from opposite sides of the rather wide heart-shaped bed and said, "Whoever took these photos was walking around the room shooting the pics. None of you noticed?"

After an embarrassing minute of silence, Jamie replied for the posse, "Hell we were in tequila wonderland sniffin' young Mexican pussy."

Big Louie shook his head in disgust as he studied the last three photos and said, more or less to himself, "A picture of a thumb, a blurry picture of the floor, and a picture of two pair of feet." He glanced over at Charles snoring away and said, "That footsie pic, looks like Charles' fancy cowboy boots. And those are great pics of the floor and that hombre's thumb. That's some set of pics. Looks to me like this mysterious photographer was as zipped as the rest of you. Was there a note?"

Jeremiah handed the first note he'd received to Big Louie and said, "This illiterate note came with the photos. You may need some help interpreting it."

Big Louie took the note and read it aloud, "Five grand, or the internet, will contact you for details. It's pretty obvious. Whoever wrote this wants five thousand bucks or he'll put the photos on the internet. Says he'll contact you with the details on how to make the exchange. Standard blackmailing procedure. You get a second note with the details?"

Jeremiah silently handed Big Louie the second note, which he read aloud, "Grants tomb Tuesday midnight." Big Louie thought for a moment and said, "Pretty straightforward. He wants you to deliver the five grand at midnight at Grant's tomb. Odd no mention about the money being in small denominations and not in sequence. It's like he's not concerned about this precaution, almost like the money's not that important. Besides, five grand's not that much for all the setup work this guy did." At this point Big Louie paused, thinking. Then he continued, "Unless he figures to milk the Doc here for more. And he don't mention turning over the photos. None of this crap makes any sense. Seems the precautions don't matter and the money's not important. Besides, like I said, five grand's not that much for all the setup work he did, unless he figures to milk the Doc for more. And he don't mention turning over the original photos. Don't make no sense, no how."

Big Louie walked over to a chair and eased his considerable bulk down and into the chair, which groaned as he did so. He sat for a moment looking at the great, heart-shaped bed and said. "It took a lot to pull this off, get you assholes to rent this-here suite and hire that Mexican sugar bush. This can't be no one-man, one-sugar-bush operation the way you were set up. And why Grant's tomb? It's far away and not all that secure."

Jeremiah slumped into a chair next to Big Louie and, looking down at his feet as he spoke, said in a barely audible voice, "I'm an adjunct professor of English literature at Columbia University and the campus is only eight blocks from Grant's tomb. Maybe that's why."

Big Louie thought for a moment and said, "That where you work now? Hell, I didn't know that. I thought you were at CCNY. Seems like those blackmailers have done their homework and know a lot about you. Why you? You and Rose ain't rollin' in dough, right?"

Jeremiah looked up in surprise and blurted out, "That's correct. I don't make much at Columbia, and as you know, Rose is a programmer and earns a good salary, but we're far from wealthy. I'd say we're comfortable, not wealthy."

Big Louie scratched his head and said, "Doesn't make sense. If they know where you work, they sure as shit know how much you earn and most likely how much Rose earns. They'd know you don't have much dough. You got to have somethin' else they want and want bad besides the money. Five thousand bucks just ain't enough for all this work and they know they can't milk you for much more. This stinks. What do you and Rose have they'd want?"

Jeremiah remained staring at the tips of his barely visible shoes and said, "I can't think of a single thing. We own the apartment, but it's mortgaged. Rose has a 401K without much in it. We own a late model Volvo. I can't think of anything else."

"No other real estate or assets?"

"Heaven's no. As you know, we live quite modest lives."

Big Louie scratched his head and looked at the ceiling mirror over the great heart-shaped bed and whistled. "Who rented this place and hired the Mexican sugar bush for so-called entertainment. She doesn't look like local talent."

Jamie point up at the image of a snoring Charles Fontaine reflected in the ceiling mirror and said, "Our Harvard hero up there rented the suite as a wedding gift for Leslie and me. And he hired the entertainment."

Big Louie looked over at the real snoring Charles Fontaine and laughed. Between guffaws, he managed to say, "He's had some fuckin' couple 'a days. Looks like prince charming over there won't be talking anytime soon. Listen, when that Harvard hero comes to, ask him how he found this place and the entertainment."

Big Louie stood and facing Jeremiah asked, "Well, you gonna pay off?"

Jeremiah hesitated and then said, "I'd like to, but I don't think I can come up with five thousand dollars cash without Rose knowing since…"

Before he could finish, Jamie interrupted, "Look, Prof, we got you into this mess and we'll get you out. If you need the five grand now, I can front the money tonight. No pro-blemo!"

"You got that kind of cash layin' around? You rich or somethin'?"

Jamie replied proudly, "I've made a lot in real estate. I'm pretty well off. I own a lot of property and…"

Before Jamie could finish, Big Louie interrupted him. "Then why the hell didn't they send the god damn photos and ransom note to you? Why the hell is the close-up of the Doc here and not you? Somethin's screwy here?"

He handed Jeremiah a business card and continued, "I take it you plan to meet with whoever shows up at Grant's tomb this Tuesday as instructed." Jeremiah took the business card and shook his head yes. Big Louie pointed at the business card and said, "Call me at my cell number tomorrow. And if you get any additional information out of sleeping beauty over there, call me right away. Any of you boys joining Jeremiah at Grant's tomb?"

Jamie, speaking for the posse, replied, "We'll be there. We got the Prof into this mess and we'll get him out of it. It's a matter of honor."

Big Louie looked at Louis, shook his head and pursed his lips in mild disgust, and said, "Louis, call your damn mother." He looked down at his watch and mumbled, "Shit, I've got to get back to the city." He double-timed it out of the Shangri-La suite with unexpected agility and speed in spite of a considerable limp, disappearing into the dark parking lot.

Jeremiah looked down at the card and read aloud, "Fazzano Collection and Protection. And we're good at it!" He turned to Louis and asked, "Exactly what services does your uncle's firm provide?"

Louis replied, "Big Louie's pretty tight-lipped about it. I heard they collect on bad debts, do some repo work and provide security. Don't know any specifics. He just says his firm picks 'em up and knocks 'em down with the best of them. What I do know is it's a pretty good idea to have Big Louie on your side and not such a good idea not to."

Midnight at Grant's Tomb brings more news from the beyond…

Jamie Steinkraus stood by Jeremiah in the shadows just beyond the brightly lit Grant's tomb and before a section of the long connected cement bench that surrounds three sides of the great mausoleum. The rest of the posse slouched in various poses close by on a section of the long cement bench.

The professor took his pocket watch from his vest pocket and held it toward a street light so that he could read it and said to himself, "10 o'clock."

From the shadows, Jonnie Hogg said to no one in particular and thus to everyone in general, "Two more hours of sittin' on these shitty benches? Christ sake, who designed these motherfuckers, the Mark da Sad?"

Jeremiah corrected Jonnie, "I think that you mean the Marquis De Sade."

Jonnie took the correction in stride, "Yeah, that bastard."

Jeremiah then went reflexively into professorial mode, "As to these benches, they're an example of what's termed community art. The artist who designed them is quite famous, Pedro Silva. He studied art at Columbia. He designed them so that the entire community could participate in both the detailed design and the execution of this living piece of art. The mosaics are like an unfurling comic book and each one of them along this serpentine bench was designed by a group from the local community."

Jonnie was unimpressed, "I mighta known, another fuckin' beaner designed these ass numers. Well one thing's certain, this Silva hombre doesn't know a fuckin' thing about benches. Those benches we sat on in the Tijuana hoosegow were more comfortable than these bastards."

The professor corrected him, "Pedro Silva is Argentinean and not Mexican. I'm sure that your friend Mr. Garcia Rosenbloom takes a somewhat different view of Pedro Silva and his work."

Out of the darkness the professor heard, "Prof, these damn benches are pretty uncomfortable regardless of where the hell this Pedro guy is from."

Jonnie remained unimpressed by Jeremiah's little lecture. "Like I really give a shit where this asshole's from. I know one thing about this Pedro Silva: he don't know a god damn thing about benches. Not only are these things hard on my ass, they're harder on my eyes. The god damn thing looks like drooling cement graffiti. Why would anyone want to surround Grant's tomb with a fuckin' unfurling graffiti comic book? And come to think of it, Prof, how come you know so god damn much about this Pedro character?"

The professor did not get angry with Jonnie Hogg for he understood that people like Jonnie were unsophisticated and did not know much about life's finer points, so he pressed on in his effort to educate the very unsophisticated Jonnie Hogg. "As to why I know so much about Pedro Silva, in 1972 I was a student at Columbia and I actually met Mr. Silva. I didn't want to come across as a braggadocio, but I worked on this piece of community art. Professors and students, such as myself, from Columbia worked hand-in-hand with members of the community, including neighborhood gang members, under Pedro Silva's direction to create these mosaic benches. Three thousand of us volunteers worked for over two years."

Jonnie was flabbergasted, "It took two years to create this piece of shit?"

"Yes. It took us volunteers two years of hard work and dedication."

Jonnie was stunned, "Why? Who overpaid for it?"

The Professor continued his lecture, "The Federal Park Service paid for it. Grant's tomb had fallen victim to vandalism and was in great disrepair. The building's exterior walls were covered with graffiti. The Park Service thought if the community had a stake in the monument, the local youth would cease their vandalism and the writing of graffiti on its walls. Pedro Silva was chosen for the project because his field of expertise was community art."

Jonnie pointed to the street lamp above them. The glass cover to the lamp had been broken and the light was out. "Prof, is that part of the community art too?" Then he pointed down the unfurling cement comic book to the next section of the serpentine bench. Barely visible were several large black letters spray painted on the bench. The letters were so stylized that no one except the spray-can artist and a few of his intimates knew what the letters actually were and what they represented. "Was that part of the original design? Looks to this redneck Okie like that grand plan of the Park Service and Pedro Silva hasn't exactly worked out. Still don't answer the question why anyone would come up with such a stupid idea."

Jamie broke in, "Look, Pig Fat, sometimes it's Chinatown and sometimes it's New York City. It's just the way it is."

Jonnie stood and stretched and said, "Well the way it is in New York City is pretty fuckin' stupid."

From the darkness, Big Louie materialized surprising Jamie, Jeremiah and the rest of the posse. He motioned for them to move with him farther into the darkness, which they all did with the exception of Charles Fontaine who was slumped across the bench sound asleep. "Leave sleeping beauty for now. He looks like a homeless bum. Fits right in." Then he said in hushed tones, "Boys, something's not copasetic here. There's a car parked down the street with a guy inside drinking coffee. I did a little reconnoitering and I recognized the car. Belongs to an NYPD detective I know. I use the bastard sometimes for surveillance work. Very suspicious. If he's here on official business, this could be a setup."

Jeremiah said in disbelief, "A setup? I don't understand. Why would a New York police detective be concerned about this particular blackmailing imbroglio?"

Big Louie added, "And more importantly, how in the hell would he know there even was a blackmailing imbro... a blackmail exchange occurring on the steps of Grant's tomb at 12 midnight? Any of you guys tell anyone else about it?"

A series of anonymous "fuck no's" with one "certainly not" emanated from the darkness. Big Louie, satisfied that no one there had leaked the information, continued, "Well I trust my nose and my nose says something stinks. Wake up sleeping beauty over there and all of you disappear. I'll do some more reconnoitering and see if I can find out what the fuck's going on."

After a long silence, Jeremiah blurted out, "But Louis, what about those rather incriminating photos of me?"

Big Louie whispered, "Not so loud and don't use my name, OK. Whoever set this up isn't going to put any of those pictures on the internet. They want somethin'. I'm not sure it's the five grand, but they want somethin'. If they put those pictures on the internet, they lose their power over you. Where's the satchel of dough?"

Jamie said, "It's over by Charles."

Big Louie retrieved the satchel and said, "You guys beat it and take sleeping beauty over there with you. There's a diner-type place a couple of blocks from Columbia. You know the Jerry Seinfeld restaurant?"

Jeremiah whispered, "I know that establishment. Leslie and I have eaten there many times."

Big Louie replied, "Good, I'll meet you guys there in an hour." He paused and then whispered, "Louis?" and a voice replied, "Yeah, I'm over here." Big Louie whispered somewhat more loudly in the direction of the 'Yeah, I'm over here', "Call your mother tomorrow, damn it!" and disappeared as mysteriously as he had appeared.

Another Jerry Seinfeld moment...

As he scraped the last of the egg yolk splattered across his plate with his last slice of toast, Jonnie Hogg looked around the restaurant and seemed to see it for the first time. He had concentrated on ordering and consuming his late night breakfast with a single-mindedness that precluded noticing much about his surroundings. A puzzled expression spread across his face as he looked around the restaurant's interior. "Hey, this ain't the restaurant in Seinfeld?"

Jeremiah, in midchew, answered, "Technically you are correct, but in actuality it is."

Jonnie's face reddened, "Technically, my ass. It don't look nothin' like the restaurant where Seinfeld ate. This dump is a tourist scam."

Jeremiah responded professorially, "I guess technically it could be considered so, but actually, as I said, it is the restaurant in Seinfeld."

Jonnie's voice began to rise, "Technically that's bullshit. Actually that's bullshit too. I've seen Seinfeld in that restaurant hundreds of times and it ain't this one."

The posse sat at a large booth hovering over what were now pretty much empty plates. The good professor, who had deposited himself in a chair at the open end of the booth's table, used his fork to delicately push the remnants on the plate of his first breakfast onto what was left on the plate of his second breakfast.

The seating arrangement was one of necessity. As with Lucille, it was problematic that Jeremiah could actually fit into a booth's bench seat, and from a culinary standpoint, it was obvious that his order would require more table space than any two members of the posse. Thus he sat in a chair at the open end of the booth's table.

All the posse's eyes had turned to the amply occupied end of the booth's table where Jeremiah sat. Even Charles Fontaine, who for the first time in days appeared awake, turned toward the professor. All of them had seen Seinfeld and his emotionally disturbed friends doing nothing in the restaurant but somehow screwing up their lives in so not doing.

Charles tried to calm Jonnie. "Look Jonnie, I think I get what the Perfesser is saying. When we walked up to the place, it looked exactly like Seinfeld's restaurant. And it was. When we got inside, it wasn't. My guess, Seinfeld was filmed someplace else. So the exterior was in New York, but the interior was someplace else."

Jeremiah added, "That's correct. As a point of clarification, the interior of this restaurant is a set in Hollywood and it is that set that you see when you see Mr. Seinfeld in this restaurant."

Jonnie tapped the table with his right index finger as he said, "Ya know, this city is full of bullshit. Nothin' is like you think it is. I'd rather be in Tijuana where you know exactly what's what."

Garcia Rosenbloom pursed his lips and nodded his head in knowing agreement. Louis Fazzano added his two cents, "Brooklyn's nothin' like this. It's more like Tijuana."

Louis's promotion of Brooklyn thoroughly confused Jeremiah, who could only say, "Brooklyn's like Tijuana?"

Jonnie turned toward Louis, "Well then I'd rather be in Brooklyn than here, because Manhattan sucks."

Jamie, who had followed the discussion with some interest, added, "Well, Pig Fat, it may suck, but there's a lot of money to be made in Manhattan. There's a very limited amount of real estate and a lot of people who want it."

Jonnie, unconvinced by Jamie's argument of the monetary advantages of living in Manhattan from an investment point of view, said, "Well that just goes to prove there's a lot of assholes who live in Manhattan or want to."

Jamie looked at his wrist watch, "I wonder where Big Louie is. It's been over an hour."

Charles, who seemed less concerned about their present circumstances and more concerned about the recent past, asked Jamie, "How's Leslie doing, anyway? I have faint memories of some kind of problem, and it's got to be pretty severe since you and she aren't honeymooning."

Jonnie Hogg elbowed Charles and said, "Where you been,

asshole?" Charles, obviously embarrassed, did not reply.

Jamie looked to Jeremiah and said, "Prof, you saw her today. I didn't. You might as well give them a firsthand report."

Charles interjected before Jeremiah could respond, "You didn't see her?"

Jamie looked down at his plate and fiddled with his knife, tapping it on the plate, and replied in barely a whisper, "No, I saw her yesterday and she became hysterical again. The psychiatrist requested that I not visit her for a couple of days."

Charles who had literally been in various stages of unconsciousness for most of the week as he recovered from his celebratory activities before, during and after the wedding, said, "Psychiatrist? Where the hell is she?"

Jeremiah straightened the napkin on his lap and kept his eyes on his fingers as he spoke up, "Rose took her to a rest home upstate, a place north of Ossining. She's had some sort of breakdown. Rose is staying up there to be close by and visits her every day."

Charles, who immediately thought his Vesuvian outburst had in some way contributed to Leslie's problem, whatever it was, said, "Damn, I'm so sorry about my behavior. I… " but before he could finish Jeremiah interrupted him, "Charles, it's not your fault. It's a very complicated problem. Today she seemed fine until one of the attendants…" he paused and then continued as his voice became fainter and fainter, "I really can't get into the details, but she seemed fine and then she wasn't. She's medicated and fairly stable most of the time."

Charles was stunned by the news and asked, "What's the prognosis? When will she be released?"

Jeremiah shook his head and said, "We don't know. As I said, it's a very complicated psychological problem. Dr. Fairchild, her psychiatrist, says that she's had some kind of transformational experience and her mind is stuck. He used another term which I've forgotten, but basically she keeps reliving some kind of seminal experience that has somehow imbedded itself into her psyche. As I have said, I cannot get into the details. They are very personal and even if I were free to do so, I would not."

Idiot-savants on the loose...

Jeremiah looked over his shoulder and there was Big Louie. He had entered unnoticed during the intense discussion about Leslie and her present condition. Big Louie pulled a chair from an adjacent table and pushed it next to Jeremiah with the back of the chair facing the booth. He straddled it, draped his arms over the backrest and said, "Well boys, the strange just got stranger." He waved to the waitress and yelled, "Cup of leaded J over here, beautiful," and then continued his tale. "I talked to the guy in that car. The one I suspected of being NYPD. Well he was, but off-duty. Like I said, I knew the bastard. He's a detective. Name's Scootch Jankowski. I done him a couple of favors, passed him some info that helped him break a case and he ended up getting a commendation. Ol' Scootch owes me big time, which was why I did him the fuckin' favor. Anyway, he was off duty like I said and workin' this private job. Hell, he lives just up the block. Says he's workin' some kind of divorce case, at least that's what he thinks."

The waitress brought Big Louie a mug of coffee. He looked up at her and said, "Thanks," as he pulled a monogrammed silver flask from his jacket pocket. He resumed, "Well my NYPD detective friend says he was supposed to hand an envelope over to a short guy with long red hair and a stubby red beard." He slowly turned the cap on the flask, removed it and poured some of its contents into his coffee, screwed the cap back onto the flask and carefully returned it to his jacket pocket. "Four Roses, boys, to sweeten the J, coffee royale, just what a man needs this time 'a night." He took a long sip from his mug and continued, "He says this guy with the red hair and beard, a guy who looked like... say Jamie over there... was to give him a bag which he was to take to some law offices in Manhattan."

Jeremiah blurted out, "Man with red hair... red beard? That's not me! I thought I was the one who was supposed to meet with those illiterate blackmailers."

Big Louie finished off his coffee royale, held up his coffee mug and yelled, "Hey beautiful, another cuppa J over here" then addressed Jeremiah, "Look, Doc, somethin's not kosher with this deal. Yer right, you shoulda been the one that ol' Scootch was lookin' for, but you ain't. Tell the truth, never understood why they'd target you, Doc, other than they got a nice shot a you muff divin'. Jamie over there's the better candidate. He's loaded and was about to be married. Money and marriage ceremonies always make for juicier victims."

Leaning over his plate, Jeremiah mumbled as he shoveled a tablespoon of late night breakfast remnants into his mouth, "For some rea… son…" He chewed and swallowed before continuing, "I feel as if these blackmail fellows have insulted me. They apparently did not think me worthy of blackmailing."

The waitress refilled Big Louie's coffee mug and Big Louie again sweetened his leaded J with the contents of his monogrammed silver flask, which he topped and returned to his jacket pocket. He took another long sip from his mug and then responded to the insulted Jeremiah, "Listen Doc, first, count yerself lucky. You won't be forkin' over no dough or havin' victim number two over there frontin' dough for you. Second, don't count yerself too lucky 'cause they still have those photos of you ticklin' that Juanita's hootchie cootchie with yer tongue and if Rose ever sees those photos, you'd a wished you'd died a painful death and gone to hell. But that's just the preliminaries."

Big Louie adjusted his stance on the chair, took another swig of his coffee royale and continued. "Well, I tell Scootch that I was workin' the other end of that divorce case. That my client's buyin' some incriminatin' photos from a third party. I held up the bag and told him my john was afraid to make the exchange at midnight with this here bag of shekels, so he hired me. Told him no need for us to climb the steps to Grant's tomb. I handed Scootch the equipment bag with the dough and he handed me this here envelope." Big Louie reached into his back pocket and pulled out a large manila envelope he'd folded and stuffed there. As he tapped the envelope on the table he said, "I tried to pry some more details out of the bastard, but he clammed up on me."

During the discussion, the waitress had cleaned off the table and given the posse and Jeremiah refills of their coffee. Big Louie continued tapping the envelope on the table and said, "Before we look at the contents of this here envelope, I still have a couple 'a questions. Doc, remind me how you came into possession of the first two notes and the photos?"

Jeremiah looked a bit bewildered to again be in the spotlight but managed an "I found both envelopes in my cabin. Slipped under the door. Lucky Rose wasn't there."

"See, that don't make no sense whatever either, if yer the person bein' blackmailed. If it was you and Rose saw them photos, they'd have shot their wad. More proof yer not the object of their affection."

Jamie's eyes widened, "It all makes sense. I originally rented the TR, that's the name of the cabin, for me and the rest of the posse. At the last minute I decided we'd stay at the lodge to be closer to the reception. We had a couple of unused bedrooms up there and since that's where we'd be partying, I thought staying there would make life a whole lot easier. So I phoned the desk and told them to give the cabin to Rose and the Perfesser."

Big Louie finished off his coffee royale and pronounced, "Mystery number one solved!" He turned his eyes toward Charles and said, "Now to mystery number two. Mr. Fontaine, how'd you choose Juanita and her strong-arm photographer for the entertainment?"

Charles scratched the back of his head and thought for a minute, then responded, "When I went to the Adirondack Motel to reserve that suite. I was feeling pretty good, having tested that Brand XXX tequila. This squirrely-looking Hispanic dude follows me into the office and stands behind me. He's dressed in a business suit. Looks like a young stockbroker type except for a stupid mustache that looked fake. Looks to be in his late 20's. He asks me if I was organizing a bachelor party. I tell him I am and he hands me an envelope."

Big Louie interrupted, "How'd he know you're there to rent a place for a bachelor party? Who told you about the place anyway?"

Charles thought some more and said, "I think the girl at the desk at the retreat told me. I asked her where I could rent a room where some guys could party without too much interference. She recommended the Adirondack Motel. Later I thought it'd be a great place for Leslie and Jamie to start their honeymoon."

Big Louie pounded the table with his fist, "Damn, that girl at the desk, she was workin' with the blackmailers. Had to be. That's how come the bastards knew that Jamie and the rest of you assholes were supposed to be stayin' at that cabin. She just didn't get the news that Jamie'd changed his plans. And that's how she knew chances were good Charles would be bookin' a room for the bachelor party at the Adirondack. It weren't no rocket science."

Charles pushed back in his chair, looked up at the ceiling and grasped the back of his neck with his hands as if seeking divine guidance. "I never suspected a thing. After I made the reservations, that squirrely-looking dude said he'd give me an excellent deal for the entertainment at the bachelor party and I bit. I open the envelope and there was Juanita in that outfit. Her face looked a little young but, damn, that body. She was wearing a little Mexican outfit, didn't cover much, and her eyes…" Charles stopped, took a breath and continued, "Well, it seemed like that squirrely-looking Hispanic dude with the fake mustache was giving me a great deal. Two hundred bucks for the night. I paid him on the spot."

Big Louie couldn't contain himself, "Did that Harvard education of yours make you fuckin' stupid." He slowly shook his head back and forth and said, more or less to himself, "What a mook" and then asked, "You paid the two hundred up front?"

Charles brought his hands down to the table and stared at them, obviously embarrassed, and replied, "Yes. I paid the two hundred up front. That squirrely-looking dude said we could negotiate for something special later if I was so inclined. About six, at the motel, this other guy shows up with Juanita. Says his name is Garcia. Mean-looking, muscular Mexican dude. Asks if I want to negotiate something special. That's where the tequila body slams came in. Paid an extra two hundred."

Big Louie started to laugh and after a couple of good guffaws said, "Damn, these bastards are good. They got you to pay them to blackmail you. That leaves only one outstanding piece of info. Why'd they set up the exchange for Grant's tomb if Jamie's the target?"

Jamie broke the silence that followed Big Louie's question. "I may know the reason."

Big Louie shot back, "Go for it!"

And Jamie went for it. "I own an apartment building off Broadway on 116th. I live in one of the apartments. It's where Leslie and I are going to live."

Big Louie scratched his head and asked rhetorically, "Why would blackmailers consider where their target lives? Usually they don't give a shit." He thought a moment and said "That don't make no sense. Maybe Scootch wanted to make his job easier. Hell, that don't make no sense either." Then he blurted, "Fuck! We still have some unanswered questions." He tapped the envelope on the table and said, "Let's see what else is hidin' in the bushes." Out slid two sheets of paper and a photo. His first word was, Shit!" followed by another "Shit!" followed by yet a third "Shit!"

He stared at the two sheets of paper and a photo and said with an obviously forced calm, "No cell phone, no SIM card. One fuckin' photo and two fuckin' sheets of paper. Looks like a photo of a Hispanic girl, a very young Hispanic girl. Here's a wild guess. That's Juanita and her hidden hootchie cootchie. Right?"

Charles looked up at the photo and then down at his hands again and said, "Yes, I think that's the photo that squirrely Hispanic dude showed me."

Big Louie picked up the second sheet of paper and read. Then he turned the paper toward the table and said, "What's this? Looks like an invite to a bachelor party, a pretty wild bachelor party, what with that stallion about to pound the shit out of that mare. And then there's these words, and I quote, "There will be a gathering of the Posse of Little Horses to honor our own Stuntman, who after tomorrow will be a one trick pony." So you have a neked underage girl performing at a bachelor party and you use the word trick in the invitation. Look familiar?"

Charles said, "Yes, but it's a copy. The original was on a card. After I rented the Shangri-La suite and called Jonnie, Garcia and Louis to tell them where the bachelor party was, I drove back to the lodge and told Jamie. He wanted to…"

Jamie interrupted, "I thought it'd be a good idea to invite my future father-in-law. We'd only met once before this week. Thought it'd give us a chance to get acquainted."

Big Louie's eyebrows rose and parted as an expression of disbelief spread across his face and he blurted out, "Get to better know your future father-in-law, who happens to be a lit perfessor at Columbia, by inviting him to a tequila drinking, hootchie-cootchie sniffin' bachelor party?"

Jamie bit his lower lip and continued, "I had my laptop and a portable printer in my room at the lodge, always carry the setup with me, you know, to keep track of my business deals and such. And I fooled around and came up with that invitation. Showed Charles who thought it was great. Then I took it over to the registration desk and stuffed it in the envelope I'd left for the future in-laws."

Big Louie shook his head in disbelief, picked up the second sheet of paper and read aloud, "You big trouble. Girl 15. Sell or jail. More coming." His eye brows scrunched together yet again. He pulled the monogrammed silver flask from his jacket pocket, slowly unscrewed the cap, which he placed on the table, and took a long swig from the flask. He set the flask on the table and his lips mouthed the words of the note a second time as he silently read it to himself. Then he said to Jamie, "If that Juanita is really fifteen, you guys could be in deep shit if this little escapade goes public." He thought for a moment and said, "What they want you to sell?"

Jamie raised his hands palms up and his eyebrows and replied, "I do not have a clue."

Big Louie looked down at the note again and reread it silently a third time. "These bastards are either the dumbest fuckers in the world of blackmail or the smartest. They're like those idiot-smart guys."

Jeremiah interjected, "Idiot-savants."

Big Louie continued without missing a beat, "Yeah, idiot-savants. First they nail the set up and get Charles over there to hire this Mexican jail bait for entertainment. Chalk up one point in the savant column.

Garcia Rosenbloom took a pencil from his shirt pocket and wrote at the top of a napkin the words Idiot and Savant and drew a line down the napkin between the two words. He put a mark in the savant column and said, "One good ticky."

Big Louie continued, "Then they deliver the first note and the muff-diving pics to the cabin where Jamie was supposed to be, but wasn't."

Charles interrupted, "But that's understandable. Jamie changed the reservations at the last minute, so these guys could still be pretty competent at their profession. Even a short stop like Julio Lugo makes errors."

Louis interrupted Charles. "And you graduated from fuckin' Harvard? That Red Sox asshole makes errors because he sucks! You shoulda said Derek Jeter. That'd make sense."

Big Louie raised his hands as a sign of peace, "Boys, we're not here to argue Red Sox-Yankee bullshit, but Charles has a point. No points on the idiot-savant tally either way."

Garcia succinctly summarized the situation with a "No ticky." Big Louie continued, "Then the bastards take pictures of Doc here inventin'… what'd you call it?… the tuna burrito… with some blurry shots of the rest of you idiots rootin' him on. Then there's those great shots of a thumb, the floor and a bunch of feet."

Jamie explained, "Well it's understandable why they didn't get a picture of me goin' down on that Juanita babe because I never did. I kept my body slam pretty much around Juanita's belly button. Jeez, I was getting married the next day."

Big Louie looked over at Jamie and said, "Listen, this bandito got some blurry shots of you watchin' Doc here playin' tequila slurpy with that girl's snatch. A really good operation woulda got a shot of you tonguin' her belly button. That'd be incriminatin' enough to do the job. And from the condition you assholes were in, that wetback bad guy there coulda asked you guys to pose neked and you'd a done it. That's a point on the idiot side of the scale."

Garcia marked the napkin and said, "Bad ticky."

Big Louie looked down at the note again. "And then there's these stupid notes."

At the word notes, Jeremiah's bushy eye brows rose and he put in his scholarly two cents, "Yes, the notes. They are so illiterate, so poorly written, that it's difficult to determine what these dastardly bandito fellows actually want. We could interpret them to some degree, but because they were so illiterate in construction, we could have easily misinterpreted them, which would have negated their initial purpose."

Big Louie considered Jeremiah's point and said, "At first I thought that the bastards were being clever and hiding their identity, but the Doc here's right. We coulda misinterpreted the notes and not done whatever it was they wanted by mistake. Another point for the idiot side."

Garcia marked the napkin and said, "Bad ticky."

Big Louie continued his analysis. "And then there's this business of needing five grand. I never heard of a blackmailer sayin' they needed shekels. They want them. So fuckin' strange, in fact, that they get another point in the idiot column."

Garcia marked the napkin and said, "Bad ticky."

Big Louie looked over at the napkin and asked, "Where we stand?"

Garcia counted the marks on the idiot-savant scale and said, "Three to one, idiots lead."

Louis added, "You forgot about the part where they had Charles pay them to set us up for the blackmail."

Big Louie smiled. "Right! You assholes paid that dynamic bandito duo and their young snatch to set you up for those incriminatin' photos. In fact, you paid them extra. A point on the savant side!" Big Louie pointed at the envelope and said, "And they arranged a clean exchange and got the dough they said they needed. Another point on the savant side. And they arranged it in such a way that we made the exchange with an off-duty NYPD detective. So we have no idea who they are. Another point on the savant side."

Garcia made three marks on the savant side of the ledger and said, "Three good tickies." He looked up and said, "Good tickies ahead, four to three."

Big Louie pointed at Jamie and said, "And they went through all of this bullshit to buy something from you? And you don't know what in hell's name they're tryin' to buy? That's gotta be a pretty big mark on the idiot side of the ledger over there." He looked over to Garcia who marked the last ticky on the napkin and asked him, "Where do we stand?"

Garcia counted the ticky marks with the point of his pencil and said, "Tie, four-four."

Big Louie grimaced in frustration and shook his head from side to side, "Shit, these bastards remain idiots and savants."

Jamie asked in frustration, "What do we do now? Seems like we know less with every note."

Big Louie said, "What do you guys do? Nothin'. That's what you do. You wait. The savant side of that operation said more comin'. They'll contact Jamie here. Probably at that apartment of his." As he screwed the cap on his flask and placed it in his jacket pocket, he said, "I know where Scootch lives. I'll tail the bastard tomorrow and see where he drops off that bag of money that the idiot side of that operation said they needed." And with that Big Louie rose from his chair, limped out the door and disappeared into the night.

Sometimes two plus two make four, sometimes it don't…

Big Louie Fazzano watched from his parked black Escalade, actually his double-parked black Escalade, his eyes trained on a car also double-parked half a block ahead. He rubbed his eyes with the heels of the palms of his hands. He was exhausted for he had been up all night. He mumbled to himself, "Do somethin' you son of a bitch." As if scripted, the off-duty NYPD detective Scootch Jankowski, to whom he had given the bag of money in exchange for yet another illiterate ambiguous blackmail note, jumped out of his car and trotted down the sidewalk away from Big Louie with the bag of blackmail money dangling from his left hand. Big Louie yelled "Fuck!" and grabbed a bunch of large printed signs on the passenger's seat. He quickly shuffled through them, grabbed the one that said Courier Service and threw it on the dash. He threw open the door of the Escalade, jumped out, slammed it shut, and quickly crossed the street. He limped down the opposite sidewalk with an unexpected light-footed grace, rare for a man of his size with a bum leg to boot, in surreptitious hot pursuit of his prey. As he trotted along, he mumbled to himself, "Where the fuck is ol' Scootch goin' with that dough?"

Mr. Scootch Jankowski trotted past two buildings and slowed to a brisk walk. Big Louie slowed his staccato trot and said to himself,

"That's right shithead, take me to your leader!" He didn't have to go far, for his prey had entered the next building, a large, modern office building. Big Louie walked down the opposite sidewalk past the entrance. From across the street he read the rather large, elaborate gold lettering on the building's façade. His lips moved as he silently read, Oglethorpe and Fernandez, International Law. He hustled back to his Escalade, removed the courier sign from his dash and took off for Jamie's apartment.

Manhattan traffic was heavy and it took him over an hour to drive from the Wall Street district north to Jamie's place. He double parked and threw a sign on the dash that read Handicapped and attached a handicapped tag to the rear view mirror. He got out of the Escalade and looked up at the building, whistled and said to himself, "Shit, this is one fine building." He checked the directory on the wall by the entrance, found the apartment for Mr. Jamie Steinkraus and thought: "Top floor. Nice location." He pushed the buzzer for that apartment. A voice blasted forth, "We didn't order no pizza, fat man." Big Louie thought to himself: Don't sound like Steinkraus, and yelled, "It's Fazzano, you asshole, buzz me in." When the door buzzer sounded, he pushed his way into a rather well-appointed lobby and took the elevator to the top floor. The elevator slowed and came to a stop. When the doors opened, there before him was an elaborately decorated foyer. He was surrounded by a fresco depicting reveling, scantily-clad young men and just as scantily-clad full-breasted, Rubenesque young women dancing about a rather well-muscled, much larger man in a loin cloth holding out a huge bunch of purple grapes. Emblazoned across the fresco in one of those banners that often appear in such works of art were the words "In Vino Veritas." He walked up to a large black door with a gold-relief mosaic depicting another large bunch of grapes. Above the bunch of gold grapes were the words, also in gold, Bacchanalian Wine Imports. Big Louie took a step back, read the words on the door, and scratched the back of his head in thought. He smiled, stepped forward and pounded several times on the door. The peep hole on the door opened and Big

Louie yelled, "For Christ sakes, who'd you think it was, the fuckin' Easter Bunny? Open the god damn door."

The door swung open and there stood Jonnie Hogg smiling from ear to ear. "Big Louie, on the rag?"

Big Louie said, "That's some fuckin' way to greet someone. Coulda been one of the tenants."

Jonnie laughed and replied, "We knew it was y'all from the security cameras."

Big Louie pushed by him and said as he passed, "You're a gen-u-ine Okie redneck asshole" and continued into what appeared to be a large living room. Jonnie laughed, pleased to have gotten under Big Louie's skin.

Big Louie peered around the room and there was the posse, schlumped about in various poses of relaxation on the large dark brown leather chairs and couches spread about the room. He took a couple of steps into the room, stopped in his tracks and whistled. The living room was dominated by a large, very old dark-stained table. The thick table top was supported by what appeared to Big Louie to be some type of carved Aztec figures. The wall to his left was covered with shelves and the shelves were covered with tequila bottles, hundreds of them, of every shape and type imaginable. Two very large maps decorated the opposite wall: one of northern Mexico and the southwestern United States, and another of Route 66 from Chicago to San Bernardino. A number of red pins tacked to various locations decorated both maps.

Jamie yelled from the far side of the room, "Big Louie, you able to tail that NYPD detective?"

Big Louie, taking in the entire room, said to himself but quite loudly, "Some layout," and then responded to Jamie, "Bingo! Ol' Scootch took that bag of dough into an office building off Wall Street, big fuckin' place. Offices of an international law firm, Oglethorpe and Fernandez."

Jamie waved for Big Louie to follow him and led him into a room off the living room that looked like a miniature NASA Command

and control center. There were monitors mounted on the far wall, a bunch of them, which Big Louie recognized as part of a rather sophisticated security system. An L-shaped table ran below the security monitors and along the wall to the right. The table was covered with computer monitors, printers, several key boards and some equipment which Big Louie did not recognize.

Big Louie whistled as he scanned the monitors and said, "That's some fuckin' security setup."

Jamie pulled a chair from the table, and said over his shoulder, "Yeah, it came with the building. The previous owner installed it." He turned the chair so that he faced Big Louie and sat down. He cupped his hands on his knees and looked down, biting his lower lip. He looked as if he had something to say but couldn't quite put it in words.

Big Louie scratched the back of his head and moved his hand down to his neck and rubbed. He waited for Jamie to speak, but no words came forth. Finally he said, "What's up?"

Jamie started talking without taking his eyes off his knees, "Jeremiah called. He's upstate visiting Leslie. Look, I don't want the rest of the posse to know about this, but the Perfesser gave me some bad news, and something that could make things a lot worse."

Big Louie couldn't imagine what could possibly make matters much worse and said "Shoot. I'm all ears."

Jamie continued, "Did you know that we put Leslie in a rest home yesterday?"

Big Louie shook his head no and said, "But I thought you'd have to do something. Where?"

Jamie said in a barely audible voice, "A place north of Ossining about 50 miles from the city." He paused and then continued, "Seems like she attacked one of the attendants last night… well attacked isn't quite the right word. She tried to get this black attendant to… you know… do her."

Big Louie said, "Do her?"

Jamie looked up and said, "Do her. You know, do her. She was naked and tried to get this black attendant to… screw her. The attendant got the hell out of her room and reported the incident. Leslie's out of her fucking mind. What if the blackmailers get a hold of this?"

Big Louie thought for a moment and said, "Ain't good. Look at the big picture. We don't know what the bastards want yet, but they're obviously setting you up. Sounds to me that they're tryin' to paint you as some kind of perv leading a bunch of other pervs in strange sexual rituals with underage girls."

Jamie, obviously hurt by what he took to be an insult, said, "Damn it, it was just a god damn bachelor party. She looked old enough. Besides, other than the Prof falling into her snatch, we kept above her bush. Just tequila body slams like everybody does. Hell, they do body slams in bars. Nobody ever screwed her."

Big Louie raised his hands, palms up toward Jamie, and said, "Look kid, I'm not sayin' you did screw her or that you and your buddies including that idiot nephew of mine were out to get some Mexican jailbait, but those bastards can paint a pretty bad picture. And if they have credible proof that Conchita there is fifteen, you guys could go to jail for a long time. You'd be classified as sexual predators. You'd do hard time, if you know what I mean, and then be labeled pervs for the rest of your lives. And now there's this business with Leslie. Can you imagine the kind of picture the tabloids could paint if they get a hold of this story?"

Jamie shook his head in worry. "What do we do?"

Big Louie said, "Look, I'll put one of my guys on it. We got to move her. We got to put her in some kind of a rest home that's way the hell away from here. She ain't far enough upstate. It's got to be someplace discrete and under an assumed name. Rose is probably embarrassed as hell and it should be an easy sell. You got the dough to cover this?"

Jamie raised his left hand and waved it across his body, "Look around you. I've been very fortunate. If I can afford this, I can afford to foot the bill."

Big Louie cleared his throat and said, "Well, since we're talkin' money, this family favor of mine is turnin' into a major operation. I'm goin' to have to charge you."

As he spun in his chair before one of the computer monitors, Jamie said, "Put me on the clock. Like I said, money's no problem." Big Louie watched as Jamie manipulated the mouse. Screens flashed on the large computer monitor before him. Without looking up Jamie asked, "Oglethorpe and Fernandez?"

Big Louie said, "Yup."

As Jamie typed he said, "I think I've heard of the bastards. They do a lot of international real estate contracting stuff." The words Oglethorpe and Fernandez in fancy script flashed onto the monitor before them. Jamie kept his eyes glued to the computer screen and said to Big Louie who stood behind him and to his left, "Knew the name sounded familiar. Here's their web site and it's a nice one." Jamie manipulated his way about the site, reading some text here and there and jumping to another screen as he worked his way through the site.

Big Louie tried to follow Jamie's progress on the monitor but could not. He was exhausted from lack of sleep. He lowered his head, rubbed his eyes with the thumb and index finger of his right hand and looked up trying to again follow Jamie's path through the site but could not. Finally he gave up, slouched into a nearby computer chair and waited for a report from Jamie on his findings.

Jamie finally spun about in his chair to face Big Louie and said, "That outfit is huge. Like I thought, they're an international law firm that specializes in international trade contracts and real estate transactions for companies here and in South and Central America. They've got offices in both regions and in the U.S."

Big Louie sat up in his chair. "What's a big, prestigious international law firm doin' handling bag money for some two-bit blackmailers?"

A fourth carta tan bella from the beyond...

The posse sat around Jamie's living room looking pretty glum. The room darkened as night fell. Finally Charles Fontaine stood and said, "This place feels like a fucking morgue." He walked over to the panel of switches controlling the apartment's lighting and just about every other service in the place. Just as he touched the light switch for the living room, the buzzer sounded. He jumped back, throwing his hand in the air yelling, "I didn't break anything!"

Jonnie Hogg yelled, "Doin' the Mexican hat dance, asshole?" The posse broke out into laughter.

Jamie ran into his computer room, looked up at the security monitors and yelled back, "Looks like a courier service!" As he ran to the apartment's entry he yelled, "We're a go!" He waved Charles back from the apartment's control panel and pushed the intercom button. He said with a forced calmness, "Who's there?"

A voice replied, "Mercury Courier Service. Delivering a package for Mr. Jamie Steinkraus. Somebody's got to sign for it."

Jamie switched off the intercom and said over his shoulder, "I'm goin' down there to get the package. Don't want that messenger seeing the inside of the apartment. We got no idea who this guy is. Charles, you come with me. One of you guys watch us on the security monitors." He pushed the intercom button again and said, "Be right down." He and Charles ran to the elevator and took it down to the building's foyer. On the way down, Jamie whispered to Charles, "You pretend to be me and sign."

Charles asked, "Why?" but before Jamie could reply he said, "Got it. Slick move."

The elevator door opened and there stood a rather distinguished-looking older man dressed in a courier's uniform. He had a clipboard in his hand and a large manila envelope tucked under the other arm. He held out the clipboard and said, "Mr. Jamie Steinkraus?" Charles stepped forward and rather ceremoniously took the clip board which had a pen pushed under the clip. He removed the pen, used it to sign for the package, shoved it back under the clip and handed the clipboard back to the courier. The courier handed Charles the package, said "Thank you, gentleman," and left.

After they entered the elevator and the doors closed, Charles handed the large manila envelope to Jamie who held it face up and read aloud, "Oglethorpe and Fernandez. Surprise, surprise."

Charles leaned over and read the large return address on the upper left-hand corner of the envelope and said, "Isn't that the law offices where that off-duty NYPD detective dropped off the bag of money?"

Jamie smiled and said "Sure is. We're about to find out what those bastards want me to sell them."

Once back in the living room, Jamie carefully placed the envelope down on the large dark table in the center of the room and gently centered it with his finger tips. The posse surrounded him, all except Louis who remained snoring loudly on the couch on the far side of the room, as he had been all evening. Jamie stood silently looking at the envelope. Finally Jonnie Hogg said, "Well ain't y'all gonna open the damn thing?" Jamie shook his head as if breaking a meditation, took out a Swiss army knife from his pocket, pulled out the long blade and slowly slit the top of the envelope open. Then he carefully pushed the blade back into the pocket knife which he slipped into his front pocket. He reached into the envelope and pulled out a large packet of papers. The first sheet was a cover letter which was clipped to two stapled documents.

Jamie quickly read the cover letter to himself. Charles asked, "What's it say?"

Jamie pursed his lips, scratched his scraggily red-bearded chin with the thumb and index finger of his left hand and replied, "It says that a real estate representative wants to buy that vacation home I bought east of San Diego, that mountain chalet in the middle of nowhere that I gave to Leslie as a wedding present. They offer exactly what I paid, down to the penny, including all the taxes, processing and legal fees. I remember exactly what that whole transaction cost me and that's what they're offering."

He quickly checked the first document attached to the cover letter and then the second. He tossed the documents back onto the table, put his hands on his hips, whistled and then said, "This is a standard contract and a nondisclosure agreement. This is the kind of transaction that's negotiated when a real estate group is fronting for a large developer who's trying to buy parcels of land for a major project. Done all the time. The nondisclosure agreement keeps the outstanding parcels they want from skyrocketing in price by keeping the purchases they've already made secret. As a real estate practice, it appears to be on the up-and-up as far as I can tell. But in this case a nondisclosure agreement seems like legal overkill. The chalet sits in the middle of a national forest, so there's no more land to be bought. And second, it's only a postage stamp of a plot. It's not much land at all."

Jonnie Hogg asked, "What about the tuna burrito pics and that beaner babe?"

Jamie said, "No mention. Yup, looks like standard stuff. Nothing about blackmail money, incriminating photos, sex with underage girls. None of that stuff." He retrieved the documents from the table and carefully pushed them back into the envelope, returning the envelope to the table. "I've got fifteen days to respond." He walked over to the big leather chair he'd spent most of the evening in, plopped down with a whoosh and stared at the envelope on the table.

Garcia Rosenbloom, who had been pretty much silent all evening, broke his silence with a rather cryptic, "Fernandez is Hispanic, San Diego is close to Mexico."

Jonnie Hogg said, "And that hot tamale had a hairy snatch. So what?"

Jamie sat up and said, "Well, my fellow caballitos, Joobie's onto something. It's time to palaver and put two and two together. Let's see if we can come up with something approximating four."

Charles stood and spoke with the stentorian voice of a great and committed orator, "Friends, Romans and fellow caballitos, before we begin this arduous journey into the dark underworld of the ne'er-do-wells, I think it appropriate that we toast the effort."

Jonnie Hogg immediately jumped to his feet and yelled, "Fuckin' A, Charlie-O! Let's get it on!" which startled the sleeping Louis Fazzano into semiwakefulness. Agreement quickly swept through the rest of the posse, for it never took much to get support for a proposal of this nature. Even the just-awakening Louis supported the idea of a toast whole heartedly without hearing Charlie-O's stentorian justification. In his mind, the toast was reason unto itself and thus self-justifying.

Jamie left the living room and a short time later he returned with a tray on which sat a bottle of Brand XXX tequila, a plate of lime slices, five salt shakers and five caballito shot glasses. He set the tray down over the envelope and the posse gathered about the great Aztec table.

Charles said, "Lead the way, Stuntman." Jamie reverently picked up the bottle of tequila and said as he removed its cap, "My fellow Little Horses, this is the last bottle of Triple X." He carefully filled his caballito and passed the precious bottle to Charlie-O who did the same and passed the bottle to Hog Fat, who passed it to Joobie, who passed it to The Guinea, who remained both quite uninformed and enthusiastic. Each member of the posse now stood before a full caballito of Brand XXX tequila.

The Posse of Little Horses licked the back of their left hands above the middle finger, grabbed a salt shaker from the tray on the Aztec table and poured salt on the wet spot, returning the salt shakers to the tray on the Aztec table. The five Little Horses then thrust their right hands above the coffee table, clentched their hands into fists, all fists meeting above the center of the Aztec table. As the fists met, the five Little Horses shouted in unison, "We don't need no stinkin' badges!" Then they snorted the salt off their left hands, grabbed their caballitos with their right hands, slammed the tequila down, and slammed the now empty caballitos onto the Aztec table, all in unison. Without hesitation they quickly and again in unison grabbed slices of lime from the tray on the Aztec table with their left hands, raised the slices of lime and squashed juice from the slices of lime into their left eyes. They then threw the spent lime slices onto the tray on the Aztec table, raised their right arms and as their hands met shouted "Fuck you!" shooting their right fists into the air with their middle fingers pointing to the ceiling in yet another single-finger salute.

Jonnie Hogg asked, "What about Joobie's idiot statement about Hispanics and that Mexico is close to San Diego?"

Jamie smiled, "Good a place as any to start. Why would a prestigious law firm be handling a real estate purchase for a bunch of blackmailers?"

Charles replied, "Money. And lots of it."

Jamie added, "And that law firm, Oglethorpe and Fernandez, specializes in international trade negotiations and real estate contracts. They got offices all over Central and South America. Read it on their web site when Big Louie was here. So the money's coming from south of the border."

The posse took another slam of tequila. After his slam, Charlie-O yelled, "The truth will out!" And to help the truth out, the posse took yet a third slam.

Charlie-O sang, "South of the border... down Mexico way."

The posse took another slam of tequila to sharpen its wit for the great and deepening intellectual task before them. The Guinea added, in his cogent ignorance, "Well we know where that property they want to buy is. It's east of San Diego."

Jamie added, "And some asshole's willing to blackmail me and offer me money to get it. Why the fuck is this property worth so much risk? The damn place is literally in the middle of nowhere."

Joobie, yelled, "Oadrita Riptita!" ("Road trip!")

The posse started chanting, "Oadrita Riptita! Oadrita Riptita! Oadrita Riptita!" And their course of action was determined, for they were, as Willie Nelson sings, going *on the road again*.

The state of affairs way upstate…

Rose sat in the waiting room facing Jeremiah and asked him, "Why did we admit Leslie into this place? It's nice enough, but it's a foot and a half from Canada. I expect it to start snowing anytime. And the drive from the city took forever."

Jeremiah straightened his pince-nez and replied, "I think that you exaggerate a bit, dear. After all, it is July and it doesn't snow in July even in Messina. Big Louie's guy found this place. It's a precaution. Leslie can remain anonymous and get the treatment that she needs here. Her problem is… well… quite embarrassing for all concerned."

For the first time in Jeremiah's memory, Rose looked careworn. She had lost her commanding demeanor. She brought a tissue to her eyes and said, "I'm so worried about poor Les. I guess you're right. It's best to keep her as anonymous as possible what with her rather embarrassing problem and all. Where's that idiot husband of hers anyway?"

Jeremiah feared that Rose would read his thoughts as he was sure she had done many times in the past, but he knew that he had no choice but to answer. He hoped that her worry and preoccupation with Leslie's problems had dulled her ability, as Stephen King would put it, to shine. He said somewhat tentatively, "He's on a business trip. He's asked me to call him on his cell phone and let him know how Leslie's doing. As soon as the psychiatrist says it's safe for him to see her, he'll fly back as quickly as is humanly possible."

An older, quite distinguished looking man in a white lab coat entered the waiting room. He peered over his glasses at them, smiled and said, "Hello, I'm Dr. Evers Peersome. I believe that Dr. Fortunato told you that I'd be handling your daughter's case."

Rose and Jeremiah rose from their chairs. Rose immediately walked over to Dr. Peersome and shook his hand. Jeremiah stood for a moment as if collecting his thoughts and shambled over, standing behind Rose. Dr. Peersome looked over to Jeremiah and greeted him with a knowing nod of his head. He gestured with his hand toward an office just off the waiting room and said, "Please. We can discuss my preliminary diagnosis in my office."

Rose and Jeremiah followed the doctor into his office where he gestured for them to be seated before a large steel desk. Rose looked down at the two chairs where they were to sit and asked, "Here?" The chairs were small and short-legged like those used for grade school students. The doctor again gestured toward the chairs and said, "Please." Rose easily maneuvered herself into a seated position. Her skirt pulled up on her thigh a bit and she tugged the hem down and sat sidesaddle on the tiny chair, her knees facing the other chair. Jeremiah awkwardly squatted over the other chair and slowly lowered himself down. The chair groaned under his weight but held as a goodly portion of his lower anatomy hung over the sides of the tiny seat and his knees pressed against his more than ample belly.

Dr. Peersome took his seat behind his imposing steel desk. From this height, he commanded the area before the desk where Rose and Jeremiah sat. He peered down at Rose and Jeremiah, took an already-sharpened pencil from a cup of pencils before him and inserted it into an electric sharpener alongside the cup of sharpened pencils. The pencil sharpener whirred as he pushed down on the pencil. He took the pencil from the sharpener and gently brushed the wood shavings that clung to the pencil's head into another cup using a small brush which he had taken from the breast pocket of his white lab coat. Then he placed the re-sharpened pencil in an empty cup alongside and matching the one holding the rest of the already-sharpened pencils.

He looked down at Rose and Jeremiah and said, "First, Leslie shall remain anonymous while at the Saint Lawrence Institute for Mental Efficacy. We at S-L-I-M-E frequently treat celebrities who request anonymity during their stay with us. For example, we are treating Alexander DuMonte the 3rd, the wealthy Canadian financier, for kleptomania under the name of Alex Doe. That information is, of course, confidential." He took another already-sharpened pencil and carefully placed it in the pencil sharpener. Over the whirring of the sharpener he said, "I shall refer to Leslie as Leslie Doe during her stay here at S-L-I-M-E to insure her anonymity." As he repeated the process of brushing off the just re-sharpened pencil, he said without looking up, "All documents pertaining to her treatment shall be so labeled, except, of course, for those dealing with billing in the business office. I hope that's acceptable."

Jeremiah shook his head in agreement. Rose, however, squirmed a bit and rolled her legs over so that she sat sidesaddle, her knees now facing away from Jeremiah. Dr. Peersome peered intently at Rose as she readjusted her seated position before continuing. He silently read from notes on a clipboard before him as he reached for a third already-sharpened pencil. As the pencil sharpener whirred away he said, "Leslie's case is quite interesting and unique. We have surveillance cameras in all of our patient rooms so that we can monitor the behavior of our patients and insure their safety. If at all possible, we do not begin treatment for 24 to 48 hours so that we can establish baseline behavioral patterns. Yesterday, Leslie masturbated seventeen times in a twenty-four-hour period. About the only times she wasn't masturbating was during your visit and while she slept."

Jeremiah's face reddened as he listened. Rose nervously shifted her seated position again, rolling her knees forward and then to the left so that her knees again faced Jeremiah. Dr. Peersome watched Rose intently as she shifted her position before continuing. He continued his pencil sharpening ritual with a fourth pencil and said over the whirring of the sharpener, "Your daughter's compulsive masturbation or CM is an obsessive compulsive disorder called sexual compulsivity. Such a condition is more common with males, but it does occur in females. As is often the situation in OCD cases such as this, she also suffers from depression."

Jeremiah remained silent, reddening even more brightly. Rose asked, "Isn't all that… you know… self indulgence… going to hurt her?"

Dr. Peersome reached for another pencil to re-sharpen and said, "There are deleterious effects from such behavior. There is of course the risk of infection in Leslie's vaginal area from the irritation caused by all that friction. But from my observations, she has a masturbatory technique, I believe it's called watering-the-flower in common parlance, that minimizes the friction and she does have the ability to come to orgasm quite quickly which also minimizes the amount of friction suffered during each masturbatory incident. From the utterances she shouts as she's masturbating, she appears to be having some strange fantasy about a Zulu fertility dance which seems to aid her."

If Jeremiah had become any redder, it would have been a precursor to his head exploding. Rose reshifted her position so that she faced forward and hugged her knees under the watchful eyes of the doctor. He continued, "I've read through the literature and I came across a condition called racial fetishism. It seems to apply to Leslie's condition but it's a condition that occurred with Caucasians in post-colonial Africa. This is all quite puzzling."

Rose looked up and relaxed her grip on her knees as the Doctor looked down at her intently. She took a deep breath and said, "You spoke of deleterious effects, plural. Are there others?"

The doctor tapped the pencil he was holding on the clipboard and said, "Actually several. There's the obvious effect of such behavior on her daily life. With all that masturbating she has little time for anything else. It is hard to imagine that she could live anything close to a normal life and establish any kind of personal relationships given such obsessive behavior."

Rose leaned back on her chair, bit her upper lip and sighed as she looked up at the ceiling and allowed her hands to fall to her side. She looked back at the doctor, who appeared to be staring between her legs, which she quickly clapped closed. She pushed back into her chair, rested her hands in her lap and asked, "What else?"

The doctor pushed the pencil he was holding into the sharpener and as it whirred away said, "The obsessive masturbation also causes changes in the brain chemistry. Technically, the brain is drained of acetylcholine and the acetylcholine is replaced with stress adrenaline. This change in brain chemistry causes memory loss and the inability to concentrate. The change is not permanent and is quickly reversed when the compulsive masturbatory activity is brought under control. And then there's the accompanying depression for which we have a number of effective therapies."

Rose smiled for the first time since arriving and said, "Well, that's a relief, Dr. Peersome. What treatment is required?"

Jeremiah looked to Rose and asked, "What did he say? I could not hear over the pencil sharpener. What does watering flowers have to do with Leslie's problem?"

While still looking intently at Dr. Peersome and consciously squeezing her thighs together she said, "Jeremiah, I'll explain later."

Dr. Peersome sat back and rested his elbows on the arms of his chair. He brought his hands together rhythmically tapping the fingers of his hands against each other as he thought. He peered down at Rose and said, "Actually, Leslie will require bimodal treatment involving both psychological and pharmacological therapies for her sexual compulsivity, after, of course, the development of a more extensive personal and family profile. We can begin treatment for her depression immediately." He looked down at his watch and shook his head saying, "I'm sorry. I have a scheduled therapy session with Alex Doe in ten minutes. Things did not go well during the last session." He tapped the breast pocket of his white lab coat where he had carefully placed the brush he used for his pencil sharpening ritual. "The man actually tried to steal my pencil brush. I've got to watch Mr. Alexander DuMonte the 3rd like a hawk during our sessions. Can we meet again tomorrow? I'd like to discuss the bimodal therapies I'm considering and develop a family profile."

Jeremiah squirmed on his chair and said, "I'm afraid I cannot. I must return to Columbia University. I'm chairing a seminar on D. H. Lawrence during the summer session and it begins day after tomorrow. Rose will be staying in Messina, so she'll be here. Perhaps we can arrange for a joint appointment later next week and you can work with Rose in my absence."

Dr. Peersome smiled broadly, "Excellent. Rose, same time tomorrow here in my office?" Before Rose could reply, he was out the door and down the hall.

Rose turned to Jeremiah and said. "Did it look to you like that old goat was peering up my skirt? He's an odd one."

Jeremiah rolled forward onto his knees, grabbed the steel desk before him and pulled himself to his feet before replying, "Rose, he's a licensed psychiatrist, reputed to be one of the top men in his field. Admittedly a bit eccentric, but isn't that often the case with brilliant men?"

Rose popped to her feet and said somewhat distractedly, "I suppose."

Jeremiah rubbed his more than ample posterior with both hands and said, "Those are the most uncomfortable chairs I've ever sat in. What was all that talk about watering flowers? I missed a lot of what he said with all that pencil sharpening."

Rose ignored Jeremiah's question, put her hands on her hips and said with some conviction, "Tomorrow I'm wearing a pantsuit."

Jeremiah leaned against the steel desk, pulled his cell phone from his belt and dialed. He looked up and said to Rose, "I'm calling Jamie to give him a status report on Leslie's condition and treatment." He put the cell phone to his ear and listened intently then said, "Hello, Jamie, it's Dr. Wright... Jeremiah. I'm calling from the

Saint Lawrence Institute for Mental Efficacy... You're where?... Chicago?" He listened for a bit and then gave a somewhat cryptic version of Dr. Peersome's diagnosis involving seventeen times, self-indulgence and Zulus. He said yes several times and ended the call with, "I'll call after we learn more from Dr. Peersome," and hung up.

Rose looked surprised at the news that Jamie was in Chicago and asked, "What in heaven's name is our idiot son-in-law doing in Chicago?"

Jeremiah stood and rubbed his more than ample posterior a second time and said to himself, "The feeling's starting to return. Those chairs are most uncomfor..."

Rose interrupted, "Jeremiah... Chicago?"

Jeremiah replied, "Oh, Chicago... something about some real estate deal he made last year. He said it was complicated."

Sunday, July 6

Rose prepares to re-engage the world of psychiatry with the aid of reinforcements...

The following morning, Rose sat in the waiting room awaiting her second appointment with Dr. Peersome. She had not slept much and did not look forward to another meeting with the noted psychiatrist, this time alone. This was not how she wanted to spend her Sunday morning, and it would be the second week in a row that she had missed mass. She brushed her pant leg absentmindedly and uttered to herself, "I'm glad I packed several pantsuits."

She heard laughing and loud chatter in the foyer and turned to see Janey Toussaint and Angel Bangor pushing the entrance door open. Angel shouted to her, "Hi, Miz F-W. How's Leslie doing in this godforsaken place?"

A startled Rose stood and yelled, "What in heaven's name?"

Before she could continue, Janey Toussaint said, smiling from ear-to-ear as she approached the flabbergasted Rose, "You didn't think we'd abandon the damsel Bookers in her time of distress, did you?"

Rose stood unable to respond. Angel looked around and said, "This place looks kinda creepy. And this town is at the end of the earth. Doesn't look like a very neat place to spend a vacation."

Janey Toussaint amplified, "We're on vacation and thought we'd take some time to see how Leslie's doing. We drove all night to get here. Kind of a last minute thing."

Angel added, "It took forever. Lots of the time there wasn't any place to stop. We had to pee outdoors three times. Makes me kinda itchy." She scratched herself through her skirt. "We changed to skirts to make it easy." She put her hand to her mouth and whispered, "We went commando. I haven't peed outdoors in years. It felt kinda exciting."

Rose sat back down and Janey and Angel sat on a couch facing her. Rose looked puzzled and asked, "How did you girls ever find out about this place? It's supposed to be a secret."

Angel giggled and said, "Oh, it wasn't that hard. Janey and I went to visit Leslie at that place in Westchester and they told us she's been moved and where she's been moved to was confidential. On the way out we saw one of those medical vans. The van was running and the driver was sitting there listening to rap. Janey here asked him how things were going."

Janey interrupted, "Boy, was he was pissed! Said he had already taken one long squirrel run this week and now he had to take another."

Angel in turn interrupted Janey, "And I asked him where he took the first squirrel run and he said it was confidential and he couldn't tell me and he turned the van off and ran into the office. He had a clipboard on the dash where he logged his squirrel runs. The last entry said 'Leslie Fazzano-Wright, Messina, NY, 350 miles.' See, it wasn't all that hard. There's only one mental health institute in Messina and this is it."

Janey added, "And here we are! How's Les, anyway?"

Rose was buoyed by the reinforcements and felt the need to unburden herself . "Leslie's got several severe emotional problems. Dr. Peersome, that's her psychiatrist, says she has an obsessive compulsive disorder called sexual compulsivity."

A look of great concern spread across Angel's face and she put her hand to her mouth, "Oh my, that sounds very bad. What's it mean?"

Rose hesitated and looked down at her lap in embarrassment before replying but then managed a quiet, "She...indulges herself... you know down there."

Angel's expression changed from worry to confusion, a short trip often taken, and said, "I don't understand. Indulges what down where?"

Rose tried to be more specific and the best she could come up with was, "You know... she comforts herself... intimately."

Janey realized what Rose was trying to say and that Rose found the topic very embarrassing. She nudged Angel with her elbow and whispered, "She was checking for squirrels. You know, playing with herself."

Angel said, "Oh!" and then asked, "Is that why that driver called it a squirrel run?"

Janey said, "I don't think the two squirrels are related, but who knows." She turned to Rose and asked, "Why is that a problem? Everybody does it."

Rose's face turned a deep red and she said, "It's a matter of frequency. Poor Leslie indulges herself a lot."

Janey asked "How much is a lot?"

Rose looked up but could not look directly at Janey and Angel and said, "At last count, seventeen times a day."

Angel blurted out, "Wow, that's got to be some kind of record. When I was twelve, I did it five times in one day when I found out how to do it, but I had to stop. Made me sore."

Rose replied without hesitation this time, "Well Leslie can't stop. That's the problem or at least the main one."

Janey asked, "What's the other one?"

"She's depressed."

Angel again looked puzzled, "Why depressed? I didn't get depressed. I just got sore."

Rose explained, "But you could stop. Leslie can't. She didn't have this problem until the wedding, at least that I knew of. Dr. Peersome wants to get more information before he recommends a specific treatment. Do you have any idea what happened? Apparently she mumbles something about a Zulu dance of some kind whenever she does it. Maybe it has something to do with her doctoral thesis."

Angel shrieked, "No. It has to do with Jamal! She's talking about Jamal."

Rose asked, "Jamal? Jamal the chauffeur?"

Janey explained to Rose about the bachelorette party and Jamal's exotic dance routine where he dressed as a Zulu warrior. Rose was stunned and finally said, "Jamal's an African-American. What was Leslie's reaction when she saw his exotic dance routine?"

Angel smiled in her best imitation of a knowing way and said, "She did more than watch. She got up close and personal. She was a little tipsy. We all drank some wine and smoked a little pot before Jamal showed up in that Zulu warrior costume of his, even Leslie. She didn't smoke or drink much, but it musta been enough for her to get high. And when Jamal danced in front of her, she yanked his sausage, moaned and fainted. Scared the hell out of poor Jamal and deflated him PDQ if you know what I mean."

A look of puzzlement combined with embarrassment came across Rose's face as she asked, "Sausage?"

Janey pointed down below her waist and answered, "You know... his package... Jamal's johnson."

Rose put a hand to her mouth and said, "Oh my." She paused as the information sunk in. Then she stood and all but yelled, "Girls, Dr. Peersome has to hear about this. It ties a whole bunch of things together. It doesn't explain everything, but it explains a lot. It's at least a very important clue as to how Leslie got into this situation." She looked down at her watch, "I'm supposed to meet with him at 10, in fifteen minutes. You girls have to tell all this to him."

Angel looked up at Rose and said, "Gee whiz, I thought it was just good clean fun. Who'd a thunk?" Rose slumped back into her seat and all three fell into silence awaiting Leslie's psychiatrist.

Rose re-engages the world of psychiatry with the aid of reinforcements...

Dr. Peersome, as if reprising a role in a movie, entered the room. He peered over his glasses at them, smiled and said, "Hello, remember me? Dr. Peersome... Leslie's psychiatrist."

Rose stood and walked over to him, but this time she did not shake his hand. She gestured toward Janey and Angel and said, "Doctor, these two young ladies are friends of Leslie's, Janey Toussaint and Angel Bangor. They were brides maids at Leslie's wedding. I think you should hear what they have to say."

At first the good doctor frowned as he noticed Rose's attire but then he looked over at Janey and Angel, both dressed in skirts, and smiled. "If these two young ladies have pertinent information concerning Leslie, by all means, I'd like very much to hear it. Please..." He gestured toward his office just off the lobby and said again, "Please..."

Dr. Peersome entered the office before Rose and her reinforcements. He quickly pulled a regular-size chair from a side table and placed it on the far side of the two grade school chairs that Rose and Jeremiah had sat in the day before. "Rose, you can sit here. The two young ladies can sit there" as he gestured toward the two grade-school chairs. Rose, without thinking, followed the doctor's directions and quickly seated herself in the regular-sized chair.

Angel looked at the two small chairs and said, "Neat, just like kindygarten." Janey and Angel eased themselves into the short-legged chairs. Janey pulled her skirt around her thighs and sat side-saddle as Rose had done the day before, squeezing her legs together. Angel sat without a care in the world. Dr. Peersome sat down at his steel desk and peered down at them smiling broadly. He reached to the breast pocket of his white lab coat and a look of panic spread across his face. He said, "That Alexander DuMonte the 3rd had better not..." Then he smiled and looked much relieved as he reached into his shirt pocket beneath his lab coat and retrieved a short-handled artist's brush which he placed on the desk top before him.

Dr. Peersome reached for an already-sharpened pencil in the cup already full of them and pushed the already-sharpened pencil into the electric pencil sharpener on his desk. The pencil sharpener began to whirr as he spoke, "Well, young ladies, what do you have to tell me?" Reprising his pencil sharpening ritual of yesterday, he pulled the re-sharpened pencil from the pencil sharpener, picked up the short-handled artist's brush he'd retrieved from his shirt pocket and carefully brushed the pencil shavings still clinging to the pencil head into another cup. He then carefully placed the newly re-sharpened pencil into the cup next to and identical to the cup of already-sharpened pencils as he had done the day before.

Angel, who watched the doctor's pencil sharpening ritual with great interest, said, "What did you say? I couldn't hear you over that pencil sharpener." She paused as if in thought and asked, "Why are you sharpening that pencil anyway? It's already got a point on it. You're only making the pencil shorter. Seems like a big waste of pencil."

Dr. Peersome, with some annoyance, replied, "Young lady, we're not here to discuss how to preserve pencils." He looked down at Angel intently and added, "We are here to discuss Leslie Fazzano-Wright-Steinkraus and her rather severe emotional problems" as he reached for yet another already-sharpened pencil.

Angel, unruffled by the rebuke, said, "No problem, Doc. Just trying to be helpful. They're your pencils."

The good doctor regained his composure, as he sharpened yet another already-sharpened pencil, smiled and said, "Ladies, what is it you'd like to tell me about Leslie?"

Janey and Angel told the psychiatrist of the bachelorette party attended by the seven ladies in distress, of the smoking of marijuana, of the drinking of wine, of Jamal the exotic dancer and his Zulu routine, of Leslie's touching of Jamal and of her fainting. After carefully brushing off the shavings from the most recently re-sharpened pencil, Dr. Peersome used it to take extensive notes as Janey and Angel

THE ADVENTURES OF THE POSSE OF LITTLE HORSES

told their tale of the inadvertent fall of Leslie from grace.

When they had finished, Dr. Peersome flipped through several pages on his clipboard and read. Then he said, while intently watching Angel, "Rose, according to Leslie's medical records, she was already taking diazepam for panic attacks. Is that correct?"

Rose asked, "Diazepam?"

The doctor answered her question, "Yes, diazepam, commonly known as valium."

Rose replied with a curt, "Yes. Leslie took valium as prescribed by her doctor."

Dr. Peersome read from his recently-taken notes. He looked up and asked, "At this bachelorette party, did Leslie smoke any marijuana with you girls?"

Angel replied, "Yes, just a little. And she took some sips from a glass of wine too. Actually she spilled most of her wine. She was pretty nervous."

Dr. Peersome looked intently at Angel and said, "She's a very lucky young lady. Marijuana or alcohol when consumed with valium can cause severe medical problems. In fact, valium when combined with recreational drugs and alcohol can be fatal."

Angel put her hand over her mouth and said, "Oh my God!" In her excitement, she relaxed her legs giving Dr. Peersome a good look at her down under. He smiled and nervously reached for yet another already-sharpened pencil.

Dr. Peersome read some more from his notes as he nervously sharpened another pencil, then peered down at Rose's reinforcements and asked, "I take it that this Jamal, the exotic dancer, was African-American," to which Janey and Angel shook their heads yes. He scribbled in the margin of his original notes and asked Rose, "Did Leslie have any close friends, perhaps even a boyfriend, who was African-American?"

Rose answered curtly, "No, not to my knowledge, and I would have known. Les kept no secrets from me. We were very close." Rose thought for a moment and added, "She did write her doctoral thesis on African tribal dance traditions. She recently received her PhD in anthropology from Columbia University. She did take one short field trip to Africa and she watched hours of video. Did a large number of interviews on the subject. Read tons of books and articles. Worked her butt off."

Dr. Peersome took more marginal notes and asked, "When exactly did she earn her PhD? Nowhere in her medical records is she referred to as Dr. Leslie Fazzano-Wright-Steinkraus."

Rose looked down at hands as she fiddled with a tissue and said, "She received her PhD last month, just before the wedding."

The psychiatrist took some more marginal notes and asked Rose's reinforcements, "To your knowledge was Leslie ever, well, intimate with an African-American?"

Janey said, "Intimate with an African-American? I don't think she was ever intimate with anyone. Not an African-American, not Jamie. Hell, I don't think she was ever intimate even with herself. She was a nervous Nellie, a regular goody two-shoes bookworm type. We called her Bookers because she was such a study freak."

Angel burst in, "I don't think she ever checked for squirrels, at least until after the wedding, if that's what you mean."

Dr. Peersome looked up with surprise, "Checked for squirrels?"

Angel pushed her skirt between her legs with her hands and said, "You know, scratched her itch, parted the petals of her flower."

The light dawned on Dr. Peersome, "Oh, you're saying that you don't think she ever masturbated. Checking for squirrels... I've never heard that slang term before. Rose, do you have anything to add?"

Rose's face had turned beet red during the discussion. She fiddled frantically with her hands, slowly grinding the tissue that she held, and without looking up said, "I have nothing to say about this topic."

Dr. Peersome said, "Hmmm," and took more marginal notes. He looked up and said, "I'm getting a clearer picture of what we're dealing with. I have just a couple of points that need clarification." He addressed Rose's reinforcements, "You said Leslie touched this Jamal fellow during his exotic dance. Could you describe the situation in more detail?"

Janey looked over at Angel. The two of them muffled their giggling with their hands and said as a chorus, "She touched his sausage!"

Janey described the scene: "Leslie was kneeling in the center of the room as Jamal danced around. He was wearing one of those African tribe kinda costumes like you see in the movies. Did you ever see that flick Zulu? Like that. My old boyfriend loved that movie. What a drip... Well Jamal had kind of a costume failure. His sausage, you know, his big ol' johnson, came free and there he was standing over Leslie. She looked that one-eyed monster in the eye, stroked it a couple of times, moaned and fainted. Scared the crap out of poor Jamal."

Angel eagerly added, "Looked to me like she blasted off... big time."

Dr. Peersome asked, "So you think she had an orgasm?"

Angel yelled back, "You betcha, Doc. She shot her rockets!"

Rose was mortified by the discussion. She stared intently at the tissue she held in her lap as she tore it into tiny pieces and said nothing. Unlike Rose, her reinforcements were excited and energized by the discussion. Angel leaned over to Janey and whispered, "That dirty old man keeps looking up my skirt. Let's wink at him." Janey smiled and the two girls leaned back, spread their thighs and gave Dr. Evers Peersome a long hootchie-cootchie look. Angel said, "Smile, Doc, we're taking your picture."

Dr. Peersome became unnerved and broke the pencil he was about to re-sharpen. He was sweating profusely. He mumbled, "Sorry, ladies, but I can't show you out. I have... notes... lots of notes to review." He turned toward Rose and said nervously, "I'd like to meet again Monday to discuss my recommendations for treatment. Leslie's friends can join us if you wish since they've had so much input and are such close friends."

As Rose ran from the office, followed by her giggling reinforcements, Dr. Peersome yelled, "Same time... same place... tomorrow!"

Monday, July 7

Is a star about to be born…

"Where the fuck are you?" Big Louie yelled into his cell phone. "Yeah, I got the key… I'm there now… but where the fuck are you?" He looked up at Jamie's apartment building and yelled, "I'm lookin' at the god damn place right now… for the third time, where the fuck are you?" He paused and leaned back against his double parked black Escalade. "Chicago? Why the hell are you in Chicago? You can't tell me? I'm your god damn security. How the hell can I keep you secure if I'm in Manhattan and you're in Chicago, and you can't, or just plain won't tell me why? Are you out of your fuckin' mind? Check for a package? OK… OK… I'll check. What kind of package? Say again? Envelope? How the hell did you find out about this mysterious package anyway? Text message. OK. I'll call you back, but look… you better be careful. These blackmailers obviously know a lot about you… like your cell phone number for starters. Hell, they probly know where you are like I didn't."

Big Louie fumed as he let himself into the building's foyer and took the elevator up to the top floor. He got out of the elevator and was greeted by Bacchus and the scantily-clad, chubby nymphs who danced around the great god's feet. He paused and looked at the fresco of the mythical god before him and muttered to himself, "How in the hell could a giant like that ever screw one of those little nymphos? He'd split 'em open. He's got to be hung like a stallion…

unless he's a god damn Greek needle-dick bug fucker."

He snapped out of his mythological reverie and saw the manila envelope leaning against the great black, Bacchanalian door. He muttered to himself, "The bastards got into the building this time," as he picked up the envelope and let himself into the apartment. He walked over to the Aztec table and placed the envelope on the table face-up. He inspected the envelope and printed on it were the words Jamie Steinkraut. He said to himself, "The bastards misspelled his name again. Idiots… what'd Doc call 'em… savants? Yeah, the idiot-savants… the idiot part strikes again." He turned the envelope over and inspected the back, finding nothing. He carefully opened the unsealed envelope and dumped the contents onto the table. Out spilled a DVD which slid across the table coming to a stop at the table's far edge. He muttered to himself, "Not good," and retrieved the DVD.

He looked around the living room and sure enough, there was an entertainment center with a DVD player and a large flat-screen TV on the far side of the room. He walked over, turned on the TV and the DVD player, slid the DVD into the player and watched.

He stood before the large screen and was stunned by what he saw. There was Leslie, in all her naked glory, knees up, legs spread, fingers buried in a healthy patch of pubic hair, strumming away and moaning as she did so. He listened carefully and heard her mutter something about deflowering and a great warrior, then something about welcoming a new life. He pushed the fast-forward button on the DVD player and there was more of the same. He said to himself, "Over an hour's worth of my dear niece, the newly minted Mrs. Jamie Steinkraus, wackin' off. Damn… she's got a nice bod, I'll give her that… and she's pretty good at it." He sat back on one of the big leather chairs and watched as the spectacle continued, giving a running commentary to himself as he thought out loud, "Security cameras from above… time-stamped… three days ago… a hospital room… video edited. Looks professional. Shit, if this ever hits the internet, my dear niece can kiss her old life goodbye. She'll be a fuckin' porn star and Jamie'll be out of the real estate business and into the porn business whether he likes it or not. So much for movin' her to a secure fuckin' location."

As he continued to watch, he pulled his cell phone from his jacket pocket and called Jamie. "Listen, Jamie, we got ourselves a big problem. That envelope… it contained a DVD… that's right only a DVD, nothin' else… it's of Leslie wackin' off… I'd say about an hour's worth of her friggin' herself… Ain't nothin' left to the imagination… Listen! I thought we'd moved her to a secure location… Look I don't run the CIA here! Yeah… yeah… I know… it don't take a genius to figure out there's a leak someplace. The DVD obviously came from that institute up in Messina. I'll try to find out how those bastards got their hands on it. You still in Chicago? O-K, I'll call you back when I have somethin' to report."

He dialed again. "Benny? That you? Where the hell are you? You still in Messina? On the way back? Well turn around and get yer ass back up there. The cover's blown. I'm watchin' a DVD of my niece friggin' herself. She's buried knuckle-deep in her pussy moaning like a bitch in heat… obviously out of her fuckin' mind. Looks like security video. She's in a hospital room. The video's time stamped three days ago. Musta come from up there. See if you can find out how the bastards got the video." Big Louie listened for a moment and yelled into his cell phone, "Don't move her again. It's too late, you asshole. Just find out who got that video and how they got it." He slammed the cell phone shut and swore quietly to himself.

Big Louie watched the rest of the video to gather any additional clues if indeed there were any to be gathered. There were none. After the video ended, he sat staring into space for several minutes thinking of what he should do next. Then it struck him, "The security cameras!" He opened his cell phone and dialed. "Hey, Jamie?… No I don't know nothin' about that DVD yet. Listen, I'd like to look at whatever your security system here recorded today. See who delivered that envelope." He walked into Jamie's miniature NASA command and control center and looked up at the security monitors. "It's monitor 4? That's the one that shows the foyer? ...Listen kid, I know my way around security systems. How do I review previous recordings for camera 4?" With his cell phone pinned to his ear with his shoulder, he sat before the computer monitor on the L-shaped table. He said "Say again," and clicked the mouse several times and entered a password. "Got it, how do I fast-forward backwards?... OK. I'm there. I'll call back, maybe tomorrow, unless something breaks. Who's that yellin'? Louis? Shit, is the whole crew with you? Yeah? He drivin' that Edsel of his? ...Where the hell are you? You're drivin' around Chicago lookin' for the official start of Route 66? There ain't no Route 66 anymore. Are you out of your fuckin' mind?" He pulled the cell phone from his ear and looked at it, slammed it shut and shoved it in his jacket pocket.

He watched the security video fast-forward backwards. Then he sat up and mumbled to himself, "There's the bastard... young skinny guy in a business suit... phony-lookin' mustache... looks like the guy contacted Charles and arranged for that jailbait stripper." He clicked the mouse and slowed the video. "Not the same guy delivered that envelope from Oglethorpe and Fernandez. Wonder how the bastard got in?" He looked up at the security monitors, said to himself "Camera 1" and clicked the mouse several times. "There's the bastard, pushin' buttons. One of the tenants musta buzzed him in. Means he don't have a key." He signed off the security system, pulled out his cell phone and dialed. "Doc? Big Louie here. I'm at Jamie's apartment. Where you? Home? Could you come over to Jamie's place? I know it's late, but we got some work to do... An hour? OK, I'll buzz you in." He flipped his cell phone closed and tossed it onto the end table. Then he sat back, extended his legs, and pulled his silver flask from his jacket pocket. He stared into space as he unscrewed the top to the flask, put the flask to his lips and took a long pull. He said to himself, "Gotta find out about that delivery service. Need more info about Oglethorpe and Fernandez." He bent his head back and took another long pull from his flask and waited for Jeremiah to show up.

Was Sisyphus a sissy...

Big Louie buzzed the rotund adjunct professor of English literature into the foyer of Jamie's apartment house and awaited his knock at the front door of the apartment. He stood by the door and pulled his flask from his jacket pocket, removed the cap, took a long pull and muttered to himself, "How the fuck do I tell Doc his daughter's about to become the family's first internet porn star?"

A knock at the door ended his speculation. He let Jeremiah in and greeted him with "Hi, Doc. Have a seat," as he gestured toward the leather couch facing the large screen TV. They walked to the couch and he offered Jeremiah his flask, "Want a pull?"

Jeremiah plopped himself down on the couch and the couch cushions whooshed under his great weight. "No thank you, Louis. What has happened?" Big Louie took another pull from the flask and sat next to Jeremiah on the couch. Instead of returning the flask to his jacket pocket, he placed it in the ready position on the end table next to the couch.

"Doc, I'm afraid that I have some bad news. I don't think there's a good way to do this, so here goes." Big Louie took the remote from the end table and clicked both the TV and the DVD player on and pushed the play button. The image of Leslie frantically masturbating filled the screen. At first, Jeremiah watched without reacting other than a "My, my. I didn't realize that Jamie watched this kind of salacious material. Although I suppose young men..."

Big Louie interrupted him, "Doc, look carefully. Recognize anyone?"

Jeremiah pushed down on his pince-nez and peered intently though them. He started muttering "Oh my... oh my." Somewhere around the fifth or sixth oh my, Big Louie handed the flask to Jeremiah. His oh my's ceased when he put the flask to his lips and took a very long pull. Big Louie mercifully turned off the TV and DVD player. He explained to Jeremiah about the DVD and how it had been sent to Jamie's apartment and that it was apparently video stolen somehow from the mental health institute in Messina where, ironically, they'd moved Leslie to insure privacy. During the explanation, Jeremiah took a number of shorter pulls from the flask.

Jeremiah looked around the apartment and asked, "Has Jamie seen this horrid video?"

Big Louis replied, "No he hasn't but I phoned him and told him about it."

A surprised Jeremiah said, "Told? Phoned? Is he still in Chicago?"

Big Louie took the flask from Jeremiah and drained it. "You knew he's in Chicago?"

Looking back down at the floor, Jeremiah said, "Yes, I phoned him from the mental health institute on Saturday to inform him of Leslie's condition."

Big Louie mumbled, "Seems like everyone but me knew where he was at." Then he said more loudly, "Yeah, he's in Chicago... at least when I talked to him. His whole crew's with him, including my worthless, asshole nephew. Wouldn't tell me why he'd gone there. Any ideas?"

Jeremiah thought for a moment and then said, "He's from Chicago and I believe that that's where his home office is located. He moved back to New York because of Leslie."

Big Louie walked over to Jamie's bar and started lifting bottles and reading labels. "Shit, no Four Roses." He settled on a single-malt scotch and as he refilled his flask said, "This'll have to do." As he screwed the cap back on the flask, he said, "Bet the papers for that real estate transaction are in Chicago."

For Jeremiah, his surprises never seemed to end. "Real estate transaction?"

Big Louie explained about the last communication from the blackmailers through the offices of Oglethorpe and Fernandez and how Jamie was at a loss as to why a real estate developer would want to buy that vacation compound in the remote mountain wilderness east of San Diego, the place he'd purchased as a wedding gift for Leslie.

Jeremiah asked, "But what does that have to do with this horrid video of poor Leslie? She's quite out of her mind and..." Here Jeremiah paused searching for words, then went on, "She's never even seen that place."

Big Louie took a quick pull from his flask to test its contents and muttered to himself, "It'll have to do." As he screwed the cap back onto the flask, he continued, "Doc, that video is icing on the blackmailer's cake. Can you imagine the kind of picture those bastards can now paint with those photos of your muff-diving a defenseless, drugged young girl... to the cheers of Jamie and friends, including my idiot namesake... and then this video of Leslie enthusiastically friggin' herself? The whole god damn family looks like a bunch of perverts... even the daughter of one of the pervs who also happens to be the newly married wife of another one of the pervs... and all this perv stuff during the wedding celebration. The Post would go wild and every TV newscast in the U-S of A would lead with the fuckin' story for weeks. Think of what Letterman and Leno would do with this stuff. Your fifteen minutes of fame would last forever. This is way beyond hardball. If we don't do somethin', your daughter, my niece, is about to become an internet porn star, you're about to become unemployed and the whole lot of you, including my asshole nephew, stand a good chance of going to jail for a very long time."

Jeremiah looked up at Big Louie who now stood over him. "Jamie will just have to sell those ne'er-do-wells whatever they want. It appears to be the only way to end this terrible nightmare."

Big Louie gestured toward Jeremiah, using the flask as a pointer, and replied, "Look, Doc, Jamie may hafta do just that, but there's a whole bunch of flies in that ointment." He stopped, unscrewed his flask and took another pull before continuing, "First, how do we get that incriminatin' evidence back? It's all digital, not like in the old days when there was negatives and makin' copies of stuff was hard to do. Hell, those pricks could get Jamie to sell that place to them, give him some copies of all those photos and that video and next year blackmail him... and you... all over again with the same stuff."

Big Louie looked down at the floor scratching his forehead with the flask's top as he thought. "And then there's the problem of why the bastards want the real estate in the first place."

Jeremiah asked, "Why does it matter why those blackmailing criminals want Jamie's real estate? Let them have the place and be done with it."

Big Louie answered quickly, "Look, Doc, these blackmailers don't want Jamie's place to build a shopping mall. This operation's way too complicated for a simple real-estate blackmailing operation, besides, who puts a shopping mall in the middle of nowhere. Hell, if it were some crazy rich guy who wanted the place, it'd 'a been a lot cheaper to just offer Jamie a ton of money for the place rather than pay for all this black mailin' shit they've done already."

Big Louie sat down on the couch next to Jeremiah and took another pull from his flask. He held the flask up, looked at it and frowned, "Why do rich guys always buy shit like this... Glenfid something or other. Four Roses tastes better and costs a hell of a lot less than this expensive piss." He brought the flask down and continued, "Just think of all the coordination and dough they needed to pull off what they've done already. I'll admit that sometimes they act like idiots, but big-picture wise this whole blackmailin' operation leans toward the savant side."

Puzzlement crossed Jeremiah's face, "I still don't understand how all that expense affects Jamie and the rest of us."

Big Louie started to lose his patience, for in his mind, the why followed the what as surely and simply as two followed one. "Look, there's obviously some kind of criminal conspiracy goin' on here and a damn good one. When Jamie sells that real estate, he's knee-deep in it. If I thought about it, don't you think that these blackmailers have already? Once he sells, they can frame him and make him a part of the conspiracy. Then they've got a way into Jamie's business and he's screwed. It's like being a little bit pregnant. Ain't no such thing!"

All Jeremiah could do was return to his oh my refrain which he repeated many times as Big Louie continued, "The point is that if Jamie does exactly what those fuckin' bastards demand, instead of freein' him and the rest of you from their clutches, he may be givin' them more power over all of you… and that includes your daughter Leslie."

Jeremiah leaned his forehead on his hands as he looked down at the floor and muttered, "We're doomed. Fate has chosen us to suffer. We're modern-day Sisypheans. We're destined to forever push boulders up hills only to have them roll back again, requiring us to repeat the task endlessly until we're condemned to one of the circles of hell."

Big Louie realized that Jeremiah was becoming paralyzed by the situation and close to giving up. "Look Doc, we ain't sissies and if we push some boulder to the top of a damn hill… what we hafta do is roll that damn thing down on those blackmailing bastards and flatten 'em."

Jeremiah looked up at the determined Big Louie, "How in heavens name do we do that? They hold all the cards."

Big Louie smiled, "Look, I got no fuckin' idea what we should do right now. All I know is there's always a chink in the armor. We got to find that chink and shiv 'em through it. The ol' oriental death shiv."

Jeremiah went from despair back to puzzlement, "Shiv? Oriental death shiv?"

Big Louis responded, "Yeah, shiv, as in knife the fuckers. You know, shiv, knife, stab, slice, right through their chink! We need information. We gotta find out what the fuck they're up to. I now know where Jamie's headed even if the bastard won't tell me… he's headed for that vacation compound he bought for your daughter to see if he can figure out why that place is so valuable. We gotta do the same here… get more intel. Once we find out what they're up to, we can figure a way to roll them fuckin' boulders down on their heads and oriental shiv the bastards."

A glimmer of hope entered Jeremiah's mind through the maze

of mixed and mixed-up metaphors, "Where do we begin such an effort?"

Big Louie smiled from ear to ear, "With what we already know, Oglethorpe and Fernandez. You're gonna infiltrate the place."

Jeremiah resumed his oh my refrain as Big Louie smiled and took another long pull from his flask.

Rose's reinforcements vs. psychiatry: Round 3...

Rose sat in the waiting room dressed securely in her other pant-suit awaiting the arrival of Janey Toussaint and Angel Bangor. A man walked by and nodded to her as he passed. He looked familiar, but she couldn't quite put a name with the face. He wore a very wrinkled, nondescript dark suit and looked as if he hadn't slept in several days. In fact, it was his total non-descriptness that made him descriptive. She stared at him as he exited the building. On his way out, he passed Janey and Angel, who were giggling and talking, both at the same time, as they pushed the outer door open and entered the foyer to the waiting room.

Angel yelled, "Hi, Miz F-W," as they skipped into the waiting room. Rose stood to meet them and said, "Girls, skirts? You know what that old goat wants to do. Why the skirts?"

Janey smiled and replied, "You betcha skirts, Miz F-W! Lets us use our secret weapons. Besides, we're not commando today so it won't be all that bad. With our secret weapon, we can take possession of a man's mind any time we want. Just give him a peek and we control his thinking, you know and sometimes even his behavior. They're conditioned to react in a certain way, you know. Worked in high school, worked in college. Hell, it even works today in my office."

Angel burst into the conversation, "We call it CMC... cootchie mind control. Janey's right, works every time... with straight men. Sometimes even with gay guys. Maybe they're bi's. You never know. Anyway, know why Mr. Goat couldn't stand up yesterday at the end of the meeting? A double team CMC! That's why. We tented him."

Rose looked perplexed, "Tented him?"

Janey explained, "Yeah, when we both winked at him, you know, let him look up our skirts, we gave the old goat a big ol' woodie… a hard on. That's why he stayed in the chair behind his desk when we left yesterday. We tented him. He didn't dare stand up. He's not as old as he looks."

Before Rose could respond, Dr. Peersome entered the waiting room from the hallway into the patient care center. He peered over his glasses at the three women and smiled from ear to ear, "Good morning, ladies. Please join me. We have lots to discuss." He ushered them into his office off the lobby and said, "Please… be seated."

Chairs were arranged as they were yesterday. One regular-sized chair to the far left and two short-legged, grade-school chairs to the right before the Dr.'s big steel desk. Janey sat in the closest short-legged chair. Rose quickly grabbed the other short-legged chair in defense of Angel. Dr. Peersome stood by his big steel desk and frowned. Angel seated herself in the regular-sized chair and put her feet on the support beneath the chair's seat, thus raising her knees. Even though all skirted thighs were clapped together, the Dr.'s frown turned to a smile as he sat behind his desk.

Before speaking, he took a pencil from the cup of already-sharpened pencils as he had done yesterday. All the pencils were considerably shorter. When he placed the retrieved pencil into the electric pencil sharpener, Angel slowly spread her thighs, giving the psychiatrist a full wink. The observant Dr. snapped the pencil in two, leaving half of it trapped in the sharpener. He yelled, "Damn it!" and smiled self-consciously as he carefully removed the broken half of the pencil from the sharpener. Angel leaned over to Rose and whispered, "CMC." Rose's face reddened as she realized what Angel had done.

Dr. Peersome cleaned the shards of broken pencil from his desk and grabbed another already-sharpened pencil, regaining his composure as he did so. "I take it the three of you visited with Leslie yesterday afternoon. How did the visit go?"

Rose replied, "Quite well. She seemed pretty much her old self again, but she was a bit logy. Strange she didn't ask about Jamie the whole time."

Dr. Peersome resumed his pencil-sharpening ritual and said, "Well that's to be expected. She's selectively blocked certain memories and replaced them with others. After our meeting yesterday, I began a pharmacological therapy. I proscribed an SSRI, sertraline, so she's calmer and her symptoms are less obvious."

Rose blurted out, "SSRI?"

Dr. Peersome smiled and said, "Oh, I'm sorry. Forgive the pharmacological acronym. An SSRI is a selective serotonin reuptake inhibitor, a medication that markedly reduces OCD and depression. In Leslie's case, I proscribed 200 milligrams of sertraline. You may know sertraline by its commercial name, Zoloft."

Angel said, "Well she seemed OK. She didn't try to search for squirrels… didn't even mention it. That SSRI stuff must be working."

Dr. Peersome held his most recently sharpened pencil between the tips of the index fingers of his right and left hands, slowly moving the pencil back and forth, and said thoughtfully, "Well an SSRI such as a Zoloft does reduce obsessive-compulsive behavior, such as Leslie's compulsive masturbation. However, it doesn't eliminate it. She did search for squirrels, as you put it, several times after you left. And I doubt she'd discuss her sexual compulsivity with her mother in the room if she were inclined to discuss it at all."

Rose asked, "Well, if she takes this Zoloft long enough, will it cure her?"

"No, it will not. Unfortunately, the original obsessive-compulsive behavior, her compulsive masturbation or CM, will return full force once she stops taking the medication… which is why we must use a bimodal or perhaps even a multimodal therapeutic approach combining psychopharmacological therapies with psychotherapeutic therapies."

Janey slowly parted her thighs and said, "That's a lot of psychos, Doc. What's it really mean?"

Dr. Peersome looked down at Janey's full wink and, startled by it, reflexively pushed his fingers together, yelling, "Ouch, damn it" as he did so, for he had imbedded the point of the pencil he was holding into the tip of the index finger of his right hand. The pencil dropped to his desk top and he jammed the tip of his wounded finger into his mouth. He removed the finger tip from his mouth, and as his eye brows furrowed, he carefully rotated his hand, inspecting his wounded finger from various angles. He continued speaking, "As a start, I think we should begin a behavioral therapy to supplement the Zoloft. It is the behavioral therapy that has the long-term effects and can best control Leslie's CM."

Janey slowly closed her thighs and smiled. Rose, in a panic, whispered rather loudly to Janey, "Stop that C-M-C business. Leave the doctor's mind alone. Stop confusing him. He's trying to explain Leslie's CM. I want to hear what he has to say about treating Leslie's OCD with SSRI to control her CM or whatever else he has in mind." She turned to Angel, "And that goes for you too!"

Angel, unruffled as always, replied, "OK Miz F-W, don't get your panties in a wad."

Dr. Peersome looked up, having heard a bit of what Rose and Angel had said, and asked, "Panties in a wad? CMC? Is there something you're not telling me about your visit with Leslie? She didn't attempt any masturbatory behavior which you neglected to mention?"

Rose assured the doctor, "Heavens no, Dr. Peersome. Yesterday's visit was just fine. I just asked Janey and Angel to not interrupt you while you were speaking. You were saying something about an additional therapy?"

Dr. Peersome, while still looking at his wounded finger on his right hand, rubbed the tip of the finger with his right thumb and continued, "Yes, bimodal treatment or perhaps even a multimodal treatment..."

Angel, having abandoned her CMC efforts and now concerned about the treatment of Leslie's OCD and CM asked, "Dr., what's with the modals?"

Dr. Peersome answered, "Perhaps I'm a bit ahead of myself. I've had several rather long sessions with Leslie to better determine the nature and origin of her sexual compulsivity. Her case is quite interesting and unique. I venture to say I can squeeze several articles about her case for some of the leading medical and psychological journals."

Rose interrupted him, "I don't want Leslie's name and her problem splashed all over some journals. We admitted her to this institute to keep her condition and treatment secret. We want absolutely no publicity!"

The good doctor replied, "Rose, fear not. If I write any articles about Leslie's rather unique condition, she will remain anonymous, I assure you. It is both an ethical requirement of my profession and the policy of S-L-I-M-E."

Janey, also having abandoned her CMC tactics at Rose's urging, asked, "What's slime? Is it related to Leslie's OCD or her CM and all that SSRI stuff?"

Dr. Peersome smiled and replied, "No, Miss Toussaint, S-L-I-M-E stands for the Saint Lawrence Institute for Mental Efficacy. It's the formal name of this treatment facility. It sounds a lot better in French."

Janey could only muster a confused, "Oh."

Dr. Peersome continued, "But back to Leslie's case… she apparently fantasizes about some Zulu fertility dance that involves the ritual deflowering of a maiden. Rose told me in a previous session that Zulu dance rituals were topics covered in her doctoral thesis. For some reason she's developed this fantasy about this one dance ritual and she associates this fantasy with orgasm and thus masturbates. At first I did not consider her condition to involve paraphilia but rather a more prosaic sexual addiction of some sort. However, she's driven by a fantasy and that fantasy is apparently required for her to reach orgasm. She may be suffering from a rather rare, archaic and esoteric condition called racial fetishism, which I would classify as paraphilian."

Rose sat in silence. Her face reddened and she looked down at her lap fidgeting with her fingers. Her reinforcements did not suffer comparably. Angel asked, "Para-feelian? Is that a dangerous disease? Who does she think is feeling her up? Some black guy?"

Dr. Peersome became agitated by the turn in the discussion and reached for another pencil. As he began his pencil sharpening ritual, he replied, "Paraphilia is a form of sexual deviation. Common forms of the condition are voyeurism and frotteurism. It could involve something akin to, as you put it, 'getting felt up,' but not necessarily."

Janey chimed in, "Frotter who? Does frotter what-cha-ma-call-it involve African-Americans?"

The good doctor found himself in a conceptual corner and had trouble finding his way out, "It could, but..."

Before he could continue, Angel interrupted, "Jamal accidently frottered Leslie and right in front of us. He para-felt her up psychologically and didn't even know it. Now that she's been frottered, she's nuttier than a fruitcake and keeps searchin' for squirrels. And all because of that stupid bachelorette party and Jamal dancing around in that stupid costume."

Rose became hysterical and began sobbing uncontrollably. Angel reached over and comforted Rose, "Miz F-W, don't worry. Leslie's being S-S-R-I-ed and Dr. Peersome is going to multi-modal her until she's better."

As Dr. Peersome brushed the pencil shards from the head of the pencil he'd just re-sharpened, he said with great relief, "I think that we should terminate this session given the circumstances." He checked his appointment book and said, "Perhaps we could continue tomorrow afternoon at 1:00?"

Rose, still sobbing, shook her head yes, and Janey and Angel helped her from the office.

Tuesday, July 8

The posse chows down before rambling down Route 66...

The posse stood beneath a large, overhanging brown sign with white script lettering as they stood in a long line in the early and still cool Chicago dawn. Jonnie Hogg looked up at the sign and read aloud, more or less to himself, "This is Lou Mitchells." He paused and added, "Where the hell else would it be with that blaring away at us" as he pointed to a large neon sign on the face of the building which pretty much made the painted sign hanging above them supplemental at best. Charles, who was reading from an old, dog-eared paperback as he stood in line, caught Jonnie's attention. "What cha readin', Charlie-O?"

Charles held the paperback up and said, "It's an old paperback that I picked up at that used book store on the South Side... 'Stuff Your Momma Wouldn't Tell You about Route 66.' Some tough looking bimbo named Big Bertha wrote it. Her pictures on the back cover. And ol' Bertha looks like a woman who spent more time counting ceiling tiles than writing. Claims she worked the Mother Road from Chicago to L.A. and back and she looks it."

A waitress walked by with a basket full of donut holes, passing them out to those awaiting a table at the Chicago landmark. Jonnie grabbed a handful and began popping them into his mouth. The rest of the posse each took a discreet one donut hole, except for Charles who took none and continued reading from his paperback.

Charles looked up and said, "Big Bertha says that a waitress gives a box of Milk Duds to each female customer and if you've got a set of balls, you are a dud and get none. It's a long-held tradition. Well, in the age of equality, it's time that someone with balls gets his Duds!"

As the posse munched, Jamie said, "You'll need more than Milk Duds today, Charlie-O. Tank up boys before we hit the Mother Road west. What you need is a good breakfast and Lou Mitchell's is the place to get it after last night's…" but before he could finish, Louis Fazzano asked, "Where's Joobie?" Jamie looked up and down the line in their immediate area and there was no Garcia Rosenbloom to be found amongst the immediate living. Jonnie Hogg stepped out of line and looked down the street and yelled, "There's the bastard… standin' in the gutter up by all those Harleys facin' out!" and with that he took off down the sidewalk with an urgency appropriate for the rescue of the unaware from the potentially fatal danger posed by Chicago drivers.

When Jonnie reached the barely conscious Garcia Rosenbloom, he pulled him back from the road by the scruff of his neck and supported him as they stumbled down the sidewalk toward the posse. Jonnie encouraged Garcia's halting progress, "Hold steady, Joobie, we're almost there." When they reached the rest of the posse, Jonnie asked, "You OK?" Garcia smiled and shook his head in a manner that could have been mistaken for a sentient yes being signaled by someone suffering from Parkinson's disease. The line moved quickly and the posse found itself seated at a large table inside the iconic restaurant of the long-deceased Lou Mitchell, whose spirit apparently still hovered about the establishment.

Another waitress walked among the tables passing out small boxes of Milk Duds. Charles Fontaine asked as she passed, "Could I have a box of those babies?" The Milk Duds waitress said, "I'm afraid not. These are for women only. It's a long-held tradition at

Lou Mitchells. I've been doing this for twenty-seven years and I've never given a box of Milk Duds to a male customer and I don't plan to start today. Women only, buddy" and passed on to the next table where four young ladies, all rather tall, athletic-looking blondes, sat, each of them receiving a small box of Milk Duds from the Milk Duds waitress.

One of the young ladies, appropriately and fetchingly dressed in tight red shorts and a white souvenir tee shirt, tapped Charles on the shoulder and offered him her box of Milk Duds. "Here, you can have mine." Charles turned and his eyes immediately focused on her ample bosom. He read the motto emblazoned across the front of her tee shirt. Because of her ample bosom, this task was difficult but pleasurable. The motto read "Get your kicks on Route 66." Charles replied firmly but politely, "No Ma'am. Those Milk Duds are yours. I want my own box of those babies. Would you just turn your chair so that you look like you're seated with us? Leave your box of Milk Duds on the table by the empty chair."

The young lady replied, "Why in heavens name would I do that, sugar lover?" Charles replied, "To help a poor Boston boy get his own sugar fix."

Suspecting some fun, the young lady smiled and said, "You're on, Boston sugar lover" and pushed her chair beside that of Charles as her three friends, also similarly attired, giggled. The Milk Duds waitress walked by and Charles hailed her, pointing to the young lady seated next to him, and said, "You forgot to give this lady her box of Milk Duds." The rest of the posse shook its collective head in agreement, not quite knowing what to expect but expecting the unexpected.

The Milk Duds waitress looked down at the young lady and said as she nodded toward the table where the other three young ladies sat, "Why, I just gave that young woman a box at that table where those other three young women are seated. That's the box right there on the table."

Charles looked over at the table and said, "That lady you gave the box to just went to the men's room and this young lady is his twin sister. You neglected to Milk Dud this young lady. She was in the ladies' room when you passed by."

The Milk Duds waitress looked over at the table where the three young ladies sat and said, as she turned looking toward the back of the restaurant, presumably in the direction of the rest rooms, "Men's room? That young woman went to the men's room?"

Charles pursed his lips, shook his head solemnly side-to-side and said, "His name is Taylor and he's changing it to Tyler after the operation is complete. He's still kind of a man, plumbing-wise. He just wanted to be this young lady's twin sister instead of her twin brother. In the worst way."

The Milk Duds waitress looked down at the young lady, thought for a moment, and said, "How do I know that this here person is the one who's the woman?"

The young woman smiled at the Milk Duds waitress, began to stand and said, "Ma'am, if necessary, I'll submit to a gynecological examination to settle this question once and for all. God knows, we don't want to break the long-held, women-only Milk Dud tradition here at Lou Mitchells."

The Milk Duds lady thought for a moment and said, "Oh, that won't be necessary," grabbed the box of Milk Duds from the adjacent table and handed the box to the young lady. "Here, you can have this one. Your twin brother Taylor isn't qualified to receive his own box until the operation is complete, his name is Tyler, and he uses the ladies' room. There, I think we've solved the problem so that this young woman does not require a gynecological exam and I can still maintain my twenty-seven years of upholding Lou Mitchell's long-held tradition of Milk Duds for women only" and she walked off to complete her rounds of Milk-Duding the rest of the apparently female customers.

The ample-bosomed, yet athletic-looking blonde, laughed hysterically, as did her three companions. The posse smiled as it concentrated on the mottos emblazoned on the front of all four white tee shirts. When she caught her breath, the blonde said, "Where you boys headed? Route 66?" The posse shook its head a collective yes, still pretty much concentrating on the mottos emblazoned on the front of the tee shirts. The blonde, accustomed to this reaction on the part of males, was unperturbed by the overt ogling of her frontal phraseology and continued, "My name's Mette, Mette Anders. I'm from Minnesota." She pointed to her three companions and said, "They're my cousins from Norway. We're touring Route 66 with the Route 66 Association of Norway." She turned her back to the posse and on the back of the tee shirt was the familiar Route 66 highway shield and above it the words "Norwegians Love." She turned back toward the posse, smiling from ear to ear.

Charles could only mumble "Norwegian Route 66 Association?"

Mette replied, "That's right. The association organizes tours of Route 66 for, guess who? Norwegians! And those twenty-seven Harleys parked along the curb outside? They're ours. It's a biker tour, sugar lover."

Charles, still stunned by this information, asked "Why in heaven's name would a bunch of Norwegians tour Route 66?"

"Same reason as you. It's a chance to see America. Talk to real people. And it's fun!"

"All four of you ride Harleys?"

"Yup. Two by two. We switch off driving. Listen, I gotta get back to my cousins and order breakfast. Maybe we'll see you on the Mother Road?" She tossed the box of Milk Duds to Charles, turned back to her table and began giggling and chattering away in Norwegian with her cousins.

At first the posse sat in stunned silence, usually a rare occurrence. Eventually Jonnie Hogg gained what equilibrium he had at his disposal and said, "We just stepped in shit!" The rest of the posse shook its collective head in yet another sign of agreement.

A waitress stopped by the table to take their orders. Jamie asked, "What's the Big Al Capone special?"

The waitress said, curtly, "The Big Al? Killer of a breakfast! A frittata laced with Genoa salami and a side of hash browns topped with slices of fried tomatoes."

Jonnie asked, "What the hell's the frittata part?"

The waitress, without looking up from her order pad, said quite dryly, "It's an Italian omelet with a bunch of Italian stuff, including Genoa salami."

Jonnie smiled, "I love salami. I'll have that."

Jamie and Louis followed suit.

The waitress looked to Garcia Rosenbloom, who said, "teaksita, arerisita!"

The waitress looked puzzled, "Say again." And Garcia repeated his order louder, incorrectly believing that volume was the problem.

The waitress remained puzzled. Charles translated, "He wants a steak, rare."

The waitress asked, "Steak and eggs?"

Charles looked toward Garcia and said, "Ithwisita eggisita?"

Garcia shook his head no and said, "Oldhisita hetsita eggisita."

Charles said, "Hold the eggs for our other foreign friend." He smiled and said "I'll have the Norwegian smoked-salmon omelet."

The posse meets the mostly dead Funks...

The posse sat in Louis's parked red Edsel convertible. The top was down so all the members of the posse had a panoramic view of their surroundings. Jonnie Hogg looked around and said, "Looks like a fuckin' cemetery to me. Why we here? I'm not dead. I'm hungry and I gotta take a leak."

Jamie smiled and said, "Get out and stretch your legs and drain the dragon, Pig Fat. We've been driving for almost three hours since we left Chicago. We'll stop and get some real Route 66 chow after I take some pictures and buy a can of maple syrup."

Jonnie couldn't believe his ears, "Maple syrup? In a fuckin' cemetery? We didn't take a wrong turn, say south of Joliet, and end up in a Vermont maple syrup cemetery or somethin'?"

Jamie smiled and got out and stretched. He held a small digital camera in his left hand which he now waved above his head as he stretched. The rest of the posse piled out of the red Edsel convertible. Louis took his handkerchief from his back pocket and walked around his prized Edsel, spitting on the car's surface here and there and rubbing off spots of dirt and the dried bodies of dead, squashed bugs. Jonnie Hogg and Garcia Rosenbloom wandered off looking for a bush. Jamie and Charles Fontaine meandered among the grave stones with Jamie taking a picture here and there as the scene struck him.

Charles asked, "Aren't you worried? You only got 15 days to respond to that offer to sell your place. And we're on a road trip on old Route 66."

While still looking at the display for his digital camera as he refocused on another shot, Jamie said, "We can't let the bastards see us sweat. We got 15 days and those bastards won't do anything until the 15 days are up." He snapped a shot and continued, "Besides, before I accept that offer, I gotta know what the deal is. I'll call Oglethorpe and Fernandez tomorrow and tell them I've got their offer and am seriously considering it. That ought to keep them quiet for a couple of days. We'll be on the road for another three or four days, give or take. Big Louie's gathering information back in New York. That'll give him time to find out more about Oglethorpe and Fernandez. By the time we're in Alpine, hopefully we'll know a lot more."

Charles said, "Alpine?"

Still walking about the gravestones and reading epitaphs, Jamie replied, "Yup, Alpine, California. We'll take Route 40 to Needles, California, and then drive south to Alpine. That's not far from my vacation compound."

They meandered back to the Edsel. The post-leaked Jonnie Hogg and Garcia Rosenbloom were standing alongside one of the rows of gravestones not far away. Jonnie yelled to Jamie, "Looks to me like it ain't so good to have the last name of Funk. They all seem to be dead. Look at this," and he pointed to individual gravestones as he spoke. "Every one of these dead bastards is named Funk. And there's one with Funk as a middle name. Seems like if Funk's any place in your name, odds are you're dead."

As Jamie walked by, he smiled and said, "Well they're not all dead, Pig Fat. There's at least a couple of them who haven't kicked the bucket quite yet." As he approached the Edsel, his cell phone sounded with "Get Your kicks on Route 66." Jamie pulled his cell phone from his belt and flipped it open. As he spoke, he wandered behind the Edsel and spoke for several minutes, then flipped the phone shut and yelled, "Let's saddle up." The posse piled back into the Edsel. Louis started the engine and looked over to Jamie who rode shotgun and said, "Where to, keemosabe?"

Jamie sat staring into space and Louis repeated, "Where to, keemosabe?" Jamie shook his head, set his cell phone to the navigator function and said barely above a whisper, "It's not far. Look for a big white arrow that says Maple Syrup. It's just off Old 66." Sure enough they came to a big white arrow with the words "Maple Sirup" painted in black and Jamie said "Follow the arrow."

As they drove by the sign, Jonnie observed, "Not only are most of the Funks dead, they also can't spell worth shit. Doesn't syrup have a y?"

Jamie yelled over his shoulder, "Not in this case." He turned toward the back seat and said, "When you spell it with an 'i', it means that the maple syrup is pure, no sugar added. The Funks have been doin' this for a long time."

Charles, who had been reading from his paperback, said, "The Funks have been making this sirup with an i since 1824. They've been here a long time, which is why so many of them are dead."

As Louis slowed the Edsel down a curved dirt lane, Charles continued, "This stand of maples is worth millions as lumber, but one of the dead Funks set up a trust before joining the rest of her dead ancestors. This stand of maple trees can only be used to produce maple sirup. That's why there's still maple trees, maple sirup, some live Funks and lots of dead ones in Funk's Grove. This place is officially called Funk's Grove Sirup Camp."

Jamie yelled to Louis, "Whoa there, keemosabe, we're here!"

The Edsel screeched to a halt in a cloud of dust. The posse piled out and mosied into the Funk's Grove Sirup Camp gift shop. Once inside, Jamie walked up to the counter and bought a large tin shaped like a log cabin full of Funk's pure maple sirup and a half dozen maple sugar patties shaped like the Route 66 shield. The rest of the posse wandered about the shop looking at the items for sale. Louis stood before a map of old Route 66 and whistled to himself. He said to Charles, "There's a ton of Route 66 souvenirs. It's like a cult. The Route 66 cult." He grinned and asked, "Think they have a secret handshake?"

Charles whispered back, "I read that they sure do. Keep it quiet. Big Bertha says that when two Route 66 culters meet, they make a fist with their right hands, stick out their thumbs like they're hitch hiking and then bump knuckles. But she warns don't touch thumbs unless you want to travel up the old dirt road."

Louis looked puzzled. "Up the old dirt road? I thought that all of Route 66 was paved."

Charles whispered to Louis, "It is, you idiot. She wasn't referring to Route 66. Touching thumbs means you're lookin' for a Route 66 buddy for a queer quickie. That old dirt road."

Louis turned and said "No shit. I was only kiddin'. It's for real?"

Charles with a look of great seriousness said, "Big Bertha says it's for real and that's good enough for me. Of course, you can caress a couple of thumbs to verify it if you so desire."

Louis could only mumble, "No fuckin' way" in reply.

The posse wandered out of the gift shop and piled back into the Edsel. Jamie put the bag holding the log cabin tin of Funk's pure maple sirup and maple sugar patties on the floor. He leaned to the side facing the back seat. "Only $12.25 for the sirup. A real steal. That lady who sold me the sirup, I believe she's a Funk. The Funks are alive and well, at least some of them." He turned to Louis and said, "Get back on Old Route 66 and follow the signs to Route 55. Get on 55 south... towards Springfield."

Jonnie Hogg leaned forward in the back seat and yelled, "When we gonna fuckin' eat again? If we don't eat soon, I'm gonna start chewin' on the a-polstry."

Jamie reached into the bag on the floor and pulled out five of the maple sugar patties. He tossed three of them into the back seat where the posse's rear guard scrambled for them. He yelled over the sound of the wind as the Edsel picked up speed, "Munch on those babies." He ripped open the cellophane packaging for the fourth one with his teeth and handed it to Louis and then did the same for himself.

Louis merged the Edsel onto I-55. Jamie set his cell phone on the navigator function and yelled to Louis, "It's about 65 miles to lunch. Should take about an hour. You're lookin' for Exit 92 toward Jacksonville." The posse fell into a wind-driven sugar funk unable to say much because of the noise. The hour passed quickly and Jamie, using the navigator function of his cell phone, directed Louis off I-55. Louis made a U-turn as instructed and pulled into the parking lot for the Cozy Drive In.

Louis parked the Edsel. Jamie turned toward the back seat and said, "Gentlemen, you are about to experience one of Route 66's culinary delights, a true American culinary delight."

Charles flipped through several pages of his paperback and said, "Says here this culinary delight, as Jamie put it, was invented by a Mr. Edwin Waldmire in 1945. He actually invented it while serving in the Army Air Corps in World War II."

Jonnie Hogg said, "I don't care who the fuck invented it. It's chow time!"

Louis, not quite as impatient as Jonnie Hogg, although getting there, said, "Well… what is this culinary delight."

Charles smiled and said, "Originally Mr. Edwin Waldmire called his gourmet creation the crusty cur."

Jonnie Hogg blurted out, "Hold it. Is this crusty cur some kind of Chinese food? I'll tell you right now, I don't care how fuckin' hungry I am or how good these fuckin' crusty curs taste, I ain't eatin' no dog meat. It's uncivilized."

Jamie laughed and said, "Charles is yanking on that pork-pulled leg of yours, Pig Fat. You know the crusty cur by another name... the corn dog!"

Jonnie could hardly contain himself, "Why didn't you say so. I love corn dogs! Let's chow down, and I mean now!"

As the posse's rear guard started to arise, Charles held up his hands, "Whoa big fellas, a word of warning. Big Bertha says that if you want good service, order cozy dogs, not corn dogs. Corn dog is the generic name for the stuff you get at a county fair. Cozy dog is the brand name for the best corn dog ever deep fried."

The posse's rear guard, losing patience with the history lesson and advice, jumped out of the back seat without bothering to await the convenience of an open door. Charles looked over at Jamie and said, "I guess a posse travels on its stomach."

Jamie flipped his cell phone open and said, "Order me a couple of cozy dogs and some stick fries with a large diet Coke. I'll be in in a minute. I've got to make a call."

Agent Double Oh-my on the case...

Big Louie sat in his black Escalade watching the Oglethorpe and Fernandez building as he spoke. Jeremiah sat in the front passenger seat listening. "Do you have the business cards and the gold business card holder I gave you?"

Jeremiah held the gold business card holder up, shook it and replied a tentative, "Yes," and then asked, "Are you sure? I've never done anything even remotely like this before."

Big Louie turned to the adjunct professor of English literature and said, "Look, Doc, if I thought you couldn't do it, I'd a done it myself. It's riskier for me. I could get recognized bein' in the security field all these years and blow the chance to get more intel, but I'd 'a done it if I thought you couldn't. Look, what do you do for a livin'?"

Jeremiah answered, "Well, I teach literature."

Big Louie asked, "Ever read some of that literature to those idiot students of yours?"

Jeremiah could not figure out where Big Louie was headed and answered, "Of course, all the time. I frequently read passages pertinent to our discussions and sometimes to stir the discussions."

"How do you read them?"

"I read them in such a way as to convey the emotional content of the piece as intended by the author."

"There you go, Doc. You were acting before a very critical audience, those idiot students of yours. You been doin' this for years. You just didn't think of it as acting. But you were. Just make believe that the people you talk to in there… " and Big Louie pointed at the Oglethorpe and Fernandez building, "are your students. Act like you're reading literature to them. Talk down to them. Treat them like those assholes you teach. You got the knowledge and they don't!"

Jeremiah smiled and said, "I just never… "

Big Louie interrupted, "Doc, today you're an eccentric business man who imports millions of dollars of a specific product from Mexico and several other Central American countries, all through a series of front companies to assure your anonymity. You're extremely secretive and need both legal and security services. Every time someone tries to get you to be specific, just clam up and say that information is confidential. You're there to evaluate them to determine if they can provide you with the services you require. Not the other way around. Got it?"

Jeremiah smiled as confidence filled him, "Yes, Louis, I think I can perform as you've suggested."

Big Louie pumped his right hand and yelled, "Yes!" He continued, "Remember, you're evaluating them and not the other way around. You're the professor and they're the idiot students. It's like leading one of those discussions. Get as much intel as you can about how they operate, particularly in Mexico. That's where your primary suppliers are. I just need some leads so that I can get the big picture of their operation. You be ambiguous. Make them be specific. Like when you question one of those mushbrains you teach to try to figure out what they know."

Jeremiah, filled with confidence, strode into the Oglethorpe and Fernandez building and remained there for over two hours. Big Louie looked down at his watch and said to himself, "Doc's either hit the mother lode or he's spent the entire time in the john puking his guts out."

Agent Double Oh-my exited the building's foyer and looked up at the skyline, smiling from ear to ear. He walked around the corner as Big Louie had instructed him. Big Louie swung the Escalade out into traffic and around the corner, picking Jeremiah up on the next block.

Big Louie asked "How'd it go?" as Jeremiah stepped up and pulled himself into the Escalade.

"Wonderfully. I spoke with three different representatives, each one apparently of more importance. The last representative was a partner in the firm, a Dr. Santiago Juarez. He told me that Oglethorpe and Fernandez specialized in exactly the kind of services I was requesting and that he headed the division of O&F that provided those services." Jeremiah smiled and added, "He said that O&F provided the highest-quality, most-confidential services available and that their fees were commensurate with that quality and confidentiality. And I told him that money was no object. The quality and confidentiality of the legal services were."

Big Louie asked, "What sealed the deal and got you in the door?"

Jeremiah said, "That business card you gave me with my name. Not having an address and only a cell phone number. As you instructed, I told them to call that number and one of my representatives would take a message and phone number and I'd return the call within the hour."

Big Louie held up a cell phone and said, "And this is the cell phone and you are looking at your faithful anonymous representative."

Big Louie drove north. "Let's head for Jamie's place. I'll call him when we get there. See if he has any intel. While we're there, I can use his computer to do some more research."

Jeremiah couldn't stop smiling, "That was quite exhilarating. It's like a good spy novel. I've read all of the James Bond novels and seen the movies. It's like I'm a character in a spy novel."

Big Louie hit the brakes and yelled, "Get the fuck out of the way. This ain't a fuckin' parkin' lot." He turned to Jeremiah and said, "This place is turnin' into a third-world home-away-from-home." He swung the Escalade around a double-parked, dented white van that had seen better days many, many years ago, giving the driver of the van the one-finger salute and yelling, "Get a fuckin' green card next time you visit," as he passed.

Big Louie yelled and fingered his way north to Jamie's place and double-parked in front of the building. He swung a handicapped sign from the rear view mirror and placed a veteran's handicapped sign on the dash. Jeremiah gave Big Louie a bewildered look as Big Louie did so. Big Louie looked at Jeremiah and said, "What? I earned this fuckin' sign the hard way. I was wounded three times in Nam. Killed me a whole bunch of those fuckin' slopes. If you ask me, we still got some unfinished business over there."

Jeremiah remained discreetly silent as they entered the foyer and took the elevator to Jamie's apartment. Once inside, Big Louie immediately limped over to the bar and picked up a bottle of single-malt scotch. He read the label aloud, "Glenfidich?" As he filled his flask, he said to Jeremiah, "Guess I'll just have to get used to this expensive piss." He took a swig from the flask. "Well, Doc, what else you got?"

Jeremiah plopped into the leather couch and pulled a moleskin notebook from his jacket pocket. "As you instructed, I refused any preprinted material and told the O&F representatives that I preferred to take notes. The first two representatives seemed a bit flustered, but when I talked to that partner, Dr. Santiago Juarez, he just nodded his head like it's what he expected."

"Good move, Doc. You're a natural."

"The first two representatives didn't seem to know much and

I got sent to Dr. Santiago Juarez quickly. At first I felt as if I were getting the bum's rush, but after I gave the first representative my business card, he quickly passed me to the second representative. When the second representative said that an initial retainer of one hundred thousand dollars would be required to begin the necessary background work, I said, 'Is that all?' and I got immediately passed to Dr. Santiago Juarez. Louis, those offices are appointed most expensively and by the time I got to Dr. Juarez's office, I thought I was entering the oval office."

As he listened, Big Louie took another swig from his flask and said, "Doc, who'd 'a thunk? Dr. Jeremiah Wright: undercover agent! I could not 'a handled the situation any better. What's their deal?"

"The firm has what Dr. Juarez termed 'affiliates' in many cities. He said they work very closely with these affiliates. I asked about San Diego and Tijuana as you had suggested and he gave me the names of two firms… in San Diego." Here Jeremiah looked down at his notes, "Schmidt and Wilder, and in Tijuana… Garcia and Schmidt. I asked for assurances that the confidentiality of my businesses and the services that I required could be maintained with such an organization and Dr. Juarez assured me that these affiliates were very closely tied to O&F. He leaned over and whispered to me that their affiliates only did work for O&F, so the tie was much closer than appeared on the surface. I smiled and knowingly shook my head and he seemed to be the one reassured."

"How about security services?"

"I asked and he said that they used a number of firms. I asked for a name and he said Tangent Services. Ever hear of them?"

"Christ! Tangent, they're one of the heavy hitters. That little blackmailing operation we're investigating is just the tip of a very large iceberg. We're in deep shit, Doc, deep shit."

Jeremiah nervously shoved his moleskin notebook back into his jacket pocket and mumbled, "Oh my, oh my, oh my."

Big Louie interrupted Jeremiah's oh-my chorus, "You were in there a long time, Doc. What else you talk about?"

"He reviewed the contract and the fee schedule. I acted like I understood every word and when he reviewed the fee schedule, I acted like it wasn't all that important. We had café con leche and talked about our passions as he put it. I told him that my passion was collecting first editions. You know, Louis, I've always wanted to, but I've never had the resources to really amass an extensive collection. I do have several D. H. Lawrence first editions. Well, I talked about my passion and for some reason that impressed him."

"What's his passion?"

"Louis, you are not going to believe this." Jeremiah pointed to the wall of shelves displaying tequila bottles of all shapes and sizes. "He collects those."

"God damn! One for us! Where'd you leave the deal?"

"I told him that I had some more work to do before deciding which firm I'd be contracting with and that I'd get back to him in a week or so and, if he had any additional questions that did not breach my confidentiality, he could call my representative and I'd get back to him."

"Great work, Doc. Time to give the wanderer a call." Big Louie flipped open his cell phone and made the call. "Jamie? Yeah… Where the hell are you and that damn posse of yours?... Funk's Grove?... Funk's what?… What state?... Illinois? What the fuck are you still doin' there?" Big Louie looked up at Jeremiah and said in exasperation, "You're not gonna believe where those assholes are. They're in a cemetery in a place called Funk's Grove taking pictures." He turned his attention back to his cell phone conversation with Jamie, "Ah-huh, ah-huh… That name sounds real familiar. Hold on a second." He looked up at Jeremiah again and asked, "What was the name of that O&F affiliate in San Diego again?"

Jeremiah replied, "Schmidt and Wilder."

Big Louie yelled into the cell phone, "You're not gonna fuckin' believe this. That law firm handling that offer to lease your property, Schmidt and Wilder, they're a front for Oglethorpe and Fernandez. I had Doc here do a little undercover work this morning. OK, I'll call later with more details after I do a little more research. I need to get on the internet. You got a guest signon. What's the log-on and password? OK, got it. Ciao."

Big Louie flipped his cell phone closed. Jeremiah asked, "Did Jamie have any new intelligence regarding Schmidt and Wilder? How did he know the name of the firm?"

"Doc, while Jamie was screwing around in New York, he received a request to lease that property he bought as a wedding gift for Leslie. His secretary in his Chicago office never forwarded the request, misfiled the fuckin' papers, so our wanderer never responded. And guess what? The request to lease came from Schmidt and Wilder. Jamie came across the request when he retrieved the file for his original purchase. That's where the papers got filed."

Jeremiah reprised his oh-my chorus as Big Louie took a swig from his flask and headed for Jamie's miniature NASA command and control center.

Crusty curs by any other name still taste as sweet...

Jamie entered the Cozy Drive In and the posse was already chowing down with great enthusiasm. Charles yelled, "One calls for another," and pointed to two cozy dogs snuggling in a cardboard container accompanied by an order of stick fries and a large diet Pepsi. "Diet Pepsi will have to do. No Coke."

Jamie pulled a chair up to the end of the booth and asked, "Where's the mustard?"

Garcia Rosenbloom slid a paper plate with a mound of mustard toward him and pointed at it. Jamie said, "Community mustard dip?" as he dipped the tip of his first cozy dog into the mustard. Garcia Rosenbloom shook his head a perfunctory yes. Jamie asked, "Joobie, you said anything lately?"

After a period of silence, Jonnie Hogg answered, "Naw, he ain't said nothin' since Chicago. He did fart once on 55... while we were drivin' here. It weren't no S-B-D either, a real thunder clap. It's the only sound he's made. He's livin' proof a man shouldn't have beef for breakfast. Damn good thing we had the top down."

Jamie asked, "A real thunder clap? That true, Joobie?" Garcia shook his head yes, this time proudly, and then smiled from ear to ear. Jamie bit off the mustard-covered tip of his cozy dog, chewed and as he chewed he shook his head from side to side. He closed his eyes and swallowed. "Damn that's good. A Route 66 delicacy!" He held up his partially eaten cozy dog and said, "Here's to Mr. Edwin Waldmire, the man who created fast food on a stick."

The posse consumed a whole mess of Edwin Waldmire's invention and piles of stick fries, and as they consumed, they talked, often while they chewed.

Charles asked Jamie, "That song you use for your cell phone ring, what is it?"

Jamie took his cell phone out and played his ring song. He let the entire song play. The posse listened with great interest as they chewed with equal enthusiasm. When the song finished, Jamie said "That's Bobby Troup singing "Get Your Kicks on Route 66." He wrote the song, I think in 1946, while drivin' Route 66. As the man says, 'When you make that California trip, get your kicks on Route 66'."

Jonnie Hogg listened to the song and said, "I know that song. The Stones sing it."

Jamie stopped eating. "Lots of people sing that song or play it. I looked it up. Over 250 different versions have been recorded. It's a great song. I listened to a bunch of them on You Tube the other day. Originally Nat King Cole sang it and made it a hit. I think in 1946. But hell, a 70s rock group, The Feelgoods, do a great version. And there's this babe in Argentina, and she's a real babe, with one name, I think its Chenoa, who rocks. There's even a version done by a bunch wearin' cowboy hats, Asleep at the Wheel. And every damn version is different. It's like a universal song. Lots of people sing it or play it. Every version's different, some great. It's good jazz, good rock, good blues, good country. It's a universal song!"

Louis chomped off about a third of his third cozy dog, and said through a full masticating mouth, "Where we goin', all the way to California like the song says?"

Jamie dipped the blunt end of his partially-eaten cozy dog into the community dipping plate of mustard. "Right! We're taking Route 66 to Needles, California, and then we're driving south to Alpine. That's not far from my vacation compound."

Louis continued chewing and talking, "So we're gonna end up at your vacation compound? Tell me again why we're goin' there."

Jamie took a sip from his diet Pepsi. "I gotta find out what's so attractive about a place in the middle of nowhere, a place so god damn attractive that someone would blackmail us to get it. There's that old saying, the three things that determine the value of real estate are where it is, where it is, and, you guessed it, where it is. I've made a lot of money knowing where it is, but my vacation compound, actually Leslie's vacation compound, is literally in the middle of nowhere. Why the hell would someone go through all that trouble to get their hands on a small piece of property in the middle of nowhere?"

Garcia spoke up, "Where's the middle of nowhere?"

Charles yelled, "He speaks! The Sphinx has a tongue!"

Jamie raised his hands toward the ceiling and said, "Finally! I was wondering when one of you assholes would get a little curious about the actual location of our final destination. Joobie, it's in the Cleveland National Forest, south of Alpine, California."

Jonnie Hogg asked, "Where the fuck's Alpine, anyway?"

Jamie replied, "Well it's east of San Diego. I'll show you guys on a map when we get to the motel."

Jonnie bit into his fourth cozy dog and said in a voice somewhat muffled and garbled by his chewing, "Shit, that's not far from tequila country."

Charles had finished his cozy dogs and looked up at the wall behind their booth. The wall was covered with pictures, news articles, and hand-written posters, most of them about Route 66. He said to Jamie, "You know all this stuff about Route 66. Why's President Eisenhower's picture up there with all this Route 66 stuff?"

Jamie sat back in his chair and wiped his mouth with a napkin before replying, then said, "Well, he was president when Route 66 was the main road to the west. He signed the bill that created the interstate road system. Changed America. Lots of people don't know that. He's famous for beating the Nazis in World War II and when he was president, he stood up to the Commies. My dad said that lots of people called him a do-nothing president but he changed America right under their noses. And that interstate road system ended up replacing Route 66. Hell, I said we're taking Route 66 but actually we're taking Route 55 and Route 44 and Route 40. Every now and then we're on old Route 66."

Jamie bit off another large chuck of cozy dog and chewed for a while. He swallowed and pointed the remnants of his cozy dog on the stick at the picture of President Eisenhower, "The irony is he actually killed Route 66. All these abandoned gas stations and restaurants and motels that we passed used to be thriving businesses. Hundreds of thousands of people drove Route 66. Then old Route 66 was slowly replaced by the new interstates, pretty much bypassing all these little towns and killing the businesses. The interstate road system changed where it is to where it was!"

Charles asked, "Why the hell do you know so much about Route 66, anyway?"

Jamie took another bite from his last cozy dog and chewed a bit before replying. "My Grandpa Gus drove a truck along Route 66 before it was Route 66, from Chicago to St. Louis and back, for some Chicago outfit. He spoke with such a heavy German accent that the other drivers nicknamed him Kraut. Eventually he worked his way up to manager of the outfit's entire trucking operation." Jamie paused and sipped his diet Pepsi. "Well, that outfit went bellyup and Grandpa Gus needed a way to make a living. He looked around and saw that Americans were becoming car crazy and drove every where they wanted to go. Pretty much stopped taking trains. Eventually thousands of cars and trucks were driving to California on Route 66 and almost as many driving back. Cars, trucks, of all descriptions."

He took another sip of diet Pepsi and pointed to the map of Route 66 on the wall. "People driving in those cars and trucks along Route 66 needed to gas up their cars and trucks, eat and sleep. Whole new industries grew up along the route to meet the need. Fast food stops, restaurants, motels, gas stations were popping up all along Route 66. Hell, fast food and motels were invented on Route 66. So Grandpa Gus emptied his savings account and set up his own company, Route 66 Restaurant and Hotel Supplies, to sell all kinds of stuff, whatever was needed, to these restaurants, motels and gas stations, all the new businesses popping up all along the route. As the traffic moved west, so did his company's route. He was an American success story. He emigrated from Germany in 1925. He worked hard, founded a business and made a fortune selling the supplies these new businesses needed." Jamie held up the container used to serve the cozy dogs, "Like these cardboard containers. The Steinkraus family ate, drank and slept Route 66 from Chicago to L.A. and back again. When Grandpa Gus died, my dad took over the business."

Jonnie Hogg said, "Are you done eating and drinking and talking? Where's the dive where we'll be sleeping?"

Jamie sucked the diet Pepsi from his cup until the straw made that whooshing sound and said, "Right, let's hit the road." The posse cleaned off the table and headed for the Edsel.

A guy was leaning against a 1967 Mustang admiring the red Edsel convertible. As the posse gathered around the Edsel, the stranger said, "That Edsel's cherry. Never saw one in that good a condition."

Louis smiled with pride, "She's a 1958 two-door Edsel Citation with a rag top and an E-475 V8 engine. Fully restored. Only nine hundred thirty of these babies were built and there's only a hundred fifty left."

The man said, "Well she's a beauty, got a decade on my Shelby here, but your Edsel's in as good a shape, maybe better." He waved at the posse and walked into the Cozy Drive In.

Louis looked up at the dark and cloudy sky and said, "Looks like rain," and without further explanation, the rest of the posse helped him put the rag top up.

After the rag top was secured, Jonnie Hogg looked toward Garcia Rosenbloom suspiciously. "You don't feel a fart comin' on, what with all those cozy dogs you et? Puttin' the top up could be a death sentence for the rest of us if you generate another gas attack."

Garcia smiled and shook his head yes confidently. Jonnie asked, " Yes you do or yes you don't?"

Garcia shook his head an even more confident yes to everyone's satisfaction and the posse piled into the Edsel. Jamie grabbed a map from the dashboard and studied it as Louis pulled the Edsel out of the parking lot. "Get back onto 55 south. We'll be on 55 for about eighty miles. Look for Exit 10."

Louis stepped on the gas said, "Got it, chief," roared onto 55 and asked, "Where we headed?"

Jamie smiled and said, "The Munger Moss Motel, my man, Lebanon, Missouri… Lebanon, Missouri. It's about four hours from here, give or take. About two hundred and sixty miles."

Louis checked the odometer and gas gauge and said, "The way I figure it, we got about a hundred miles before Lucille here needs a drink."

Jamie checked the map again and said, "That'll take us close to St. Louis. We can gas up there."

Rose and her reinforcements enter the belly of the beast...

Rose and her reinforcements sat in Dr. Peersome's office awaiting his arrival. Rose had taken the regular-sized chair on the far left while Angel and Janey sat in the grade-school chairs before the good Dr.'s great steel desk. Dr. Peersome entered and quickly sat behind his desk. He looked down at Rose and her reinforcements and frowned. Rose was dressed in a pantsuit and Janey and Angel were dressed in jeans. As he looked up, he noticed that Janey and Angel also wore halter tops. He muttered to himself, "All is not lost," as he reached for an already-sharpened pencil. The pencils were so short now that he had to reach into the cup holding them in order to retrieve one. He looked at Rose and said, "How are you feeling today, Rose? Things got a little tense yesterday."

Rose answered, "I'm sorry about yesterday's emotional outburst. I feel a little better today, but all this business with Leslie has been quite trying, and I'm having some difficulty understanding both her condition and the therapies you're recommending."

Angel looked over at a large bouquet of flowers on the side table. "Doc, those flowers are beautiful."

The doctor frowned and replied, "Yes, they are. They're from Leslie's husband. The card that accompanied them is quite provocative. I'm not sure she's ready for an expression of passionate love from her husband and how much he misses her. Could create more anxiety. I've decided to allow the flowers to be delivered, but without the card." He began his pencil sharpening ritual as he spoke, "I'm sure it has been trying and a bit confusing for you Rose. I'll be as clear about Leslie's condition and the therapies I'm recommending as is humanly possible." Without pausing he continued, "We've already spoken of the psychopharmacological therapy, the SSRI... serotonin... Zoloft... two-hundred milligrams daily. Today, I'd like to elaborate on the second part of the bi-modal approach I hinted at yesterday... the psychotherapeutic therapy we must employ so that Leslie can fully control her SC OCD CM. As I said, the SSRI will reduce the symptoms, but not eliminate them, thus the need for psychotherapeutic therapy."

Angel blurted out, "Psychotherapeutic?"

Dr. Peersome looked down at Angel, somewhat disappointed and continued, "That's right. I'm recommending a psychotherapeutic therapy which we call covert sensitization or CS."

Angel said, "So you're using an SSRI so that Leslie doesn't go searching for squirrels as much because of her SC OCD CM, and now you're going to bi-modal her with CS?"

Dr. Peersome looked surprised, "Yes, Angel, that's it in a nut shell. You're summary is excellent."

Angel smiled, "Oh Doc, I've always been good with numbers."

Dr. Peersome looked a bit befuddled by Angel's explanation concerning her powers of memory. Angel reached down to scratch her ankle and straighten her ankle bracelet, exposing much of her pendulous breasts as she did so. The Dr.'s expression went from befuddlement to confusion.

Rose immediately knew what had happened and whispered to Angel, "I told you no CMC today."

Angel turned to Rose while still scratching her ankle, her breasts jiggling with each scratch, and whispered back, "Miz F-W, I'm not CMCing. I'm wearing jeans. It was more like an accidental BMC, you know, a Boobie Mind Control kind of thing." She continued her explanation as she continued fiddling with her ankle bracelet. "A BMC is usually not as effective as a CMC, but it can be with some men. I didn't mean it."

Rose whispered back, "It doesn't matter whether you meant it or not. If you don't stop scratching your ankle, we'll never find out about this CS business that's going to cure Leslie. For heaven's sake, sit up."

As Angel sat up, the Dr.'s confusion waned and he continued, "CS or covert sensitization is a behavioral psychotherapeutic therapy based on learning theory. We teach Leslie to think of a nauseating or anxiety-producing situation every time she begins her maladaptive behavior, in this case her sexual compulsivity, her compulsive masturbation. The nauseating or anxiety producing image causes the maladaptive behavior to become unpleasant and she stops."

Angel became excited by the explanation and said, "You're going to teach Leslie to make herself sick in order to get well and that way she'll cure herself!"

Dr. Peersome beamed with delight. "Exactly right in a roundabout way! However, the learning and conditioning process will take several counseling sessions and the effectiveness of the covert sensitization will in a large part be determined by Leslie's ability to identify a suitable unpleasant image."

Janey smiled and said, "Doc, we got it made in the shade! Leslie's scared of all sorts of things. She's bound to have a bunch of images that make her sick."

Angel broke in, "But Doc, we don't want to make her too sick of that CM business… just the C part. A little bit of the M part can be a lot of fun and then there's always the real thing. We just want her to turn herself off a little bit. No?"

Dr. Peersome looked down at a pencil he was brushing off and said to himself, "I seem to be missing a number of pencils." Without looking up, he replied, "Well I guess that's one way of expressing it. But right now, I'm most concerned with the entire CM, as you put it. The conditioning process takes some time and isn't always effective." After depositing the pencil he'd just re-sharpened and brushed off into the cup of re-sharpened pencils, he reached into the cup holding the already-sharpened pencils and came up empty. He muttered "damn" to himself and continued his explanation, "Leslie's case is a bit more complicated than usual. Later this afternoon, I'll work with her to teach her the CS process and develop a suitable negative image. However, …"

Before he could continue, Rose interrupted and said in worried tones, "However what? You said you had those psycho what-have-yous to cure her."

Dr. Peersome raised his hands in a gesture to quiet Rose and said, "Rose, these therapies aren't guaranteed to work all of the time. They work much of the time with differing degrees of effectiveness. Leslie's case is quite unique. She appears to be also suffering from a racial fetish, a rather esoteric paraphilian condition. But don't panic, we can move to a multi-modal approach if necessary. In the literature I came across an additional psychopharmacological therapy to treat CM using Naltrexone and Mirtazapine in conjunction with CS."

An attendant, a large, well-muscled African-American, burst into the office and said, "Doc, that klepto of yours has gone nuts again. He was walking funny down the hall, like he had a load in his pants. We stopped him and found these stuffed in his drawers." The attendant held up a bunch of rather short pencils. "Must have been real uncomfortable. Anyway, when we took the pencils away, he started bouncing off the walls."

Dr. Peersome replied, "Javarious, I'll be right there. Restrain Mr. DuMonte." The attendant rushed out of the office and into the patient care center. Dr. Peersome turned to Rose, Angel and Janey and said, "Sorry ladies, but I must attend to this emergency. Rose, call me later."

Rose shook her head yes as the doctor hurried from his office and into the patient care center.

Rose's cell phone rang. She reached into her pocketbook, grabbed her cell phone, flipped it open and said, "Hello?" She listened for a moment and said, "Jamie? Where are you? Illinois? Leslie? We just talked to Dr. Peersome, her psychiatrist. She's a little better but still kind of out of it. Yes, the flowers arrived, but the doctor thought that card you sent with the flowers was too… well, too provocative. He's going to allow the flowers to be delivered without the card this afternoon." Rose listened for several minutes shaking her head yes. She then said, "I'll ask, but don't expect anything too soon. Dr. Peersome's beginning some kind of psychotherapeutic therapy later today. I'm to call him later and I'll ask." She said a final OK and flipped her cell phone closed.

Janey asked, "What's up, Miz F-W? That Jamie?"

"Yes. He's very upset, as you'd expect. He wants to see Leslie. I'm to ask Dr. Peersome when he can fly in to see her."

Janey said, "He's been very patient with Leslie. He's got to be worried sick."

Angel bent to scratch her ankle and said, "You know guys, I don't think it's such a good idea to have that big black nurse hangin' around Leslie. He's a chunk and a half. No tellin' what the sight of him will do what with all that fetish business in Leslie's head."

The Great Jack Daniels Caper...

Louis looked down at the gas gauge and announced, "Boys, Lucille needs a fill. She's runnin' on fumes. And I'd like to get some TLC for the lady. It's been a while and I don't want her to get out of sorts."

Jonnie Hogg yelled from the back seat, "TLC? Out of sorts? Lucille's a fuckin' car. Not some bitch on the rag. If someone needs some TLC, it's yours truly, as in I need a brewski."

Louis replied indignantly, "Pig Fat, you gotta be a little more... well... polite... when talking about Lucille... particularly in her presence. She needs her oil changed."

Pig Fat's neck started to redden as often occurred in these situations, and he returned fire, "Lucille's still a fuckin' car, for Chrissake. She ain't no human woman. She ain't goin' to threaten to not cook you dinner and she sure as shit ain't goin' to refuse to put out."

Jamie interrupted the two verbal combatants and yelled, "Gas station ahead on the right!"

Louis slowed down and pulled into the gas station which Jamie had spotted, parking in front of the gas pumps as the bing-bing of the customer alarm sounded. He turned to Jamie and said, "Wow. Looks like we drove into the 1950s. I ain't heard that bing-bing in years."

The gas station had two old-fashioned pumps with frosted-glass tops. The frosted-glass tops were lit and on each one the word SHELL was spelled in large, dark red letters. The building looked new but could easily have been on the set for Mayberry, USA. And sure enough, as Lucille set off the bing-bing of the customer alarm, a goober in uniform walked out of the office adjacent to a two-bay garage. He smiled as he approached and yelled, "Welcome to Herman's Route 66 Shell. Herman at your service."

Louis asked, "What year is it?" and the goober smiled as he admired Lucille from stem to stern and replied, "1958, my man, 1958."

Louis smiled back and said, "Well, my '58 Edsel, Lucille here, needs to get her oil changed and a good fillup."

The goober continued admiring Lucille and said, "V8?"

Louis grinned from ear to ear, "Bingo! 1958 two-door Citation convertible, eight-cylinder E475 engine."

The goober put his hands on his hips and whistled. "Golleeee! It'd be a privilege to service Lucille, but I gotta warn you. We charge an arm and a leg. It's the price for relivin' history."

Louis could hardly contain himself, having run into a kindred spirit, "No problemo, my man. Mind if I stick around and watch?"

"Heck no, I understand. If Lucille here was my automobile, I wouldn't let her out of my sight either."

Jonnie yelled from the back seat, "While the two of you drool over Missy here, is there a place around here where a guy could get himself a tall one?"

The uniformed goober replied without taking his eyes off the Edsel, "Sure is. Try Egan's Rat Hole over there" as he pointed in the general direction of what looked like a large Victorian house across the street. Mr. Colbeck had his grand opening last week. He's open for business."

Louis sat gently running his fingers along Lucille's steering wheel as the rest of the posse jumped out of his pride and joy. The goober pointed to one of the garage bays and yelled, "Pull over to the lift and we can make Lucille happy as a clam."

As the goober directed, Louis drove his precious into the garage for servicing. The rest of the posse wandered across the street and up the front-porch steps of what looked like an unoccupied but very well-kept residence in spite of the large old-fashioned neon sign by the roadside advertising "Eagan's Rat Hole -- fine food and drink." There on the large, ornate double-door entrance was a small, white sign with neat black script which read "Please use rear entrance." Having puzzled over the mysterious sign for several minutes, the posse wandered around the side of the house. As they turned the corner into the back, there before them was a small parking lot filled with cars and behind the parking lot was a long narrow building that looked suspiciously like an old-fashioned motel. Charles Fontaine murmured, "Holy shit, what kind of establishment is this, anyway?"

Jamie smiled and said, "Boys, we just walked from 1958 into the thirties. It's a restored speakeasy. Gotta be. "

Charles added, "And an old motel where the clientele could sleep it off after an all night bender of bathtub gin and rubbing alcohol."

The posse walked past the parked cars to a set of steps that led down to a black steel door. Jamie jumped down the steps and read aloud the sign posted on the door, "Knock 3 times. When the peephole opens, yell Dint sent me." Jamie knocked as instructed and waited. Becoming impatient, he slammed the door three more times with his fist. The peephole finally squeaked opened and he yelled, "Dint sent me!"

The large steel door swung open and there stood an older man with a large, black handlebar mustache. He was dressed in a formal white shirt with a red bowtie and a large white apron. He smiled and said, "Welcome to Egan's Rat Hole!"

Jonnie, Garcia, and Charles followed Jamie into the dark recesses before them. Music blared in the background. Jonnie, his ever-impatient self, yelled, "Hey buddy, we need a beer."

The man yelled over his shoulder as he waved them forward, "Follow me!"

The posse squinted as their eyes adjusted to the darkness. Slowly the interior came into focus. From behind a long oak bar, the man who had greeted them at the steel door, twirled the tips of his fine handlebar mustache and waved them forward to the bar. As the posse settled onto their bar stools, he yelled, "What'll it be, boys?"

Jonnie yelled back over the blaring music, "Some suds! What you got on tap?"

The barkeep yelled back over the music, "On tap... Kinney's Lager. My own brew. Best in the Midwest!"

Jonnie yelled, "Pour four!"

As the barkeep poured four large mugs of the ostensibly best of the Midwest, his own Kinney's Lager, the posse swung around on their bar stools and cased the joint. There were no windows, not even those small, cellar casement windows. The interior walls were wood-paneled. Dim lights with green glass lampshades hung from the ceiling. Off to the right was a dining room about half full of customers. Before them loomed a table covered with a red and white checked table cloth. On the wall behind the table hung a large framed picture of a group of men and a single woman seated about what looked like the table above which the picture hung. The picture was a tinted antique brown and the faces of the men and the one woman difficult to make out in the dim light.

The barkeep spun each of the mugs of cold Kinney's Lager down the bar as if he were dealing cards, each mug spinning down the bar coming to rest before a seated member of the posse. The boys turned to the bar, grabbed their mugs of Kinney's Lager and took long draughts.

Jonnie wiped the foam off his mouth with his sleeve and yelled to the barkeep, "Great suds, great suds!"

Charles slammed his mug down and looked around, "Hey keep, what tune is that?"

The barkeep yelled back, "March of the Hoodlums. It's by Irving Mills and His Hotsy Totsy Gang. They were pretty popular in the late 20s and early 30s. The temporarily immortal Legs Diamond even named his Broadway speak the Hotsy Totsy Club back then. Thought the tune rather appropriate for this establishment."

Charles yelled over Mr. Mills and his Hotsy Totsy Gang, "Exactly what kind of place is this establishment? A restored speakeasy?"

The barkeep walked down his side of the bar until he was opposite the boys. He placed his hands on the bar and, giving an excellent imitation of Jackie Gleason, growled, "Well, technically speaking, boys, in the parlance of the times, this place was no ordinary blind pig. It was what's called a lid club. What you might call a gentlemen's club in the loosest sense of that term."

Jonnie took another long pull on his mug and said, "What the fuck's a blind pig?"

The barkeep continued smiling. "A blind pig establishment is not a whore house with a stable of ugly prostitutes with bad vision. In the parlance of the times, a blind pig was slang for a speakeasy."

Jonnie thought for a moment and then asked, "What the fuck's the difference between a blind pig and a lid club?"

The barkeep twirled the ends of his handlebar mustache yet again and said, "A lid club was a place where a man could not only get his thirst quenched but his ashes hauled, regardless of his visual acuity or the visual acuity of those who hauled said ashes."

Charles smiled, "So that isn't a restored Route 66 motel out back."

The barkeep laughed and managed to say, "I guess you could say the place was a motel, if by motel you mean a place where a men drove up in cars, rented rooms for at least an hour and the rooms came with all the usual amenities, a bed, a bathroom, towels and..." as he broke out in guffaws, managing to say "... a woman."

Jonnie finished off his mug of Kinney's Lager and said, "I get it. Egan's Rat Hole was a combination speakeasy and whorehouse."

A bell rang and the bartender turned, walked to the end of the bar and threw open a small door in the wall behind the bar. He pulled a tray of covered plates from the opening behind the bar, placed the tray on the end of the bar and yelled "Helen! Order up!"

He walked back to where the boys were seated and said, "That's a dumbwaiter. The kitchen's upstairs. This place used to be a high-class lid club. The Egan mob in St. Louis ran the club in the 30s. The bar and dining room were in the basement like many illegal clubs. It was called The Topper back then but the locals referred to the place as Egan's Rat Hole. The stable of whores were called Egan's mice. Local law enforcement raided the place every now and then and arrested a couple of the mice to keep the good citizens happy, but the Egan mob was always tipped they were coming and hid the booze. The officers of the law were not... shall we say... very diligent in their duties during these raids."

He walked to the end of the bar and pulled at a section of shelves built into the wall. The section of wall swung open revealing a large vault door. He pulled the door's handle down swinging the heavy vault door open. "This old bank vault is where the Egan mob stored their booze and cash. We don't use the cylinder lock anymore. I disabled it when I restored the place, for safety reasons, but the Egan mob kept the vault locked when they ran the place. They sold rum and whiskey to the speakeasies in the greater St. Louis area. This is where they kept the good stuff. Excellent Caribbean rum smuggled up the Mississippi from New Orleans and the best bonded whiskey smuggled down from Canada. The good stuff was literally worth its weight in gold. The vault is huge. Had to be to accommodate the stock sold by Egan's Rats. I have it set up as a private dining room"

Jamie, who had remained silent after entering the building, pointed to the picture on the wall and asked, "Keep, who's in the picture... some mobsters?"

The barkeep said, "Listen boys, call me Cole. No need to use my formal title. That picture... mobsters? Well, it's mobsters all right, but not just any mobsters. It's the mobsters." He walked around the bar and stood pointing at the picture. "See that chubby guy sitting at the end of the table..." He turned and pointed at the table behind him, "this very table... that's Scarface himself, Big Al... Capone."

Jonnie jumped off his bar stool and yelled, "You're shittin' me. Al Capone?"

Cole laughed and said, "That's right... Mr. Alphonse Capone."

Jamie slid off his bar stool, walked closer to the picture and stared intently at it. Jonnie yelled above the music, "They musta pulled off something big what with those shit-eatin' grins plastered all over their mugs."

Cole smiled and said, "Correct. They have shit-eatin' grins, as you so poetically put it, because they just closed a deal and everyone in that picture made a huge chunk of money, literally several million bucks in 1935 dollars, and that was real big money back then."

Charles grabbed his half-full mug and walked to the table, plopping down on a chair at the table facing the picture. He took another swig of Kinney's Lager and asked, "What kind of deal?"

Cole took a seat at the table facing Charles. "A deal involving 894 barrels of uncut pre-Prohibition Jack Daniels whiskey. They just pulled off what's called the great Jack Daniels milking caper."

Charles asked, "Why in heaven's name would there be one barrel of Jack Daniels whiskey anyplace, given that Prohibition was in full force, let alone 894 barrels of the stuff?"

Cole replied with his own shit-eating grin decorating his face, "Prohibition law allowed doctors to proscribe whiskey for, quote, medicinal purposes, end quote, so already existing stocks of whiskey were kept for this purpose. It was the medical marijuana of its time, and there were 894 barrels of Jack Daniels kept in a bonded warehouse on Duncan Avenue in St. Louis. State Senator Mike Kinney got his brother Willie appointed as the official gauger for the warehouse. Willie's job as gauger was to check the whiskey to be sure it remained uncut and to supervise the bottling of the whiskey should there be any."

The good Senator comes to his old buddy and fellow Irishman Dint Colbeck, the boss of Egan's Rats, with a proposal to steal the 894 barrels. That guy sittin' next to Capone, that's Dint Colbeck. Dint needed time to sell the barrels after they'd been stolen. Sellin' off 894 barrels was a big job and if his mob just robbed the joint at gunpoint, they'd never have enough time to move all 894 barrels. The problem Dint had was how to boost the whiskey over time and in such a way that no one knew the whiskey was gone. Ol' Dint, a clever old Irish hood, comes up with this scheme to milk the barrels."

Cole stopped his tale of the great Jack Daniels milking caper and asked, "You boys sure you want to hear me blather on?"

Garcia Rosenbloom, who had not uttered one word for hours, said quietly but clearly, "You betcha keemosabe!"

Cole gave his handlebar mustache yet another twist and continued, "Well Dint cases the neighborhood. There's an abandoned building about 150 feet from the bonded warehouse. Drawing on his knowledge as a former plumber, he develops this plan to use a series of metric pumps to siphon off the whiskey and pipe the stuff into barrels in the abandoned building. Then he'd have the empty barrels filled with water and resealed. Since it was Willie Kinney who as gauger checked the content of the barrels, no one would find out that the whiskey was gone, at least not until it was all gone and Willie had quit the job. It was a great plan but a very expensive one. Like any good American entrepreneur, Dint sought investors. He needed about a million bucks in today's dollars to rent the abandoned building, purchase the equipment, hire the men, surreptitiously lay the pipe, get the trucks necessary to transport and distribute the barrels of stolen whiskey and pay off all those who had to look the other way."

Cole pointed back at the picture. "That squirrely lookin' guy standin' next to Capone, that's Jake "Greasy Thumb" Guzik. He's the business manager for Capone's Outfit. Somehow Guzik hears about this caper and goes to Capone recommending that the Outfit invest in it. Dint Colbeck promises a $3000 return on each $1000 invested. Capone OKs the deal and invests $110,000 in return for one hundred barrels of the whiskey which he plans to water down, bottle and sell to his high-end customers in Chicago for a fortune."

Charles interrupted Cole and asked, "Not to cast aspersions on your tale, but how did you get all this information?"

Cole answered Charles without missing a beat. "My name's Michael Kinney Colbeck. Cole for short. Dint Colbeck was something like a great uncle three times removed. At least that's what I think his relationship to me was. I'm named after Michael Kinney. He was the longest serving senator in the history of Missouri's state senate. Hell, he served one term while in jail. I came across Dint Colbeck's notebook when I was cleaning out the vault. Dint had a secret hideaway in the back of the vault where he kept all his documents. That's where I found the negative for that picture."

Jamie asked, "What was the take? How much did they make on this deal?"

Cole thought for a moment and said, "Well, the barrels of uncut

Jack Daniels sold for approximately $3,400 each. That's in 1935 dollars. I figured out what that is, in today's dollars… $42,000 a barrel. Who knows how much Capone made when he watered down the whiskey and bottled his 100 barrels? You can bet it was a lot more than $42,000 a barrel."

Jamie whistled and walked closer to the picture. "Who's that sitting at the end of the table with that woman sitting on his lap?"

Cole got up and walked over to where Jamie stood. "According to the envelope where I found the negative, that's someone named Kraut. I think he was one of Capone's men. The woman on his lap is one of Egan's mice. She's a nice-lookin' gal."

Jamie walked even closer to the picture and ran his finger around the image of Kraut and the nice-looking Egan's mouse on his lap. "Damn, that Kraut character looks an awful lot like my Grandpa Gus and that mouse… hell, that's Grandma Gert."

Cole put his hands on his hips and whispered, "You sure? Did your grandpa work for Capone?"

Jamie stood silently for a moment and then said, "My grandpa was called Kraut. When he immigrated to the States from Germany, he settled in Chicago and got a job driving a truck for what he called some outfit. He was known as Kraut, as he told it, because he spoke with a heavy German accent. According to him, he worked his way up to become the supervisor for a large trucking operation. I've got an album of old pictures my dad gave me. I swear to God that's Grandpa Gus and Grandma Gert. This is a little shocking… my grandpa was a mobster and my grandma, a whore… a bit fucking disconcerting to say the least."

Cole put his arm over Jamie's shoulders to comfort him. "Look, every family's closet is full of skeletons. Look at me. I'm named after one of the most corrupt state senators in the history of Missouri and my ancestors ran Egan's Rats, a mob many historians consider the most vicious in the history of American crime. You know, it was members of Egan's Rats who did Capone's dirty work. They machine-gunned Big Al's competition. You may have heard of it…

the St. Valentine's Day massacre. Look at it this way… these mobsters were rugged individuals who established businesses in a highly-competitive, high-risk market with products and services that the public desperately wanted and paid premium prices for. In a twisted sort of way, they were the rugged individualists and entrepreneurs of their time, working in a market created by an overreaching government. The risks were high but the rewards were commensurate with that risk. Ironically, bootleggers are a sort of left-handed tribute to our free enterprise system."

Jamie sat on a chair facing the picture. "Yeah, but my grandpa was a mobster and my grandma was a whore."

Jamie's cell phone buzzed the song Get Your Kicks on Route 66. He flipped it open and listened. He yelled "What" several times and "You're shittin' me" at least twice into his cell phone before flipping it closed. He turned to Cole and said with great urgency, "Listen, I don't have time to explain right now, but we gotta hide from some Mexican bad guys. We haven't done anything illegal. We were just at the wrong place at the wrong time." He yelled over to the rest of the posse, "Our friendly Mexican bandito and two of his amigos are on the way."

Cole smiled, "No problem, boys. It'll be like old times. The ghosts of Egan's Rats will be proud." He escorted the boys over to the still open vault, reached in and tuned on the overhead lights. He yelled over his shoulder, "In here. I'll get you after they've left." The boys ran into the vault and Cole closed the door behind them.

The haunting past…

As the great vault door closed behind them, Jonnie yelled, "What the fuck just happened?"

The posse grabbed chairs around the large table in the center of the vault and sat. Jamie looked at each of the members of the posse and then said, "Louis called me from across the street at that service station. He was in the service bay and Lucille was up on the lift when this black Suburban pulls up and out jumps what looks like our own Pedro, his buddy Garcia and a third amigo. Louis tells the station attendant if they ask about the red Edsel convertible to tell them that we got gas and drove off towards St. Louis. I guess the banditos decided to have lunch before continuing their pursuit."

Charles smiled and said, "How ironically appropriate for members of a Mexican drug cartel to dine at a restored speakeasy!"

Jonnie quickly corrected him, "Lid club. That barkeep said it wasn't a speakeasy but a lid club because of the… what'd he call the whores?… Egan's mice. Yeah, Egan's mice."

Jamie put his elbows on the table and held his head between his hands, "And my Grandma Gert was one of Egan's mice. A god damn whore… knowing this changes everything. Turns out I didn't know my grandma at all, just like I didn't know Grandpa Gus. Grandpa Gus wasn't an American success story. He was a bootlegging criminal… a mobster in Capone's Outfit. This changes everything. Changes all my memories. Changes who I am." Jamie raised his head and asked, to no one in particular, "Do you think that my dad knew?"

Charles answered, "What difference does it make. Your grandma is still your grandma, your grandpa is still your grandpa and your dad is still your dad."

Jamie shook his head slowly from side to side, "But I thought they were somebody else. I tried to do as Grandpa Gus said… after all, to me he was the great American success story… at least I thought he was… and my dad… all those times Grandpa told me to work hard… to obey the law but be sharp about it. It all turns out to be a lie. And here I am sitting in a bootlegging vault to prove it. Hell, Grandpa Gus probably worked right where we're sitting, moving those stolen barrels of Jack Daniels to his truck."

Jonnie said, "Look, none of this shit changes the past. It's already happened and you can't change what's already happened."

Jamie shot back, "Oh yes you can! Knowing this changes everything… everything. My memories weren't what I thought they were. I can't go backwards and forget what I just learned. Now I wonder about what my dad knew… and my mom… she died when I was a baby… who the hell was she? I was raised by Grandma Gert… a god damn whore. I was raised by a god damn whore who used to walk across that parking lot out back to that building with a john and put out for money. I don't like the pictures that are coming in my head."

The posse fell silent as long minutes passed. Finally Joobie said in almost a whisper, "What do you think those banditos are going to do if they find us?"

Jonnie replied, "Well I don't think they're going to shake our hands and wish us a pleasant fuckin' day! Look, we know guys like this kill people and we know they're pissed at us. I don't want to find out what they might do. You can bet they're armed to the teeth, and we're not, as if I give a shit!"

Charles reached across the table and grabbed Jamie's arm, "Jamie, come out of it. If we don't do something, your trip down memory lane's going to be a short, violent one and it's not going to end well."

Jamie looked up. His eyes were red with a distant and quite unpleasant look. He was preoccupied with the images in his head that he did not like.

Jonnie interrupted, "Look, this ain't some problem for an Einstein. We need a couple of 12-guage shotguns and pistolas all around. And we need to ditch that fuckin' red Edsel."

Jamie snapped out of his not-so-pleasant reveries and conjectures. "Jonnie's right. I can rent something. Hell, I can buy something."

Jonnie pounded the table, "My old man lives south of Oklahoma City, a place called Pauls Valley. It's about 50 miles south of 40 off 35. He's got a fuckin' arsenal."

Jamie's eyes became fixed, "I'll rent or buy something in St. Louis. Louis will have to store Lucille. Once we're out of Lucille, we'll be hard to spot. Then we can drive to Jonnie's dad's."

The vault door swung open and the barkeep stood smiling before them, hands on hips. "Well, boys, those bad guys you don't want to see are long gone. Saw them drive off."

Jamie asked, "Did they say anything?"

The barkeep smiled and said, "They sure did, in Spanish. By the time they left, they were slurring in Spanish too. I set them up with mugs of Kinney's lager followed by tequila shooters. The big, mean-lookin' fella with the black mustache, the two others called him Garcia, asked for a luncheon menu but after three lagers and tequila shooters, one on the house, they pretty much forgot about eating and just drank. They were arguing like hell when they staggered out of here. The young one, they called him Pedro, seemed to be in charge. He was really pissed about something. I gave them a good half hour before I opened the vault. They should be long gone by now. Why those guys after you, anyway?"

Jamie replied, "Cole, we're not sure. It has something to do with a land deal and not drugs, at least not directly."

The barkeep laughed, "It's like déjà vu all over again. Dint Colbeck rented an abandoned warehouse to pull off that Jack Daniels milking caper and these guys want some land and they sure don't plan to grow corn on it. It's all about the money!"

Jamie's cell phone buzzed "Get Your Kicks on Route 66." He flipped the phone open and turned away from the barkeep. "What! Are you shittin' me?" He listened intently and then said, "Get your ass over here. We've got a lot to do."

The barkeep asked, "What's up?"

Jamie turned and smiled from ear to ear. "You're not going to believe this. Those banditos rammed that Suburban into a pole just down the road. Louis heard the crash and ran out to the road, saw the Suburban roll onto its roof. Looks like one of the banditos got trapped behind the steering wheel. Then the short, skinny bandito and the big one crawled out of the wreck. The big one pulled a gun, fired several shots into the overturned Suburban and the two took off on foot."

Bad news from the belly of the beast...

Rose sat on the bed in her motel room hugging her cell phone to her ear with her shoulder. Janey sat in the room's desk chair facing Rose while Angel sat on a stuffed chair also facing Rose. Angel

— 191 —

said, "That hunk at the counter says there's a real good seafood place not far from here." Rose answered, "Sounds good to me…" then she raised her hand to the girls and spoke sideways into her cell phone, "Hello? Dr. Peersome?… This is Rose Fazzano-Wright. I'm calling to find out how your session with Leslie went." There was a long pause. Then Rose shouted "What!" After another long pause, she grabbed the cell phone with her right hand and shouted, "Are you nuts? What with her… what'd you call it… that racial fetish business… you had that black nurse deliver the flowers to her?" She paused listening intently and then yelled, "This isn't a civil rights issue." She listened again and screamed, "I don't give a damn about your being an equal opportunity employer. Are you out of your mind? What did you expect her to do?… Tomorrow at 10:00?… Fine, tomorrow at 10:00!" She slammed the cell phone closed and threw it into her open purse.

Janey said, "Doesn't sound good."

Rose said, "It is distinctly not! I need a drink."

Angel said, "Sounds like Dr. Peersome had that Javarious nurse deliver the flowers from Jamie. He's a chunk and a half. I'd love to see him do the Jamal."

Rose, not quite understanding Angel's remark, said, "The Jamal?"

Janey interrupted and said, "What exactly happened?"

Rose's face was beet red with anger, "That idiot Peersome had that male nurse, that black guy, Javarious, deliver the flowers from Jamie without the card. What'd Leslie think? That the flowers were from the nurse!"

Angel scrunched forward on her chair and said, "What'd Leslie do?"

Rose reached into her purse and pulled out a tissue and started frantically wrapping and unwrapping the tissue about her fingers, intently watching her fingers as they twirled the tissue. "This is so embarrassing. She got on her knees and offered herself to him. And started playing with herself… you know."

Angel said, "Searching for squirrels?"

Rose replied without looking up, "Yes, that searching for squirrels business… apparently frantically."

Janey said, "What'd that asshole Peersome expect? What with her condition and all."

Rose, still concentrating on her fingers as they twirled the tissue about, said, "He told me the institute was an equal opportunity employer and never considered race when making assignments of personnel. It's their policy. Only in extreme cases do they deviate from that policy and he assured me that Javarious was gay. As if that makes it OK."

Angel asked rather innocently, "They have a policy for assigning deviats to jobs? That sounds pretty silly. I thought they were treating deviats."

Janey added, "Well, there doesn't seem to be much difference between the deviate patients and the staff at that slimy place. Let's get the hell out of here. I need that drink too."

Goodness has perverse consequences…

Rose, Janey and Angel sat at their table sipping glasses of the house white wine. It was their second glass and they had yet to order their meals. Angel looked around the dining room and said, "This is a pretty nice place."

Rose looked up from her glass of wine and froze. She motioned with her head and whispered, "That guy over there, the one dressed in a suit and tie, the guy on the cell phone. I recognize him. I saw him leaving the institute the day you two arrived. I can't quite place him but he looks familiar."

Angel turned and looked directly at him. Janey kicked Angel under the table and whispered, rather loudly, "Don't be so obvious."

Angel yelled "Ouch! That hurts!" She leaned over and rubbed her shin and said, "I was only lookin' for cryin' out loud."

The three ordered their meals. Rose and Angel also ordered a third glass of wine. Janey volunteered to be the designated driver and ordered a club soda. Rose nibbled at her meal but obviously wasn't very hungry. She said, "All of this business, you now, the squirrels thing. And well, you know, I was taught never to talk about it. It's very embarrassing. I guess I'm pretty old-fashioned. After all, most of that stuff is a sin in the Catholic church."

Angel's appetite was unaffected by the events of the day and she dug into her meal with great gusto. While chewing on a bit of salmon, she said, "Miz F-W, it's not all that embarrassing. Besides, it feels real good."

Rose pushed her fork about her plate and said without looking up, "One is supposed to control desire. Intimacy is a gift from God and should not be wasted in casual relationships. It's not just about feeling good. It's about being good."

Angel bit into another piece of salmon, chewed and thought for a minute, then observed, "How are you to use this gift if you never open the package? Seems like until you unwrap the gift and practice using it, you can't really be very thankful for having it or very good at using it. And the suspense would kill me if I had this package and I was told it was a great gift and all I could do was look at the wrapping for a bunch of years before I could open the damn thing."

Rose said, "Angel, it's not supposed to be easy. It's your life and you have to work at it. You're supposed to discover the gift and practice, as you put it, with your life's partner."

Janey asked, "Doesn't all this waiting cause lots of problems. Look at poor Leslie. She waited too long and she now wants some fake Zulu warrior to open her package and she's practicing all the time and for all the wrong reasons. It's like the wrong person pulled the ribbon off the wrapping around that package of hers."

Rose put her fork down, "I don't know all the answers and God knows I'm no expert on the subject, but for some unfathomable reason Leslie loves Jamie, at least she used to, and somehow that's gotten lost."

Janey added, "And that goofy Dr. Peersome, what with his constant pencil sharpening ... "

Angel interrupted, "And always tryin' to get a peek. What's with those little chairs, anyway? He's set up his office so that he can look at a person's package. What a perv! And he keeps giving poor Leslie all those drugs. It's no wonder she doesn't know up from down."

Janey continued, "Maybe we should get Leslie out of here."

Rose finished off her third glass of wine and said, "I'll call Jeremiah when we get back to the motel. It's only right for him to know what's going on, although he's never one for making a decision."

Angel pushed her now clean plate back and said, "Maybe you should call Jamie too. He's the one's supposed to open Leslie's package."

Time travel, Route 66 style...

A dented 1999 Dodge Ram pulled up to Herman's Route 66 Shell Service Station, made a U-turn and parked in front of the gas pumps, now facing west, the direction from which it had come. Jamie lowered the front-passenger side window and yelled, "Hey, you assholes, it's us."

Herman walked out of the station's office, followed by Jonnie, Charles and Garcia. Herman yelled to Jamie as he approached, "Ram 3500 Quad Four-by-Four, right... '99?"

Louis yelled from the driver's side, "Co-rect amundo, my man! Fill'er up!"

As Herman filled 'er up, Jonnie, Charles and Garcia piled into the back seat. Jonnie asked Jamie, "Where'd you get this baby?"

Jamie yelled over his shoulder, "St. Louis. Found 'er on Craig's List. Cash on the barrel head."

Louis added, "She's got one-hundred-eighty-eight thousand on her but she's in great shape in spite of the bumps and bruises. Great shape mechanically. We left Lucille in storage where she'll be safe and sound."

Jamie leaned out the cab to pay Herman for the gas and said, "If anybody asks, you never saw us in this Dodge Ram, in fact, you never saw us again," as he handed Herman three one-hundred dollar bills." Then the posse took off down Route 66.

Jamie yelled over his shoulder, "We're headed for the Munger Moss Motel, about two hours and change. Relax and enjoy. There's a couple 'a cases of Bud on the floor. Pop one for me." Many popping sounds erupted from the back seat as several cans of Bud found their way to the front seat and the Dodge Ram meandered its way to Route 44 and eventually the Munger Moss Motel.

"There it is. That big, red neon sign with yellow letters... Munger Moss. That sign's a damn landmark." Jamie pointed at the brightly lit neon sign with the enthusiasm of a kid spotting an ice cream stand.

As Jamie eased the Dodge Ram into the parking lot before the motel's office, Jonnie yelled from the back seat, "What's got them panties of yours in that big ol' wad, Stuntman? It's a god damn motel."

As the Dodge Ram glided to a stop, Jamie said, "Oh no it's not. It's a portal into the past. We're about to walk back into the sixties. The Munger Moss Motel is one of a kind. My dad stayed here many times as he traveled his distribution route." His brow furrowed, "Hell, my Grandpa Gus, my fucking gangster grandpa, probably stayed here. Maybe with my whore grandma. Anyways, I stayed here with my dad a couple of times during summer breaks when I rode with him as he serviced his customers. After he sold the business, we stayed here on our last trip down the Mother Road. He was a dedicated roadologist. Loved driving Route 66. We didn't get far that last time. He started to feel ill and we had to drive back to Chicago. I did the driving. He died two weeks to the day we checked out. Heart attack."

The posse scrambled out of the pickup and stretched. Charles walked towards the office and yelled back to the rest of the posse, "Guys, you are not going to believe this," as he waved for the rest of the posse to join him. He pointed along one of the motel's buildings and there, parked in a long row, was a line of Harleys. "I'll bet that Norwegian nookie is holed up in one of those rooms. Did we step in shit again or what?"

Remembering America's first no-tell motel...

Jamie held up a key and said, "Gentlemen, you don't see real motel keys like this anymore, except of course at the Munger Moss Motel." He carefully pushed the key into the keyhole and opened the door to their motel room. There before them were two double beds, each covered with a bright pink satin bed spread.

The posse entered the room and stood before the two beds. Garcia whistled and said, "Histito lacepito ooklisito ikelito a-ito horewito ousehito." ("This place looks like a whore house.") Charles pointed to the light on the table between the beds which had a bright red lamp shade, "There's even a red light. Subtle."

Jamie sneered back, "Fucking right on, Joobie, fucking right on. This is the Coral Court Room. Commemorates the first no-tell motel in the U-S of A, the Coral Court! Had a very bad rep, a place where guys went with hookers and girlfriends to get laid on the sly. Hell, I'll bet my gangster grandpa took my whore grandma to the Coral Court for oldtime's sake."

Jonnie Hogg asked, "Did yer dad ever stay there?"

Jamie sneered back, "What the fuck do you think? It was probably a family tradition, the one I didn't know about."

Jamie pointed to a series of nine pictures neatly hung on the wall above the two beds. "There's pictures of the god damn place. It was located just west of St. Louis. Was torn down years ago."

Charles walked between the beds to get a closer look at pictures over the bed. "Interesting architecture. Has a kind of Art Deco feel to it. Looks to me like there's two attached units separated by two attached garages."

Louis took out a large comb and started running it through his hair as he observed, "Hell, a guy could drive in with his rent-a-honey, park his car in the garage and no one would know he was there bangin' his rent-a-bimbo."

Jamie yelled "Like my fucking grandma! Ain't this fucking cute? We're staying in a room co-mem-or-a-ting another family whore house."

Charles put his arm over Jamie's shoulder and said, "Look Stuntman, maybe we should stay in another room? This one's bad karma."

Jamie shrugged off Charles' arm and said, "Got no choice. This was the only room left. Let's get something to eat. There's a bowling alley across the street. Makes great pizza."

Louis was the first out the door, "Hot pie, suds, and bowling balls. Hell, I could be in Brooklyn!"

A dead bandito and the hootersitos...

The posse pretty much staggered across the street and into the bowling alley/pizza parlor. Seated at the far side of the room were the Norwegian Route 66 babes. Mette Anders, their titular leader, yelled to Charles, "Hey, sugar lover!" and waved. Her three equally titular companions giggled. Jamie ordered four large hot pies and a couple of pitchers of beer and the posse wandered over to the Norwegian babes. Charles smiled and said, "Mind if we join you?"

Mette smiled back, "Sure enough, sugar lover." The posse pulled up chairs and sat. Mette drained her glass of beer. "Have you guys turned on that funky TV in your room? You only get three stations. I haven't seen TVs like that except on old TV re-runs. Anyways, it's all over the news. Some guy got murdered outside St. Louis on Route 66. Just west of where we gassed up, Herman's Shell Station. Seems like the driver hit a pole with this huge SUV and turned the thing over. The driver got trapped behind the steering wheel. Two guys crawled out of the wreck and one of them shot the guy trapped behind the wheel. Put four bullets in his head. He's deader than two doornails. Then the shooter and the other guy took off on foot and they haven't caught them."

Garcia drained his recently poured mug of beer and said, "Hatito hootersitos... sito terafito suito." ("That shooter is after us.")

Mette pointed at Garcia, "Did that wetback say something about our hooters? What language is that?"

Charles laughed, "Who? Garcia? He's speaking in tongues. It's a religious thing. He's actually from an ancient Aztec clan. He's a shaman. 'Hootersito' means 'the beauty bestowed on woman by great mother earth' in the dialect he speaks. Roughly translated, what he said means 'The great Mother Earth has blessed you… plural you meaning you and your three companions… with great beauty.'"

Garcia smiled and slowly shook his head in agreement with Charles' explanation while not having paid any attention to what Charles had actually said.

Mette smiled, "Why thank you, Mr. Garcia. Look guys, we got to get a very early start tomorrow, and we need our beauty rest to maintain our, what was it your shaman friend called it… our hootersitos." Mette looked at Charles and passed him a folded piece of paper. "Here's my email address, sugar lover. Send me a email sometime and I might reply. Maybe we'll see you guys down the road."

And the Norwegian foursome left.

Charles mused to himself, but most likely speaking for the entire posse, "I like to see them walk away but I hate to see them leave."

The past is never dead. Hell, it's not even passed…

The posse settled into the Coral Court room after their meal of pizza and beer at the bowling alley across the street.

Charles was spread out on one of the double beds reading from the used paperback he'd picked up in Chicago. He yelled to Jonnie, who was seated on the floor next to the beer, "Toss me a Bud!"

Jonnie did so and asked, "What you readin'?"

"It's that paperback by Big Bertha, 'Stuff Your Momma Wouldn't Tell You about Route 66.' She has a whole chapter on the Coral Court Motel, titled 'Life at America's First No-tell Motel.' Claims she made a damn good living there providing what she calls a discrete personal service." Charles flipped to the paperback's title page. "Musta been published before the place was torn down." He read some more and said, "She writes about this case involving the Coral Court, this kidnapping, the Bobby Greenlease case. Happened in 1935. Apparently one of the kidnappers stayed at the Coral Court with a couple of whores, this guy named Carl Austin Hall. He and his girlfriend, a Bonnie Heady, kidnap this kid, Bobby Greenlease, whose old man owned a bunch of Cadillac franchises from Texas to North Dakota. He was a very rich son-of-a-bitch. Anyways, according to Big Bertha, right after they kidnap the kid, he was only six, Carl Austin Hall murders him. Later says he just wanted to dispose of the evidence. It wasn't personal."

Jonnie interrupted Charles' telling of the tale, "Well I guess it was pretty fuckin' personal for that kid and his family."

Charles read some more and said, "You're not going to believe this. After Heady and Hall kill the kid, they drive to a bar and drink themselves silly before they send the ransom note. Apparently they were alkies and spent most of their conscious hours drinking whiskey, even when kidnapping and killing. I believe that drinking copious amount of whiskey while on the job is not good professional business practice for killer kidnappers."

Louis waved to Jonnie who tossed him a Bud which Louis deftly caught and popped open as he asked, "How much ransom the kidnappers ask for?"

Charles scanned the chapter and said "Six hundred grand, that's what, over six million today… some payoff. Hold it, hold it. Big Bertha says they sent the ransom note by mail and misaddressed the envelope." Charles read some more, "But the ransom note got delivered to the right place anyway, which Hall and Heady didn't know."

Jonnie started to guffaw but managed to blurt out, "Assholes!"

Charles interrupted him, "You're not going to believe this. They send a second note to the right address which instructs the Greenleases on where to drop off of the ransom. Hold it… Hold it… Those two assholes decided on how much to demand by weight. Big Bertha says they figured that they could carry about eighty-five pounds of money, which in tens and twenties is about six hundred thousand. They calculate that a million bucks in cash weighs too much. Can you beat that? Sounds like that idiot-savant stuff. And guess who helps the Greenleases put together the ransom money?

Arthur Eisenhower, President Eisenhower's brother. Of course, this was way before Ike was president."

Charles read some more and chuckled, "Listen, they have to send three more notes, at least I think it's three, on how to deliver the ransom money. The first couple of instructions didn't quite work out. I quote the fifth ransom note as quoted by her Miss Nibs: 'Go back to J-t (Viona Road)-- Go west to first road heading south across from lum reek farm sign. Drive in 75 feet leave bag on right side of road. Drive home, will call and tell you where you can pick up the boy.' The Greenleases tried to follow the instructions, but because it was dark and raining and there were several unmarked farm roads, they had difficulty finding the right location. Well, they drop a duffel bag with the six hundred thousand seventy-five feet up a farm road but apparently the wrong one. Hall calls them and says he can't find the money."

Jonnie crushes his empty beer can and pops another. "Sounds like the assholes that wrote those blackmail notes the Prof got at the wedding. What is it with these assholes?"

Charles read some more and then said, "After, I don't know, four maybe five more attempts to arrange the drop-off of the ransom, after a week of notes and phone calls, Heady and Hall finally get their hands on that duffel bag of cash. The drunken bastards, seven days after the kidnapping and murder."

Garcia smiled, "Ni-ito hiskeywito, tupidsito!" ("In whiskey, stupidity!")

Jamie had remained silent for some time but was obviously following Charles' telling of the tale of the whiskey-soaked kidnappers, "What's all that got to do with the two whores and the Coral Court?"

Charles read some more, then looked up. "Seems that when the dynamic duo returned to their apartment, ol' Bonnie Heady, who was now drunk out of her mind, starts giving Hall a hard time about their shoddy surroundings. So Hall cold cocks her and takes off with that eighty-five-pound duffel bag full of tens and twenties. He hires a cab driver to drive him around to a bunch of bars and the drunker he gets the more generous he gets."

Jamie was becoming impatient, "How do those whores figure in all of this?"

Charles read some more. "Well, it appears that Hall gets the taxi driver to round up a couple of whores and drop the three of them off at the Coral Court. The taxi driver eventually drops a dime on Hall and a couple of cops arrest him and take possession of the eighty-five-pound duffel bag of tens and twenties. The whole plot unravels. Hall gives up his sweetie, who is still drunker than a skunk back at the shoddy ranch, and his sweetie describes how her paramour murdered the boy."

Jamie asked, "What about those god damn whores?"

Charles looked up. "Turns out one of the whores testified against Hall. She said that Hall was so drunk that nothin' happened at the Coral Court. The jury found both of Hall and Heady guilty of capital kidnapping. They were executed in the gas chamber eighty-one days after they committed the crime."

Jonnie looked up with disgust, "Today it'd take eighty-one years to execute the fuckin' bastards. We've turned into a bunch of pussies."

Charles smiled, "And, again according to Big Bertha, when Carl Hall and Bonnie Heady were strapped into the gas chamber side by side, gas seeping into the chamber, Bonnie says, 'Are you doing all right, honey?' and Carl says, 'Yes, mama'."

Jonnie finished off his beer and said with great disgust, "Ain't that fuckin' cute!"

Charles read some more. "And guess what? When those two cops that arrested Hall and Heady turn in that duffel bag, it only weighed forty-two and a half pounds. J. Edgar Hoover spent fifteen years trying to find out who took those tens and twenties, all sixteen-thousand-nine-hundred and seventy-one of them. The FBI knew the serial numbers and eventually found one hundred and fifteen of those bills, which means, roughly speaking, sixteen-thousand-eight-hundred and fifty of them are still out there some place, maybe hidden where the real Coral Court was." Charles tossed the paperback onto the night table between the two double beds

Jamie threw his empty beer can at the wastepaper basket, banking it off the wall and into the basket, yelling, "And he hits for three. Charles, that's sixteen-thousand-eight-hundred and fifty-six still out there. J. Edgar's boys found seven and two-thirds bills a year. Not very efficient. Some things haven't changed. We still got fuckin' stupid criminals and we still pretty much catch them, but we don't have the guts to execute them. Jonnie's right. We're a bunch of pussies today. Today some whining asshole would be defending those two killers saying it was a disease, alcoholism, that caused the crime and society is responsible for not helping them. What about that kid. It's like nobody's responsible for what they do, except of course for the rest of us. It's like murdering that kid Bobby Greenlease was an act of nature that the rest of us could have prevented. What fucking pussies!"

Charles yelled down to Jonnie, "You want the bed tonight?"

Jonnie said, "Naw. I'd rather sleep on the floor like I always do. Beds are too soft." He held up a sleeping bag and said, "This'll do just fine. Just throw me a pillow."

Wednesday, July 9

A slimy plan for shock therapy…

D r. Peersome looked down from his great steel desk at Rose, Angel and Janey. Unlike all their previous meetings, he did not begin his pencil-sharpening ritual, but instead looked down at his audience and gently shook his head from side to side. He said, in an almost inaudible voice, "I fear that yesterday's incident with the flowers has caused Leslie to suffer a major setback. I tried to calm her down and begin the CS psychotherapy after the incident, but she was totally unresponsive."

Rose began sniffling and yelled, "It's all your fault. What did you think would happen when her racial fetish thing kicked in when that Javarious nurse delivered those flowers? She didn't know they were from Jamie!"

Dr. Peersome grabbed a very short pencil from the jar of already-sharpened pencils and placed it into the pencil sharpener, pressing down on the eraser until the pencil disappeared into the whirring pencil sharpener. Without looking up, he said, in a voice barely audible above the whirring pencil sharpener, "Rose… Rose… that's water under the bridge. It's over and done with. We have a new situation that we have to deal with."

Rose dabbed her eyes with a tissue she'd pulled from her purse and said, "Well what should we do now? She's apparently getting worse… a lot worse."

Dr. Peersome raised the pencil sharpener, turned it over and shook it until the pencil, now a mere nub, fell onto his desk. He picked up the pencil nub, inspected it carefully and then said, "We need a new radical approach, something to shock her, something to reset her emotionally. I think that a bit of psychodrama would do the trick very nicely."

Janey interrupted him, "Like re-enacting that fake Zulu dance ritual with Jamal?"

Dr. Peersome smiled and poked the pencil nub at Janey as he spoke, "Exactly, young lady... exactly! Can I count on the three of you to make the necessary arrangements to get the participants in the original ritual to gather here for the reenactment?"

Angel smiled and yelled, "Yup! I'm sure that the rest of the Seven Damsels in Distress will join us and do whatever is necessary to help a fallen sister. And Jamal will do whatever we pay him for."

Angel added, "He might even do it for free. I know he feels very bad about what happened."

Friday, July 11

The ghost of Captain Ahab, once removed...

Charles Fontaine stood a bit unsteadily on the bank of the lake looking down at the rest of the barely visible posse now chest-deep in the lake's muddy water. It was early in the morning and the sun had yet to rise, but, with the courage provided by their present state of sobriety or lack thereof, the rest of the posse had jumped into the muddy lake in the reflected light of a full moon as if they were jumping into a motel pool for a midnight swim.

Unlike said rest of the posse, the more cautious Charlie-O did not. He was dressed in the outdoor sartorial splendor that only L. L. Bean could provide with his ankle-high hiking boots, calf-high yellow socks, neatly pressed khaki cargo shorts and matching khaki shirt of many mysterious pockets. In his left hand he held an open bottle of tequila and in his right, his own personal caballito. He yelled down at his much damper compadres, "This is fucking noodling? Back at that place where we stopped yesterday... Bob's Pig Shop... I asked if it was some kind of culinary contest, you know, one of those Southern cooking festivals and you said yes. Now you want me to jump into a fucking lake in the fucking dark and wrestle some humongous cat fish with my bare hands. Are you out of your fucking mind?" Unlike his lesser-educated and much-damper compadres, the erudite, Harvard-educated Bostonian always pronounced the full i-n-g to all words so ending with a clipped Bostonian accent no matter how inebriated, making his use of the vernacular seem more educated and, well, somewhat less vernacular.

Jonnie Hogg looked up at the better-educated Charlie-O and yelled, "Get yer ass down here. It is a fuckin' Southern culinary festival, but first you gotta catch what yer culi-natin' and that, my asshole friend, is a catfish… a big ol' flathead. First you catch, then you cook and then you eat."

From their much damper environs, the rest of the posse started chanting "Noo-dal dick! Noo-dal dick! Noo-dal dick!" The adamant Charlie-O stood his ground and slammed another caballito of tequila. "No fucking way!"

Undeterred by Charlie-O's lack of enthusiasm to participate, Jonnie Hogg yelled, "Well, get that flashlight back at camp and give us some light down here!" Charlie-O disappeared into the mist.

Garcia smiled like a cat of the Cheshire variety, Louis Fazzano, carefully keeping his elbows above water, continued to comb his hair with a large black comb and Jamie asked, "What do we do now?"

Jonnie pointed to the shoreline, "There's holes in that there bank. My daddy and me noodled this place fer years. Kep it a secret. The way it works is I poke my hand into one of them holes and wiggle my fingers like they're wet noodles. With any luck, a big ol' flathead's in there guardin' his eggs. He sees my wigglin' fingers and attacks. I ram my hand down his throat and out his gills and pull him free. Then y'all jump the bastard and throw him on shore."

Jamie looked at Jonnie and then at the river bank and asked, "What if it isn't a catfish hiding in there?"

Jonnie replied, "What do I look like, an idiot? I take precautions. I feel the sides of the hole and if it feels slimy, I get the hell out. Could be a beaver or muskrat den and those fuckers bite. Could even be a snapper or a no shoulders."

Jamie interrupted him, "A no shoulders?"

Jonnie continued, "Yeah, a no shoulders, a water moccasin, and they bite worse. Any ways, regardless, I pull my hand the hell out of there pronto. If it's sandy, nine times out of ten, it's a big ol' cat wigglin' over them eggs of hisin and spreadin' bottom sand around the hole."

Unconvinced of the efficacy of the aforementioned safety precaution, Jamie asked somewhat skeptically, "Nine out of ten?"

Jonnie smiled confidently and said, "Yup, and them's damn good odds for a noodler."

By now, Charlie-O had worked his way back to the shoreline and was shining a huge flashlight down at them. Jonnie pushed his way to the lake's bank and yelled behind him, "Get yer asses behind me… get ready to pounce!"

Garcia yelled "Ewito howito re-a-ito bouta-ito otito atchwito ouyito iedito alutesito ouyito!" (We who are about to watch you die salute you!)

Jonnie ducked his head under water. There was some thrashing about and then his head bobbed up and he spit out some water and yelled, "I heard the damn thing growl. There's a big 'un down there. Get ready!" and he ducked back under the water. After some furious thrashing of the water, Jonnie appeared on the surface with a huge catfish stuck to his arm. The huge catfish thrashed about furiously pulling Jonnie about the muddy water. He yelled, "Grab the bastard you assholes. Throw the motherfucker on shore."

At first stunned by the thrashing muddy water and the sudden appearance of Jonnie with a huge catfish attached to his arm, the posse stood watching as the big fish pulled Jonnie back under water causing them to wonder exactly who had caught whom as Jonnie again disappeared beneath the surface of the muddy water. He reappeared and yelled, "He's drownin' me." This last scream brought the boys to action and they attacked. As Jonnie bobbed to the surface again, the three virgin noodlers grabbed the huge catfish. Jonnie screamed as he yanked his arm from the monster's mouth. The now not-so-virgin noodlers strained to throw the monster onto the shore where it flopped about and skidded into the slower-moving

Charlie-O, toppling him forward and into the muddy lake head first.

Charlie-O's scream ceased as he disappeared beneath the surface of the muddy water. The posse hooted and howled with delight as Charlie-O reappeared, somewhat damper, screaming "fucking assholes" many times at a furious rate, carefully pronouncing his i-n-gs each time. When he regained what little equilibrium he possessed, having pretty much fucking-assholed himself out, he yelled, "That was no fish… that was Moby Dick's fucking cousin, once removed… by you assholes."

Jonnie smiled as he pulled himself up the bank of the lake, "That baby's over 60 pounds. Feels like a record. You boys did good. You ain't no virgin noodlers no more. Yer noodlin' cherry's been broke, excepta course for Sir Charles, the posse's own royal virgin pain in the ass. Get yer asses out of the water. We gotta drag Moby Dick's cousin here back to camp. We can get him weighed tomorrow at Bob's."

Charlie-O, still chest-deep in the lake, held up his caballito, now full of lake water and yelled, "To a modern day Ahab, who lived to whack his Moby Dick!" He laughed and slammed his caballito of lake water.

Fertility right redux…

Dr. Peersome looked up at the closed-circuit TV monitors and said, "The ritual is about to begin." He fiddled with the controls on the panel before him and adjusted the angle and focus of the closed-circuit cameras.

Rose, who sat next to him, reluctantly looked up and asked, "Are you sure this will work? It's not the same. There's no alcohol or marijuana. It's not even the same room."

Dr. Peersome asked, "Did you take the medication that I prescribed for you? It will calm you down and help you through this procedure."

Rose robotically shook her head yes.

Without taking his eyes off the TV monitors, the good doctor said, "Relax Rose. Let the event happen. We don't have to recreate the exact physical environment. All we have to do is create the same psychological environment for Leslie, which I believe we are doing. She's medicated and is in much the same emotional state as when she first experienced the ritual."

The faint pounding of African drums began over the speakers of the closed-circuit TV. Leslie knelt in the center of the semicircle formed by the Seven Damsels in Distress. Off to the right, Jamal, dressed in his Zulu warrior costume, danced his way into the semicircle, his ankle bracelets jingling as his bare feet hit the floor. He swirled forward until he stood over Leslie as he had before. He peered down at her.

Dr. Peersome focused one of the closed-circuit cameras on Leslie. As the beating of the tribal drums quickened and became much louder, Leslie looked up at Jamal and then down at the floor. Dr. Peersome readjusted the focus of the camera to close in on Leslie's face. Sweat formed on her forehead and her breathing quickened. Jamal swirled around Leslie, his belled ankle bracelets beating time to the rhythm of the drums as his feet struck the floor. He stopped before Leslie, towering over her. The tribal drums grew louder and louder as Jamal beat time to the rhythm of the drums with his heels, bells jingling away. He thrust the short stabbing spear forward towards Leslie three times.

Rose could not take her eyes off the monitors. As she intently watched, Leslie placed her hands between her legs, Rose instinctively did the same, pushing her right hand into her crotch. She felt a spreading wetness and could not take her eyes off the camera focused on Jamal as he raised the stabbing spear above his head and shouted. With his other hand, palm up, he motioned for Leslie to rise, which Leslie did slowly and somewhat unsteadily. From his spread stance, his hips slowly undulated forward and back as Leslie arose. Leslie's hips slowly undulated forward and back in response. Her now sweaty tee shirt clung to her breasts and the nipples of her breasts became pronounced through the clinging tee shirt.

Rose felt her fingers slowly and involuntarily push deeper into her crotch and slowly massage the wetness between her legs. She raised her other hand to her breasts and rubbed her thumb slowly over each nipple. Her breathing quickened.

Dr. Peersome, oblivious to Rose's movements and unable to hear her heavy breathing over the sound of the pounding drums, remained focused on the TV monitors, concentrating on controlling the angle and focus of the closed circuit cameras through the control panel before him.

Jamal swirled about the room, but unlike the first ritual, the damsels in distress remained silent. After circling the room, as he did before, Jamal stopped in front of Leslie and motioned for her to kneel, which she slowly did. He swirled so that he faced away from her and slowly danced about the semicircle, facing the other damsels. As he had done before, he reached across his waist and pulled the clasp to the belt holding up his loincloth. As before, the belt swung free and dangled from his raised hand. With a wide stance, he bent at the knees and began rising on his toes and then hitting his heels on the floor in rhythm to the tribal drums as he danced about the semicircle of quiet and subdued damsels. Slowly the loin cloth fell to his feet. Unlike the first time, he now stood naked. He beat time to the rhythm of the drums with the heels of his feet as his great phallus bounced in curious counter-rhythm.

Rose intently watched the monitor focused on Jamal. She discreetly pulled up the hem of her loose-fitting summer skirt and pushed the fingers of her right hand deeper into her crotch as Jamal swirled and faced Leslie. As he hopped towards Leslie, his huge black phallus continued to bounce in counter-rhythm to the beat of the drums. Rose's breathing quickened. Jamal stopped, towering over Leslie, who looked up at him. She smiled and raised the palms of her hands, gently cradling his huge black scrotum with her hands as she had before. Dr. Peersome adjusted the cameras so that they captured all the movement. Rose rhythmically moved her fingers quickly, rubbing the upper crease of her panty-covered vagina. Heat ran through her body and centered in her groin. She rhythmically tightened and relaxed her stomach and thigh muscles and the muscles of her groin and buttocks in response to the undulations of Jamal as he stood over Leslie.

Leslie lowered her head and looked at the great phallus and then ran her fingers along its length to its root where a leather ring clasped the base of the uncircumcised monster. Rose felt the total loss of control as Leslie smiled up at Jamal, pulled back the foreskin of Jamal's great phallus, and gently kissed its wonderfully shaped head. As Leslie's lips touched the head of the great phallus, Rose felt the muscles of her groin and buttocks involuntarily contract rhythmically and intensely as an orgasm grasped her body with an intensity that she had not felt in years, if in fact she had ever felt at all.

Dr. Peersome remained focused on the action on the monitors and the control of the cameras. He did not notice Rose and her heavy breathing at least in part because of the continued blaring of the African drums over the loudspeakers.

He yelled, "Bingo!" as Leslie rose, gave Jamal a peck on the cheek, whispered something into his ear and walked over to Janey and Angel chattering away. The other damsels joined the three and the chattering intensified to the apparent pleasure of the participants. Rose adjusted her skirt and looked down at the wet spot between her legs, her face reddening even more deeply with shame.

Are you off your noodle...

Big Louie's eyes were glued to the TV as Fox's Shepard Smith reported live, interviewing one Jonnie "Pig Fat" Hogg, this year's winner of the Okie Noodling Contest, the natural single-catch category. Mr. Hogg, as Shepard Smith called him, stood next to his record-breaking flathead catfish, which hung from the branch of a tree. Jonnie was saying in reply to a question that Shepard Smith asked, "We caught this sucker last night, actually early this morning. He weighs in at seventy-two and four-tenths pounds... a record. The bastard almost drowned me, but my buddies grabbed the monster and saved me. They called him Moby Dick's cousin once removed. I guess the removal part being by us."

Shepard Smith asked, "What happened to your left arm? I notice that you're bandaged from your wrist to your elbow."

Jonnie smiled into the camera and held up his left arm, "Oh this! It's nothin'. Comes with the territory. Just a scrape I got when I yanked my arm out of the mouth of Moby Dick's cousin here... once removed... by us."

As Shepard Smith said, "Well congratulations Mr. Jonnie 'Pig Fat' Hogg on your record noodle... Shepard Smith, reporting on the road live from flyover country... Pauls Valley, Oklahoma," Big Louie screamed into his cell phone, "Jamie, are you out of yer fuckin' mind? I just saw that asshole Jonnie Hogg on Fox news winning some fuckin' fishing contest. He's a champion noodler? Know what this means? There's a chance that those Mexican drug cartel bastards know where you are... Bob's fuckin' Pig Shop in the thriving metropolis of Pauls Valley, Oklahoma."

Big Louie listened for several minutes and then said, "OK, OK... They might not be lookin' at Fox News and they might not know Jonnie Hogg's name, but if they are, they might recognize him from that idiot bachelor party. It's a chance you shouldn'ta took. They're playin' for keeps. You know they were followin' you. Hell, they wrecked their SUV on Route 66 just outside St. Louis. Saw it on the news. Two survived the crash and one of the bastards wacked the injured driver, probly to keep him from talkin', then escaped. They were Mexicans, the dead one was illegal with a record longer than yer arm, and you can bet that the two that escaped weren't no angels neither." Big Louie paused and then said in disbelief, "You knew about that... and went to that Okie bullshit fishing contest anyway?" He listened some more and then said, "OK, OK... Just get yer asses out of there. Don't take the southern route down through Texas onto 10 and 8 along the border. That's too close to Mexico and there's too many long stretches of nothin'. Go back to 40 and ditch that stupid red Edsel."

He listened for several minutes and then said, "Good... a Dodge Ram... good. And you're armed to the teeth. You guys know what yer doin'?... Well shootin' at some deer ain't exactly combat experience. Deer don't shoot back. Listen, only use yer weapons if you can't run." Big Louie paused to listen and then yelled in disbelief, "Fuckin' paintball? You guys are champion paintballers? Like that matters! Just be careful. Don't take any chances. There ain't no do-overs and timeouts in the game yer playin' now. Listen... Jeremiah and me are flyin' out to San Diego tomorrow. We're gonna meet with those lawyers out there, the ones that sent you that lease for yer property...

Yeah, we'll be OK. They think Jeremiah's a shady importer lookin' to avoid import duties. Those crooked lawyers want his business. And I got an old Nam buddy out there can help us. I'll call you and let you know what we find out. Oh, one last thing. Jeremiah heard from Rose last night and that psych up there is goin' to try some kinda reenactment to shock Leslie out of whatever it is that's making her crazy. Rose says she'll call you after they're done and tell you how it went."

Strangers in a strange land…

Jamie pulled the Dodge Ram into the Big Texan Steak Ranch as a huge, old-fashioned cowboy smiled down at them from the establishment's neon sign. Jonnie Hogg, his ever-cheerful self, yelled to Jamie from the back seat, "I could eat one of them fuckin' Texas steers whole. I need meat and lots of it."

Jamie yelled over his shoulder, "Jonnie, you're about to get your wish! Listen, we'll check in and then go to dinner. We'll stay here tonight. The Big Texan is a motel, restaurant and resort of sorts. Hell, they even have a hotel for horses. My dad loved the place. Best steak in Texas!"

Jonnie yelled, "A hotel for horses? Why the fuck do they have a hotel for horses?"

Jamie yelled back, "Because we're in fucking Texas… Amarillo, Texas. That's why. There's over a million head of cattle in the stock pens around here and there's cowboys all over the place. And where there's cowboys, there's horses. If you want the business from one, you've got to accommodate the other. You figure out which is which."

Jamie stopped at the motel office, rented a couple of rooms for the night and then parked the Dodge Ram in front of their rooms. "Let's dump our stuff and mosey over to the restaurant."

Charles asked, "Mosey? What exactly is a mosey, anyway? Is that something between a walk and a gallop? Is there some kind of steps per minute ratio that we must obey in Texas?"

Jonnie, hungry and impatient, yelled, "What the fuck does it matter? All we got to do is get our asses from here to there and eat."

Charles, with a twinkle in his eye and a smile, neither of which Jonnie could see, threw some live bait into the conversation. "Jonnie, I think that we should follow the customs of the country. We're in what amounts to a foreign country. This place is nothing like Massachusetts or Illinois or even Oklahoma. And although I am a bit fuzzy on the details, I'm pretty sure it is nothing like Manhattan either."

Jonnie took the bait, "What? Are we goin' to get arrested by the mosey police or somethin'?"

Charles answered, "Look, it's a matter of respecting the customs of a different culture and the members of that culture."

Garcia added, "It's like wearing a yarmulke in a synagogue."

A now puzzled Jonnie Hogg, still unaware that one of his legs, if not both, was being vigorously pulled and that if he didn't come to this realization soon, his mosey to the restaurant would be more like a series of metaphoric limps on a metaphoric bum leg, said, "A mosey is like a yarmulke? That makes no fuckin' sense. One involves the head and the other the feet."

Charles replied, "That about sums it up, my man!" And the rest of the posse broke out in guffaws.

Jonnie, now realizing he was the brunt of a joke, yelled, "Mosey yer ass to hell!"

Louis asked, "Do you think they have meatballs and spaghetti?" as the posse exited the truck.

Sometimes even cowgirls give the blues...

After a walk-this-way non-Texan mosey to the restaurant led by a somewhat staggering and thus awkwardly ambulating Jamie Steinkraus, the posse entered a building that looked like a cross between a large ranch bunkhouse and a tourist trap. It was a taxidermist's dream with buffalo heads, deer heads and sundry other animal heads plastered all over the walls. There was even a whole ferocious bear standing guard over nothing in particular. A second floor balcony with additional tables rimmed the main dining room. The place was huge. Louis stared at the décor and mumbled, "There's nothin' like this in Brooklyn."

Charles added, "And that's because we're in Texas, Louis. Different country, different natives, different customs, different décor and, I suspect, no spaghetti and meatballs."

A waitress, who looked more like a cowgirl, showed them to a table on the main floor. She was dressed in a buckskin skirt, boots and spurs, which jangled as she walked. A well-used cowboy hat was smashed down on her head. She did not look like she was dressed in a costume. She smiled like sunshine and said, "Welcome to the Big Texan Steak Ranch, boys. My name's LuLu and I'll be yall's waitress. What'll you have?"

Without looking at the menu, Louis said, "I feel like spaghetti and meatballs."

LuLu put her hands on her hips, her spurs jingling as she tapped her foot in mock anger, and said, "Honey, you can feel anyway you want, but you ain't gettin' no spaghetti and meatballs in this here place. This is Texas. We herd steers. We don't herd no spaghettis, and the only meat balls we serve are prairie oysters."

Charles spoke up, "Ma'am, you'll have to forgive him. He's from Brooklyn."

The waitress smiled down at Louis and said, "Poor thing. I guess we can't all be blessed. Look, honey, let me order you up a nice chicken-fried steak. It'll make you forget all about that I-talian food in Brooklyn."

A mortified Louis shook his head yes and looked down at the table.

LuLu looked over at Jonnie Hogg and asked, "And what'll y'all have, honey bun?"

Jonnie said "I could eat a horse."

The waitress pointed her pen at Jonnie and said, "Looky here, you're still in Texas and in Texas we don't eat no horses like them Ruskies. There's no stallion steaks on these menus. We ride horses and we eat steaks. What steak would you like, big boy?"

Jonnie sneered, "Give me a Big Texan Ribeye."

LuLu asked, "Which cut?"

Jonnie replied, "The god damn Houston cut!"

LuLu smiled and said, "Well, if we don't have a man right here with a Texas-sized appetite. Y'all know the Houston is thirty-six ounces. It's a big hunk of meat. You sure that's what you want… real sure?"

"Damn right I'm sure that's what I want. I could eat two of the bastards."

"Well, honey bun, why not take the challenge. If you can eat seventy-two ounces of steak, why not do it for free… big man like you."

Jamie whispered to him, "Go for it, Jonnie. If you finish the whole seventy-two ounces, it's free. If you don't, I'll pay for your meal and…"

LuLu interrupted Jamie, "Whoa there, cowpoke. If Jonnie here enters the Big Texan seventy-two ounce steak challenge, he's got to also finish off one baked potato, one salad, one shrimp cocktail and one bun with butter. Gotta eat it all, big boy. Gotta eat it all. And in one hour… a skinny sixty minutes."

Charles said, "Surely the challenger has some say in the matter. Otherwise it could be a set up."

"Yup. He sure does get some say. He gets to say how he wants that big hunk of steak cooked and he gets to eat one chunk before the challenge so as to be sure it's cooked the way he said. If it ain't, it's recooked until he says it's OK. He don't have to eat the fat and grizzle. And there's one more thing… if he pukes, he loses." She pointed to the front of the dining room and said, "Oh, and you gotta sit up there at the challenge table."

Jonnie, now boxed by his own bragging, felt honor-bound to take the challenge. The rest of the posse gave LuLu their orders. As she wrote the last order down, she dropped her pen and said to Jonnie, "Be a good cowpoke and pick up that pen for me."

Jonnie, miffed at being trapped into the challenge, said, "Why should I? Your legs broke or somethin'?"

LuLu answered, "No, they ain't broke, but there's somethin' every cowgirl learns real quick in Texas."

Jonnie asked, "Yeah? What's that?"

She smiled and said, "Don't ever squat while wearin' spurs. The results could be very devastatin'… par-ticly if you squat at the wrong angle. Ouch!" Jonnie bent over, picked up the pen and gave it to LuLu who finished writing down the last order. She flashed Jonnie one of her Texas smiles and said, "Good luck with that there challenge, honey bun."

Bitin' off more than you can chew, Texas style...

Jonnie found himself seated at a table facing the dining room. One of the waiters, acting as challenge referee, spoke into a microphone, "We have a challenger. Does anyone else wish to take the Big Texan seventy-two ounce steak challenge? Come on folks, it's not all that difficult. We had one challenger finish off his steak in just over nine minutes. We even had a seventy-year-old grandma do it. Any additional challengers?"

A woman yelled from the balcony, "I will… to defend the honor of Norway!" Loud cheers arose from the balcony. The posse looked up in the direction of the voice from above and there stood Mette Anders.

With the two contestants now seated at the challenge table, the referee reviewed the rules. Two waiters brought out the meals for the two challengers and the referee asked each contestant, "Is your steak cooked as you requested?" Jonnie Hogg cut a huge piece off and stuffed it into his mouth. After chewing for some time, he shook his head yes. Mette cut a much smaller piece which she carefully chewed and said, "OK." She looked down at Charles who stood with a large cheering crowd before the challenge table and said, "Sugar lover, don't bet against Norway! Vikings kick ass!"

A bell rang and the contest was on. Jonnie cut off huge chunks of steak which he stuffed into his mouth, quickly chewed and swallowed. Mette cut smaller pieces, chewed and swallowed, her strategy being to eat more slowly and much more methodically.

Jonnie took an early lead and quickly ate almost half the steak in the first twenty minutes. The posse cheered him on. Mette kept her methodical pace but was quite a bit behind Jonnie. As the clock ticked on, Jonnie's pace slowed. He cut off another huge chunk of steak and stuffed it into his mouth, but now his jaws moved much more slowly as he chewed. His face turned ashen as he swallowed. Mette kept her methodical pace, eating small pieces of steak at a steady pace. Jonnie cut off another huge chunk of steak which he stuffed into his mouth. His jaws moved even more slowly and suddenly stopped. His face turned an even paler shade of white and he dove under the challenge table gagging. The referee quickly moved between Mette and the gagging sounds to shield her from what was obviously Jonnie's involuntary admission of defeat.

Unperturbed, Mette kept her steady pace, eating a forkful of salad or a shrimp from time to time and punctuating her chewing with frequent sips of water. One waiter grabbed the bucket from beneath the table and quickly removed it while another helped an obviously depressed Jonnie up from behind the table and walked him to the men's room as the crowd cheered and jeered his semi-noble effort. Mette kept chewing away. At the fifty-two minute mark, Mette had consumed her entire steak, the salad, the baked potato and the shrimp cocktail. She picked up the bun, carefully buttered it, and with a broad smile ate the last of her meal, her official time clocked at fifty-three minutes and twenty-eight seconds. She looked out at the cheering crowd which included the entire Norwegian Route 66 gang, stood, pumped her fist in the air and yelled, "Vikings kick ass!" Which she had in fact just done, gastronomically speaking.

Charles approached her and said, "Well done! What's your secret?"

Mette looked him squarely in the eye and said, "Mastication. Rhythmic and steady mastication."

Charles could barely hear her above the din of the cheering

and jeering crowd and asked, "Masturbation? You masturbated? You Norwegian women are something else. Before or during the challenge?"

Mette replied, "During, sugar lover. Why would I do it before the challenge? There'd be no point. I couldn't masticate with nothing in my mouth?"

Erotic images exploded into Charles imagination. "How'd you do it? Rub your legs together as you chewed? Both your hands were occupied."

Matte eyes sparkled and she started to laugh, "Why sugar lover, what did you think I said? I said masticate... m-a-s-t-i-c-a-t-e."

The images in Charles' imagination imploded as he mumbled, "Oh."

Meta smiled down him and said, "How's that email comin'?"

Sunday, July 13

Even south of the border, stupid is as stupid does…

Big Louie blinked, adjusting his eyes to the explosion of light as the hood was yanked from his head, and pulled at his hands which were tightly bound behind his back. He looked over at Jeremiah, whose hood had already been removed, and poor Jeremiah had a look of absolute terror burned into his face as his bushy eyebrows met in the middle of his forehead. Big Louie then surveyed the room as he stretched his arms downward. It was a very large room and looked more like the office of a CEO for a major corporation than that of some leader of a Mexican drug cartel. Both he and Jeremiah were surrounded by a number of heavily-armed men. Before them stood a short, well-built Mexican in an obviously very expensive tailored suit. He looked at Big Louie and said, "Mr. Big Louie, we know all about you and your imposter professor friend. We know about Fazzano Collection and Protection and your little run-ins with the law. And we know all about this Jeremiah Wright and his cover as a professor of literature. Do you think that we are blind to those who would steal our business from us? Do you think that we are stupid?"

Big Louie replied, "To tell the truth, sometimes yes, sometimes no. What makes you think we're stealing from you?"

The Mexican laughed cynically and replied, "We know that your organization has refused to lease or sell that property to us and we know that a party of your representatives drives out to California as we speak, probably to secure that property. The only thing we are unsure of is… are you a part of the Gulf Cartel or are you independent? If you are truthful with me, things will go much easier for you. I do not have the time or desire for any prolonged entertainment, but I will do what I must to get the information that I seek. Are you affiliated with the Gulf Cartel?"

Big Louie looked down at his feet and was relieved to find that they were standing on an obviously expensive carpet and not a plastic sheet. Whatever was to happen to them would not happen here. They had a little time. He looked directly at the Mexican and said, "We didn't realize we were dealin' with yer organization. The individual we were dealin' with was… an idiot. Actually he was one of those… idiot-savants, favoring the idiot side. When the bastard first contacted us, we couldn't figure out what he wanted. We thought he was yer run-of-the-mill blackmailer… even after several of his idiot notes." Jeremiah's bushy eyebrows separated and rose at the very mention of the blackmail notes and he interrupted Big Louie, for he felt more secure now that they were speaking about language and communication, his bailiwick. He said, rather indignantly, "Those blackmailing notes were illiterate. We didn't know that you wanted to buy that property. We had no idea. We aren't connected to anybody."

The Mexican started swearing in Spanish. He calmed down and said in English, "So you are not connected to the Gulf Cartel. Then you must be independent operators. I am tired of all this. My stupid little brother Pedro can get nothing right. He is family and I must tolerate his inefficiencies, but he tries my patience. This matter should have been settled last year. He was authorized to make a very generous offer."

Big Louie said quietly, "We received no generous offer. When we finally figured out what this Pedro character wanted, he offered exactly what was paid for the property… down to the penny. That's when we suspected there was a fly in the ointment. How would an ordinary schmuck blackmailer know the exact price paid for the damn property? Then again, how could he be so fuckin' stupid to send notes no one could figure out? We had no fuckin' idea what the hell he wanted."

The Mexican said to one of the armed men, speaking in English, "Pedro should be back. I arranged for a private flight from St. Louis. Tell him to clean up this mess and set things up with El Pozolero. Make sure that Garcia goes with him. I do not want to upset the Americano federales and what they do not know cannot upset them."

Big Louie asked, "What'd ya want that property for anyway? It's a small chunk of real estate. Not enough land to do much with and there's national forest all around the god damn place… after all it's in the Cleveland National Forest. There's plenty of unused remote land out there. Why that particular place?"

The well-attired Mexican smiled, placed his hands on his hips, thought for a moment and then said, "It matters not, but I can satisfy your curiosity since what I tell you will not go beyond your ears." He walked behind his large mahogany desk, opened a drawer and pulled out a forty-five automatic. He said something in Spanish and the heavily-armed men guarding Big Louie and Jeremiah left the room, closing the heavy metal door behind them. The Mexican resumed speaking in English, "I am rather proud of our organization and rarely get to tell anyone about it. Our enterprise, which we call El Equipo de Tijuana… perhaps you have heard of us… is divided into a number of divisions, much like General Motors, 3M or, better yet, like Mr. Capone's Chicago Outfit. We made a careful study of how to organize most efficiently."

Big Louie blurted out, "Al Capone? You studied Al Capone?"

The well-attired Mexican smiled and said, "Of course. Mr. Capone was the CEO of a very successful enterprise… a very successful criminal enterprise. His success was not achieved through luck."

Big Louie interrupted, "But ol' Scarface got caught. He couldn'ta been that great an example."

The Mexican replied, "It is best to learn from another's mistakes rather than from one's own. It is much cheaper." He brushed his pant leg with his free hand, wiping away some imaginary lint and continued. "Mr. Capone suffered from syphilis, which seriously affected his judgment over the years and eventually caused his death. In the end, it was really the syphilis that brought him down and not your Mr. Elliot Ness and his federales."

Big Louie, who was very familiar with organized crime, asked, "Why not study the mafia? They outlasted Capone by decades. Hell, they're still in operation, weakened, but still operating."

The Mexican smiled and said, "And do you think that the Outfit does not still control Chicago and its politics? We studied the mafia as well… We studied all forms of business organization. However, the mafia was severely limited because it would only admit Sicilians into its organization. This brought more security of a sort, but severely limited the talent that they could draw upon to direct and manage their enterprise."

Big Louie's brow furrowed, "And what did you learn from Capone?"

The Mexican asked, "Who did Mr. Capone appoint his CFO and business strategist?"

Big Louie asked, "His money man?"

The Mexican replied, "Yes, his money man."

Big Louie thought a moment and said, "Probly Greasy Thumb Guzik."

The Mexican replied, "Yes, Mr. Jack Guzik. Do you know much about him?"

Big Louie thought for a moment and then said, "I think he was from Poland. Yeah, he was a short, dumpy Polish Jew and he had the reputation of smelling like a pig."

The Mexican smiled again, "Yes, and that's Mr. Capone's genius. He hired and promoted competent, trustworthy people. They did not have to be Italian or even well-groomed, for he viewed a criminal organization as an enterprise, a kind of unfettered capitalism. Such an enterprise, like all enterprises, required the best people to be successful, particularly given the high-risk nature of their business. And if you were faithful to Mr. Capone, he was faithful to you. Did you know that Mr. Capone killed a man who had berated Mr. Guzik with anti-Semitic insults while beating him? For the security of his Outfit, Mr. Capone and Mr. Guzik never allowed the right hand to know what the left was doing… a business practice that I have instituted here at El Equipo de Tijuana. There is only one big picture of our organization and it is in my head and my head only."

Jeremiah, who listened intently to the conversation, asked, "But what about those illiterate and unintelligible blackmail notes? Your brother Pedro does not seem to be… how should I put this… very efficient."

The Mexican shook his head slowly from side to side. "First, I hope you realize that Pedro is not his real name. Not that it matters much for the two of you. But, yes, my brother is not very efficient presently, but he is new to the business. I still have high hopes for him. He is very smart and did quite well in school. He recently graduated from Columbia's School of Business. I thought that perhaps he could develop into our own business strategist, but his extended academic education seems to have made him less intelligent rather than more so. My hope is that exposure to the more practical aspects of our enterprise will allow him to apply his academic knowledge so that we can keep our business model current, efficient and profitable… for my stockholders, unlike those of General Motors and 3M, are not as forgiving of failure. This is a very dangerous business. I must deal with law enforcement on both sides of the border, the competition and even factions within my own organization. One can never be too careful."

Big Louie asked, "But what about that property? Why that small piece property?"

The Mexican said, "The water, Mr. Big Louie… the water! But

there's no need to bother with buying or even leasing that land now. I'll put a stop to all those legal initiatives. We no longer need that insurance." He smiled and held up the forty-five automatic. "Now, this is all the insurance that I need." And with that, he pushed a button on the phone on his desk and the heavily-armed men entered and escorted Big Louie and Jeremiah out into the hallway.

Cookin' pozolli Equipo-de-Tijuana style...

Big Louie pushed against the wall and lowered his shoulders to relieve the pressure on his wrists which were bound with plastic cuffs behind his back. Both he and Jeremiah were sitting on the ground with their backs against an old stone wall. Jeremiah was also cuffed. Their legs were free, enabling them to scrunch about the ground.

Jeremiah looked up at a thatched ceiling and asked, "Where are we?"

Big Louie watched the fat Mexican laboring before them, observing his every move. Without moving his head, he whispered to Jeremiah, "In very deep shit, my friend. Very deep shit."

The Mexican wore rubber gloves and poured gallon bottle after gallon bottle of an acrid smelling liquid into an old, oversized porcelain tub in the center of the room not far from where Big Louie and Jeremiah sat. After every second or third gallon bottle, the Mexican pulled a pint bottle from his back pocket and took a long swig of what Big Louie thought was probably tequila.

He was a jolly looking fellow with a quick smile even as sweat poured from his brow. He frequently wiped his forehead dry with the sleeve of his shirt as he went about his work. He turned to Big Louie and Jeremiah and asked, "Do you Americanos know who I am?"

Big Louie replied, "Who gives a fuckin' god damn rat's ass."

The fat Mexican frowned and said, "You Americanos are vulgar and irreverent. One should not take the name of God in vain." He paused and looked at the stack of gallon bottles yet to be emptied into the large tub and shook his head in disgust. He said to no one in particular, "This is very hard work, but I do it as best I can. Normally I use just a barrel."

Jeremiah grunted as he adjusted his legs and asked, "Pray tell, my friend, who are you?"

The fat Mexican smiled, "I see that you are a gentleman, unlike your vulgar friend. I am known as El Pozolero. Perhaps you have heard of me."

Big Louie spit to the side and said, "God damn fuckin' right I have!"

The Mexican smiled and took another long swig from his pint bottle and swayed a bit as he did so. He leaned against one of the ceiling support posts as he stuffed the pint bottle into his back pocket. He looked over at Big Louie and asked, "Do you know what El Pozolero means in your language?"

Big Louie pushed against the wall to straighten up as best he could, "It means fuckin' stew maker. God damn right I heard of you."

The fat Mexican's brow furrowed, "You are such a vulgar man. Your speech is difficult to tolerate. However, you are right. I am the stew maker and, my vulgar friend, you are to be the pork in my pozolli. Perhaps you would like to be accompanied with some chili peppers, a bit of maize!" He burst into laughter as he returned to his labors.

Jeremiah looked over at Big Louie and said rather quizzically, "Stew maker? Pozolli? Chili peppers? What does he mean?"

Big Louie remained focused on the fat Mexican and whispered, "He's preparing an acid stew and we're goin' to be the meat. This asshole's a legend in Tijuana. He disappears people… literally."

Jeremiah began muttering to himself, "Oh my, oh my, oh my."

The fat Mexican's breathing became more labored. He pulled the pint bottle from his back pocket and plopped down to the ground resting his back against a ceiling support post. He took another long swig from the pint bottle and said, "The schedule is off. Rarely do I get to talk with those whom I must service. You should have been ready for disposal when I arrived. Instead I must await that ignorant

Garcia. He must do his job before I can do mine. A man in my position must follow procedure. I have scruples."

Big Louie watched the fat Mexican intently. Jeremiah, somewhat befuddled, asked, "Scruples?"

The fat Mexican smiled and took another long swig from the pint bottle. "Yes, my well-mannered friend. I am not a common murderer like young Garcia. He is young and ignorant. I do not believe in killing. It is a very great sin, but young Garcia does not care. He is going to burn in hell for eternity."

He drained the pint bottle and threw it against the stone wall above Big Louie and Jeremiah. Shattered glass rained down upon the two of them as they ducked their heads as best they could.

"Oh, my friends, I am sorry about that. I fear that I have had a bit too much tequila to drink. I am not like that ignorant Garcia. I find this business quite distasteful. But a man must provide for his family. I do the best that I can and I have scruples. I avail my services for men only. I will not avail my services for women and I will not avail my services for children under the age of fourteen. Sometimes it is difficult to tell, but I do my best. Mistakes are made. After all, I am but a poor man."

Jeremiah began to shake. The fat Mexican's brow again furrowed, "Do not worry, my well-mannered friend. It will be painless. That ignorant Garcia is very good at his job and of course, I do not provide my services until he has provided his. I am told that we must be very efficient as you are Americans and we do not want to upset your federal government."

Big Louie whispered to Jeremiah, "Keep talking. Keep him occupied."

Jeremiah took a deep breath and asked, "Isn't that a rather large tub?"

The fat Mexican staggered to his feet with difficulty. "Yes it is, my friend. I usually use a barrel for this work, but there are two of you and you are very large men. I have had to bring many bottles to fill this tub."

Jeremiah squirmed against the wall. His stomach growled and a look of distress and then profound embarrassment spread across his face.

The fat Mexican grabbed two gallon bottles from the stack and staggered toward the tub. He stopped in front of Big Louie and turned to look back at Jeremiah, sniffing the air like a beagle. He began to laugh. "Well it appears that someone has shit his pants. I can smell it even over the smell of the acid. Is that you, my well-mannered friend? Did the thought of becoming the pork in my pozolli scare the shit out of you?" He threw his head back in boisterous laughter throwing him off balance.

Big Louie kicked out his legs at the laughing fat Mexican, knocking the fat Mexican's feet out from under him. The off-balance fat Mexican tumbled backwards into the tub striking his head hard against the tub's side as he splashed into the tub of acid. His body twitched violently for several moments and then settled, motionless, beneath the surface of the liquid filling the tub as bubbles spread over the surface.

Big Louie pushed his back against the wall and slowly worked himself into a standing position. He spit towards the tub and yelled, "Hey, Mr. El Pozolero, how's that fuckin' stew now? Still like the home cookin'?" He looked around the shed and hobbled over to the ceiling support post. "We gotta get the hell out of here before that Garcia asshole shows up." He spotted a rusty nail on the ceiling support post, turned his back to the post and slowly rubbed the plastic cuff against the rusty nail until the plastic snapped freeing his hands. He hobbled over to a workbench where El Pozolero had placed a large knife, a handgun, and the keys to their rented SUV along with the contents of their pockets, which included their passports and wallets. Big Louie checked the pistol's clip to be sure it was full and mumbled, "Shit... armor piercing five sevens," pushed the clip back into the handle and stuffed the pistol into the back of his pants. He mumbled "An F-N Five-Seven USG. Christ, nothing but the best for these assholes." He stuffed their passports and wallets into his shirt, grabbed the knife and cut Jeremiah free, pulling him to his feet after he did so.

Jeremiah stood somewhat unsteadily rubbing his wrists. He stared with horror at the decomposing remains of El Pozolero and said, "That stew is quite odiferous."

Big Louie yanked Jeremiah out the shed's door and yelled over his shoulder, "We gotta vamoose pronto! No tellin' how many banditos ignorant Garcia will have with him. They usually travel in packs armed to the teeth. The SUV's behind the shed. We gotta get back to San Diego and call Jamie. You can get cleaned up when we're at a safe distance from this fuckin' place."

A former pozolli ingredient spices up a conversation...

Big Louie hurriedly punched a number into his cell phone. As he did so, he yelled at Jeremiah, who drove their rented and rather large SUV, "Prof, keep the god damn vehicle on the road!" for Jeremiah had never driven so large a vehicle before, in the dark no less, and had difficulty controlling it. Big Louie yelled again, "Faster! Floor the fuckin' thing! I'd rather get pulled over by the California highway patrol than those Equipo bastards." Jeremiah, reminded of his quite recent opportunity to become the main ingredient of an El Equipo pozolli, developed an uncharacteristic need for more speed and slammed his foot down on the gas pedal, for fear can be a potent motivator and the greater the fear, the greater the motivation.

Big Louie yelled into the phone, "Jamie?...Yeah, it's Big Louie. The Professor here and me just escaped from those cartel bastards. I'll give you the details later. Let's just say the only good lawyer is a fuckin' dead one. That drug cartel that's tryin' to cook our asses, they're called El Equipo de Tijuana. And that asshole that's chasin' you, well, he ain't chasin' you no more. Ol' Pedro and his homicidal sidekick Garcia are back in Mexico with his older brother, Mr. Numero Uno, who runs the fuckin' cartel."

Big Louie listened and then said, "Alpine? Meet you in Alpine? Where the fuck's that?" He listened again and then said, "OK, got it! We're stoppin' at one of my Nam buddies east of San Diego. We'll probly camp out there tonight. He's armed to the teeth. He'll lend me whatever armament I'll need. Listen, I got two pieces of intel. First, that Pedro character, the asshole who tried to blackmail you, screwed up. He was supposed to make what his big brother called a very generous offer. My guess, the asshole low-balled you to impress his brother with what a sharp businessman he was. You're not goin' to believe this. That Pedro character actually grageated from Columbia School of Business. Probly magna cum fuck up. Explains a lot. Anyways, intel item number two… those bastards want yer property for the water. What kinda water you got on that property?"

Again Big Louie paused as he listened to Jamie and then said, "A well? A deep, spring-fed well? Too bad there ain't no cars to wash. Well that's what the bastards want. They want the water, not the property." He asked rhetorically, as much to himself as to Jamie, "Why the hell would they want water in the middle of a fuckin' national forest?" He paused and then said, "Listen, the coast is clear for you and yer idiot buddies for the next couple 'a days what with Pedro the fuckup back in Mexico with his bandito buddy, but they'll be back with a bunch of their friends and armed to the teeth. Be careful! They know who you are and they know where yer goin'. And they know the Doc here and me, and we know some more stuff Mr. Numero Uno don't want spread around, so we're toast too."

Life's just a big ol' tuna burrito of the mind…

The posse got a very late start, having spent most of the night celebrating what they viewed as the ignominious retreat of their murderous bandito pursuers, and thus they did not make much progress on their drive to California. Jamie stared down at a map and said to Louis, "Pull off at Exit 22. We'll stay at the El Rancho Hotel tonight. We need some recovery time after last night. Besides, it's on old Route 66 and it's a neat place. My dad and I stayed there a bunch of times."

The posse had downed a number of beers during the relatively short ride in a valiant and overly aggressive, hair-of-the-dog strategy to overcome the effects of last night's tequila sunrise celebration, paradoxically extending rather than eliminating the condition that caused their tardy departure from the Big Texan. As they pulled into the El Rancho, Jonnie Hogg asked, "They got a restaurant here? I could eat a... " and before he could finish, Charles interrupted, "Whoaa there cowpoke, careful what you wish for. Have you heard of the El Rancho's great burrito challenge?"

Garcia added, "Dan-ito tito inta-ito erye-ito dinaryorito igbito leo-ito airyhito unatito urritobito, istermito owpoke-cito." ("And it ain't yer ordinary big ol' hairy tuna burrito, mister cowpoke.")

Jonnie couldn't follow what Garcia said and asked Charles, "What'd he say?"

Charles, with a look of great seriousness, said, "Something about El Rancho's great tuna burrito."

As Louis pulled the Dodge Ram into a parking space, he asked, "They serve a tuna burrito special here?"

Charles could barely hold back laughter as he said, "Yeah! A big ol' tuna burrito inserted into a bed of spaghetti oozing with red sauce. A once-a-month special!" Unable to hold back any longer he doubled over in hysterical laughter.

Jonnie crushed the empty beer can in his hand and yelled, "Fuck off, asshole!" much to the pleasure of some members of the posse and the confusion of the others as the entire posse piled out of the truck and into the El Rancho Hotel.

Did someone say the Marx Brothers...

Charles yelled across the hotel room to Jonnie, "Pig Fat, pass me another blaster!" Jonnie, who sat on the stack of three cases of Budweiser beer representing the posse's remaining supply, yelled back, "Fuckin' A." He reached between his legs and pulled up a can of Budweiser from the open case on top of the stack of cases upon which he sat. He popped the Budweiser can open, took a long sip, poured whiskey from a bottle of Four Roses into the can, refilling it to the top and dutifully passed to Charles the requested Budweiser blasting cap, or blaster as the posse so fondly referred to what had quite recently become their second favorite drink.

Charles took a long swig and said, "No tequila tonight, right? Gotta stay sober, right?"

Jamie tossed his exploded blasting cap into the tall trash can across the room. As the dead blasting cap clinked into the nearly-full trash can joining a regiment of its brothers, he yelled, "And Michael Jordan hits for three as the Bulls destroy the Celtics again." He pointed to Jonnie and said, "Pass me another live one," which Jonnie did. Jamie sucked the foaming suds from the blaster's top and then said, "Yup. Gotta hit the road at a reasonable hour tomorrow. No tequila!"

Louis watched the others as they continued to toss dead blasters into the tall trash can. As was his habit, he had stopped drinking some time ago. He set a limit of around four or five blasters for himself, since as the designated driver he thought it best to be sober in the morning, although he defined sobriety much more loosely than did the laws of virtually every state in the union. He asked "Jamie, where we headed tomorrow?"

Jamie took a long swig from his still live blaster and said, "Even though those two cartel assholes aren't chasing us, I'd still like to get to Alpine tomorrow night. It's about a twelve-hour drive, but if you assholes get up at a reasonable hour tomorrow, we can make it easy. We'll take Route 40 to Needles, California, and then work our way down to Alpine. It's about six hundred and eighty miles."

The posse shook its collective head yes in agreement to this detailed plan for the morrow and took long draughts from their still live blasters to celebrate the plan and affirm their commitment to it.

Jonnie looked around the suite and said, "This is some fuckin' place... and that lobby... long-horned furniture... a player piano... big ol' stone fireplace, and all those damn Indian rugs on the walls. I thought that the Big Texan looked like the Old West with all those animal heads nailed to the wall and that wooden furniture and all, but this place has it beat by a mile."

Garcia smiled his usual inscrutable smile and said, "Ightricita, istermita owpoke-cita! Igbe-cita exanti-cita ookedle-cita ikeli-ci-ta Dolcita Estwita. Histita lacepita sita Dolcita Estwita." ("Right, mister cowpoke! Big Texan looked like Old West. This place is Old West.")

Charles took a swig from his blaster and set it on the table before him. He leaned his chair back and plopped his feet on the table, making sure his feet and his blaster could peacefully coexist on the table's surface. He held a dog-eared paperback open with his right hand. He quickly read the pages before him and said, "Not so fast, Joobie. Know who built this place?"

The inscrutable Garcia shook his head a quite scrutable no.

"Well my friend, it says here that this place was built by D. W. Griffith's brother in 1937."

Jonnie crushed his dead blaster with one squeeze of his left hand and said, "Who the fuck is D. W. Griffith?"

Charles reached for his blaster, took a swig and carefully set it back on the table. "He was a famous movie director. A Hollywood pioneer. Ever hear of Birth of the Nation?"

"Nope. What's that got to do with his brother?"

"Well, his brother built this hotel as a place where the movie stars and crews could stay since Hollywood shot so many movies out here. Directors liked the western landscape. Says here D. W.'s brother, R. E., built a hotel of quote rustic elegance end quote to attract the movie stars."

"How come these assholes go by initials instead of names?"

Charles continued, ignoring Jonnie's question, which he couldn't answer, "Says here that John Wayne, Katherine Hepburn, Spencer Tracy, Errol Flynn, Kirk Douglas, Gregory Peck, Humphrey Bogart and Richard Widmark... to name a few... all stayed here. Over eighty movie stars shacked up at the El Rancho while making movies. Hell, it says two presidents, Reagan and Eisenhower, slept here."

"That'd explain all those fuckin' autographed pictures of movie stars lining the walls. What book is that yer readin' from?"

"It's that Big Bertha paperback about Route 66, the book I found in that used bookstore in Chicago. Says here that over three-hundred films were shot in New Mexico, most of them westerns." Charles read on and then yelled "Whoa, you're not going to believe this. Ever see the John Ford classic Cheyenne Autumn? The one where Richard Widmark and the cavalry drive the Cheyenne on a forced march back to Wyoming, killing a lot of them along the way… that trail of tears business. Well that was shot around Gallup, some of it north of here in Monument Valley, the four corners… you know… where New Mexico, Colorado, Utah and Arizona meet. Here's the kicker! No Cheyenne live around here. Hell, they're several states away, so Ford hired a bunch of the local Navajos for the movie to play the part of the Cheyenne. I guess he figured an Indian is pretty much an Indian, at least as far as a movie audience is concerned. He dressed the Navajos up in war bonnets, armed them with lances and then filmed the Hollywood cavalry herding them around and beating the crap out of them from time to time. Well these ersatz Cheyenne, when they negotiate with the movie's cavalry colonel and the other cavalry officers, speak in Navajo. Says here they talk in what appears to be somber terms about their plight. The Hollywood crew think the Navajo are following the script, discussing supposedly weighty tribal matters in an Indian language, any Indian language would apparently do. But instead of talking about the terms of treaties and such, the Navajo are discussing how small the cavalry colonel's dick is and something like how he couldn't satisfy a desperate female rabbit. Since none of the Hollywood crew speak Navajo, they just role the cameras and record all that raunchy Navajo dialogue which ends up in the movie. The movie's a cult classic here on the Navajo reservation."

Jonnie smiled. "Well times have fuckin' changed. Didn't used to pay to be an Indian, but now it sure does. They sell us the whiskey and they sell us the cigarettes and they shit all over us… at their crap tables. They don't even have to force march us to the reservation. We haul ass there as fast as we can so they can shit on us."

Jamie said, "And all those autographed pictures of movie stars like Richard Widmark, plastered all over the walls, well the owner of the El Rancho decided to name all the rooms here after the Hollywood stars who stayed in them."

Jonnie popped another can of Budweiser and a took long swig, replaced the consumed contents of said can with Four Roses whiskey and then took another long swig from his newly-created blaster. "So this place ain't the authentic Old West, just like those Navajos ain't the Cheyennes. It's the fuckin' Hollywood Old West. I shoulda known. So whose fuckin' rooms are we in?"

Jamie chuckled and said, "The Marx Brothers suite, Chico. Sleeps five."

Petrified is as petrified does...

The small talk slowly slipped into silence until Jonnie laid a huge fart, which reverberated like a clap of thunder through the suite of rooms. He smiled and proudly proclaimed, "Hey Joobie, thanks to them burritos, I just topped y'all!"

Jamie yelled, "For Chrissake, get that ass of yours under control. You know, Pig Fat, you're offensive at both ends!"

Jonnie, proud of his contribution to the dying conversation, said, "It's the smartest thing said around here in a long time."

Jamie grabbed his nose, "Somethin' must a crawled aside a you and died" as he and Louis, who had been sitting on the floor on either side of Jonnie, moved to the far side of the room. Garcia smiled inscrutably.

Charles took a long sip from his blaster, "We gotta get Pig Fat's mind, what there is of it, off his intestines if we're to survive the night." He held up a DVD and said, "Thought we could take advantage of the room's DVD player to help us chill, so I rented this movie down at the gift shop, The Petrified Forest, the great Bogie's first hit, since we'll be driving by there tomorrow. It'll be interesting to see

Hollywood's take on the place. I've seen the flick a bunch of times. Great movie! Studied it at Harvard... a course about twentieth-century American film."

Jonnie asked, "A film with a great bogie man? Is it a horror film?"

Charles replied, "Horror film? No! Not a great bogie as in a mispronounced boogie man, but the great Bogie as in Humphrey Bogart, you idiot. Surely you've heard of him. Pig Fat, you've spent too much of your wayward, redneck youth under water with all that noodling. It's rotted your brain. You've managed to turn that poor, underutilized hunk of gray matter between your ears into a vestigial organ. Watch the damn movie, my flatulent friend."

Charles, who now stood before what could be called an entertainment center of sorts, turned on the TV and DVD player, slid the DVD into the player, returned to his seat at the table and started the movie with the remote. The posse's eyes intently focused on The Petrified Forest as the credits rolled.

A long shot appears on the screen. A man walks briskly along a desolate and dusty desert road as a car passes him. He walks closer, punctuating each step with a long walking stick, as the camera focuses on him. Another speeding car flashes on screen. The man quickly turns and sticks out his thumb as he walks. The second car speeds by him raising a cloud of dust. The man who had stuck out his thumb stumbles forward and resumes his brisk walk down the lonely, dusty road into the distant desolation, punctuating each step with his long walking stick.

The posse watched intently.

The scene shifts to an old rundown gas station and restaurant, oddly named the Black Mesa Bar-B-Q, apparently the last chance to gas up your automobile and get a meal before the long drive west across the desert on old Route 66. Two linemen are finishing their lunch. The waitress is the owner's daughter, Gabrielle Maple, or Gabie as she's called by the locals. Her grandpa engages the two linemen in conversation over the objections of her rather annoying father, and gramps tells his oft told tale of being shot at by a drunken Billy the Kid in the old pioneer days when men were men. Gramps announces that the vicious criminal Duke Mantee and his gang, who are attempting to escape after murdering six people in Oklahoma City, are believed to be in the area.

The linemen exit stage right leaving the restaurant empty. Gabie walks out the restaurant's front door, sits on the steps of the restaurant and begins reading from a book of poetry. A young man called Boze, who's the hired attendant for her father's gas station, plops down next to her as she sits reading. He makes a rather awkward pass at her. She gets up indignantly and walks over to the gas pumps. She stops and bends over to tie her shoes, presenting her fine derrière in silhouette to the camera.

Jonnie mumbled as she bent over, "Who's that? She's got an ass that won't quit. I can't wait to see that baby uncovered."

Charles answered, "That's Bette Davis and that's the most you'll see of her derrière. This movie was made in 1936 and back then they didn't show nudity. In fact, this scene was considered quite daring by the Hayes Commission, Hollywood's self-censoring board, and they almost demanded that it be deleted… because of the fear that it would cause the exact reaction with the audience that you just had."

Jonnie, obviously engrossed by the movie, said, "Too fuckin' bad. It'd be fun watchin' that Boze idiot bang her doggy style. Does he at least get to bang her behind closed doors? I'll bet she's a screamer."

Charles smiled and said, "Watch, my flatulent friend, watch, only time will tell."

The entire posse watched intently hoping to eventually hear Bette Davis scream in orgasmic joy.

The man who walked down that dusty desert road shows up at the Black Mesa Bar-B-Q. Gabie is obviously intrigued by the man, Alan Squier, who is a failed writer and self-proclaimed intellectual.

Jonnie said, "That Alan character looks like a fairy. He couldn't handle that Gabie bitch."

Charles said, "That's Leslie Howard playing Alan Squier."

Jonnie said, "Shit, he's even got a girl's name. Before that Leslie character could settle into the saddle for the ride, ol' Gabie'd buck him off with one thrust of those hips of hers."

Charles admonished Jonnie, "Cut the wisecracks. It's not that kind of movie."

Jonnie answered, "Says who?"

The posse watched the movie, anxiously awaiting the entry of Bogie and Bette Davis's screams of orgasmic joy. The posse, excepting Charles, thought that perhaps Mantee was the man for the job, for they were now sure that Boze wasn't and Alan couldn't.

Alan Squier reads the menu and asks about the day's special, bar-b-que. Gabie replies, "Here it's a hamburger and vegetables. It's pretty good."

Jonnie yells, "Hold it. Bar-b-que ain't ever a hamburger. Bar-b-que's bar-b-que. Whoever wrote this stuff didn't know what the hell he was talking about."

Charles answered, "Well Robert Emmet Sherwood knew enough to win three Pulitzers for drama."

Jonnie answered, "Never heard of him. Any of you assholes ever hear of him?"

The rest of the posse shook its head a collective no, as the movie played on. The plot continued unfolding and it unfolded without the appearance of Humphrey Bogart as the evil Duke Mantee.

Jamie finally asked, "Where the hell's Bogart. If he doesn't appear soon, he'll miss being in the movie. I thought he was the star."

Then Bogart appears with his gang on that dusty, remote road. It's night and their automobile has broken down. Mantee orders his gang to hide as he stops a passing automobile, forces the occupants out, one of whom is the hitchhiker Alan Squier. Mantee and his gang commandeer the automobile and drive off toward the Black Mesa Bar-B-Q.

Jamie mumbles a barely audible, "Finally."

The posse watched intently as the plot thickened. Mantee and his gang take over the Black Mesa Bar-B-Q and Alan Squier reappears at the restaurant to warn Gabie, obviously concerned for her safety.

Squier enters the restaurant and walks to the luncheon counter behind which Gabie stands. As he warns Gabie about Duke Mantee and his gang, Gabie tries to warn him that Mantee and two of his henchmen are already there, unnoticed by Squier, on the far side of the room. Mantee shuffles into the scene with his arms hanging limply forward.

Jonnie asked, "What's with Bogie's walk? He looks like a gorilla with a load in his pants."

Charles leaped to Bogart's defense, "He studied John Dillinger's walk and copied it."

Jonnie, in disbelief, asked, "Dillinger walked like gorilla with a load in his pants?"

Charles added to his explanation, "That walk's the walk of a sociopath, a man of pure evil, a man who could erupt into violence at any given moment."

Jonnie said, "I get the point. I guess if Dillinger had to walk around with a load in his pants, he'd get pretty pissed off. Could make a man pretty violent, so I get it. Bogart's a violent hombre."

Charles corrected Jonnie, "That's not Bogart. That's Bogart playing Duke Mantee."

Jonnie ended the repartee with, "Sometimes it's hard to tell the difference." The posse's eyes returned to the unfolding plot.

Mantee takes all those present captive and a frustrated Boze refers to Manatee as a gangster. Grandpa Maple indignantly corrects him, "Mantee ain't no gangster. He's an American. He's a desperado. Gangsters is foreigners."

Louis yelled, "Hold it! That's not right. That's anti-Italian. Capone was as American as Mantee. Hell, Scarface was born in Brooklyn. You don't get any more American than that!"

The movie played on with its various twists and turns.

The now-captive Alan Squier, who has fallen in love with Gabie, makes her the beneficiary of his life insurance policy, his only asset, so that she can travel to France and study art. He calls Mantee "the last great apostle of rugged individualism" and asks Mantee to kill him so that Gabie can get the money from the insurance policy. Mantee agrees and before escaping from the sheriff and his posse, he shoots Squier who dies in Gabie's arms. Gabie proclaims that Alan Squier will be buried in the Petrified Forest as he wished.

Jonnie yells, "What a fuckin' coward. Ol' Leslie ain't no hero. All he does is to get someone else to kill him so that a girl he just met can go to France to study art. He's a coward and an idiot. The only one with any guts in the whole damn flick is Mantee. He does what he says he's gonna do and he ain't no phony like all the other idiots in the movie. Leslie there belongs in a petrified forest. He'll be right at home with the rest of the petrified wood."

Charles replied, "Pig Fat, you've overlooked a lot of the subtlety of the movie and the shadow of inevitable doom over both Squier and Mantee. They're both trapped by life."

Jonnie took a long drink from his blaster and said, "Yeah, that may be true, but one of those trapped bastards has balls and one of them don't and it don't take no Harvard education to tell who has the balls and who don't."

Monday, July 14

Oh, the irony of life: a strange bedfellow learns from history so as not to be buried by it…

Big Louie yelled over a blaring TV, "Doc, get yer ass in here! You gotta see this!" Jeremiah shambled into the room, huffing and puffing. Big Louie pointed at the TV, "Those three bastards are dead!"

The TV news anchor continued as the pictures of three individuals appeared on the TV screen, "The head of the Mexican drug cartel Equipo de Tijuana, his younger brother and an associate are believed to have been assassinated by another faction in the cartel in a struggle for control of the organization. Mexican authorities believe that the three were gunned down by their own bodyguards early this morning south of Tijuana."

Jeremiah stared at the TV, "Which three bast… errr… individuals… got… have become deceased."

Big Louie jumped to his feet and yelled, "Hoooeeeee!" as he pumped his fist into the air and then he yelled, "Numero Uno, his asshole brother Pedro and that homicidal maniac Garcia… that's who!"

Jeremiah stood motionless and started mumbling "Oh my… oh my… oh my…"

Big Louie turned to Jeremiah, "Know what this means? We're free, that's what it means. Nobody else in that fuckin' cartel knows about us or that blackmailin' operation Mr. Numero Uno's asshole brother Pedro was runnin'. So much for that clever fuckin' business strategy of Mr. Numero Uno. The bastard didn't learn as much from Capone's Outfit as he thought. I'll bet ol' Scarface's ghost is wanderin' around Chicago's Southside with a shit-eatin' grin plastered across his ugly face as we speak."

Big Louie's buddy, who sat quietly watching the TV, asked, "Is this the trouble you were in?"

As he carefully lowered himself back onto the couch, Big Louie replied, "Yup! This be the trouble, my man. I thought I'd keep you out of it but there's nothin' to keep you out of now."

With a thud, Jeremiah plopped onto the couch next to Big Louie and said, "I'd like to thank you for accommodating us, Mr. McMann, especially given the circumstances in which we found ourselves and my rather deplorable and embarrassing condition."

Big Louie's buddy said, "Call me T-S. No need for formalities here. Listen, it's the least I could do. That fat bastard sittin' next to you saved my ass more times than I care to count."

Jeremiah asked, "T-S?"

"Yup, just T-S."

Big Louie added, "And it don't stand for Tough Shit. Stands for Thai Stick."

A puzzled Jeremiah asked Big Louie, "Thai Stick?"

"Yup. Thai Stick. Ol' T-S got the label back in Nam. He supplied his buddies with weed, for a price of course. Had connections all over the god damn delta. Hell, he supplied the whole fuckin' division with weed."

McMann turned to Big Louie and said, "As I recall, you didn't do many joints. You pretty much stuck to booze."

Big Louie smiled, "I never really got into drugs, except of course for my drug of choice... alcohol."

McMann added, "Which you drank by the fuckin' gallon. I didn't make a dime off you."

After a long silence, as the TV droned on, McMann asked, "What's with this blackmailing deal?"

Big Louie said, "Well it's a little complicated but dead Pedro, the younger brother of the equally dead Mr. Numero Uno, was blackmailing the Doc's son-in-law here, Jamie Steinkraus, to get possession of some land not far from here, at least we thought they wanted the land even though there wasn't much of it. Couldn't figure out why he went through so much trouble to get such a small chunk of land. Turns out the recently air-conditioned Mr. Numero Uno told us he didn't want the land at all. He wanted the water. Jamie's place has some kind of deep spring-fed well. He could run a carwash at his place. Unfortunately the well's in the middle of nowhere."

McMann asked, "Where's this land?"

"Cleveland National Forest, apparently not too far from a place called Alpine."

McMann smiled, "Well, my good buddy, the Doc's son-in-law may have hit the mother lode. Look, I know a lot about what goes on around here. Things haven't changed much for me since we left Nam."

Big Louie immediately knew what McMann was implying, "So you still distribute the stuff?"

McCann replied, "Between me, you two and the recently departed, I never quit distributing."

Jeremiah remained in the dark, "Distribute what?"

McMann said, "Dank, weed, pot... you know, marijuana. The really good stuff. I only deal with bulk. No end user stuff. I arrange to have the product moved from point A to point B for a fee. The legit business world would call me a factor. I rarely touch the product, just arrange to have it moved from seller to buyer... as I said, for a fee."

Big Louie asked, "Where's the stuff come from?"

McMann answered, "Before I get into that, you should know a fact or two about the business. It'll help you understand the sitcheation you and the Doc here and his son-in-law are in. Did you know that marijuana is California's biggest cash crop? Last stats I saw, the marijuana crop in California's worth over 35 billion bucks annual, and it ain't the weed your hippy momma toked. Today's dank is hybrid, the stuff they grow around here is called California Gold. It's genetically engineered. Grows quicker, matures in two months. Tolerates adverse conditions and produces ten times the product. You can't kill the stuff with pesticides. Hell, the only way to kill the stuff is to pull it out by the roots. Rumor has it the California Department of Agriculture working with several of the California state universities developed the stuff for what they claimed was medical marijuana production. And if you believe they developed the hybrid for medical marijuana production, I've got a bridge in Brooklyn to sell you. There's a huge market for the stuff."

Big Louie asked again, "So where do you get this hybrid product you factor?"

McMann pointed out towards the forest that surrounded them, "Right there, good buddy, right there. The locals used to grow the stuff in small batches on their property and I'd gather up the batches and have it moved north in bulk. But law enforcement started law enforcing, much to the dismay of the local population, as a bunch of them got busted. So guess what, in the age-old entrepreneurial spirit of America, they moved their grow plots to someone else's land, and that someone else was Uncle Sam and his little buddy, the state of California."

Big Louie took a pull from his flask and said, "Like the Cleveland National Forest?"

McMann smiled and said, "Yup. It's a great place to grow the product, particularly this hybrid California Gold. They grow the stuff in forest areas so that the plots can't be detected from the air. Federal and state drug enforcement guys fly helicopters over the forest areas all the time, at least they used to. Every now and then they'd find a plot, but what they find is only a drop in the bucket."

Jeremiah asked, "Why doesn't California just make marijuana legal? After all, the state of California developed the hybrid these growers use. How ironic. First they develop the hybrid that growers use, and then they have all this law enforcement trying to eradicate it. It could stop all this helicopter flying and law enforcement by just making marijuana legal. I've read that the state could close its budget gap just by taxing marijuana and eliminating the expense of all this helicopter flying and law enforcement."

McMann answered, "Doc, no fuckin' way do we want marijuana made legal. If it's legal, the price will come down and I'm competing with Wal-Mart. Every time there's a ballot initiative to legalize the stuff, I donate mucho denaro to the anti-marijuana people. Hell, I'll bet dollars to donuts that the cartels do the same. The last thing they want is for the stuff to be legal too. Look, we ain't stupid. Those who don't learn from history are doomed to repeat it. When they repealed prohibition, they killed the bootleggers, put them out of fuckin' business. Legalization is the last thing we want."

Jeremiah's bushy eyebrows rose and he said, "More delicious irony! The drug dealers and the anti-drug forces are allied to prevent the legalization of drugs."

McMann laughed and said, "That's right, Doc. The world is made up of strange bedfellows. Happens all the time. It's the happy alliance of economics and morality! I'm surprised the cartels haven't taken more forceful and direct action and knocked off a couple of the wealthy bozos who pretty much fund the legalization movement. It's like a religion and this religion could use a couple of martyrs as far as I'm concerned. What'd that pimp say in that Tom Cruise movie? Don't fuck with a man's living. Well they're fucking with a whole lot of people's very good living."

Big Louie asked, "What's all this got to do with Equipo de Tijuana wanting a source of water and willing pay a pretty penny for it?"

"Well, here's where it gets a little more complicated. The water is the easy part. Grow plots in the middle of the forest need water. The hybrids tolerate drought, but they need water to maximize their growth and thus the value of the crop on the grow plot. That's where the need for water comes in. Why the cartels are growing the stuff here is a little more complicated."

Jeremiah said, "Well why don't the cartels just grow their product, as you call it, in Mexico where they pretty much can do whatever they want. I should think that there would be less risk in so doing. Then all they have to do is smuggle the product into the U.S., which as I understand it, is not that difficult."

"There's where you're wrong. Times have changed and the cartels are changing their business strategies and operations to accommodate those changes. Here's a question for you: how has our federal government's change in policy to keep illegal aliens out of the U.S. caused the Mexican drug cartels to move production into the States?"

Big Louie smiled, "Bingo! Because the increased border security to keep illegals out not only stops the wetbacks. It stops everything coming across the border illegally and that includes drugs. Right?"

"Mostly right, but let's not overestimate the efficiency of the organization that brought us the post office and Amtrak. The bastards didn't seal the border. They just tightened it up some. The cartels still smuggle billions of dollars worth of cocaine and meth across the border. But marijuana's a bulk product. It's more difficult to smuggle. And thanks to the California Department of Agriculture, the stuff can now be grown almost anywhere. No brainer! Grow the stuff in the national and state forests where there's lots of land, lots of cover and not much law enforcement."

Jeremiah's eyebrows rose to new heights and he shouted, "Another irony!"

McMann continued, "The cartels have the muscle and investment dollars to dominate growing the weed here in the U.S."

Big Louie interrupted him, "I understand the muscle part, but investment dollars? What's it take to grow these hybrids, anyway?"

"To maximize the yield, you have to water the plants, like I said, and that involves two things. First, a source of water. Second, an irrigation system. Thanks to marijuana being illegal, the profit margin is so high on each of these hybrid plants that it pays to invest in an extensive system of pipes and pumps and generators to move the water thousands of feet to grow plots. Depending on the supply of dank at the time of distribution, a single marijuana plant yields a street value of between two and four thousand bucks. The profit margin is so high that these extensive irrigation systems are only used once and then abandoned. The investment is pretty large for a small operator, but for a Mexican cartel it's peanuts."

McCann started to laugh, "And there's an added irony, Doc, perhaps the most ironical irony. Those grow fields use lots of potent fertilizer and that burns the shit out of the soil, and all that irrigation… that causes lots of erosion and then there's all that garbage and abandoned pipe and equipment littering the forest floor. How's this for irony, Doc, the assholes in Hollywood protesting global warming and the pollution of our national forests are the ones buying up this shit by the fist full for a pretty penny. They're the fuckin' market. God, I love America and those Hollywood assholes hold a special place in my heart and… my bank account!"

Big Louie asked, "Why would Mr. Numero Uno want to buy or lease that land Jamie owned? He could just use it and then abandoned the place when he's done."

"I'm not sure, but my guess is he wanted it for insurance… wanted to lower the risk. There was no telling when Jamie would show up. If Mr. Numero Uno's got a bunch of grow plots up there, the yield could be worth millions dollars… forty, maybe fifty million dollars. A hundred thousand here, a hundred thousand there, that's peanuts, relatively inexpensive insurance for such a high return."

Big Louie whistled and said, "Did you say forty to fifty million?"

"Sure did. That's forty to fifty million!"

Jeremiah mumbled, "Oh my… oh my… oh my…"

Living the petrified life...

The posse sat in the Dodge Ram pickup looking out at the land. Jamie opened the window and said, "Well this is it, the Petrified Forest."

The posse piled out of the pickup and stood scanning the

landscape. There were petrified logs scattered about like gigantic pickup sticks dropped from the sky by a drunken Bacchus. Jonnie asked, "What petrified the fuckin' forest?"

Charles, reading from his copy of Stuff Your Momma Wouldn't Tell You about Route 66, leaned his back against the pickup and said, "Big Bertha apparently was no idiot. She says here that millions of years ago these trees were growing along a river bank. The river bank eroded and the trees fell into the water and were carried into swampy lowlands."

Charles stopped, shaded his eyes with his right hand and looked out at the land, looked down again and continued reading, "The trees became submerged under volcanic ash rich in silica. Eventually the silica replaced the wood turning it into stone. The rainbow colors are actually stains caused by minerals." He looked up and said, "And there were dinosaurs running around here too, from the late Triassic Period, 200 million years ago. That's even before those Jurassic Park dinosaurs were munching on the local homo sapiens. But these Petrified Forest dinos were small, about the size of a man. They were meat eaters and hunted in packs bringing down the larger plant eaters."

Jamie bent over on his haunches, picked up a handful of the sandy soil and let the soil run through his fingers onto the ground. "Well there's no river running through it now. This place is a desert. In a million years a lot can happen. I guess whatever happened was meant to happen and some of it happened here. This place is like the where it is, where it is, and where it is of paleontology." The song "Get Your Kicks on Route 66" interrupted him. "Oops, my cell." He stood, flipped his cell phone open and walked behind the pickup.

Jonnie smiled, "So what happened involved volcanoes. There's always volcanoes. In the movies, the damn things are always exploding as a bunch of dinosaurs chase a bunch of humans who are running like hell for their lives for some cave as the volcanoes kill the dinosaurs who are trying to eat the humans."

Charles interrupted Jonnie, "You know that we've only been

around for two hundred thousand and not two hundred million years. Humans and dinosaurs never coexisted."

"Well they do in the movies! And one of those humans running around like a chicken with its head cut off is always a real good lookin' piece of meat wearing an animal skin that barely covers her big ass, her huge tits, and that hairy tuna burrito you'd like to sink yer teeth into. It's frustrating to watch her run around. You'd think that animal skin would slip off or at least move around so you'd get to see the parts of her you'd really like to see, including a lucky glimpse of that hairy tuna burrito of hers. But nooo, it never happens."

The inscrutable Garcia shook his head a scrutable yes for a change.

Jonnie asked, "What else that book say about the Petrified Forest. So far you ain't said nothin' any momma wouldn't say."

Charles continued, "Well, says that early pioneers resorted to dynamite to break up the petrified logs since they couldn't cut them up with saws. They actually used the petrified wood to construct buildings, and of course polished smaller pieces for jewelry to sell to assholes like us. Here's a handy tidbit from Big Bertha… conservation-conscious American tourists steal a ton of the stuff every month, so if you don't want to pay an outrageous price, grab a hunk and hide it in your vehicle. No one will miss it."

Jonnie walked beyond the scenic overlook where they'd parked. He looked about his feet, picked up several pieces of petrified wood and yelled back, "Great advice!" He walked back to the pickup and after carefully inspecting the pieces of petrified wood he'd found, he shoved one piece into his back pocket. Then he tossed each of the discarded pieces back into the desert. After each toss, he shaded his eyes and watched the piece he'd just thrown as it landed. After his last toss, a surprised look came across his face and he said to Charles, "Ya know, this don't look anything like what we saw in that movie last night."

Charles yelled, "Bingo! Nice observation, Pig Fat! Big Bertha says here there's no Petrified Forest in the movie of the same name.

OXBOW LAKE THE 2ND

Says the whole movie's a scam. That opening scene where that hitchhiker, Alan Squier, walks along that road through the Petrified Forest, well, that's not the Petrified Forest he's walking through. It's Red Rock Canyon State Park outside L.A. And it's not even Leslie Howard doing the walking. It's a stand-in. She says here Warner Brothers thought that it'd be too expensive to film on location, so they trucked tons of sand onto Sound Stage Eight in Burbank and filmed the rest of the movie there."

Jonnie said, "You had to learn that by reading from some old paperback you bought at a second-hand bookstore in Chicago by some educated whore named Big Bertha? Didn't those Harvard asshole's who studied the film, one of which was you, happen to notice that the whole movie was a fake?"

Louis, who had been checking the oil in the pickup, slammed the hood closed ending the discussion. He yelled to Jamie, who had just flipped his cell phone closed, "What's up, Stuntman?"

Jamie walked to the rear of the pickup, pulled down the tailgate, jumped up and sat. The posse gathered around him. Louis said, "The chariot's A-OK. We're ready to roll. Where to next?"

Jamie shook his head from side to side with an expression of disbelief. "I'm not sure. We got to palaver. You're not going to believe what Big Louie just told me." He spit into the desert and continued, "Those two assholes that were chasing us, Pedro and Garcia, well Pedro was the little brother of Mr. Numero Uno, the asshole who ran that cartel, Equipo something or other. Seems their bodyguards put lots of holes in all three of them. Looks like some of Mr. Numero Uno's investors took a dim view of his management style. Big Louie and Jeremiah actually talked with the bastard and managed to get away with their skin intact."

Charles asked, "So where's that leave us?"

"I'm not sure. Big Louie thinks that we may be in the clear. He thinks that the only ones in the cartel who knew about us and that offer to buy my land were the three assholes who got air-conditioned."

Jonnie pumped his left arm and yelled, "Yippeee! I feel a celebration coming on!"

Jamie held up his hands, palms forward. "Not so fast, keemosaabe, there's more. Big Louie says that Numero Uno wanted my land for the water, that deep well on my property, to irrigate what his Nam buddy thinks is a huge marijuana grow field that the recently air-conditioned Mr. Numero Uno was keeping secret from his business partners. Big Louie thinks he was skimming money from the till to pay for it and got caught. Anyway, Louie says his Nam buddy, who knows about this stuff, said that this secret grow field could be worth millions of bucks. You heard me, maybe forty... fifty million bucks. And most likely those pissed off business partners of the former Mr. Numero Uno have no idea that the marijuana grow field exists."

The inscrutable Garcia said inscrutably, "There's more gold in them California hills!"

Charles asked, "Are you smelling a business opportunity, Stuntman?"

Jamie scratched his chin beneath his scruffy red beard and said, "I'm reluctant to get involved. It's dangerous. It feels too much like bootlegging, and it is illegal."

Louis pulled a rag from his back pocket and wiped his hands. "Look, my uncle Big Louie will find out what's what. And if there's fifty million bucks on the table?... well you can split that a whole bunch of ways and each one of us would still get a pretty big chunk of cash. Sounds good to me." He looked down at his hands and said, "I'm tired of bein' a god damn grease monkey."

Jamie held up both hands, "Whoa there, Guinea, we don't know if there even is a grow field. One step at a time. But I'll tell you guys right now, I'm reluctant to get involved. Mr. Numero Uno and his two stooges ended up dead, not unlike a lot of those bootleggers. Besides, there's this little thing about the state cops, the Feds, the DEA. Look, Big Louie and his buddy are going to do some recon and see what's up. He'll call as soon as he has more intel. Until then, we wait."

Going Native American in a 60s kinda way…

Louis pulled into the parking lot and glided the pickup to a stop. There were a number of vehicles parked in the lot, including an old, faded, multicolored Volkswagen bus and a beat-up, equally faded and multicolored school bus that'd seen better days several decades ago, joined rather oddly by a couple of BMWs, an Audi, several Lexuses and a Mercedes. Louis peered over the steering wheel. "Christ, there's a Mercedes SL Class. This motel looks like a dump, a real tourist trap, only it's in the middle of nowhere. But the place seems to be kinda popular with people who drive very expensive cars."

Garcia said, "Veryeplacesita roundasita erehisita sita nita hetisita iddlemisita fo-sita owherenisita." ("Everyplace around here is in the middle of nowhere.")

Louis looked back at him and said, "Yeah, but this place is in the middle of nowhere in the middle of nowhere." He looked up at an old, faded sign over what appeared to be the motel's office, "There's a reason they call this place the Lost Navaho Indian Camp Motel."

Jamie finished off his blaster and tossed the dead soldier unceremoniously to the floor of the pickup. He peered out the pickup's window at the screen door to the motel office. "My dad delivered supplies here. I stayed here with him a couple 'a times. Seemed like he arranged his delivery schedule so that he'd end up here for the night. I was only a kid the first time, thought it was neat. The Lost Navaho Indian Camp Motel, a bunch of motel rooms, each room a separate little building set up like a Navaho hogan, with electricity, but no indoor plumbing." He pointed to his left at a rectangular concrete block building and said, "The johns and showers are in that building over there. I loved it, but like I said, I was just a kid. When I got a little older and the novelty of the place wore off, I couldn't figure out why my old man stayed here all the time, but a lot of people did. It wasn't all that cheap either. It was out of the way, and it wasn't all that well maintained. It was OK, but hell, lots of places are OK, and after you've stayed here once, you've pretty much had the experience. I guess a lot of people just like staying in fake hogans, my dad included. I'll say this, when we parked that big ol' white box truck of his here, we got the royal treatment. You'd think we were delivering gold bars."

The posse jumped out and stood around the pickup. Jamie and Jonnie walked toward the office while the others stayed behind. Jonnie asked, "You think there's a liquor store anyplace around here? We're gettin' kinda low."

As they entered the office, Jamie replied, "Dunno. Looks like there's no place close by, but we can ask."

An older, very tall, very thin man with a scraggly, salt-and-pepper beard and shoulder-length, white hair held in check with a rainbow-colored head band squinted down at them through gaunt, sunken eyes as if they were a thousand miles away. He towered over the counter behind which he stood. Jamie thought he looked oddly like a 60s version of Abe Lincoln, now a hippy gone to seed after having freed the slaves. The man said, "I su-spect you two'd like a ho-gon. Right?"

Jamie smiled, "Actually, we'd like two, sir."

"Sir? Hey man, no need for for-malities. Judy Rabinowitz at your service. Call me by my Indian name, Angry War Lance. You got a label other than young man?"

"Jamie… Jamie Steinkraus."

"And I'm Jonnie Hogg with two g's."

Angry War Lance scratched his scraggly beard and murmured to himself, "Steinkraus?"

Jonnie gave the tall, thin man the careful once-over from waist to headband and said, "No insult intended, Mr. Angry War Lance, but you sure don't look like no Indian. You're too tall and way too skinny for an Indian. And ain't no Indian I ever heard of named Judy Rabinowitz. You look more like a old hippy."

"Peace, brother. No insult taken, Mr. Jonnie Hogg with two g's. Lots of people hint that and every now and then someone with a pair of chestnuts says it. I guess they expect a real live redskin to check them into a place called the Lost Navaho Indian Camp Motel." From behind the counter, he started tapping his hand against his mouth yelling, "Woo… woo… woo!" as he pumped his long, thin legs up and down in place behind the counter simulating an Ichabod Crane-ish sort of Indian war dance.

Jamie and Jonnie, at first stunned, looked at each other and broke into Indian warwhoops of their own, pumping their legs following Angry War Lance's lead as they danced in a tight circle before the counter.

Angry War Lance stopped his war dance and thus theirs, put the palms of his hands up in front of him, gave his head several jaunty shakes from side to side and said, as he smiled from ear-to-ear, "That make it any better? Well that's as close to a real Indian as you're going to get… namely me, A-K-A Angry War Lance doin' his war dance. Customers are probably disappointed, but hell, it don't bother me none. I'm used to it. I did marry an Indian and she weren't no maiden, believe me, at least once I got done with her. She called a certain part of me a great angry war lance, but the name sorta stuck for all of me. Anyway, she's off to those happy hunting grounds in the sky or as you white people would say… she's dead… and I'm not. You said two of them ho-gons? That's a hundred bucks a night… fifty each. How many nights?"

Jamie replied, "Just one," as he pulled his wallet from his back pocket, shuffled through it and took out a credit card, which he offered to Angry War Lance.

Angry War Lance held up his huge right hand and with his left pointed to a sign taped to the front of an ancient cash register settled in dust on the counter. The sign read "cash only, all transactions final."

Jamie pulled back the offered credit card, pushed it back into his wallet and then pulled out two fifty-dollar bills, which he handed to Angry War Lance. Angry War Lance ignored the dust-covered ancient cash register, folded the two fifties and shoved them into his shirt pocket. As Jamie fiddled with his wallet, Angry War Lance handed Jonnie two keys, which were attached to large, flat pieces of plastic shaped and decorated like tom-toms. On one of the tom-toms, in heavy black marker, the number five was crossed out and the number two written above it. On the other, the number six was crossed out and the number eleven written above it. "You got ho-gon number two and ho-gon number eleven. They're right next to each other."

Jamie asked, "You're not going to check the fifties."

Angry War Lance smiled his gaunt smile and said, "Naw. We got our own kinda don't ask, don't tell policy here at the Lost Navaho Indian Camp Motel. We take our chances with you. You take your chances with us."

Jamie asked, "Where's the guest register to sign?"

Angry War Lance replied, "We don't keep a register. It's part of our 'don't ask, don't tell' policy. We're a no-tell motel."

Jonnie looked down at the two keys. "Hogon two and hogon eleven? What happened to three through ten?"

"They're here, only not between two and eleven. And then there's twelve through fifteen and they're not next to each other either. One night me and the squaw... she hated to be called a squaw, rest her luscious fat red ass... well, we were inspired by a random number-ing kinda idea that came to us late one night while we were smokin' and watchin' the stars, so we renumbered all the ho-gons. Seemed pretty cool at the time. Turns out we couldn't be completely random in order not to have any numbers next to each other, but it was the randomness idea that inspired us. Any ways, I keep the numbering scheme in her honor."

Jonnie looked down at the keys, a bit dismayed, recovered what for him was a sort of rational equilibrium and asked, "There a liquor store anywhere around here, say less than a day's drive?"

"There's a bunch of them way over at Holbrook, but we dis-courage the use of the proverbial firewater here at the Lost Navajo Indian Camp Motel. It's unhealthy to drink alcohol, particularly for

Indians. We promote organic health here." He pointed to a rack of cigarette papers at the far end of the counter and said, "But we do sell those. We got all kinds of brands and flavors. We're very proud of our selection. We got our own peace pipes for sale, too. We even got some carved from petrified wood." He pointed to a shelf on the wall behind them with several racks of small multicolored pipes. "And we sell toe-bacco, our own special blend, and other smoking materials, as they say, but we don't display them." He cocked his head to the left and through squinting eyes stared at Jamie as if something were slowly echoing through his mind from the distant past. "What you say your name was?

"Jamie... Jamie Steinkraus."

"You ever stay here before? I don't recognize you but that name sounds kinda familiar."

"I stayed here with my old man a couple 'a times when I was a kid. He used to sell motel and restaurant supplies along Route 66, stayed here a lot. We delivered supplies here in a white box truck. A big sucker."

Angry War Lance smiled and pointed at Jamie. "I remember you. Your old man went by the handle Kraut Two. We sure do miss him here at the Lost Navajo Indian Camp Motel. Got smoke signals a couple of years back that he died." He pointed toward the ceiling with the index finger of his left hand and said, "He's probably up there in the happy hunting grounds with my big-assed squaw lookin' down at us laughin' their asses off. Kid, things ain't been the same around here since your old man quit his route."

Jamie and Jonnie turned to leave and Angry War Lance said, "Look, I'm here all night if you want to buy somethin'." Jamie and Jonnie turned and looked back. "If you don't see me, bang on this here war tom-tom." He pointed at a small drum next to the rack of cigarette papers. "Bought it at the Phoenix airport... must be ten years ago. Customers get a big kick out of bangin' on the damn thing." Jamie and Jonnie turned back towards the screen door, pushed it open and walked from the office. The screen door banged close behind them.

Jonnie asked Jamie as they joined the rest of the posse standing around the pickup, "What the fuck was that all about?"

Jamie looked back at the office, "I'm not sure. So my old man was Kraut Two. Christ, you learn something new every day. I get the distinct impression that Mr. Angry War Lance's special blend of toe-bacco, as he calls it, contains no nicotine."

Jonnie said, "Let's get to Holbrook before the liquor stores close."

Jamie shook his head no. "Look, we got a bottle of tequila, a bottle of Four Roses, two full cases of beer and a cooler full of bologna, rolls and mustard. We don't need to drive to Holbrook. We're only staying here tonight and if we run out of Bud and Four Roses, we can buy a folder of cigarette papers and some of that special toe-bacco from Mr. Angry War Lance there."

Charles asked, "What's with all that shouting, anyway? Who's Mr. Angry War Lance?"

Jamie looked back at the office, "Angry War Lance? He's the hippy who runs the motel, which apparently includes a full-service head shop."

Charles looked somewhat confused. "Angry War Lance is a hippy? You know Big Berth's little tell-all book here." He held up his old, dog-eared paperback. "Well, it has at least a paragraph on every place we stopped except this one. There's nothing on The Lost Navajo Indian Camp Motel. Strange. Place like this ought to be featured."

Kraut Two? Who knew...

Jamie wandered back from the rectangular building toward hogan number 2 after taking a much needed dump. As he passed the motel office, Angry War Lance, who sat in the shadows on the steps to the office, yelled, "Hey Steinkraus! Hold up a minute."

Jamie stopped and turned. He saw a detached, bright-red dot bouncing rhythmically about the dark to the words that he heard. He walked towards the detached, rhythmically-bouncing, bright-red dot. As he approached, he could see that the floating red dot was attached to a pair of lips by a joint. As he moved closer, the dark image of Angry War Lance appeared in rough outline, barely illuminated by a dim nightlight in the office. Angry War Lance said, "Take a load off Fannie, kid. Have a seat." Jamie could hear a song hitting into the night from the office:

> *One toke over the line sweet Jesus*
> *One toke over the line*
> *Sittin' downtown in a railway station one toke over the line*

Jamie sat. "Who's that singing?"

Angry War Lance said, "Brewer and Shipley, my man, Brewer and Shipley. Me and Mourning Flower used to sit out here late at night listening to them, smokin' the good shit. After, we'd make love. She was always enthusiastic when I mounted her, as they say." He looked up at the sky. "Things ain't been the same down here since she passed. It's been seven years. I sure do miss her, and she was my best friend too." He handed Jamie the joint he was smoking. "Have a toke on me, man. It's good shit, California Gold. Best mary jane available."

Jamie took a long drag and Angry War Lance said with a muffled sense of urgency, "Hey man, don't Bogart that joint! I said take a toke. California Gold is hard to come by. All I can usually get is the local shit."

Jamie smiled and passed the joint back to Angry War Lance. "I haven't heard this stuff referred to as mary jane in years. And 'don't Bogart that joint?' Hell, some of my posse don't even know who Humphrey Bogart was, no less the meaning of 'don't Bogart that joint'." Brewer and Shipley sang on:

> *I sailed away a country mile,*
> *And now I'm returning and showing off my smile*
> *I met all the girls and loved myself a few*
> *And to my surprise*
> *Like everything else that I've been through*

It opened up my eyes
And now I'm one toke over the line, sweet Jesus
One toke over the line
Sittin' downtown in a railway station
Don't you just know I waitin'
for the train that goes home sweet Mary
Hopin' that the train is on time
Sittin' downtown in a railway station one toke over the line

Angry War Lance toked his joint and pointed to his head with the index finger of his free hand. "Yeah, man, time passes slowly up here in the mountains. But times they have already changed, man. It's too late. They've already changed."

He passed the joint back to Jamie, who took a short toke this time and passed it back. "You said you knew my old man?"

"Yeah, knew him pretty well. He was a prince among scumbags."

"Why'd you refer to him as Kraut Two? I never knew he went by Kraut Two."

"I pretty much understood the Kraut part given the Steinkraus, but I couldn't figure out where the Two came from. I asked him, why Two? Musta been a One somewhere in the wood pile. He said it was a family tradition."

Jamie smiled and said, "Yeah, there was. My grandpa. He was known as Kraut by his associates, one of whom was Al Capone. I just learned the other day that my upstanding grandpa was a bootlegger during Prohibition. Ran Capone's trucking operation. His bootlegging buddies called him Kraut. Surprised the shit out of me."

Angry War Lance took a roach clip clipped to his shirt pocket and clipped his joint. "No shit... one of Capone's bootlegging truckers? The acorn didn't fall far from the tree. Explains a lot."

Jamie asked, "Explains what?"

Angry War Lance took short, quick tokes from the end of the roach clip to avoid burning his lips and then said, "You didn't know?"

"Know what?"

"About your old man's business?"

"Yeah, I knew. He sold restaurant and motel supplies for his company, Route 66 Restaurant and Hotel Supplies, along the Mother Road from Illinois to California. Delivered them himself in that big white box truck."

"Well that's what he delivered on the way out to California. On the way back he delivered weed, in bulk. He was the most dependable, reasonable distributor me and the squaw dealt with. A real business man, not some low-life scumbag like I gotta deal with today. You know how hard it is to score this stuff today, reliably and reasonably. Impossible. I just got word that my supplier is out of business for a while. She's goin' up the proverbial river for a spell, a long spell. The skank was an idiot. Hell, I wouldn'ta fucked that bitch with yours."

Brewer and Shipley were on their way through the song a second time...

Whoooo do you love, I hope it's me
I've bin a changin', as you can plainly see
I felt the joy and I learned about the pain that my momma said
If I should choose to make a part of me,
surely strike me dead
And now I'm one toke over the line, sweet Jesus
One toke over the line
Sittin' downtown in a railway station
One toke over the line
I'm waitin' for the train that goes home sweet Mary
Hopin' that the train is on time
Sittin' downtown in a railway station
One toke over the line

Jamie sat silently listening as darkness slowly overtook him, for he was now many, many unbearable tokes over his line.

Fulfilling an unexpected destiny...

Jeremiah's cell phone ring awakened him. It was early morning and the sun was just rising, an event he rarely witnessed. He felt blindly about the bed table with his left hand while his eyes remained shut and his hand finally came across an object which he believed, correctly, to be his cell phone. He grabbed the cell phone, flipped it open and mumbled a sleepy, "Hello?" He listened and then his great bushy eyebrows shot upward as he yelled, "Rose, please repeat that!" He listened again and then screamed, "This cannot be!"

Big Louie, who was already up, heard Jeremiah's screams and hobbled on his bum leg to the doorway of Jeremiah's bedroom where he stood listening to one half of an apparently very intense conversation as he sipped his morning coffee.

"She left a note? Is it clearly written? What does the note say?" As Jeremiah listened, he looked up in Big Louie's direction with an expression of dumbfounded disbelief. He whispered a barely audible, "Have you told Jamie?" He listened again and then said, "I have to think about what we should do. I will call back within the hour."

Big Louie leaned against the door frame and asked, "What's up, Doc?"

With great effort, Jeremiah pulled his corpulent body up and leaned his back against the bed's headboard. He stared off into the distance and said, "Rose just called. Leslie's run off with that Zulu imposter. Apparently she slipped by the security desk early this morning. Security cameras caught her meeting that fellow in the parking lot. They drove off in his SUV."

Big Louie straightened up and said, "What? Leslie did what?"

"Ran away with that African-American exotic dancer. Jamal something-or-other. He performed at her bachelorette party."

"You're shittin' me? Jamie know?"

"No, not yet. Rose wants me to call him. She's too upset."

"Any more details?"

"She left a note."

"And?"

"She wrote something to the effect that she has found her destiny and must fulfill it."

Big Louie yelled "Fuck" several times and then asked, "How's Rose?"

Jeremiah looked directly at Big Louie for the first time and said, "She's come unglued. She appears to be incapable of acting."

Big Louie said, "We gotta get you back to New York. Is Rose alone?"

"No. Those two bridesmaids, Janey Toussaint and Angel Bangor, are with her."

"Good. We'll get you a connecting flight to Albany A-SAP and they can pick you up at the Albany airport. I'll call Jamie and talk with him after we make your travel arrangements. I'll have one of my guys meet you at the airport."

Shit just happens... a lot

After putting Jeremiah on a flight that would eventually land him at the Albany airport, Big Louie sat in his rented SUV and stared at his cell phone for some time. He dreaded making the call he knew he must make, thinking back to the difficulty he had informing Jeremiah of that blackmailing DVD showing Leslie masturbating with great enthusiasm and endurance. It seemed like a century ago. He shook his head and mumbled to himself, "Hell, that was..." He thought for a moment and said "Monday after last. Seems like two lifetimes." He finally decided to do as he had done then, just say what must be said and let the chips fall where they may.

He dialed Jamie's cell phone and waited. Finally someone answered. "That you, Jamie? Listen, I got some bad news about Leslie." He paused a moment and said, "There's no way to sugarcoat this. Leslie's run off with that Jamal character, that black exotic dancer from Leslie's bachelorette party. Yeah, he was the chauffeur too. She escaped from that institute early this morning." He listened carefully for a response and heard none. "Hello, hello? You there?" After what seemed another eternity, he heard a loud bang causing him to pull the phone from his ear and look down at it. Finally another voice answered and he said, "Who the fuck is this? Charles? Where's Jamie?"

Charles informed him that Jamie had gone berserk and that Jonnie Hogg, Garcia Rosenbloom and his nephew Louis Fazzano had jumped him and were holding him down after he attempted to destroy what little there was to destroy in their motel room. He could hear Jamie in the background yelling "That fucking bitch!"

Big Louie explained what had happened to Charles and while the details were few, there were enough of them to make it quite obvious to all that Jamie's world had been rocked to its very foundations. Big Louie paused and listened, then said, "Jeremiah? He's flying to Albany. He's already taken off. Rose and those two bridesmaids are meeting him there. I'm sending one of my guys to help them find her. When Jamie calms down, tell him what I told you. I'm at the airport and I'm headin' back to my Nam buddy's now. He knows the area and we're gonna do some recon and find out what the hell's goin' on at Jamie's property. I'll call back when I've got more intel." He flipped his phone closed and sat for some time trying to make sense of all that had happened. Unable to do so, he pursed his lips, shook his head slowly from side to side and started the SUV. As he drove off, he said to himself, "I guess shit just happens... a lot."

Shit not only happens a lot, sometimes it gets on your shoes...

Big Louie and TS hugged the ground behind some low bushes looking down at a barely visible camp fire in the partial moonlight. Clouds wandered across the moon and the night darkened. TS scanned the area with night-vision binoculars. "Looks like three soldiers. There's four tents, a large one and three small ones. No visible weapons. The assholes just finished eating and are passing around a bottle, taking short swigs, probly tequila. The bastards drink a lot of the stuff when they're stuck out here." He put the binoculars down and mumbled, "Only three. Keep drinkin' boys!"

Earlier in the day, Big Louie and TS had set up a carefully-con-cealed base camp about a half mile away on the other side of the trail leading to Jamie's property. They hadn't had time to survey the mari-juana grow field or fields but TS thought there were probably several given the size of the irrigation pipe they had discovered protruding from the well on Jamie's property.

They had come across the camp set up by the El Equipo soldiers almost inadvertently as they had followed the irrigation pipe. First they had stumbled into the area where the El Equipos dumped their garbage and trash. Big Louie had looked at a pile of empty cans and bottles and said, "Looks like they been livin' on beans and tequila."

Then as Big Louie and TS had approached the camp still in the distance, they had stepped in several piles of crap and had found themselves surrounded by many piles of the stuff, each pile capped with soiled white toilet paper. Big Louie whispered, "Fuck! I thought we were in a field of flowers." TS snickered, "Yeah, shit carnations. Should have known. No flowers I know of smell like this." As they had worked their way to the side away from the trash dump, they had inadvertently discovered the clearing that the El Equipos used as a latrine. Having uncovered the general layout of the encampment and covered their boots with actual El Equipo shit in the process, they had quietly retreated to plan their next move and to clean off their boots, for as Big Louie had said, "If we don't clean the shit off our boots, those Equipos will smell us coming a mile away."

The two grey-haired commandos settled into their previous spot on high ground behind the crest of the hill after determining that there were only three El Equipo soldiers and that all three were ac-counted for. Big Louie sat up and looked down at his shit-covered boots and muttered, "Fuck." He rubbed his bum leg and said, "I'm too old for this shit. I'm not used to sloshin' through underbrush with a field pack, a rifle and all the other crap we're carryin'. Thank God these assholes ain't VC."

TS sat up facing Big Louie and took a small container from

the breast pocket of his camos and popped it open. He carefully shook the container until two pills tumbled into the palm of his free hand. He tossed the two pills into his mouth and as he chewed, he passed the container to Big Louie, saying, "Take two and hit to right, good buddy," as he did so. Big Louie did as TS had done and passed the container back to TS, who capped it and returned it to his breast pocket. TS then pulled a small flashlight from the same breast pocket, turned it on and stuck the blunt end in his mouth, holding the flashlight in place with his teeth. Having learned the layout of the El Equipo encampment, he pulled a topographical map from his back pack and flung it on the ground. He centered the light from the flashlight on the map and studied it.

Big Louie noticed a newspaper sticking out of TS's field pack and said, "Hand me some of that newspaper. I don't wanna get beaner shit all over my hands."

TS looked up and pulled the newspaper from his field pack and carefully read the first page using the flashlight to illuminate the paper. He pulled the double-fold sheet of the front and back pages from the rest of the newspaper, carefully folded it and stuffed it in the breast pocket of his camos as Big Louie watched. A puzzled Big Louie asked, "What's so special about those pages?" TS said nothing in response and handed Big Louie the rest of the newspaper. Big Louie pushed the newspaper into the light from TS's flashlight and said, "What the fuck are you doin' with a Spanish newspaper? You buy this at the 7-11?" TS pushed the newspaper out of the light and said in garbled English as he held the flashlight with his teeth, "Good buddy, I read and speak Spanish. Have to. Required by my profession," as he returned to studying the topographical map.

As Big Louie carefully rubbed the shit off his shoes using several sheets he'd torn from the newspaper, TS turned off the flashlight, stuffed it in the breast pocket of his camos, carefully folded the map and put it back into his field pack. He said to Big Louie, "Clean all that beaner shit off your shoes?" Big Louie grunted a disgruntled, "yes." TS continued, "Good. Now for the plan. Look, it's always easier and safer to jump a guy when his pants are down and he's concentrating on pushing out turds. Nobody shoulders a rifle while taking a crap. Let's work our way back to where they crap. We can take the same path we took before. Eventually one of the bastards will have to take a shit. When he does, we'll jump him and even the odds. Then we can work our way to the camp and jump the other two, one for you and one for me. They should be pretty much pickled by then. That ain't 7-Up they're passing around."

Big Louie passed the rest of the newspaper back to TS, who said, "Why the newspaper?"

Big Louie said, "To wipe the shit off yer boots."

TS said, "Why would I bother to do that? We're walkin' back into that field of flowers, as you so poetically put it, to ambush the first El Equipo shitter that shows up to take a crap. Hell, why bother to clean off the shit. In a couple of minutes we'll be knee deep in the stuff again, and in the dark."

Big Louie smelled his hands, grimaced and said, "You son-of-a-bitch."

A shit eatin' grin spread across TS's face and even though Big Louie couldn't see it, he knew it was there.

A man at his most vulnerable...

Big Louie and TS crouched in the underbrush just beyond the latrine area where the freshest piles of shit showed their moist glistening in the partial moonlight.

Big Louie looked out at the fresh piles of shit. "Looks to me like the bastards are working their way back towards their camp shit by shit."

An El Equipo staggered toward them barely able to keep his balance. As he reached the clearing, he pushed his pants down and squatted. A huge fart broke the silence. The man grunted approvingly and started to shit. As he did so, Big Louie grabbed the shitting El Equipo around the neck from behind with his right arm and pulled the El Equipo back and to the ground, covering the man's mouth with his left hand. The man continued to shit, unable to hold back what his bowels had so obligingly begun and his fear now accelerated. TS stood over the still shitting man, held a knife to his face and snarled, "Yell y morir. Permanecer en silencio y en vivo!"

The man shit even more.

Big Louie turned the man onto his belly and pushed his head into the dirt as TS knelt on the man's back, pulled back his arms and cuffed his wrists with plastic handcuffs. Big Louie yanked a bandanna from his neck, knotted it in the middle several times and gagged the man who then turned his head sideways and whimpered. Big Louie stood and whispered, "Jesus Christ, there's got to be a better way to neutralize a bad guy than to grab him while he's taking a god awful bean shit."

TS stood and put his foot on the back of the cuffed El Equipo. "If he'd only been from Wisconsin."

Big Louie whispered in disbelief, "Wisconsin? What the fuck does Wisconsin have to do with it."

TS smiled. "They'd be cheese eaters. Anyway, now it's two on two."

Big Louie followed TS toward the camp muttering to himself, "What the fuck does cheese have to do with it. Shit's shit and it don't smell any better if the shitter's from Wisconsin."

They trotted slowly towards the tents and camp fire, Big Louie going to the left and TS to the right. As they circled the tents, with their rifles in the ready, they came upon the two remaining El Equipos sprawled out on the ground snoring away. They pushed the sleeping men on their bellies and cuffed them as they had the first one. Neither man resisted.

Big Louie looked down at his shit-covered boots. "For Chrissake, TS, all we had to do was walk in here and cuff the bastards. That 'take a bad guy while he's shitting' strategy… well it stinks!"

Wednesday, July 16
No shit, there's gold in them thar hills too…

As the sun rose, the three El Equipo soldiers sat cross-legged before the dying fire with their hands cuffed behind their backs. They reeked of piss and shit and, most prominently, fear. TS stood over them and said, "They know we're not law enforcement and they're literally scared shitless. They think we're going to execute them." He pulled the newspaper pages he'd saved from the breast pocket of his camos and spread the front page out as he knelt on one knee before the three cuffed men. He said, "Conoces a estos hombres?"

Big Louie asked, "What's that?"

TS looked up and said, "It's a front page article from the local Spanish paper about the assassination of those three assholes that were running El Equipo de Tijuana. There's a picture of each asshole."

Big Louie looked down at the front page and said, "Christ, those are head shots from the morgue. Looks like those death photos they used to take of outlaws in the Old West after a posse put a bunch of holes in 'em."

TS smiled, turned to the men and asked again, "Conoces a estos hombres?"

One of the men, apparently the man in charge, shook his head yes. TS moved the front page closer to the man to enable him to read the article. "Puede usted leer?"

The man shook his head yes again and read. After finishing the article, he turned and then explained to the others in Spanish what the article said. He then said to TS in English, "Are you going to kill us too?"

TS stood and looked down at him and said, "That, my compadre, depends on you. Were you working for those three men?"

"We worked for the young one, Pedro. The other one, Garcia, was always with him. I never saw the third one before."

"How long have you been here?"

"Over three months, I think."

"When's the last time you saw Pedro and Garcia?"

"It has been many weeks. They were supposed to resupply us every two weeks and inspect our work, but we have not seen them for a long time. We feared leaving. That Garcia is... was... a very dangerous man. If we left, he told us he would track us down like dogs and kill us in most unpleasant ways. There was another who worked with us. He argued with Pedro about money and Garcia shot him in the head."

"Down to beans and tequila?"

The man shook his head yes.

"How many grow fields do you have?"

"Three. It is a very large operation and most difficult to maintain with only three men."

"How many plants?"

"I am not sure. Many thousands.

"Any weapons... rifles... pistols?

"One rifle with one clip. That's all Pedro and that Garcia would let us have."

"Where's the rifle?"

The man motioned with his head toward the large tent and said, "Are you going to kill us now?"

"No, we will not kill you now and if you continue to cooperate, we will not kill you at all. You no longer have to fear Pedro or Garcia. As you can see from the newspaper, they are both dead. Your family will not have to mourn your death… at least not today."

The man looked up and said, "No one will mourn me or my friends" as he nodded with his head toward the other two cuffed men. "We have no family. It is very sad. No one will mourn for us."

The man turned to the other two and repeated in Spanish what TS had said. The men smiled, looked to the heavens and muttered, "Gracias a Dios".

Big Louie sipped from his flask and offered it to TS who stood, took the flask and said, "What's your take?"

Big Louie said, "These poor devils weren't goin' to live past the harvest. Pedro had to make sure that no one else found out about this operation. I'm sure he'd have Garcia put a bullet in each one of them after all the heavy lifting was done. Hell, that Pedro asshole took all the precautions. He even recruited soldiers for the job with no family, no one for them to talk to back home, no one to miss them when they're dead."

TS took a long swig from the flask and said, "We're sitting on a gold mine here and nobody knows about it except those three, you and me and that posse of assholes. This is the chance of a lifetime. One and done… for life. But we still have a major problem… a problem that could get us all killed." He stared at the three cuffed El Equipo soldiers squatting on the ground. "We gotta find a way to keep those cartel beaners from squealing to whoever's running the cartel now. If the cartel finds out about us and all this product, we're as good as dead." He motioned with his head toward the three cuffed men. "And we can't just kill them. I'm not into killing people. I did enough of that in Nam."

Opportunity's ghost knocks at the back door…

Big Louie took the satellite phone from TS and dialed Jamie's cell phone. Someone answered on the other end and yelled, "Who the fuck's this?"

Big Louie yelled back, "It's the fuckin' Easter Bunny, asshole. Who the fuck else would be callin' you at this time."

"I suppose that asshole associate of yours got pictures of my wife fuckin' that nigger."

"Jamie, get yer feet under you. What is… is. I'm sorry about what my niece has done, but right now we got a dangerous sich-e-ation here."

"Fuck your dangerous sich-e-ation."

Big Louie heard a scuffle and then, "Big Louie? This is Charles. Jamie's still drunk as a skunk. We gotta sober him up. Oops, there he goes. He's ralphing into a trash can as we speak. He got double whammied yesterday. You're not goin' to believe what he found out."

"No time now. Fill me in later."

"OK. I'll give you the details later. What's up?"

Big Louie told Charles of the El Equipo encampment, the three marijuana grow fields, the three El Equipo soldiers they'd captured and then said, "We gotta make some decisions and quick. Everyone's gotta be in on it. A lot's at stake. Where you at now?"

"We're outside a place called Holbrook, I think." Big Louie heard Charles yell in the background, "Where we at? What state?" Then Charles spoke into the phone, "We're in Arizona, yeah, Holbrook, Arizona. I think the name of the dump is the Lost Navaho Indian Camp Motel. Believe that?"

Big Louie asked "How far you from Alpine?" He heard some muffled conversation in the background and then Charles said, "According to Louis, it's about a ten-hour drive if we drive straight through, but given Jamie's condition and piss breaks, it'll take a couple more hours."

Big Louie said, "Look, my buddy TS and me got lots to do here. I'll call you back at this number in a couple of hours. Sober up that drunken bastard and hit the road. Ten-four." Then he hung up.

TS asked, "What's up?" and Big Louie explained the situation concerning Jamie and his new, crazy and recently runaway bride, where the posse was presently and that it'd take at least ten hours, probably twelve, for them to get to Alpine.

TS said, "The Equipo sergeant over there says they got coffee and sugar in the supply tent but not much else other than several dozen cans of beans. He asked if they could clean up and make coffee. I think that we should let them wash and change out of those stinkin' clothes, one at a time, and make some coffee. If they want, they can have some more of those beans you're so fond of. Then we can have them backpack those supplies in we got back at our base camp."

Big Louie looked up through the trees at the sky. "Don't we have another problem? Didn't you say that the Feds and state law enforcement use helicopters to search for grow fields?"

TS said, "Yup. But the worry's not as great now. One of the benefits of the state of California going bankrupt. Their drug enforcement guys don't have enough fuel to fly their copters around. A guy I know who works maintaining their copters says the state can only afford rescue missions now and the Feds stopped regular patrols last year. All their assets are on the border. The ranger units are understaffed and there's no recruiting to replace those that left."

Big Louie shook his head in admiration, "Damn, you got all the bases covered."

"Yup. It's my job and I do it well. It's why I ain't been caught. Ya gotta know the enemy's logistics. Just like Nam. Nothin' happens without supplies, fuel, transport and, most important, people. We still have an exposure, hikers and campers. But a lot of this area is privately-owned and posted so the public tends to stay away. It's why this place was chosen in the first place. Looks to me like somebody else did his homework too."

Thursday, July 17

One and done, again and again...

McMann looked down at the posse who slouched in various poses about the table. The three former Equipo soldiers sat along the wall on the floor. Big Louie stood behind McMann as McMann addressed the group, "Listen, I've dealt with the cartels. For them there's too much money to be made in the now and the time they don't spend selling drugs, they spend avoiding law enforcement and killing each other. Their leadership changes violently and often. They have short institutional memories. We can do this. No one left in El Equipo de Tijuana even knows about this operation."

Big Louie spread his arms and held out his hands, "And we can use Jamie's place here as our base. It's on privately owned land. It's remote and hidden by trees. People are supposed to live here, so our presence won't be all that odd. Hell, it even has a generator. This is some fuckin' place."

McMann tapped the table with the index finger of his left hand. "If we can keep this operation secret... if what we say here stays in this room... we can move this product without attracting too much attention... I know how to do this... we can pull this off. It'll take time, but there's a lot of money to be made. It's a one-and-done operation."

Jamie pointed at the former Equipo soldiers sitting on the floor along the wall. "What about those assholes? Won't they squeal?"

McMann said, "Hold it, Jamie. They're more afraid of the cartel than we are. They're associated with the former head of the operation, the so-called Mr. Numero Uno, and they know it. If they go to the new bosses, if they're lucky, they'll be killed. If they're unlucky, they'll be tortured and then killed. And they know that too. Besides, that Pedro character chose them because they have no family, no ties back in Mexico. Keeping the operation secret is why they were chosen."

Louis pulled his chair up to the table and asked, "How much we talkin' about?"

McMann pushed his chair back from the table and leaned his right elbow over the chair's backrest as he squinted his eyes staring toward the ceiling. "Well, I did a preliminary survey earlier today. There's three grow fields tucked along Jamie's property. I'd estimate about three thousand plants per grow field, that's nine maybe ten thousand plants, with a street value of between twenty-five and thirty-five million dollars, give or take. This is premium product, top value."

Louis asked, "How much for each of us?"

McMann said "After all costs of preparation, distribution and overhead, divided eleven ways, that's probably about a million each."

Charles asked, "Eleven ways? There's only seven of us."

McMann pointed to the three former Equipo soldiers, "They're in and they're equal."

Jamie said, "OK, that's ten. Who's the eleventh?"

Big Louie replied, "Jeremiah. He's got to be. He almost became an ingredient in a human stew gathering information about this operation. He's earned it. He doesn't have to know what's going on, but he's got to be in. He's family. I'll take care of handling him."

Jonnie Hogg yelled, "Seven come eleven! Who gives a shit. A fuckin' million each? That's good enough for me. God damn! Count me in."

Louis chimed in, "And me!"

Jamie held his hands up in a gesture for silence, "Hold it,

McMann. Do you mean to tell me that the cartels, particularly those El Equipo de Tijuana assholes, will let us sell this stuff to their customers? They're not stupid, you know. They'll find out and once they do, what do you think they'll do, just sit idly by and let us invade their turf?"

McMann turned toward the table and slapped his left hand down on the table with a bang. "Look, Jamie, I've been at this business a long fuckin' time. Before you have us all iced, listen to my business plan. You're a business man yourself from what I've heard. Just listen." Jamie held up his hands, bit his lower lip and nodded his head to the side indicating he was reluctantly willing to listen.

McMann continued, "We don't want to compete with the cartels and their distribution networks. You're right. If we did, they'd find out and come after us and we'd all probably end up like those three Equipo assholes that got gunned down. The cartels distribute primarily through gangs, mostly in urban areas. We should concentrate on the markets they ignore or are unable to reach. Rural areas, professionals, doctors and lawyers, accountants, even judges, people who just wouldn't purchase marijuana from gangs. Hell, those judges have probably seen a lot of those gang members come before them in court. And there's a lot of small colleges and universities stuck in the boonies. Knowing these secondary markets is how I've survived all these years without so much as a bruise. I know these markets. I have the contacts. I've been doing it for years."

Charles said, "Count me in." and Garcia shook his head a most scrutable yes.

McMann said, "The Mexicans are already in so it's a go except for you Jamie. In or out?"

Jamie sat back and folded his arms. He started laughing. "What the fuck! I take a sentimental journey down Route 66 and find out that my law-abiding grandpa went by the name of Kraut and ran Al Capone's bootleg trucking operation, and that my grandma worked in a whorehouse outside of St. Louis before she married him. Hell, looks like ol' Kraut met her in that whorehouse. Then I find out that my dear old, very upstanding dad went by the name Kraut Two and distributed marijuana along Route 66 using his motel and restaurant supply company as cover… big time. And then my wife runs off with a nigger exotic dancer with a big dick before we even get to the honeymoon. Here we are sitting in the place I gave her as a wedding gift, and now there's a cool million just sitting here at the end of this fuckin' rainbow." He yelled, "Fuck yes, I'm in! What the hell, I'm following a long standing family tradition. God damn fuckin' right I'm in. Step in shit and call me Three… Kraut Three. Charlie-O, break out the tequila!"

McMann stood up so suddenly that he pushed his chair over and it banged onto the floor. He said, "You're the son of the legendary Kraut Two?"

About the Author and His Novel

I believe that I have done a lot in my life. Unfortunately I cannot remember much of it, indicating that most of what I have done is not very memorable or possibly that my memory's gone bad on me, both being very likely. Obviously those of my deeds which may be memorable, I am unable to write about since I cannot remember them. I do remember having a mother and father, three brothers and a sister and playing in the fenced-in grounds around the walls of Sing Sing prison where my father held the unofficial title of Captain of the Death House and where he apparently enjoyed his work very much. He celebrated his joy every evening by drinking copious amounts of Piels beer and smoking packs of Camel cigarettes. My mother was nice but never left the house for some reason. That pretty much sums up my childhood.

I did go to high school at a place that nick-named itself the Ossining Indians, but to eliminate the possibility of insulting a tribe of Indians that no longer existed and all of whose tribal members had been deceased for a very long time, some board of education removed the "Indians" part of the nick-name.

I've been married several times and am presently married and have a bunch of kids and step-kids and two to three grand-kids. During much of this time I worked at IBM in the Hudson Valley and never really fit in there but did manage to make a lot on money writing things that I believe may have destroyed my memory. I did go to college at Albany State or SUNY at Albany or the University at Albany (I can't remember which) and I believe that I did graduate with a major in English literature. I think that I taught in high school for a year at some place on the Hudson River named after Henry Hudson's boat before having my memory destroyed at IBM.

I got laid off by IBM and took a course in writing at Columbia University taught by the now deceased novelist Raymond Kennedy who wrote one of my favorite novels, *Ride a Cockhorse*. IBM apparently felt bad about forcing me into what became an early retirement and paid for the course.

The Adventures of the Posse of Little Horses is my first novel. It's pretty long (97,000 words, give or take a word or three). It's my best to date and may win an award. When I first attempted to get the novel published, I originally described it as a "hardboiled detective novel" of sorts for reasons I do not remember. When I got no takers from that debilitated and incestuous industry, I re-described it a "softboiled detective novel"… again to no avail. Anyhow, now that the wonderfully perceptive publishing mogul Robert A Ward III, the CEO of Ship Wreck Publications, has agreed to publish the novel, I call it a "satiric humorous crime novel" for reasons I can't explain because I don't understand why these words are any better than any others.

This great novel was inspired by at least three novels. The first two novels are humorous, wonderful and distinctly hardboiled in their fashion, but surely not hardboiled detective stories: Raymond Kennedy's aforementioned *Ride a Cockhorse* and John Kennedy Toole's *A Confederacy of Dunces*. The detective hardboiling of this mulligan stew, at least what there is of it, came from reading Steve Hamilton's wonderful and very hardboiled detective novel *A Stolen Season*. I could probably have listed any of Hamilton's Alex McKnight novels as inspiration, but since *A Stolen Season* is his latest hardboiler and I think his best, I credit it. When he reads my claim that he inspired me, he'll probably ask me to remove his name, but it will be too late! Ha, ha!

I originally gave my *opus erectus* the title *The Universal Posse*. I was never quite satisfied with this title and slowly but surely it became a kind of not-working working title. However, I could not think of a better one. Kennedy, Toole and Hamilton had come up with such wonderful titles making mine seem rather pale and prosaic in comparison.

Then rather serendipitously, someone copied me on an email with the following tag line: "When a true genius appears, you can know him by this sign: that all the dunces are in a confederacy against him." -- Jonathan Swift." Ironically, the author of the email is a lifetime member of the confederacy posing as a true genius. One has to be suspicious of individuals who even hint that they are true geniuses, for they are more than likely undercover agents for the dreaded and ubiquitous confederacy.

I feel obligated at this point to interject that I do not claim myself to be a "true genius" in the Swiftian sense of those words, but I do believe that I am not a member of the much dreaded confederacy. However, in all humility, I leave it to others to make this determination.

Anyway, the quote from Swift made it quite clear where Toole got the title for his novel. This was news to me. I suspect that my rather forgetful mind had known this at one time but forgot to inform the rest me, for as that great Irish-American Indian troubadour Jimmie Dale Gilmore sings "my mind has a mind of its own" and my mind, in particular, often operates as an independent entity. On its own initiative, having been inspired by the Swiftian barb, my mind marched forth, bad memory and all, to seek out a better and more appropriate title for me.

This inspiration took my mind to perspiration (thank you very much, Mr. Edison) and off went my soon-to-be perspiring mind in search of this better title. On the internet, my mind found a site of famous quotes. It went to the site's compendium of famous quotes by Jonathan Swift, who as it turns out, said a shitload of memorable things. Undaunted by volume, my mind plowed through them, apparently thinking that if Swift were good enough for Toole, surely he was good enough for the rest of me. But according to my mind, no combination of the words that could be strung together to form a better title for my novel ever passed through the Reverend Swift's lips, modestly or otherwise... at least as far as my mind could determine from that Irish malcontent's blasts of irreverence as documented on this website.

My mind thought that perhaps it should investigate the quotes of Oscar Wilde, for like Swift, he too was Irish and said a whole bunch of pithy criticisms of mankind's follies. (What is it with the Irish, anyway? They've surrounded me: Kennedy, Toole, Swift, Wilde and Gilmore. Even Hamilton, I suspect, has a touch of Irish blood. They all are so clever, pithy and... malcontent, each in his own way. My mind always thought that the Irish deserved each other, even when they're alone, and here I was intellectually encircled by a mob of them.)

Anyway, my mind ditched the Oscar Wilde gambit for me on the grounds that the frilly Mr. Wilde was much too literary and far too clever by three-quarters for someone such as the rest of me. Then the name Mark Twain popped into my rather independent mind. At first my mind was a bit suspicious of someone who had to use an alias to become famous, but then concluded that this need for anonymity was evidence of the severity and social unacceptability of his quotes and so off my mind went, stomping through the fertile ground of the quotes of Mark Twain, AKA Samuel Clemens. After reading many of his barbs, my mind concluded that Mr. Twain or Mr. Clemens, take your pick, must have been of Irish descent too, and if his biography claimed otherwise, there was surely an undiscovered Irishman somewhere in his family's wood pile, as they say.

Then my mind came across these words of Mark Twain: "Against the assault of laughter nothing can stand." My mind, now drenched with sweat, jumped (metaphorically speaking) high into the air and yelled at the rest of me, "You silly bastard, make your title out of those words." Unfortunately try as I might, I could not, and so in desperation I re-titled my novel *The Adventures of the Posse of Little Horses* after a kind of shot glass.

You may wonder why and how I adopted the pen name of Oxbow Lake? Unfortunately the name Ward A Bobb the 3rd, which happens to be an alias, is all too common and more prosaic than my non-working working title, even when adorned with an undisclosed middle name and a 3rd at the end. For example, I often get calls from someone in Oklahoma looking for a long lost relative with the alias of Ward Bobb, which isn't me. To overcome this anonymity through commonality while still preserving some anonymity at the same time, I have decided to adopt a pen name. The big question was: which one?

I enlisted my mind again even after considering the job it had done finding a more intriguing title for me. After all, what choice did I have? My mind thought it might be useful to search around the term mark twain since it was Mark Twain's words that had inspired my novel's inscription in a back-handed sort of way. After fumbling about the internet searching for Mississippi river boat terms and some safe water words I could use, my mind stumbled upon the rather mysterious and undefined term oxbox.

My mind knew not what the term meant and decided to google said term. Fortunately, it misspelled or mistyped the term, incorrectly entering the term oxbow, which, as serendipity would again have it, is the first word of a term used on rivers throughout the world, including the Mississippi. The full term is oxbow lake. An oxbow lake is a small lake located in a former meander loop of a river. It is generally formed as a river cuts through a meander neck to shorten its course, blocks off the old channel, and then migrates away leaving a lake behind, an oxbow lake. Eventually, oxbow lakes silt up to form marshes and finally meander scars. There's a bunch of them in various stages of oxbowness decorating the lower Mississippi.

Could there be a better pen name for the likes of such as me, particularly when writing in the shadow of the likes of a Mark Twain, et al? I think not! So here I am: the newly minted Oxbow Lake, a writer more or less left behind to eventually silt up literarily speaking to become a meander scar, but it is my beautiful scar.

Note: I added the "2nd" to the end of my pen name in case there was already a "1st".

www.ingramcontent.com/pod-product-compliance
Lightning Source LLC
Chambersburg PA
CBHW052015020726

47501CB00004B/1080